"YOU EQUATE A CALM NATURE WITH A LACK OF PASSION?"

"I guess I do." Petra's voice had sunk to a husky whisper, she noted, dismayed. It sounded positively seductive. "What are you doing?" she suddenly inquired.

"This," Dan answered.

She had been kissed before by men who were skilled at lovemaking, as skilled as this man seemed to be. She had kissed in return, her body quick to the passion of the moment. But she had never felt an aching in her bones as she felt now. She had never known a mouth could brush against hers with such gentle pressure, yet steal all the breath from her body, so that her heart, starved of oxygen, would pound so fiercely.

Seconds later, he slowly released her. "Is that enough passion for you?" he murmured, with a satisfied glint in his eye.

Rosalind Carson
LOVE ME TOMORROW

Harlequin Books

TORONTO • NEW YORK • LONDON
AMSTERDAM • PARIS • SYDNEY • HAMBURG
STOCKHOLM • ATHENS • TOKYO • MILAN

Published July 1984

First printing May 1984

ISBN 0-373-70123-3

Printed in Canada

For my friend, Clydelle Smith

CHAPTER ONE

HE BOARDED THE PLANE in Chicago. Petra, waiting to check his boarding pass, watched him stride confidently toward her along the covered ramp. The man was tall, slim and athletic looking, smartly dressed in a well-cut blue pin-striped suit, immaculate white shirt and dark tie. His hair was thick and light brown, its tendency to curl expertly trimmed into neat submission. He carried a black leather briefcase.

Her first thought was that there was something predatory about him. She wasn't sure why she felt that. Perhaps it had something to do with the expression on his sharp-featured face, or the unmistakable aura of power about him. Power and money. Automatically she fitted him into a slot in her mind. The executive type. Ambitious. Ruthless. Mid-thirties, probably.

She could imagine him chairing a meeting of the board of directors, standing at the head of a long gleaming table in an air-conditioned office with nervously respectful faces looking up at him like flowers drawn toward the sun. "Gentlemen, our agenda this morning...." No women present.

She felt a flash of resentment. Though she had always envied that aura of authority—of *presence*—

she knew few women could attain it. And she knew from bitter experience that few men appreciated authority in women. Especially men like this one. Warning signals started flashing in neon inside her brain: *avoid at all costs*.

As he approached her, she realized that he'd been studying her just as intently. It seemed almost as though he was inspecting her navy blue uniform jacket and skirt for creases or flecks of lint. Self-consciously she checked with one hand that her floppy bow tie was straight under the collar of her blue-and-white striped shirt and that her dark curls were no more riotous than usual.

"Hello, Petra McNeil," he said after glancing at her name tag.

The greeting was a little too familiar, the voice too intimate. Surprised, she shifted mental gears, refiling him under the heading of "in-flight Lothario." She sighed inwardly. She was in no mood to bother fending anyone off on this trip. The farewell party her friends had given her the night before had lasted until midnight, and this flight from Seattle to Boston had already offered more than its share of irritations. This was her last working flight, she reminded herself. She didn't have to worry about offending anyone.

"Good afternoon, sir." Assuming the frosty smile she employed when dealing with overly friendly males, she glanced at his boarding pass. First class, naturally. When he hesitated as though he wanted to stop and talk, she gestured him by abruptly, pointing out his seat in 3A.

He didn't move. "Will you have a chance—" he began, but she cut him off.

"Excuse me, sir," she said coldly, leaning around him to look at the next passenger's boarding card, trying to make it clear with voice and manner that she wasn't encouraging advances.

The other passenger, a woman, moved around him, but he just stood there, smiling faintly. There was nothing predatory about him now: he was all benign self-confidence. Even though he was getting in the way he was demonstrably not worrying about it.

Again she felt a spasm of irritation, followed by a moment of doubt. He was acting as though she ought to know him. Was he somebody famous? Was she supposed to recognize him instantly? Did he expect special consideration? She looked more closely at his face and her eyes met his. He had green eyes; not hazel, but light green, ice green, cool spring green. Devastating.

A sudden and totally unexpected shock of awareness went through her like a jolt of electricity, charging the air and making it vibrant with danger. She felt as if she'd just walked out onto a high-dive platform and had looked down to see that there was no water in the pool. No, she thought immediately, without knowing quite what she was denying.

He felt the shock wave too. She saw his eyes widen with an expression of astonishment that might have been comical if she'd been in the mood for comedy. His smile faded abruptly. For a second, he stared at her blankly and then he moved on, and she had the sensation of free-falling through thin air. Her heart rattling around like a wild thing, she turned in confusion toward the rest of the approaching passengers, repeating inwardly, no.

The usual busyness of pretakeoff rituals forced her to recover her composure instantly, but inside she was still in chaos. That zinging response that had arced between them had been purely sexual. It was the kind of instant chemical reaction that occasionally happened between a man and woman, the kind of reaction she had sworn to avoid.

She found herself muttering—almost chanting as if it were a prayer—the vow she'd made recently: she was not, repeat not, going to let herself be attracted to any man for some time to come.

He seemed to be suffering from shock himself. That moment of awareness had surprised him as much as it had startled her. She was sure of that. He kept staring at her, his gaze following as she went through the cabin checking seat belts, catching her eye when she began to demonstrate safety and emergency procedures. He watched her with narrowed eyes as if she might do something unexpected—turn a somersault maybe, or at least stand on her head.

She felt unusually conscious of her body. She found herself constantly glancing down at herself to see if her blouse buttons were undone, her skirt zipper in place.... Her exposed feeling reminded her of a common recurring nightmare in which she walked around in public without any clothes on. She was beginning to feel angry—an emotion she welcomed. There was safety in anger.

Nervously stealing a glance at him, she noticed lines on his lean, lightly tanned face that she hadn't noticed before, lines that were emphasized by his frowning expression: one vertical groove between his eyebrows, two deep lines bracketing his well-shaped mouth, a few more radiating from the corners of his eyes. Why was it, she thought, annoyed, that lines on men's faces only made them look more interesting, while on a woman they just made her older? Damn! He'd caught her looking at him. That faint smile was hovering around the corners of his well-shaped mouth again. The mouth didn't quite match the rest of his business-like appearance, she noticed. It was a sensual mouth, full lipped and relaxed—a mouth made for kissing.

She had to look away from him; her knees were disintegrating. She was relieved when she was through with her demo and could take her seat for takeoff. Deliberately she took some deep breaths and exhaled slowly, following procedures for dealing with stress that she'd learned from a doctor friend.

As the engines came up to full power, she noticed her friend and co-worker, Janie Lincoln, seat herself next to the man. With any luck at all, he'd switch his attentions to Janie and she could relax. Most men relished the young Southern blonde's mischievous attitude to life. Why should he be an exception?

"That's some gorgeous man," Janie whispered as they prepared the drinks cart after they'd reached cruising altitude.

"What man?" Petra said, affecting an airy tone.

"Y'all don't know him? I thought surely you were old friends."

Petra groaned. "What did you say to him?"

Janie smoothed her swinging blond bob into place behind her ears and put on her wide-eyed innocent look. "I didn't do the talking, honey. He wanted to know if you'd be off duty when we get to Boston."

"You didn't tell him I'm going on to Cape Cod?"

"I surely did. He's going to the Cape himself. He's real interested in you, Petra. Seriously interested. He asked loads of questions about you. All I told him was that you were quitting your job and you and your kid brother were going to run some old colonial inn on Cape Cod that your uncle left you. Stuff like that."

"You don't call that talking?"

Janie had long ago perfected a Marilyn Monroe pout. She used it now. "Where's the harm?" She rolled her eyes. "Isn't he something? He reminds me of the man in the Barclay cigarette ads—the one who's always looking sideways. Did you ever see such eyes? And that mouth. Mmmm—sexy!" She glanced slyly at Petra. "His name's Dan Halliwell. Mean anything to you?"

"I've never heard of him."

Janie sighed. "Me neither. But he surely looks like he's somebody."

"Or thinks he is."

"Well, he likes you a whole lot. I thought he must be a friend of yours. He knows your name."

"Of course he does. All he had to do was look at my name tag. God, Janie, what else did you tell him? You know I'm not...oh, what's the use—" Petra broke off as they began wrestling the drinks cart along the aisle. Janie refused to believe she'd sworn off men. It was no use trying to convince her. Janie didn't see how any woman could exist without men, especially a woman who'd reached Petra's age. From Janie's twenty-year-old standpoint, twenty-six was bordering on pension time. Where she came from, Janie was fond of declaring, women bloomed early and married before the freshness could wear off.

HE HAD RECOVERED his poise. He gave her a knowing smile when she asked him if he wanted anything to drink. Then that too-intimate glance of his flitted over her again and she wished she hadn't taken off her jacket. After a moment his eyes met hers again, and again she felt a potent, almost overpowering surge of attraction between them. Mesmerized, she couldn't tear her gaze away from those devastating eyes of his. For a second or two he stared up at her, apparently just as hypnotized. Then Janie giggled and he hurriedly collected himself once more. "Yes, thank you. Coffee. Black."

When he took the cup from her, she noticed his hands. They were wonderfully capable looking, with long slender fingers and the appearance of strength. His face seemed strong too: that was a very assertive jaw. But then, so was her own.

"I understand a storm delayed the flight," he said evenly, totally in command of himself now. "There wasn't much evidence of it on the ground, but it must have been fairly turbulent to make you three hours late." His accent was pure Boston, bringing to mind

Ivy League schools, old family money and a nanny in the nursery.

Petra seemed to have lost her voice. That leaf-green gaze was still intent on her face, and her heart had begun drumming again so that she could barely hear anything else.

"We got ourselves stuck in the holding pattern over Minneapolis center and ran low on gas, Mr. Halli-well," Janie confided when Petra didn't answer him at once. "We were diverted to Rockford to refuel and the storm hit right after we landed. We had to wait it out. I guess it was worse there than in Chicago."

He looked politely at Janie while she talked, but as soon as she finished, he looked at Petra again. He seemed to be waiting for her to say something, but she couldn't think of anything to add to Janie's explanation.

Janie, however, wasn't suffering from any inhibitions. Irrepressible as always, she babbled on while they served nearby passengers, telling him all about the unaccompanied eight-year-old boy Petra had shepherded from Seattle to Chicago. The little monster had smuggled a kitten on board in his jacket pocket and had let it out during their enforced stay in the Rockford terminal. The cat, unnerved by her prolonged confinement, had leaped, claws extended, onto the lap of a sweet but nervous old lady, causing her to shriek like a banshee, which in turn had sent the cat hurtling across the floor to hide herself behind an enormous fixed trash container in a corner, where she'd resisted all of Petra's efforts to extricate her.

Petra had spent half an hour on her knees on the cold tile floor, trying to coax the kitten out. She had finally dragged her out by her tail, spitting and clawing. By that time she'd been in a mood to do some spitting and clawing herself.

"You should have put down a saucer of milk, or food; something to tempt her out," Halliwell said at the end of Janie's recital.

Know-it-all, Petra thought, annoyed because she hadn't thought of such a simple solution herself. But then neither had anyone else.

"It seems you've had a bad day," he said when she didn't speak. Was that a patronizing note in his voice? He was smiling faintly again, eyes crinkling attractively at the corners. He was probably imagining how asinine she must have looked on all fours, trying to catch that stupid cat. As indeed she had.

Still trying to recover her composure, Petra forced herself to respond calmly. "Some flights are tougher than others."

He nodded in apparent sympathy, then raised one eyebrow. "I suppose that's why you were so short with me earlier."

The nerve of him! Her heartbeat steadied abruptly, its former erratic behavior overcome by a flash of indignation. "I wasn't aware I was short with you," she said coldly, barely restraining herself from imitating his accent. "I'm just doing my job, sir. I don't have time to chat." She tugged at the cart so hard she almost pulled Janie off her feet. Janie grinned knowingly at her, and Petra had to bite her tongue to keep from blasting out at her. "Enjoy your coffee, sir," she said frostily as she moved on. "We'll be serving dinner directly."

BRAD PALMER, the flight attendant who usually spent most of his time wooing attractive female passengers, for once helped Petra and Janie yank dinner trays out of the containers in the rear galley. "Who's the guy in 3A?" he asked mildly.

Petra let out an explosive breath. "I don't know who he is and I don't care," she snapped.

Brad's sandy eyebrows rose. His handsome face was filled with lively curiosity. "No need to bite my head off, sweetie. The guy's had his eye on you since he came on board. Even I could feel the vibrations. You can't blame us for wondering what's going on."

"His name's Dan Halliwell," Janie informed him. "He's real curious about our Petra, but she doesn't care a bit. She froze him out like he was her all-time enemy.

"You've got to watch that temper of yours, honey," she added earnestly to Petra. "Vinegar never did catch the best flies." She sighed dramatically, looking at Brad and rolling her eyes. "How come all you good-looking men are always interested in feisty women like Petra? That don't-you-dare-touch-me look makes you all roll over and play dead every time."

"A discarded lover, maybe?" Brad persisted.

"I've never seen him before," Petra said curtly.

"Sure you haven't," Brad teased. He raised his eyebrows at Janie. "He looks like a good catch, don't you think? Smart cookie like the Professor here ought to be able to land him with one hand tied behind her back.''

Janie grinned. ''Didn't you know, Brad? Petra's sworn off men.''

''Is that a fact? You sure they haven't sworn off her?''

Ignoring both of them, Petra headed up the aisle, balancing trays, smarting over the snide note in Brad's voice. Sour grapes, she decided. She'd dated Brad once and they'd argued heatedly over his far-right politics. She'd destroyed his arguments one by one, using the Socratic method of reasoning that would have made her father proud.

Like most of the men she'd known, Brad was intimidated by a woman who had a mind equal or superior to his. He'd called her ''Professor'' ever since. And he had never asked her out again. That was no loss to Petra. She wasn't interested in Brad. She wasn't interested in any man. Not for a while, anyway. So she wasn't about to give Dan Halliwell, whoever he was, a single inch that he could turn to his advantage. She wished she didn't have to serve him. He was just biding his time, she felt sure, waiting for a chance to make a pass at her.

His chance came an hour later. Just as she had decided everything was under control and she could relax for a while, she heard a page in the first-class section and had to hurry toward it, hoping it wouldn't be Dan Halliwell. It wasn't. He was leaning back in his seat, reading an in-flight magazine. As she came abreast of his seat section, he looked up, caught her eye and smiled faintly, almost hopefully. Probably he thought she'd come up there just to look at him. She turned her back on him.

The page had come from the Oriental woman in the opposite seat. Her small daughter wanted her doll from the overhead bin. Could Petra get it for her? Petra smiled at the adorable little dark-haired girl, glad the request was so simple.

But when she opened the bin, she found the doll was wedged on top of a tote bag and a raincoat in the farthest corner, evading her reach. On tiptoe, she stretched as far as she could, determined not to ask Brad, now serving drinks in the coach section, to get it for her.

The tips of her fingers brushed the edge of the doll's dress. She tugged, but it didn't come free and she staggered slightly on her high heels. He was immediately behind her, holding her, his hands firm at the sides of her waist. "Why don't I get that for you?" he murmured, and reached around her, his body brushing against hers. Accidentally? Or deliberately? She felt a tightness inside her body that she tried to convince herself was caused by anger—even though she knew it had a lot more to do with sex.

He plucked the doll easily from its hiding place. Presenting it to the little girl, he clicked his heels, bowed and said, "At your service, madam."

The child promptly dissolved in giggles, one hand covering her mouth. Halliwell's eyes met Petra's. He was smiling, his left hand still touching her waist.

There was a stillness in her body, a softening in her bones. She was completely tongue-tied, shaken by feelings she hadn't experienced before, at least not with a traveling Lothario. Confused, panic-stricken, she tried to put enough words together to ask him to move out of her way, but she couldn't seem to manage the simple request as long as he was touching her. As she continued to stare at him, his easy smile gave way to a frown that reminded her of her first impression of him as predatory. "I think you'd better sit down for a minute," he said commandingly, in a voice that was probably used to being obeyed. "I want to talk to you."

Somehow she managed to shake her head, conscious that Janie had joined Brad and was standing in the aisle, looking forward, an expression of pure mischief on her face. As Petra glanced at her, she circled thumb and index finger and grinned wickedly. Halliwell turned his head just in time to catch the gesture. He looked back at Petra, both eyebrows arched. She felt heat rush to her face. "I have work to do," she said tersely. "I don't have time to entertain the passengers."

For a second, he looked taken aback. Then he inclined his head. Spreading both hands in a gesture of defeat, he stepped into his seat section and waved her past with all the aplomb of a courtier. "Try to spare me a minute later, okay?" he suggested sardonically.

Petra swept by, trying not to show that her whole body was trembling. "Not later and not ever, Mr. Halliwell," she muttered to herself as soon as she was safely out of earshot. No way was she going to dally for a minute with a man who was so dangerous to her hard-won peace of mind.

Janie preceded her back to the galley and then turned around. "Well?" she demanded. "Y'all looked mighty cosy there for a minute. What did he say?"

"I told him to leave me alone," Petra said grimly.

"Now, honey, that's no way to do. How often does a great-looking man like that come along? Least you can do is be polite." Her blue eyes took on a dreamy vagueness. "He talks like one of the Kennedys, don't you think? I saw a movie about them a while back." She sighed. "Eastern Yankee types are so adorable." She winked at Petra and started away with a coffeepot to see if anyone wanted a refill, adding over her shoulder, "If you truly aren't interested, I'll try my luck again."

"Be my guest," Petra muttered, and carefully stayed out of the first-class section for the remainder of the flight.

IT DIDN'T TAKE LONG for Petra to get through the formalities of turning in her ID card, figuring out her air time—up until the blocks were placed under the wheels of the plane in Boston—and drawing her final pay. But before she could leave the flight attendants' office, the flight specialist decided to give her a last-minute pep talk. "You do realize, Petra, that it won't be easy for you to get back into the airlines should you change your mind? Even with your good record."

Petra assured the older woman that she had no intention of changing her mind, but Cora Trenton hadn't acquired her reputation as mother hen for nothing, and it took some time for Petra to convince her once again that she was of sound mind and body and willing to take responsibility for her decision to quit.

"I sure hope I *do* know what I'm doing," she muttered to Janie as they left the office. Even though sometimes flight attendants seemed to be no more than glorified waitresses, she had really loved flying—the marvelous feeling when the plane took off and lifted her away from the world. And she'd enjoyed traveling all over the country, meeting new people. But Tony *needed* her. He was the only brother she had—almost her only relative—and she was afraid he was becoming too much of a loner, withdrawing into himself. It had seemed a good idea to take advantage of her uncle's legacy and make a home for the two of them.

She still thought it was a good idea, she assured herself. She could run the inn successfully. She knew she could.

Musing, she was startled when Janie nudged her sharply with her elbow. Mildly disoriented, she looked up and saw Dan Halliwell. He was waiting outside the baggage area, one hand braced against a pillar, the other in his pants pocket casually hooking his suit jacket open. He looked as though he was posing for a full-page fashion spread in *Gentlemen's Quarterly. The businessman's look this season is. . . .* As Petra and Janie approached, he straightened and stepped into their path, looking directly at Petra. "May I offer you a lift to the Cape?" he asked. "My car's in the car park."

Before Petra could reply, Janie erupted in giggles. Halliwell glanced at her, one eyebrow raised. "I said something funny?"

"It's the way y'all talk," she said between bubbles of laughter. *"My cah's in the cah pahk."* With a visible effort she straightened her face. "I'm sorry. I guess I sound pretty near as funny to you."

The stern expression had given way to a slightly fatuous look. "Not at all. You sound charming."

That pleased Janie. Her face flushed with pleasure and she looked at him adoringly. "My, but you're gallant, Mr. Halliwell."

"Dan."

Petra was beginning to feel like an invisible woman. Annoyed and not caring if she showed it, she hoisted her tote bag more securely on her shoulder. "We've already made arrangements," she said firmly, glaring at Janie when she opened her mouth, probably to inform him they were spending the night at the Logan Hilton.

"Your arrangements can't be changed?"

"No."

Janie was getting ready to speak again, but Petra cut her off. "If you'll excuse us, we are in rather a hurry and. . . ." She let the rest of the sentence trail away, implying other plans, other assignations.

"I see." He was looking down at her with narrowed eyes, and she wondered if he sensed that she was afraid—no, not of *him*—of the feelings he aroused in her, feelings she refused to accept.

He reached into an inner pocket of his suit jacket, brought out a business card, scribbled a number on it and handed it to her. "Please call me when you get to the Cape," he said. "Perhaps we could have dinner. I've been trying to—" His voice cut off abruptly, probably because he'd seen the change in her expression.

She had glanced at the card and frozen instantly. Dan Halliwell, *the Braden Corporation*. Well, that explained a lot. Not everything, but some of it. "I won't have time for socializing," she said bluntly. "Good night, Mr. Halliwell."

She walked off, dragging her suitcase on its wheels, hoping it wouldn't tip over as it had a tendency to do. She at least wanted to make a dignified exit.

Janie caught up with her at the taxi stand. "Petra, how could you?" she complained. "That nice man. What were you thinking of? He was real shocked. You were so rude. And there he was offering you a ride. Why, it would have saved you that whole old bus ride tomorrow. Sometimes I just don't understand you!"

"Don't try," Petra said.

She hoped her rudeness would close the conversation, but Janie was not easily suppressed. A couple of hours later, sitting on the edge of one of the twin beds in their hotel room, rosy from her shower and wrapped comfortably in her pink terry robe, she declared her intention of "getting to the bottom of all this."

Pulling her own more tailored navy blue robe around her, Petra flopped onto her own bed. "All what?" she asked tiredly.

"Your attitude to men. Why y'all hate them so."

"I don't *hate* them, Janie. I'm just soured on them right now."

"You don't give them half a chance, honey. Look at Dan Halliwell, for instance. What was wrong with him?"

"Nothing that met the eye, if you discount the fact that there was an ulterior motive behind his apparent moonstruck madness."

"What motive?"

Petra sighed. "He gave me his card, remember? He works for the Braden Corporation. A couple of years ago, the Braden Corporation wanted to buy my Uncle Will's hotel."

"That old inn he left you?"

"That one. Will's response was pretty salty. I don't blame him. There's too much of this trend of big corporations buying out independent businesses. The free-enterprise system doesn't stand a chance anymore."

Janie's pretty face had screwed itself into a puzzled expression as she tried to follow Petra's explanation. Petra waited, knowing Janie would catch on as soon as she'd thought it through. Janie made a big thing out of acting what she called Southern corn pone, but she wasn't anywhere near as dumb as she sometimes pretended.

"You think Dan Halliwell was coming on to you so he could eventually grab your hotel?"

Petra flashed her a "well done" smile. "Exactly."

"But you don't know that."

"Why else would he take such an interest in me?"

Janie shook her head, looking at her reproachfully. "Petra McNeil, you are so dumb sometimes." Narrowed, her blue eyes examined Petra minutely. "Okay, so you aren't drop-dead beautiful," she said with devastating honesty. "But still you've got that great body because of all the working out you do. And then you have those enormous dark eyes and that straight little nose, not to mention your curly black hair and your sexy voice and. . . ."

"And my big mouth."

"Yes, well there is that, isn't there?" Janie agreed solemnly, making Petra laugh, which made her feel much better. She'd felt disappointed when she'd found out Dan Halliwell had an ulterior motive for approaching her. And that was absolutely stupid, when she'd sworn she wasn't going to have anything to do with him anyway.

"Okay," Janie conceded. "We can scratch Dan Halliwell, I guess." She sighed. "Too bad. That is one gorgeous hunk of man."

"I wouldn't call him a hunk," Petra objected. "Attractive maybe—in an urbane way." She was pleased with the indifferent note in her voice and congratulated herself on her acting ability. The man had made her indignant, even furious, but certainly not indifferent.

"I'd call him a hunk," Janie insisted. "But all this still doesn't explain to me why you've turned yourself off men. Not every man you meet wants to buy your hotel. You have to admit that."

"True." She hesitated. "I guess there's something wrong with me, Janie," she said lightly after a while.

"I seem to be attracted to the kind of men who don't want me on a permanent basis, not the whole me anyway. I always go for a strong ambitious man who either admires me for my mind and never notices I have a body, or is attracted to my looks but wants me to put my brain in cold storage."

"So why don't you?" Janie waved a hand as Petra started to protest. "Forget I said that. All the same, it wouldn't hurt you to pretend you're a dumb bunny for a little while, at least until you've got a man hooked."

"That wouldn't be honest."

Janie's wide-eyed look was much in evidence. "Who made a rule that you have to be honest with a *man*?" She laughed along with Petra. "All right, let's talk about the men you've had in your life since college. From the meager bits of information you've shared with me, I know you've had at least two serious relationships. Who was the first? The high-school principal?"

Petra nodded. "Ted."

Ted had wanted to be the youngest high-school principal in the state, if not the country. He'd made it too. Petra had worked at the same high school, teaching English and English lit. She smiled reminiscently, painfully. "Ted was such a lovely bear of a man. He smoked a pipe." She paused, sighing. "I love pipes. We used to have long conversations about medieval superstitions, Yeats, Milton, the Wars of the Roses—and stuff like that, as you would say."

Janie was grimacing. "No wonder you gave up on him."

"I didn't give up on him. I like conversations like that. As far as I was concerned, the only problem with Ted was that it didn't occur to him that I had anything from the neck down. I tried every way I could to let him know I wasn't the frigid intellectual he thought me, but he didn't ever make a pass at me, and then, just about the time people began making comments about us being an item, he announced he'd got engaged to someone else."

"Why?"

"What is this, an inquisition?"

"I've pondered your love life for some time, Petra. This might be my last chance to find out what makes you tick."

"But you're coming to visit me sometime."

"Stop trying to change the subject. Why did Ted decide to marry someone else? What did she have that you didn't?"

"Adoring eyes and a slave mentality. She was apparently willing to type his papers and host teas for the faculty. He'd let out a few clues that he was expecting that kind of thing in a wife and I hadn't been too receptive. He also suggested once that I should take some cooking courses. Obviously he was looking for the ideal little woman—waiting at home to fetch his slippers and that pipe, like some kind of well-trained puppy. So of course he was quite right to look elsewhere. I'm just not the type."

Janie slanted a teasing glance at her. "Maybe you *should* learn how to cook."

"You didn't like the tuna sandwiches I fixed you when you came to visit me in Sacramento?"

Janie giggled. "They were better than that casserole you made for my birthday potluck, I'll admit that." She narrowed her eyes in mock indignation. "You're changing the subject again. Proceed."

"I've told you most of this before," Petra protested.

"No you haven't. All you ever told me was that Ted didn't work out. Anyway, I'm trying to perceive a pattern—as you would say. What about the blond-headed charmer who used to meet you whenever we got into Sacramento—the guy who was running for state senator? Was there anyone between Ted and him?"

Petra shook her head. Something had twinged inside her when Janie mentioned David. Those memories still had the power to hurt. She'd really thought he might be the perfect man for her—at first anyway. "David used me," she said. "Even though he was a very intelligent man, I found I was doing all his planning, writing all his speeches, and he was getting all the glory. I finally suggested maybe I should run for the Senate myself. He laughed, uproariously, which made me mad enough to tell him he might be better off with a woman who'd be happy in a secondary role, someone who'd be content to live through him. He got very thoughtful for a while, and then agreed with me. Next thing I knew, he'd found a red-haired secretary who doesn't write speeches as well as I do, but does make him cheese blintzes for breakfast."

She took a deep breath and let it out. "Even before all of that, things weren't exactly going swimmingly with David. When I started working for the airline, he was forever complaining about my being gone all the time. Which was understandable, I guess, but I didn't feel he had the right to dictate what kind of job I should have.'' She hesitated before going on. ''Anyway, it was all over before I decided to move to Cape Cod.''

Janie was chewing on her lower lip, mulling over Petra's problems as though they were her own. Petra smiled at her. ''It's okay, Janie. I'll survive. The trouble is, you know, that even in this day and age, most men still want a woman to *belong* to them. If I ever meet a man who'll let me be my own person, maybe I'll bring myself around to making a commitment. But I'm not ready yet.'' She laughed. ''Maybe tomorrow.''

Janie was still worrying her lower lip. ''It occurs to me that you've changed jobs as often as you have men. Maybe y'all are running away from something.''

Even though Petra knew Janie was smarter than she let herself appear, the younger woman could still surprise her. Because the truth was that she'd often felt she was running through life, though she'd never taken the time to sit down and figure out why she felt that. She'd never wanted to take the time to figure it out any more than she'd wanted to figure out why she had such problems relating fully to men. She suspected that something inside her prevented her from falling head over heels in love and that she was using her desire for independence as a cover-up for that inadequacy. But she wasn't going to admit that to

Janie, or explore it herself—not at the moment anyway.

Long ago, she had stolen a convenient philosophy from Scarlett O'Hara. Whenever anything really painful came up, she simply told herself with emphasis and lots of melodrama, "I'll deal with that tomorrow." The sound of her own voice proclaiming in such an absurd way was usually enough to make her laugh and feel better. But the habit was, she honestly admitted to herself, a type of running away, as Janie had so shrewdly guessed. She drew in a deep breath, sat up and clasped her knees with her arms. "I don't know that I'm running away from anything specific," she said slowly. "I just get bored, I guess."

"You're too bright for your own good," Janie said matter-of-factly.

"Not bright enough to figure out what I want to do with my life. I'd like to have the kind of job I could feel good about—the way men seem to. Something I really loved, something that would shape my life and give it meaning, so I wouldn't have to depend on other people for happiness."

"Men, you mean."

"I suppose I do." She shrugged. "I'm missing some kind of chemical in my brain, I guess—the one that makes a woman try to be the person a man wants her to be."

Janie gazed at her with mock despair. "Love isn't just a bunch of chemicals, Petra."

"Maybe not, but all the same, when you know it's going to end one way or another, it hardly seems worth the effort of starting. However it ends, you get involved in scenes and arguments and recriminations, which can be exhausting and definitely nonproductive." She sighed. "You've heard the expression, once bitten twice shy? Anybody would be stupid to keep coming back for more punishment. And whatever else I might be, I'm not stupid. So I've made up my mind that I'm going to stay away from men for a while and concentrate on getting my ambitions straightened out. A sabbatical, you might say. A few months free of the stresses of romance."

Her voice was pontifical, deliberately poking fun at herself. No way was she going to let Janie suspect that after each of her "romances" had ended she had hurt so much she hadn't been able to breathe properly for months. The pain of rejection, she thought, was surely the most acute pain anyone could suffer.

Janie sighed. "I guess I'll just have to hope that being settled in your hotel will change your mind. At least you'll be in one place for a while. Maybe that will help."

Glad the subject had been changed, Petra made a determined effort to sound more positive. "The inn is quite a challenge. It needs a lot of work." Then she laughed wryly. "That's an understatement if ever I heard one. Only five of the ten guest rooms are even habitable. The roof has leaked for years, and the water has stained the ceilings and walls in three of the rooms pretty badly. Then a guest got careless smoking in bed and set fire to a rug in number four—blistered the floor and half a wall. The fifth room had a fireplace that didn't draw properly. My dear

eccentric Uncle Will simply closed off each room
when it became unlivable. He couldn't be bothered
fixing them up, according to Sarah Merriweather.
She's the housekeeper. She says she nagged him all
the time, but he just wouldn't budge. But I'm sure I
can get the inn back in shape and make a success of
it. I've been there several times, the last few months,
checking on financing and so on. Mrs. Merriweather's a very competent woman. She worked for
my uncle for years. A Scotswoman. A bit on the sour
side, but kind.''

She lay back on the pillows and closed her eyes,
suddenly feeling very weary. It had been a long, hard
day. ''I'd better get some sleep. That bus leaves fairly
early.''

Janie didn't answer, but Petra rambled on, talking
mostly to herself. ''Maybe I should have rented a car.
No, it makes more sense to rent one when I get to
Falmouth.''

Her voice was fading. *She* was fading. She barely
heard Janie mutter, ''Well, you could have had a
ride, if you weren't such a bullheaded old thing.''

Was she really bullheaded? Her Aunt Sophia, who
had taken care of her and Tony after their parents'
accident, had told her often enough that she was. Her
parents had too. No, they hadn't used that word.
''Stubborn,'' her mother had said, furiously. ''Don't
be so damn stubborn, Petra.'' She could hear her
easygoing father's voice protesting mildly, ''Let her
be, Gina. She has her own life to live.'' Her own life.
Their lives had ended. Ten years ago. The pain of
loss was still sharp. She pushed the pain back into the

depths of memory where it belonged, wondering what had possessed her to allow it to surface. Oh yes, she'd wondered if she was really bullheaded. She certainly didn't think of herself that way. Determined to succeed, perhaps. Determined to be independent.

Dan Halliwell. The name popped into her mind from nowhere. There was a man who knew what he was doing and where he was going. She could tell just by the way he walked, and looked, and smiled down at her. *Down* at her. Superior height, superior smile, superior attitude. Why couldn't she have that much confidence in herself? Confidence wasn't strictly male territory. It only seemed to be, sometimes. Confident or not, Dan Halliwell was a rat, making a play for her so he could soften her up and attempt to take her hotel away from her. He'd better not try it. He'd find out she could be just as salty as Will McNeil.

"He surely was gorgeous," Janie said sleepily, evidently reading Petra's mind.

An image of Halliwell's lean tanned face and cool green eyes appeared behind Petra's closed eyelids. She shouldn't have walked off like that. She should have stayed and told him what she thought of his underhanded tactics. Next time. She was certain there would be a next time. He'd make sure of that.

"He's even got *me* convinced he's a winner," she muttered to herself. And sighed. And slept.

CHAPTER TWO

WAITING IN LINE at the bus station the next morning, Petra longed for Dan Halliwell—not for himself, but for his car. If he hadn't annoyed her so, she could have accepted a ride out to the Cape. If she'd known him better, and if he hadn't been connected with the Braden Corporation. She shrugged. Too many "ifs."

The terminal was crowded with tourists of every shape and size. Older couples milled about in Bermuda shorts and T-shirts, the women gossiping together and the men standing back looking bored, their arms folded across their ample waistlines. Harassed young mothers carried squirming toddlers and held others by the hands. Fathers wrestled with suitcases and paper bags, and a couple of teenage boys ogled a pretty young girl. Everybody was acting out his typical role, Petra thought nastily, and then stopped herself short. She was getting altogether too cynical lately. Just because she was soured on love right now, there was no reason for her to take it out on the rest of the world.

The crowded bus depot smelled of sweaty socks and stale cigarette smoke. It was too bad she hadn't been able to make this move before tourist season

started, but it had seemed best to do it while Tony
was out of school for the summer. So here she was on
a hot July day, feeling totally disoriented, claustrophobic, lonely and suddenly sure that this whole venture was a terrible mistake. She'd been mildly
depressed ever since she had waved Janie goodbye
earlier. They'd shared a cab as far as the airport.
Then Janie had gone off, looking smart and pretty as
always in her uniform, taking with her Petra's uniform, which she'd arranged to turn in, and leaving
Petra behind in a "civilian" dress, whose bright
yellow cotton hadn't cheered her up at all.

The bus ride improved her spirits. She had a seat to
herself, and the sky was the impossible blue of a
child's finger painting, with fleecy white clouds
breezing across it. The scrub pines crowding the
edges of the highway looked clean and fluffy as
though each needle had been combed into place.

When the bus crossed the Bourne Bridge over the
sapphire-colored Cape Cod Canal, her recovery was
complete. Each time she'd visited Cape Cod recently,
she'd felt that same lift as soon as she arrived, as
though all problems connected with the mainland
had been left behind and any difficulties ahead could
be solved with time. On the Cape there always
seemed to be plenty of time. As the bus rattled along,
she imagined the Cape in her mind as it showed on a
map, like an arm poking out of Massachusetts, bent
at the elbow and flexing its biceps muscle. Her mind
wandered to picture the lonesome stretches of pale
sand bordered with marsh grass, the quaint villages,
the bays and inlets, and the pine woods. Yes, she def-

initely felt that she was coming to a place she would
love, a place she would be able to think of as home.

The bearded young man from the car-rental agency who picked her up at the Falmouth bus depot was
talkative. He told her it had rained more the previous
day than it had in the entire month of June. She
groaned, thinking of the inn's leaky roof. One whole
section had to be replaced—and the last she'd heard,
Carter Mansfield, the contractor she'd hired, hadn't
even started on it.

The Cape was getting crowded, the young man
complained. The usual influx of summer people was
well under way, which meant petty crime had also increased. Vandals had broken windshields and poured
sand into the gas tanks of four cars in his lot the previous night. She was lucky to get a car at all, he added.
This was the only undamaged car they had in the shop.

A nice car, Petra thought after sympathizing with
the man. It was a tan Dodge, clean and tidy and apparently in good running condition, though larger
than she'd hoped for. She'd have to buy a car soon.
She'd sold her beloved old sports car when it started
costing more than it was worth.

"Where're you heading?" the young man asked as
he drove through Falmouth on the way to his office.

Petra had her head craned out of the window, re-
acquainting herself with the charming Main Street,
the triangular village green with its stately elm trees
and white-painted cypress fence, the old stone
Church of St. Barnabas, and the quaint-looking
shops and restaurants. "The Captain McNeil Inn,"
she answered absently.

There was a silence. Then he glanced sideways at her from under the bill of his Pennzoil cap. "Pretty girl like you'd be better off at the Pine Village Resort," he said. "Best place hereabouts. Built about a year ago. Regular swinging singles kind of place. Indoor-outdoor tennis, indoor-outdoor swimming pools, great food. They'll even serve drinks to you on the beach if you want. Got a nightclub too, with big stars sometimes. And dancing every night. Anyone stays there doesn't have to leave for anything. They've got it all."

Petra's ready temper had slowly been rising throughout this recital of the Pine Village Resort's virtues. She knew the place all right. It adjoined her newly acquired property at Pine Point, and it belonged to the Braden Corporation, an organization that had thought it would be a neat idea to offer their guests 2000 feet of silver sand—their own private beach—instead of the measly 1850 feet they had acquired from former residents.

"This inn belonged to my father and his father before him, not to mention the rest of my ancestors," Will McNeil had written to the corporation. "You want to put up a fence between your place and mine so your guests can have their blasted privacy, go right ahead, but you aren't getting my property."

Petra had laughed, reading the letter among her uncle's papers soon after he died. *Good for you, Will,* she'd thought, wishing she'd known him better.

"I'm the new owner of the Captain McNeil Inn," she told the driver, adding dryly, "I hope you won't sing the praises of the Pine Village Resort to my guests if any of them rents cars from you."

"I wondered when you said your name," he said, not a bit put out by the gaffe he'd made. "Relative of old Will's, are you?"

"His niece. My brother Tony's arriving in a couple of days. We're going to run the inn together. Until Tony goes back to school, that is. Then I'll be on my own."

"The old place is pretty run-down. Heard tell the roof leaks." He glanced at her and then away, pulling down the bill of his cap. "Sarah Merriweather sometimes goes to quilting bees with my mother."

And Sarah Merriweather was a gossip, Will had often told her in his letters, though not in such polite terms.

"I'm going to have the roof repaired," Petra said firmly. "I've already talked to a contractor. We're planning on repainting and repairing the whole place. It'll be as good as new in no time. You can pass that around town."

"Sarah's staying on?"

"She's talked of leaving?" Petra was filled with alarm. Without Sarah the task that already loomed so large would be almost impossible.

"Not in so many words," the young man said in a soothing tone. After another sideways glance he added, "Seems a big job for a girl."

Petra swallowed back the angry retort that sprang to her lips. She was going to need all the friends she could get, so she couldn't risk alienating anyone.

"I'm not as young as I look," she said mildly. "I can do just about anything I set my mind to."

"Uh-huh."

They had reached the car-rental office, and she didn't have a chance to think about the young man's comments until she'd signed the necessary papers and was on her way to the west coast of the Cape. None of her co-workers had thought it was a good idea to take over the hotel either. Neither had Sarah Merriweather, nor Aunt Sophie, really, though she'd agreed it might be good for Tony to have a new environment. "It's one thing to take him to Cape Cod," she'd said, "but to run a hotel?"

"I worked at the front desk of the Holiday Inn for two summers when I was in high school," Petra had reminded her.

"It's hardly the same thing, dear." Sophie's head was bent. She was brushing her heavy mass of black hair into its usual neat coil around her head. She had been getting ready to go to a benefit for the art museum where she worked. "I suppose you can't come to any real harm," she'd finally allowed. "But I really don't understand this nonsense of wanting a home of your own. I know I haven't been too successful in the mother department, but I've been delighted to have you and Tony living with me. You know you're welcome to stay with me until you get married."

And if I don't get married? Petra had wondered, but hadn't said. She was fond of her aunt, had always been grateful to her for taking in her and Tony when their parents died, but she'd never felt truly at home in Sophia's house in Sacramento. Kind as Sophia was, she hadn't really known how to handle either Petra or Tony. She'd alternated between strict discipline and benign permissiveness, depending on her mood, and how involved she was with one of the ultrasophisticated, intellectual men with whom she'd spent her spare time since she'd divorced her husband twenty years before.

Petra rolled down her window so she could smell the salt-kissed pine-scented air. Away with memories, she decided. Happy or unhappy, the past was over. This was the here and now. She had a home of her own now, and she wasn't going to listen to any more pessimistic talk about what a tough job she'd taken on. She was going to show all the naysayers just what Petra McNeil could do.

This brave attitude lasted only until she arrived at the Point. Parking the Dodge at the side of the inn, she walked around to the front of the hotel, wanting to see how it looked to her now that she'd committed herself to the place. She tried to see it as a stranger might—a stranger who expected to pay good money to stay there.

It looked *dingy*. The huge gilded wooden eagle that hung over the front door was peeling. The once-white shiplap siding was salt pitted in places, blistered in others and stained here and there. The green shutters sagged at almost every window, upstairs and down. "I'm a mite lazy," Will had written on more than one occasion. "Someday this place will fall down around my ears."

There was moss growing around the shingles on

the roof, and even a small section where several shingles had blown away in a long-ago storm. That was the first chore—the roof. And she should probably do something with the carriage house, which was attached to the inn by a breezeway. She'd looked into it on her last visit and didn't want to look in there again until she felt stronger. It was filled from wall to wall with the furniture from the damaged rooms: beds and dressing tables and marble-topped washstands all piled together with no covers or protection of any kind.

Her shoulders slumping at the thought of all the work that had to be done, Petra deliberately turned her back on the inn and looked at the view instead.

Beyond the expanse of lawn—which needed cutting—steps led down the bluff to the beach. Such a wonderful beach! The sand glinted silver in the sunlight. The full yellow skirt of her dress billowing around her legs in the breeze, she walked to the edge to look down. Below her, an elderly couple in swimsuits snoozed in deck chairs, newspapers shading their heads. The Inn had *some* guests then, unless the old couple had wandered over from the resort next door.

Waves were tossing gently, showing whitecaps as frothy as beaten egg whites. Close to shore the water had a greenish tint, but farther out in Buzzard's Bay it was as blue as lake water, reflecting the sky. The sky was hazy in the distance, so she could barely make out the opposite shoreline. New Bedford? She wasn't yet sure of the geography of the place. Her recent visits had been taken up with lawyers and bank

managers and she hadn't had time for sightseeing.
Her one visit as a child was an indistinct memory.

Reluctantly, she allowed her gaze to travel along
the beach to the resort area. Several shapely young
people were playing at the water's edge, while a few
swam farther out. On the beach itself, wooden
chaises topped with foam mattresses stretched in
rows, with almost every chair supporting a reclining
oil-glistened body. Sun-tanned beach boys circulated
among the chaises, adjusting striped umbrellas and
putting down mattresses for new arrivals.

Dominating the bluff, but screened by maple trees
so that she couldn't see them distinctly, were the
resort buildings. Designed to imitate traditional Cape
Cod style, the main hotel was very large, three stories
high, attractive and luxurious looking, surrounded
by wide verandas and flanked by dozens of small cot-
tages—"villas," the resort's rather pretentious
brochure called them. Between the buildings and the
edge of the bluff, a huge swimming pool glinted tur-
quoise between the trees. Given the choice, Petra
thought, she would probably choose to vacation
there herself.

She sighed, then turned back to her inn again. It
had a kind of old-world charm, she told herself
staunchly. Especially with Sarah Merriweather's
brave show of geraniums and petunias in the window
boxes. And the building was very sturdy. It had stood
there since 1812, when her great-great-great-great-
grandfather, Josiah McNeil, had built it as his
private residence after he wearied of deep-water
whaling. For more than a hundred seventy years, its

two rows of multipaned windows had looked out to sea. And now the inn was hers. She felt a sense of history, of family, standing there gazing at the sturdy white building, as though the inn were welcoming her home.

Forget Pine Village Resort, she ordered herself. Forget the Braden Corporation and Dan Halliwell. Forget all the people who had no faith in her abilities. This old inn was going to look as good as it must have when Josiah surveyed it himself, or she would die in the attempt!

SHE WAS GREETED inside the cool, somewhat dim lobby by Sarah Merriweather, who was sitting behind a small rolltop desk, writing in a ledger. The lobby was spotlessly clean, Petra noticed thankfully. The planked floor gleamed. The braided rug didn't have a speck of lint on it.

Sarah's greeting was hardly effusive. She looked up over her half glasses, stretched her mouth in what Petra took to be a smile and said, "So you're here," rolling her *r*'s as though she'd just arrived from Scotland, though she'd actually lived on the Cape longer than thirty years.

Petra nodded briskly, determined not to let her spirits be dampened any more. "It's good to see you again, Sarah."

Sarah's mouth tightened as though she doubted that and then she stood up, letting her glasses fall on the black cord that held them around her neck. She was a sturdy, somewhat plain woman of about fifty-five, shorter than Petra by a couple of inches, with a long sober face that seemed to hold a disapproving expression more often than not, and graying brown braided hair wound in a tight knot at the back of her head. "I've no doubt you're hungry," she said. "You'd best come to the kitchen as soon as you've washed your hands. I've a meal waiting."

Dutifully Petra freshened herself up in the downstairs bathroom, then followed Sarah into the back regions of the hotel, feeling much like an unruly pupil summoned to the principal's office.

The kitchen was totally efficient, modernized at Sarah's request some ten years ago, but it had retained most of its old charm. Its early-American-style furniture included a large antique dresser and a round pine table and chairs. It was as immaculate as the lobby. The table was draped to the floor with a yellow cloth and set for one with white ironstone china. There was a small bowl of yellow roses on the table—Petra's favorite flowers, a fact Sarah knew from a conversation they'd had on Petra's last visit. A warm feeling crept around Petra's heart. For a moment her eyes felt suspiciously moist, but she knew if she showed any reaction to the touching gesture, Sarah would be embarrassed. She turned toward the wonderfully fishy smell that was emanating from a large pot on the stove, making her mouth water. She hadn't had time for breakfast.

"Is that clam chowder?" she asked eagerly. "It smells marvelous."

"Stuffed Quahogs," Sarah said, her Scottish accent giving an odd intonation to the word. "You mince up the meat, mix it with spices, stuff it back in

the shells and steam them. You'll find them tasty.
And there's some of my homemade bread.''

"You shouldn't have gone to so much trouble,"
Petra protested, but was silenced with a wave of one
rather bony hand.

"I make lunch for the lassies and myself—no more
bother to add extra.''

The lassies, Petra knew, were the two maids who
came in daily. She remembered them as a pair of
overendowed young women with fresh country-girl
faces and a habit of giggling together while they
worked. Sarah professed disapproval of them and
frequently complained about their "laziness," but
Petra suspected she was fond of them for all that,
though she'd have died rather than admit it. Her
latest complaint had dealt with their wanting to wear
shorts in hot weather. It had seemed a sensible idea to
Petra. The inn's air conditioning was far from efficient. And by the time the girls—Bonnie and Terry,
as Petra recalled—came on duty, most of the guests
were on the beach or off on day trips, or had gone to
eat breakfast in town.

The Captain McNeil offered only a continental
breakfast, something Petra intended to alter as soon
as she gathered the courage to suggest any innova-
tions to Sarah.

The quahogs were delicious, the bread—one-
hundred-percent whole wheat, Sarah informed her—
warm from the oven. Sarah watched her eat, not
talking until Petra reached for the coffeepot and
poured herself a cup. "I thought you might change
your mind at the last minute," she said then.

Petra grinned at her. "Thought I might, or hoped I might?"

Sarah allowed her rather pinched mouth a small smile. "Well, now, I do sound a mite disapproving, don't I? It's just that you're such a bairn. . . ."

"I'm twenty-six years old, Sarah."

"So old? How the time does pass." There was a dry, teasing note in her voice that made Petra feel a whole lot better suddenly. It was often hard to remember in Sarah's presence that she was really a good-hearted woman, because she certainly wasn't demonstrative about it. "Sour old biddy," Will McNeil had called her. But he'd kept her on for twenty-five years.

"Speaking of changing minds," Petra said, sipping the scalding coffee, "I have an idea someone might try to work on me to do just that. I met a man from the Braden Corporation yesterday on the plane. . . ."

"That would be Dan Halliwell," Sarah said.

Petra stared at her. "You know him?"

"Aye. His family used to summer on the Cape. They owned a house along the bluff there, where the new resort is now. One of those big old houses. You probably don't remember. They didn't use it for a long time before the resort was built. Rented it out. I haven't seen much of any of them the last few years, but Dan's always kept in touch with me on the telephone."

She gazed at Petra a moment, apparently thinking back. "I suppose Dan was away that time your father and mother brought you out here. His parents started taking their holidays in Europe about then. So you never did meet him. I've known him since he was a lad—such a fine, braw lad he always was. He used to spend a lot of time here. I'm fond of him, you might say, even though he is a bit of a devil. Your uncle knew him too, of course. Knew his parents—Foster and Catherine—for years and years, which made no difference when they wanted him to sell. Though why Will wanted to hang on to this place, I've no idea. He didn't like work at all. He just wanted to go fishing all the time. And he offended half the guests with that gruff way he had. He could have retired nicely on the offer they made. It was more than generous."

Petra was feeling confused. "The family made the offer? I thought it was the Braden Corporation."

"Same thing, lass." Sarah had refused so far to call her anything but lass. She didn't approve of the name Petra, given her by her scholarly father. "Outlandish name. Doesn't go with McNeil at all," she'd objected.

"It's a private corporation," she went on. "Came down through Dan's grandmother. Right now, Foster is in charge, and I do mean in charge! A powerful strong person is Foster Halliwell. But it will all be Dan's someday." For a moment she studied her bony hands, loosely clasped on the wooden table. There was an expression on her face Petra couldn't quite interpret. Could it be pleasure?

Sarah sighed. "Many's the time young Dan sat right here eating scones. 'Nobody makes scones like you, Sarah,' he used to say."

Her mouth curved upward in what looked like a

child's drawing of a smile. "You'll never guess what else he liked to do here."

Petra waited, feeling slightly stunned. She'd already suspected Dan Halliwell had deliberately taken her plane the day before, knowing full well she'd be on it, planning to give her his card and bring up the subject of the Braden Corporation's offer. But to think that he'd sat at this very table, that he'd known her uncle. Why hadn't he told her?

Before she could pursue this thought, Sarah stood up, motioning her to follow, and led the way into what she called the sitting parlor at the front of the house. It was a large bright room, cheerful with chintz and polished wood and braided rugs, crowded with soft deep wing chairs and sofas, more like someone's living room than the lounge of a hotel. Petra liked its homey feeling. Her Aunt Sophia's tastes ran to chrome and glass and leather-covered furniture—a rather sterile atmosphere that Petra had never found comfortable.

A fat leather-bound photograph album lay on the rustic pine coffee table. Sarah handed it to Petra and gestured her to a wing chair, seating herself on the arm. At Sarah's insistence, Petra had looked at this same album on one of her recent visits and had found the memories it evoked to be painful. Why did Sarah want her to look at those old photographs again, when she had unpacking to do and a million things to think about?

"Open it, lass," Sarah said, her voice brooking no argument. "It will get easier each time, you'll see."

Knowing that wasn't so, but anxious to please

Sarah, she opened the book and was immediately caught up in it just as she had been before.

The pictures were all of the McNeil family, snapshots sent to Will over the years. Petra had kept up the practice after her parents died. A lump came into her throat as she turned the pages. They had been such a happy family. There were photographs of Petra and her parents skiing in the Sierras, eating sukiyaki with chopsticks in a Japanese restaurant in their beloved San Francisco, fishing in a boat on the Sacramento River while they visited Sophia, posing in front of the Capitol building. Smiling, always smiling.

There was a snapshot of the three of them in swimsuits, sitting on a rock on this very beach, the one summer they'd come to Cape Cod. They were dangling their feet in the water, her mother slyly pushing her tall skinny father just as the photographer, Will, snapped the picture. Her mother, looking unusually chubby—she'd been three-months pregnant with Tony at the time—was laughing as her husband, already off balance, clung to ten-year-old Petra. He'd slid all the way into the water immediately afterward, pulling Petra with him.

Yes, there was that picture too: Petra and her father sprawled in water up to their necks, Petra's curly black hair soaked and dripping, both of them scowling up at her beautiful mother who was laughing herself silly. Beautiful, beautiful mother, so alive, so in love! Dad's eyes shone with adoration in spite of the put-on frown. So much love, and so much bright promise—all gone.

Petra swallowed hard and closed her eyes momentarily. Then she turned the page, relieved to see she'd reached the pictures of Tony as a baby. The first one showed him sitting upright in the old-fashioned English perambulator Gina McNeil had insisted on for each of her children. Tony's face was solemn even then. There were snapshots of him that Petra had sent, chronicling his growth. The last one, taken a couple of years ago, showed him sitting on a bench in Sacramento's Capitol Park, his long legs stretched out in front of him. He was frowning characteristically into the camera lens, his mind probably engaged with some abstruse problem in the textbook held open on his lap.

Will had obviously cherished these photographs of his only relatives. A bachelor himself—the one love of his life had jilted him and he hadn't tried again—he'd apparently depended for love on his brother's family.

As she grew up, Petra had often wondered why Will had never visited them and why they hadn't visited him more often. The brothers didn't get along well, Aunt Sophia had explained when she asked. They'd had some big disagreement years and years ago. It hadn't taken much power of deduction for Petra to finally figure out that Will had loved her mother first, and had lost out to his younger brother, Ian. Why else, over the years, would he have carefully preserved these photographs? Poor lonely man. She should have visited him herself after her parents' death, but she hadn't had the heart. Apart from that one visit, sixteen years ago, she hadn't seen him at all and could only remember that he'd looked something like her father, but hadn't laughed as much.

"Don't look so sad now, lass," Sarah said briskly. "Those were good times. All that happiness is stored somewhere. It never goes away."

"I still miss them," Petra said quietly.

"I should hope you would. That's the way people live on, in the hearts of those who love them."

Moved, Petra turned and hugged her. Sarah accepted the hug, patting Petra's shoulder in a businesslike way. Then she straightened, a faint tinge of pink in her flat cheeks the only clue to her embarrassment over such overt affection.

"You were telling me about Dan Halliwell," Petra reminded her.

"Oh yes. Well, he always liked to come in here and look at these pictures. Last time he was here, oh, maybe five years ago, he was taken by this one in particular."

She turned the book to near the end and pointed at an enlarged picture of Petra—her high-school-graduation photograph. She was leaving the auditorium after the graduation exercises, her white gown flowing around her thin boyish-looking body, white mortarboard set squarely on her dark curls, honors medal on a green ribbon around her neck.

Sarah was actually smiling. "Dan studied that picture a long time," she said. " 'She looks so sad,' he said to your Uncle Will. 'Look at those great dark eyes. There's tragedy there.' And then he laughed. 'Did you ever see such a determined chin?' he asked Will. 'You might title this picture Petra McNeil challenging the world.' "

Petra snapped the book closed. "Men never realize a woman *has* to challenge the world if she's going to get anywhere," she said curtly.

Sarah shook her head. "Och, lass, he didn't mean anything by it. He was more admiring than anything."

"I'm sure." She didn't even attempt to hide her sarcasm. Dan Halliwell seemed bent on annoying her, even in absentia. She felt invaded, knowing he'd looked into her private family life. What business was it of his? And why the hell hadn't he told her he knew who she was?

He had started to talk to her several times, she remembered suddenly, but she'd cut him off, thinking he was making a pass. She had even imagined he had a sexual interest in her. Lord, could she really have been so gauche? No wonder he'd looked amazed when she was so rude to him. All the same, it would only have taken him a second to say, "I knew your Uncle Will." Why hadn't he?

Sarah was studying her face. "What did you think of him?"

"I—well, it's difficult to say. He—I guess at first I thought he was Lothario personified."

Sarah's eyebrows were rising.

"I mean, he seemed to want to—" She broke off. "He's a good-looking man," she finished lamely. "But once I found out he was connected with the Braden Corporation I didn't want anything to do with him."

"But you do think he's attractive?" Sarah persisted.

She hesitated, aware that Sarah was eyeing her suddenly hot face with interest. "Yes, I suppose I'd have to call him attractive. I didn't really talk to him much. I didn't know at first...."

"He didn't mention I told him you'd be on that plane?"

"He did not. Why did you tell him that?"

Sarah looked sheepish. "Well, he called a month or so ago. He'd been away for a long time, in England, first, then traveling all over the place; Paris, Rome...to do with business I've no doubt. He's an ambitious man. Anyway, he'd married an Englishwoman, so I suppose he didn't want to leave her just to come here. When he did get back to Boston, he heard Will had died and he called to see if I was managing all right, or if I needed anything. He was always thoughtful that way. So naturally I told him you planned to take over the inn. He was interested. He asked me to let him know when you were coming. So I did."

Petra tried to speak casually. "He's married?" She had no idea why she should care one way or the other, but she did.

"There was a divorce," Sarah said. "I don't know what happened. Since then, I understand, he's had a different woman every other month." Her mouth had set in a disapproving line. Petra couldn't decide if she disapproved of the divorce or of the womanizing. Probably both. What had happened to her own husband? Petra wondered. As far back as she could remember, no Mr. Merriweather had ever been mentioned.

Okay, so Dan Halliwell wasn't married. But she still had no idea why he hadn't told her he knew Will and Sarah.

"Well, I suppose I'd better get back to my work," Sarah said after a moment of silence. "You'll be wanting to get yourself settled in. I've put you and Tony up in the little rooms at the end of the hall upstairs, as we agreed. Yours is on the front."

Petra nodded absently as Sarah left the room, but went on sitting where she was, wondering about Dan Halliwell.

Abruptly she got to her feet. She wasn't going to spend another second thinking about that man. She had too much to do.

Yet still she lingered, finally wandering over to the small spinet piano that stood against one wall. She lifted the lid, absently fingered a few notes, and then, following some urge she couldn't identify, rummaged through the tattered old sheet music in the bench until she found a tune she recognized: "Come Back to Sorrento." Playing it, she could almost hear her mother's rich soprano voice singing the words in Italian. It was a lovely old song, carrying echoes of her childhood, haunting, and sentimental. And romantic, definitely romantic.

Slamming the lid down, she stood up, then hurriedly left the room. Petra McNeil, hotel proprietor, had no time for such nonsense.

CHAPTER THREE

"DAMN TOURISTS," Petra muttered, ignoring the fact that she'd often been one herself.

She was driving at a snail's pace along Falmouth's Main Street, looking for a place to park—an apparently impossible task. Just as she was about to give up and go check the side streets, she saw an empty spot ahead. She had the Dodge neatly lined up with the curb before she saw the sign: Don't Even Think Of Parking Here.

In spite of her dismay she couldn't help a spurt of laughter.

"You're in good spirits this morning," a male voice drawled beyond her open window. Startled, she turned to see a long low blue car drawn up alongside, with Dan Halliwell leaning across the front seat, eye corners nicely crinkled, beguiling smile softening the sharp planes of his face.

"Follow me," he directed.

He didn't leave her a whole lot of choice. Before she could answer, he'd pulled away, leading her to a large parking lot behind the chamber of commerce that she hadn't known was there. "Thank you," she said as she climbed out, willing her voice to stay level even though she felt very awkward in his presence after what Sarah had told her. Did he still see her as Petra McNeil challenging the world? she wondered. And did he still think her eyes were "tragic"? What nonsense!

He was leaning against his car, the ultimate preppy in a white oxford-cloth shirt and khaki slacks, boat shoes and a tennis sweater tied by its sleeves around his neck. His light-brown hair was smoothly brushed from a side parting to curve neatly behind his ears. He looked delighted with himself, as though meeting her was the happiest coincidence he could imagine. Was it really a coincidence? "Are you following me?" she demanded.

He nodded without hesitation or embarrassment. "I saw you drive off. I'm staying at the resort."

She hadn't thought about where he might be staying. Naturally he'd stay at his family's hotel, site of his old house. Swinging singles, she remembered the car-rental agent saying. A man who looked like Dan Halliwell would probably do very well at such a place. She could imagine women flocking, and pictured sun-bronzed bodies in brief bikinis. She wasn't sure if it was sexual attraction or annoyance that was making her pulse beat loudly in her ears.

"Just happened to look out of the window, did you, as I drove by?" she asked.

His quick dimpling smile showed appreciation of her sarcasm. "I cannot tell a lie," he said lightly, raising both hands in token surrender. "Sarah called to tell me you were on your way into town."

"Why would she do that?"

"Because I asked her to?" He grinned. "She also told me she thought you liked me."

She was going to have a firm talk with Sarah, Petra decided.

"I hoped I might persuade you to have lunch with me," Dan continued, sounding not quite certain of success. She felt pleased that she'd finally ruffled that too-confident exterior.

"I'm sorry, Mr. Halliwell. I have a lot of errands." As though she needed to prove she was telling the truth, she pulled a list out of the pocket of her white linen blazer and looked at the paper. The chamber of commerce, the drugstore for shampoo and then she was going to try to track down the contractor. Sarah Merriweather was running out of buckets and dishpans to catch the drips in the attics. The man still hadn't shown up. According to Sarah, he was never in his office. Her phone calls were not returned.

The list didn't impress Halliwell at all. "You have to eat," he pointed out.

True. And she wanted to find out what he was up to, see if he'd finally admit he'd known all along who she was. Maybe he'd even lead up to the corporation's offer. It would give her tremendous satisfaction to turn him down flat. At the same time, she could ask him about the contractor. If he'd spent summers there, he might know the local tradesmen.

Probably she shouldn't even consider having lunch with him though. She *had* promised herself she wasn't going to encourage him at all.

He smiled, evidently amused by her indecision. His

smile was dazzling, high voltage. It lit his whole face, deepened the green of his eyes and tripled his attractiveness. He had wonderful teeth—white and even. No doubt about it, he was gorgeous. A sudden attack of weakness threatened to buckle her knees and before she knew quite what was happening, she was walking alongside him through the parking lot and across Main Street, his hand gently supporting her elbow, sending shivers of sensation along her arms. A few seconds later, they entered a delightful little restaurant that was bustling with noontime activity.

A fresh-faced young woman in a white scooped-neck T-shirt and full ruffled denim skirt showed them to a round table beside mullioned windows that looked out onto the street. Dan pulled Petra's chair out for her, pushed it in after she'd seated herself, then rested his hands lightly on her shoulders. Her whole body stilled. She could feel the touch of his hands through the fabric of her blazer and the thin cotton of her striped sundress. She wanted suddenly to lean back against him, and knew if she did his hands would tighten. . . .

"May I take your jacket?" he asked politely.

She felt ridiculous. Of course that was all he'd intended. She was acting like a love-struck teenager out on her first date with the campus hero. "I'll keep it on," she managed. "It's cool in here." Her voice sounded huskier than usual.

She concentrated on her surroundings as he seated himself. There was a small vase of wild flowers in the middle of the table. The cloth was pink gingham and the walls were hung with local landscapes featuring vistas of sand and sky and dune grass, wind-sculptured trees, and sailboats scudding across blue-green water.

Dan Halliwell's eyes were watching her as she looked around. "Okay?" he asked.

"Lovely."

Another dazzling smile. If he'd smiled like that in the airport yesterday, she'd have accepted his offer of a ride, vow or no vow. No woman on earth could have resisted that smile.

But she must not forget who he was. She wondered how he'd get around to the subject of the inn.

"Sarah's a dear under that taciturn exterior, isn't she?" he said after they'd ordered a salad for her and a bowl of chowder for him.

There was her opening. "Why didn't you tell me yesterday that you knew Sarah?" she demanded. "Why on earth didn't you introduce yourself right at the start? Sarah told me you knew my Uncle Will and that you used to spend summers right next door."

He looked distinctly uncomfortable. Good, she thought. "I intended telling you," he admitted slowly. "But then you were so busy and. ..."

The waitress arrived with their food and it was a few minutes before they had any privacy. As soon as she left, Dan completed his sentence, but not in the way Petra had anticipated. "Actually, you were damned rude," he said bluntly. "I felt like a clod. Sarah hadn't told me you were so prickly."

She could feel heat rising to her face, but she had to admit his complaint was justified. "I'm sorry," she said stiffly, then added more naturally, "You're quite right. I was very rude and I do apologize."

He looked at her directly, those cool green eyes holding her spellbound. "Apology accepted. I was at fault too," he added magnanimously. "I should have told you who I was instead of acting like a love-struck urban cowboy." He smiled and her heart started doing all kinds of somersaults again. "The problem was, you see, that I hadn't expected to start falling in love with you right away. It rather threw me off stride."

A forkful of salad halfway to her mouth, Petra stared at him. His gaze was open, candid, with the deadpan expression of a proper Boston businessman. Her hands trembled in a sudden spasm of nervousness. "That's not very funny," she said in a voice that threatened to disappear.

"It's not, is it?" he said ambiguously. "You must realize, Petra, that I've never been struck by lightning before. I'm not sure how to handle the phenomenon." He looked at her with a perfectly reasonable expression on his face, as though he was discussing the weather. "It *was* like lightning, wasn't it? Just the way all the poets have it—one look and the earth shook."

She was suddenly not quite sure if he was making fun of her or not. She did know she wasn't about to get involved in such a loaded conversation. She began to attack her salad as though she hadn't eaten in a week, while he watched her, making no attempt to touch his own food.

After a moment when Petra was sure her cheeks

and ears must be flaming, he reached across the table and lightly touched her free hand, which was clenched on the tablecloth. "I'm sorry, Petra," he said without any inflection in his voice at all. "You don't like to be teased, do you? I'll desist, I promise. But I hope you aren't going to deny the chemistry between us. I'm not going to believe you if you do."

Chemistry? Chemistry was a much safer term than love. Petra relaxed a degree or two, then said tightly, "I won't deny there's something there, but I'm not going to pursue it. I'm not interested in pursuing it."

"I see." He withdrew his hand, looked at her steadily for a moment, and then opened both palms in a peace-making gesture. "Let's forget it then, shall we?"

She raised a cynical eyebrow. "Just like that?"

"Just like that. I'll try not to offend you again. Let's talk about something more impersonal. Pick a subject. How about the Captain McNeil Inn? I understand you're planning to manage it. Have you done anything like that before?"

Here it comes, she thought, *here's where we get to the real purpose of this lunch.* But again he surprised her. As he started in on his chowder, he encouraged her to talk about her plans for the hotel, and after a few moments of faltering, she managed to get under way. He was a good listener. He kept his gaze fixed on her face so intently that as she spoke it was sometimes hard for her to swallow. She told him about her Holiday Inn experience, expecting him to laugh, which he didn't, explained that she'd gained a lot of knowledge of legal affairs when she'd helped her

Aunt Sophia work out the details of her parents'
estate, and then went on to talk about the large extension her aunt had built on her house in Sacramento.
Nineteen-year-old Petra had taken it upon herself to
supervise the work, watching everything that was
done, asking so many questions that the work crew
had groaned when they saw her coming. She'd
thought it must be a fine thing to build a house with
your own hands, to watch it take shape in the way the
blueprints directed and see it come to life.

"I'm not too worried about the repairs," she concluded, starting to feel more relaxed. "I know what
needs to be done, and *how* it should be done. All I
have to do is get the contractor started." She laughed
shortly. "That isn't as easy as it sounds. His name is
Carter Mansfield and he seems to be letting me
down. Do you happen to know him? His office is
right here in town."

He frowned. "Most of the tradesmen on the Cape
will give you good value for your money—they're a
remarkably honest group. But there's sometimes a
bad apple in the best of barrels, and Carter Mansfield
might be it." He paused, apparently conscious of the
fact that Petra's spirits were sinking lower with every
word he spoke. "However," he went on more cheer-
fully, "I don't know anything against the man. Let
me check with my father. He'll know if Mansfield's
any good or not."

She suddenly regretted bringing up the subject. She
had no desire to get the elder Halliwell involved in
her plans. A powerful strong man, Sarah had called
him. "Don't worry about it," she said hastily. "I'm

going to see Mr. Mansfield this afternoon anyway. I'll take care of it myself.''

He raised an eyebrow but didn't comment. "Running the hotel's going to be quite a challenge for you, isn't it?" he asked after a while. He shook his head. "A small operation like that isn't likely to be too profitable you know, especially without a lot of money to back it up."

Trying not to show that his pessimistic comments were depressing her, Petra said mildly, "I'm not expecting to get rich. As long as I can break even...."

"Have you any idea how time-consuming a job like that can be?" he interrupted. "How on earth are you going to handle it alone? It's not a nine-to-five commitment, you know. It means long hours, never-ending responsibility. You're never off the job even when you're asleep. Are you sure it's worth the effort? It's not the sort of job I'd advise anyone to take on, especially a young woman who—"

"I'm sure I can manage," Petra cut in. "I'm determined to give it as much time and dedication as is necessary. I'm a very hard worker, especially when my mind's made up—as it is now. And I do have a little money. My parents weren't wealthy, but their insurance money was invested for us and...." Why was she telling him all this? "Sarah's very competent, you must know that," she went on briskly. "Why is it always so impossible for a man to believe that a woman can be efficient? Even more so than a man sometimes. Will didn't do a very good job of running the hotel, you know."

She felt guilty about maligning her uncle when he

wasn't there to defend himself, but facts were facts and she was getting tired of being told she'd bitten off more than she could chew.

Dan Halliwell didn't seem impressed by her arguments. He returned her heated gaze calmly and then said, "What you're not taking into consideration is the fact that I've had some experience...."

As she continued to glare at him, he let his voice trail away. Then he looked at her in silence for a moment. *Here it comes,* she thought again. "Have you done any sailing?" he asked.

Puzzled, she frowned at him. He was studying her face, waiting for her answer. "A little," she said finally. "A school friend of mine had a dinghy. After I moved to Sacramento, I used to go out with him on Folsom Lake."

"I keep a sailboat in Falmouth harbor," he told her. "I take her out whenever I have time. You'll like her I think. We could go over to Martha's Vineyard or Nantucket. Are you familiar with the islands?"

He was taking an awful lot for granted. "I believe I told you I wasn't going to have time for socializing, Mr. Halliwell," she pointed out in a deceptively mild voice.

"Dan." His expression was full of charming appeal. "I thought perhaps you'd change your mind, now that I turned out to be an old friend of the family?"

"That doesn't make any difference to my schedule." What was he trying to pull here? she wondered. First he'd tried an apparent sexual attraction and now he was going through a friend-of-the-family

routine. Obviously he wasn't going to approach her
with the Braden Corporation offer directly. Perhaps
she ought to put him on the spot and see what happened. "Are you vacationing here?" she asked pleasantly.

He didn't answer immediately, as anyone with innocent motivations would have. For a second he looked as
though he was uncertain of how to answer her. Put on
the pressure, she decided. "A business trip perhaps?"

"Not exactly." He was smiling blandly now, and
she was getting irritated. No, not irritated. Mad!

"I don't expect to have any spare time during the
next six months," she said bluntly. Let him try to
weasel around that.

"So long?" He studied her face again, apparently
mulling something over. Then he said, "I've no idea
where I'll be in six months, but it won't be here. I
don't expect to be here more than two or three weeks.
We'll have to work something out faster than that."
He paused. "If sailing doesn't tempt you, how about
driving? There are some lovely spots to see on
the Cape. We could drive to Provincetown. That's
down Cape, you know. A lot of people think it must
be up Cape, but it isn't. When the Pilgrims landed
at Provincetown, they explored 'up the Cape' and
so it has been ever since. We have our own way of
doing things here, you'll find."

Such as ignoring everything she said?

"If Provincetown doesn't appeal to you, we might
go antiquing in Dennis. Do you like antiques?"

Hadn't she made herself clear? Was he unable to
take no for an answer?

"How about tomorrow?" he suggested.

Giving up on the rest of her salad, Petra put down her fork and looked him right in the eye, stiffening her resistance to the boyishly dimpled smile that was probably supposed to disarm her, and was almost succeeding.

"As I've told you several times already, Mr. Halliwell," she said evenly, "I don't have time. As it happens, I have to pick up my brother in Boston tomorrow."

She could have bitten the words back when she saw the immediate leap of satisfaction in his eyes. "Why don't I drive you then?" he asked. "I've seen photographs of Tony, of course. I'd like to meet him."

"I'm perfectly capable of driving to Boston, thank you."

He sighed, tilting his head to one side. "I'm not doing too well, am I?"

She refused to be affected by his deliberate charm. "No, you're not."

Unexpectedly, he laughed, then reached across the table to take both of her hands in his. "If I promise not to tease you any more, if I promise faithfully to be only your driver, a helpful friend, will you reconsider?" This man could sell the crown jewels to the queen of England, she thought, but she wasn't buying.

He'd very cannily avoided mentioning anything about the Braden Corporation, she noted. Was he planning on moving more slowly than he'd first intended? Did he think the long drive to Boston would give him a chance to soften her up some more, so he

could bring her around to agreeing with any proposal
he might make? It might be interesting at that, Petra
thought, to see how far he would go before revealing
the real purpose of his attempts to charm her.

"All right," she said abruptly. "I'll accept your
offer of a ride tomorrow. I want Tony to like it here.
Perhaps you'll help me make him feel welcome."

"I'd be delighted." As soon as she'd said yes, he'd
let go of her hands and sat back, looking completely
satisfied with himself, infuriating her all over again.
She welcomed her annoyance. It gave her something
to think about rather than the way her hands had felt
in his, safe and warm and secure.

"I have to go," she said, standing up abruptly.

He didn't try to detain her. She supposed there was
no need for him to do so now that he'd have another
shot at her tomorrow. She was tempted to blurt out
that she knew he wanted to buy her hotel, but she
managed to stop herself. Tomorrow, she thought. If
he didn't say anything by the time they reached
Boston, she'd challenge him then. She looked forward to seeing his amazement when he realized she'd
seen through him and his spurious overtures.

She felt uneasy after they parted. She'd never met
anyone quite like him before. She had the feeling he
was the type who would size up a business situation,
decide on the best method of handling it and then
march on toward his goal, stepping on or over whoever happened to be in his way. Obviously, he'd
decided the way to her vulnerable point was through
the use of his not inconsiderable charm. That was
pretty dirty business practice, and insulting to her in-

telligence. Maybe those tactics had worked with other women in his business life. He'd be surprised when he found out they weren't going to work with her.

She still felt uneasy as she went about her errands. The nice woman in the chamber of commerce must have thought her very scatterbrained, she decided as she drove toward the contractor's address. She'd been pleasant and welcoming, promising to make sure the brochures Petra had brought in would be kept on display, promising she'd tell people who asked about the inn that it would be in splendid shape in very short order, telling Petra that she admired her for her courage and was willing to help in any way she could. And Petra had enjoyed talking with her, enjoyed being treated as a serious businesswoman.

Yet at the back of her mind all the time she was talking was that image of those superconfident green eyes, that dazzling smile, those incredible words: *I hadn't expected to start falling in love with you.* A couple of times the woman had had to repeat herself when she realized Petra wasn't paying attention to her.

PETRA WAS ALMOST RELIEVED when she found that Carter Mansfield was not in his office. At least his absence made her annoyed enough to clear her mind of all distractions. "He's supposed to be working on a job for me," she told the muscular blond teenager who seemed to be the only person in the office.

The boy shrugged, looking her up and down in an unoffensive but definitely admiring manner. "I haven't seen Carter in a long time," he said. "He sort of comes and goes."

Petra stared at him. "What does that mean?"

Another shrug. "He's not often here. His partner, Matt Mansfield, does most of the work. He's Carter's nephew."

"Okay. Where is he?"

"Out on a job."

"Where?"

Her impatience had offended him. His mouth was beginning to set stubbornly. "If you tell me where he is, I could go talk to him," she said coaxingly. "At least he might be able to tell me where Carter Mansfield is. He did promise to do the job for me. The firm's reputation...."

"Well, I don't know...."

There was enough hesitation in his voice and enough of a gleam in his eyes for Petra to chance applying a little charm. Five minutes later, with an unaccepted offer of a movie date behind her, she was negotiating the tan Dodge around the winding road to Nobska Point. She stopped the car near the Nobska Lighthouse, wanting to let her mood improve before she confronted the contractor. Painted a lustrous white, the ancient lighthouse stood close to ninety feet above the water on a manicured lawn dotted with shrubbery and flowers. It offered a fine view of Martha's Vineyard across the narrows.

By the time Petra drove on to find Matt Mansfield, she felt much better, mellowed by the scents of warm earth and flowers carried on the sea breeze through the car's open window.

She found the address in an area of big old houses near the Church of the Messiah. Huge trees overlooked the water, backed by professionally landscaped yards. After she'd parked the car, the sound of hammering drew her to the back of a rather ugly contemporary house with roofs going off in several directions and a lot of glass walls. It looked very ill at ease among its mellow old neighbors, and she wondered how the other owners could have allowed such a monstrosity to be built.

Matt Mansfield, instantly recognizable because he looked like a younger version of his short, stocky uncle, was perched on one of the strangely shaped roof sections, talking to two older men who were doing all the hammering. Made furious again by the fact that someone else's roof was being worked on, Petra called the man's name more stridently than she'd intended.

He peered down at her, hands on his hips, an obnoxiously cheerful-looking young man in shapeless overalls with a white painter's cap on his head. "Looking for someone?" he called.

"I'm looking for you, Mr. Mansfield. I want to know where your uncle is. I'm Petra McNeil. I saw your uncle a couple of months back. He promised to work on my roof and siding."

"The Captain Mac Inn?"

"That's the one."

"Uh-huh." Turning, he spoke to his helpers and then started down the ladder, moving at a snail's pace.

"Pretty busy today," he said with a bright smile

when he reached the ground. "Not much time for chatting."

"I didn't come here to chat. Carter Mansfield promised me...."

"Had a storm two days ago," he said as though that explained anything.

"He told me he'd start two weeks ago," she pointed out. "There wasn't any storm then, was there?"

"No." He scratched his head, reaching up under his white cotton cap to do it, exposing a mass of tight blond curls. Then he pulled a pack of cigarettes from a rear pocket and lit one, taking his time. He was probably no older than she was, Petra decided, but he had the deliberate movements of an old man.

"It's like this, Miss McNeil," he said at last. "From time to time, Carter gets what you might call restless. He gets tired of working and goes off on what he calls a walk-around. Usually, I try to prevent him from making any arrangements with customers because he's not reliable. Not his fault—he was born that way. You must have caught him when I wasn't around. He did mention you'd been in, but didn't say anything about getting the job. Not much I can do about it. When Carter's gone, he's gone."

He said this in such a calm voice that Petra didn't register what he'd said at first. When she did, she tried several times to respond, but she couldn't quite get the words to come out. "But he came out to the inn," she managed at last. "We talked about everything that needed to be done. He was enthusiastic. He promised...."

Mansfield shrugged, still smiling genially. "He's

good at promises, Carter is. Not so good at keeping them. No knowing how long he might be gone.''

"It's your company too, isn't it?" she asked.

"Uh-huh."

"Well, then, couldn't *you* come out and do the job for me?"

He dropped his cigarette stub, stepped on it deliberately, grinding it carefully under his heel, then nodded reluctantly. "I suppose I could take a look at it."

"Fine. When?"

"*If* I had time."

She took a deep breath, and promised herself she'd hang on to her temper if it killed her. "When *will* you have time, Mr. Mansfield?" she asked politely.

He squinted intently at a large maple tree as though a calendar hung on it. "Might manage it on Thursday."

"But it's Friday today. That's almost a week away." In spite of her good intentions, her voice was rising.

His nod was as slow as his speech. He followed it with a sly sideways glance. "Might, I said now. Lots of people needing roof work."

"But I had an agreement with your uncle. It seems to me that if he's...disappeared, the least you can do is keep the contract for him and...."

His sardonic blue eyes looked at her sideways again. "Doesn't do to get yourself in a state, Miss McNeil. Might get yourself ulcers."

Petra sighed. This wasn't getting her anywhere. "I'll expect you Thursday," she said crisply. "I'll just have to pray it doesn't rain again before then."

He smiled confidently, showing remarkably strong white teeth. Then he looked up at the sky. "Won't rain for a while now."

He sounded positive and Petra looked at him doubtfully, wondering if he was relying on an islander's instincts or gauging the wind direction. "How can you tell?" she asked when he didn't offer anything more.

"Weatherman said so on television this morning." He paused. "Course, he was talking from Rhode Island."

Somehow Petra managed to remove herself from his presence without strangling him. The last she saw of him, he was gazing up the ladder, looking as though he wasn't quite sure he wanted to bother making the climb. She should really hire someone else, she thought as she drove away. Except that it was probably impossible to find someone else. It had taken her a while to find anyone who wasn't too busy, or too expensive, and Carter Mansfield had already given her a fairly reasonable estimate, which she hoped his nephew would adhere to.

Matt Mansfield was probably right anyway, she thought, deliberately trying to cheer herself up, looking up at the cloudless cornflower-blue sky as she drove back to the inn. It might not rain again for some time.

THE SOUND OF WATER rushing down drainpipes woke her at six the next morning. Hastily, muttering imprecations on the heads of Carter and Matt Mansfield, she pulled herself out of her cosy bed and stag-

gered along the hall and up the stairway to the attics.
Sarah was there ahead of her, her single wispy braid
hanging over one shoulder, clutching a blue chenille
robe closed around her sturdy figure as she carefully
checked the position of the buckets and bowls she'd
set out earlier. The patter of water sounded like a
Maxwell House coffee commercial. "I'm going to
kill Carter Mansfield if I ever see him again," Petra
said through her teeth. "And after he's disposed of,
I'm going to start on his weather-prophet smart-aleck
nephew."

Sarah gave her one of her closed-mouth smiles.
"Pity you couldn't find a woman contractor," she
said. "Men think they can take advantage when it's a
woman running things, especially if she's an off-
islander. You maybe should have lost that famous
temper of yours with this Matt Mansfield."

"I will if he doesn't turn up on Thursday," Petra
promised, then hesitated. "My temper is famous?"

Sarah seemed taken aback and Petra put her sudden suspicion into words. "You've been talking to
Dan Halliwell again?"

Sarah cleared her throat. "Aye, well, we might
have exchanged a few words."

"What exactly did you tell him?"

"I don't know that I remember."

"I hope you haven't been encouraging him
again."

Sarah said nothing but she looked unmistakably
guilty. Petra sighed, but then realized it was probably
safer to drop the subject before she unwittingly gave
Sarah any further quotes to pass on to Dan.

She went back to her bedroom, cheering up when she looked around it in the gray light that was filtering through the thin window curtains. Even the slanting rain couldn't make this room look depressing, bright as it was with hooked rugs and warmly glowing old furniture.

Sarah had put a quilt that had belonged to Will on Petra's bed, telling her the sea breezes made the nights cold. It was a lovely creation that one of the local women had made him. "They were all after him," Sarah had said with a sniff. Appliquéd with gingham flowers, it had a yellow background and a ribbon-tied edging of midnight blue. "Much too feminine for a man," Sarah had scoffed. "Will wouldn't have been seen dead under it." As she realized what she'd said, her eyes had filled and she'd had to blink several times, unwilling or perhaps unable to show sadness any more than she could show pleasure.

She had smiled her tight-lipped smile though when Petra told her she wanted all the rooms in the inn to look as warm and inviting as this one. "We can't compete with the big hotels and their fancy entertainment," Petra had said. "We can only offer our guests a home away from home."

Standing there now, she was struck with the thought that she'd created the whole theme for the inn; the focus, the heart. *A home away from home.* She'd think of all the things people missed in a large, soulless hotel and provide them if she possibly could. The possibilities were endless. She'd get started just as soon as the roof was fixed.

Damn Matt Mansfield. He could have come out earlier than the following week, considering the circumstances. He shouldn't let that uncle of his near the office. Walk-around indeed. He'd better agree to go to work right away when he did come out, or she'd ram his painter's cap down over his smug blue eyes.

The thought cheered her, and she was humming as she headed for the bathroom she shared with Sarah.

CHAPTER FOUR

"ACTUAL WORK ON THE CAPE COD CANAL was started by some of your mother's countrymen. Did you know that?" Dan asked.

Seated in the butter-soft leather bucket seat on the passenger side of Dan's car, comfortable in a red cotton shirt and cream-colored pants with matching linen jacket, Petra glanced at his handsome profile, feeling mildly puzzled. Ever since he'd picked her up this afternoon, he'd expounded on the history of every place they passed. This was interesting enough, since he was very well informed, but after she'd keyed herself up to resisting his advances, it was a bit disconcerting to find there apparently weren't going to be any.

All the same, the atmosphere between them was every bit as loaded with tension as it had been since they first met. And to compound the problem, he was looking extremely attractive in a tan shirt and slacks, with a brown V-necked sweater. He oozed virility, guaranteed to make any woman suffer from palpitations and instant sexual fantasies. She took a deep breath, let it out and tore her gaze from him. Surely all this electricity couldn't be emanating only from her?

"No, I didn't know that," she said at last.

He nodded briskly. "Four gangs of over a hundred Italian laborers worked with pick and shovel. Around 1880, I believe. Actually, they stopped after two months because the promoters of the canal ran out of money. The next company to have a go went broke too, and the next. It wasn't until August Belmont came along after the turn of the century that anything really got accomplished. Belmont was a New York financier who was known for taking on challenges. His grandfather was Commodore Matthew Perry, who opened Japan up to trade, so I suppose gumption ran in the family."

"You admire gumption?"

"Absolutely."

She pounced. "Unless it's displayed by a woman? A woman who takes over a hotel, for example, and has the gall to think she can run it successfully?"

He winced and then laughed shortly. "You're still annoyed by my warnings yesterday? I keep forgetting how prickly you are."

"I am not prickly. I just object to people who doubt my abilities before they've even been tested."

He looked at her sideways. "You're really determined to succeed, aren't you?"

"I am."

"Then I suppose all I can do is wish you well."

"That would make a nice change. I'm getting pretty tired of pessimistic outlooks."

"I've nothing against optimism, as long as it's coupled with an acceptance of reality."

"I'm not stupid, Dan."

"I didn't think you were." He accompanied this remark with a measuring glance that seemed to raise her temperature several degrees. Then he turned his attention back to the fairly heavy traffic on the highway. The wheels of the car ahead of them were throwing road mist and the rain was beating down steadily. The metronomic thrum of the windshield wipers added to the feeling of tension in the car.

Petra searched her mind for something to say, wishing he'd go on with his history lessons even though there was nothing now to comment on. All she could see through the rain-streaked windows were a lot of scrub pines and some other cars. She looked at the dashboard, which had enough instrumentation to equip a fighter plane.

"The old saw about if you don't like the weather, wait a minute and it'll change certainly applies here," Dan said, and then declaimed,

> "In winter, when the dismal rain
> Came down in slanting lines,
> And Wind, that grand old harper, smote
> His thunder-harp of pines."

The quote astonished her. "Not that it's winter," he added, "but the verse does seem to fit, doesn't it?"

"I thought I was the only person in the world to know Alexander Smith," she commented in a pleased tone of voice.

"'Time has fallen asleep in the afternoon sunshine,'" he quoted reverently from the same source. "I really admire that line. Whenever I think of it, even on a rainy afternoon like this one, I can smell the warm toast smell of sitting under a tree out of the sun, listening to bees buzz, feeling that whole marvelous languor of a summer afternoon.''

She looked at him with new interest. "You really like poetry?''

"You're surprised?''

"Yes. I—well, of course there's no reason for me to be surprised, but I haven't met many men who...''

"Liked the finer things in life?'' he finished for her. "I can see your education needs to be completed, Petra McNeil.''

There was a note of amusement in his voice. He was probably going to offer to complete her education himself. In two easy weeks—wasn't that how long he'd said he'd be around? Would she get her money back if she didn't pass the course? "I was about to say that I haven't met many men who were familiar with nineteenth-century poets,'' she said dryly.

The corners of his mouth quirked. "Try me.''

"Owen Meredith,'' she challenged.

"Ah yes. A.k.a. Edward Robert Bulwer-Lytton, Earl of Lytton. Let me think now.''

A small Buick, traveling much too fast, hurtled past in a backwash of water, splashing the windshield, so that for a second he couldn't have been able to see a thing. Petra sat up straight, heart pounding, stomach contracting with fear as the Buick cut in front of him, much too close, then swung out again with another back splash. Petra would have pounded a harsh tattoo on the horn, but Dan just raised an eyebrow, then settled himself more comfortably in his seat, before going on to quote, " 'My life is a torn book. But at the end a little page, quite fair, is saved, my friend, where thou didst write thy name.' "

Okay, Petra thought. If he could be that cool, so could she. "How about Emily Dickinson?" she asked.

He didn't hesitate this time.

> "Love—is anterior to Life—
> Posterior—to Death—
> Initial of Creation, and
> The Exponent of Breath."

His voice lingered on each word lovingly. This was getting dangerous, Petra decided, but almost as the thought came to her, he dissipated the renewed tension with a laugh. "You're forgetting Lewis Carroll," he said. " ' "You are old, Father William," the young man said", "and your hair has become very white. . . ." ' "

" ' "And yet you incessantly stand on your head—" ' " Petra joined in. " ' "Do you think at your age it is right?" ' "

They both laughed and Petra began to feel a little like Alice in Wonderland herself, not quite sure what she was doing there with this surprising man. " ' "I can't explain myself, I'm afraid, sir," said Alice,' " she murmured, " ' "Because I'm not myself, you see." ' "

" " "I don't see," said the Caterpillar,' " Dan finished for her.

Delighted to have found someone who could share both her love of the ridiculous and her love of the classics of literature, Petra relaxed her guard without even consciously deciding to do so and they spent the next half hour discussing British novelists like Thackeray and Trollope and George Eliot. "I'd love to have lived in the nineteenth century," Petra said with a sigh.

"No you wouldn't. You'd have hated being your husband's chattel, bound to home and children."

Petra looked at him wonderingly. How had he learned so much about her in such a short time? "I wouldn't have married," she said positively. "I'd have been another Charlotte Bronte, devoting myself to my writing, falling helplessly in love with a married man."

"Charlotte married eventually."

"And died soon after. There's a moral in there somewhere."

"You sound very cynical, Petra. Haven't you ever fallen helplessly in love?"

David was suddenly alive in her mind. She could see the sheen of his blond hair, the blue light of his eyes. She'd been dreadfully hurt when he deserted her for Rena of the red hair and perfect cheese blintzes. But helpless love? Absolutely not.

What about Ted? Both relationships had ended in disenchantment. All love ended in disenchantment and loss.

"I don't know that I believe in the concept of helpless love," she said. "I guess I believe the will is always in control." She hesitated. Whenever a conversation turned to love as it so frequently did between a man and a woman, all her "fight or flight" mechanisms came into play and she felt forced to either combat every suggestion of softer emotion, or to run away mentally from the subject. She knew it was ridiculous. There was nothing wrong with discussing love on an intellectual basis.

"I'm not sure I even believe in love," she continued, musing aloud. "It seems to me that when someone says he loves you, he immediately starts making claims on you and trying to change you into the person he thinks you should be. The ideal of love would be for someone to love you exactly as you are, warts and all. And I don't think anyone's capable of that kind of love." She glanced across at him and saw he was frowning as though she'd displeased him—which didn't bother her a bit. "How about you?" she challenged. "Have you ever been helplessly in love? You were married, I understand."

She felt smugly pleased when he looked surprised that she knew that. It was about time he realized Sarah's gossip could be double-edged.

"I'd have to say yes, I guess," he said slowly. "Elizabeth and I. . . ." His voice trailed away and he seemed to withdraw into himself.

Elizabeth: a perfect complexion, fine, baby-soft blond hair, china-blue eyes, petite and adorable, no doubt English, Sarah had said. *The rain in Spain stays mainly in the plain.* Terribly refined. Why did it upset her to know he'd loved his wife helplessly? Was she envious because he had the capacity to love so much when she didn't?

"The divorce is final?" she asked.

"Yes." He paused, frowning. "It was fairly friendly, but I don't ever want to go through something like that again." Those lines had been carved in his face by pain, she realized. He was more sensitive than she'd suspected. She wished she hadn't brought the subject up. "I'd strongly advise you to avoid matrimony, Petra," he said. "Independent as you seem to be, you'd probably hate it."

Obviously he didn't want to get married again either, she thought as he hesitated. "Official reason given for my divorce was that I traveled too much," he added.

"I can identify with that. I had that complaint leveled at me when I worked for the airline." She hesitated. "You said official—you mean that wasn't the real reason?"

"The reasons we give ourselves when we fail at love are seldom the truth," he said.

She was surprised by his perception, and when he fell silent, she pondered what he'd said and why it sounded so right to her, so applicable to herself. She suspected again that she hadn't given herself the real reasons for her failure to love enough in the past. But that was ridiculous, she reassured herself. The reason she hadn't loved enough was that she hadn't met a man *worth* loving enough. It was as simple as that.

She glanced at Dan. It seemed they had both had emotional troubles. Did that make her safer with him? Or more vulnerable? He was frowning, looking straight ahead through the rain-swept windshield. "Petra," he said musingly. "That's Latin, isn't it?"

She was relieved that he'd changed the subject. "My father named me. He taught Latin and classical Greek at university level. He loved everything to do with the old Romans. If I'd been a boy he'd have called me Marcus."

"How did Tony slip through?"

"He didn't. His full name is Antonius, but don't ever call him that."

"He has a temper like yours?"

She felt herself flushing, though she could hardly blame him for realizing that about her. "No," she said slowly. "Tony's a bit of a stoic like my father was. He's a typically calm Scotsman and takes life as it comes."

"I guess I must be a stoic too then."

"You don't lose your temper?"

"Only when absolutely necessary. My family doesn't consider it good form to lose control. I was trained to suppress all hostility. It became a habit, I suppose."

She could envision his parents. Sarah had mentioned their names. What were they? Oh yes, Foster and Catherine. Very proper. Old family and conscious of it. She could just imagine them standing in a receiving line, greeting guests with cool, superior smiles, observed by Dan, who was too young to join in the festivities—no, not festivities; the word implied jollity—the soire. A small ensemble would play, a few members of the Boston Symphony perhaps. Dan the child would peer through the stair rails wistfully? Jealously?

Into the silence Petra said, "I've often wondered how my mother and father managed to be so happy. They were such opposites. My mother was an opera singer; dramatic, very volatile. She threw things. My father used to just duck and laugh at her. He never got angry. That must have infuriated her. She was so passionate herself. . . ."

"You're equating a calm nature with a lack of passion?"

"I guess I am."

He laughed shortly. Then, without any warning at all, he swung the car onto a side road Petra hadn't noticed, let it roll to a stop, switched off the ignition and turned toward her.

Startled, she looked at him. Their eyes locked. She felt a sudden sense of isolation, exaggerated by the rain-streaked windows that prevented anyone from seeing them. It was as though they were trapped together in that very small space, suspended in time, shut off from the world. Her throat had tightened and she couldn't speak, couldn't move.

His gaze continued to bore into hers, and she returned his look as though she had no will of her own. There was an odd expression on his lean sharp-featured face—a mixture of helpless exasperation and amusement. Was he amused by himself? Or her?

As though in slow motion, his left hand reached toward her face. His fingers traced the line of her eyebrow, then slid across to her hair. Gently, he tugged a single fat black curl to its fullest extent, then let it go to spring back on itself. Then he smiled. His eyes were green as a cat's in the gray light.

"Your eyes intrigue me, Petra," he murmured as she stared mutely at him. "They put me in mind of Shelley's lost angel of a ruined paradise. 'She knew not 't was her own; as with no stain she faded, like a cloud which had outwept the rain.' It's impossible to see into your eyes, impossible to see what goes on in that complex mind of yours, yet I sense sadness. Why are your eyes so sad, Petra? What hurt are you hiding away back there in the dark?"

"I'm not, I don't...." Her voice trailed away as his fingers moved to her mouth, his thumb gently stroking over her lower lip, back and forth, back and forth. "What are you doing?" she asked. Her voice had sunk to a husky whisper, she noted, dismayed. It sounded positively seductive.

"This," he answered. And she was suddenly in his arms, one of his hands holding her head firmly as he bent his head to hers and brought his mouth down on her half-open lips.

She had been kissed before by men who were skilled at lovemaking, as skilled as this man seemed to be. She had kissed in return, her body quick to the passion of the moment. But she had never felt such an aching in her bones as she felt now. She had never known that a mouth could brush against hers with such gentle pressure yet steal all the breath from her body so that her heart, starved of oxygen, would pound so fiercely it drowned out the sound of the rain on the roof of the car.

Her hands were in his hair, urging him closer to her as his tongue explored the softness in her mouth. His hands were behind her now, those wonderful capable hands fumbling with her jacket, lifting it at the hem, reaching under it to slide across the curve of her waist, upward to the sides of her breasts. Strong hands, cool hands, burning through the thin cotton of her red shirt. All the time his mouth played against hers, and she didn't want ever to release him from this kiss that was turning her bones to gelatin, her blood to liquid fire.

His breath was warm against her mouth and his lips had increased their pressure. His tongue seemed driving, intrusive, demanding a response that she seemed unable to refuse. She surrendered totally, her body arching to meet his, her hands gripping his head so hard she could feel the firm shape of his skull beneath his crisp, thick hair.

She didn't want him to stop. She wanted him to go on and on. She wanted.... She wanted *him*. The air was whirling around her now, and she was being helplessly drawn into the tumult of her own emotions, out of control....

A second later he released her and she heard herself give a soft moan of loss. He drew back and looked at her with a satisfied glint in his eyes, his hands still cupping her face. "Is that enough passion for you?" he demanded.

Shocked as though she'd suddenly been doused with cold water, Petra pulled back as far as she could into the soft bucket seat, reaching for composure, aware that blood had rushed to her face and must have dyed it pink, judging by his amused expression.

God, what had she done? After all her vows, all it had taken was one kiss from an aggressive, assertive man who had thought she was questioning his masculinity and she had let herself become undone, betrayed by her own sensuality. She'd even let herself forget who this man was, what he wanted. He was looking at her now with an expression she recognized: the dominant male, sure of possession, sure of his own power.... After the way she'd responded to him, he'd expect her to go to bed with him. She could see the expectation in his eyes.

"We'd better get on to Boston, I suppose," he said at last when she didn't respond. Then he turned away, started up the car and expertly maneuvered it into a U-turn that took them back to the highway.

Her face burning with what she decided was annoyance, Petra sat in silence for a few minutes and then said, "You had no right to do that, you know."

He glanced at her sideways. Then he said in an exasperated voice, "You know damn well, Petra McNeil, that something has been going on between us ever since we first saw each other. You might as well face up to it because we're going to have to decide what to do about it. I suppose we can't decide much now, since we're almost into Boston, but after we pick up Tony and get him to the inn, we'd better go to my hotel suite and talk about our relationship and how we're going to handle it."

The word "relationship" flagged a warning in Petra's mind. "Oh no," she said flatly. "Forget it. Forget the whole thing. I've no intention of going through all that again, not with you or anyone else."

"Going through all what?" he asked blankly.

"Never mind. All you need to know is that I'm not

in the least interested in any kind of relationship with you.''

He chuckled softly in a deriding way. ''Petra, Petra,'' he chided. ''You know you want me as much as I want you. You can at least be honest with yourself.''

''I don't know how you have the nerve to accuse *me* of not being honest,'' she said in a tone that came close to emulating his sardonic drawl. ''You haven't been honest at all.''

He shot her a startled glance. ''I haven't?''

''You haven't said a thing about your real reason for tracking me down. I'd respect you a lot more if you were straightforward.''

''Petra, I have no idea what you're talking about.''

''Come off it,'' she said heatedly. ''Sarah told me you caught that plane deliberately, just to meet me. And I know the reason.''

His face had closed out all expression. ''Sarah told you that too?''

''No, I figured it out for myself the minute I saw your business card.''

Now he was looking puzzled, yet somehow relieved, which she couldn't understand. She came straight out with the accusation. ''You're after my hotel, aren't you? You and your corporation.''

She had to admit he played it very well. He appeared so startled that his grip on the steering wheel veered them across the road while his green eyes looked at her blankly. He caught himself immediately, straightening the wheel, shaking his head in what certainly looked like genuine bewilderment. ''Where on earth did you get a crazy idea like that?''

"Let me explain it to you," she said evenly, pleased that she was completely in control of the situation now. "Some time ago, the Braden Corporation offered quite a large sum of money to my uncle for his property. The idea was to create a private beach for the rich visitors to Pine Village Resort."

"Well, I suppose that makes sense," he said. He lifted an eyebrow. "I take it Will turned the offer down?"

"You know damn well he did."

He shook his head, glancing at her with a supercilious smile that infuriated her. "I believe I begin to see. In your infinite wisdom, you've decided Dan Halliwell is the big bad villain of the Braden Corporation, prowling around tweaking his mustache, waiting for the opportunity to rob the poor defenseless girl of her inheritance. Grow up, Petra. That situation has been done to death in fiction. The Braden Corporation has *some* integrity. I'm sure that if Will turned down the offer, then the whole project was abandoned. It may be that the corporation will renew the offer now that you're in charge, but if your answer is no, that will be the end of it."

"You're trying to make me believe you knew nothing about this?"

"I'm not trying to make you believe anything. I'm not involved in acquiring land. I do a lot of other things in my current role as troubleshooter for the corporation, but that's not one of them."

"Tell me this, then," she asked, sure she'd got him. "Why did you go to the trouble of boarding the plane I was on? Why were you so anxious to talk to me?"

"That's not relevant," he said hastily.

"Yes, it is. If you aren't after my hotel, there was no reason for you to get on that particular plane."

"It was a coincidence. I'd forgotten what Sarah had told me."

"All right. Why did you come to Cape Cod? Can you tell me that?"

He didn't answer for a minute. Then his gaze shifted away to one side, making her wonder if he was ever going to be honest with her. "People do take vacations, you know," he said finally.

"Not people like you, not career-minded executives. They don't take aimless vacations anyway." As she stared at him, eyes narrowed, conscious of the challenging expression that must be on her face, he stopped the car again. Alarmed, she looked around quickly, only to find they had entered the parking lot at the airport terminal. Engrossed in her argument with him, she hadn't even noticed.

His hands on the wheel, he sat still for a minute. Then he looked at her with eyes that were clear as green glass, and totally disarming. "Petra, I assure you that my presence on that particular plane had nothing to do with the Braden Corporation. As far as I know there is no pressure afoot to get your property away from you. I'm certainly not interested in doing so."

She believed him. It was impossible not to. That meant there wasn't really any reason for his advances to her. And that made her feel suddenly panicked and very, very wary. If he wasn't after her hotel, what was he after? "I'm sorry I jumped to conclusions," she said uncertainly.

"It seems we both did," he said ambiguously. For a moment he gazed at her with what looked like mild exasperation. Then he took her hand in his. "Don't look so worried, Petra, dear. Loving you as I do. . . ."

"Don't say that," she said explosively.

"You don't want to be loved?"

"You don't even know me. How can you talk about loving me?"

He looked at her in a surprised way. "Evidently you don't realize how attractive you are. But if it annoys you to talk about love, let's choose another word. How about infatuation? According to all the textbooks, infatuation is based on strong physical attraction, which we obviously have going for us. A lot can grow from infatuation, of course." He was beginning to look immensely pleased with himself. "I've taken several courses in human relationships, so I know how these things go. Relationships start off with rapport, feeling at ease with each other. They build through self-revelation. Then comes dependency on each other as each person learns the other's habits, until finally you have emotional and physical intimacy. Does that sound about right to you?"

While Petra stared at him, openmouthed and exasperated, he paused, considering. Then he gave her a wicked smile and added thoughtfully, "It's a lot to accomplish in two weeks, isn't it? Especially as you're not really at ease with me yet. In spite of the time factor, we should probably go a little more slowly, get to know each other better, as you so rightly suggested."

"I didn't say—suggest any such thing," Petra stammered.

"But you are attracted to me, aren't you?"

She sighed. After her response to him, it didn't make much sense to deny having any feelings whatsoever. "Yes," she said softly. "But—"

He shook his head to silence her, then he lifted her hand and touched his lips to the faint blue veins on the back of it, sending a thrill of sensation through her bloodstream. "I'm really quite encouraged," he said. "We've come a long way in a short time. In this one drive, we've gone from small talk to sharing ideas and attitudes and even a few feelings. It won't be long before we've established peak communication."

"We have to level with each other first," she said dryly, recovering at last.

"You've studied communication skills too?" He gave her a winning smile when she nodded reluctantly. "That ought to save us a lot of time."

"Mr. Halliwell . . ." she began, then gave in when he raised both eyebrows. "All right, Dan. I've repeatedly told you that I can't get involved with you. My plans are all made and there just isn't room for any—"

"Hanky-panky?" he supplied when she hesitated.

She sighed. "I have a lot of things to think about," she said firmly. "A lot of things to do. I don't want to be distracted or . . . ."

"You can't put life on hold," he interrupted. "It has a way of demanding action. We've already gone well beyond the acquaintance stage, which I guess makes us friends. As you're so nervous, we can take another day or two before moving on to become dating partners...."

This whole conversation was getting away from her. He certainly had a unique approach, and if she was to be honest with herself, she found his dryly teasing attitude intriguing and even—might as well admit it—exciting. But the fact remained that he was as capable as any man of changing his mind later, of getting her involved with him just to prove his masculinity and then dumping her when he found out she didn't quite suit him, because she had a mind and a will of her own.

And in the meantime, he'd have messed up her time and energy, right when she needed both. No, an affair with him wasn't to be considered.

Keep it light, she told herself—humor was often the best defense. "I can't say I've heard of anyone creating a relationship by following a psychology manual," she said.

"That doesn't mean it can't be done."

"You don't think the concept is rather cold-blooded?"

His eyes glinted. "There you go again, accusing me of a lack of passion." He sighed dramatically. "My dear Petra. I'm merely adjusting myself to your own wishes. Obviously I moved a little too rapidly for you. So I'm perfectly willing to back off and start over as friends. What do you say?"

There was safety in the word friends. The word established boundaries. Perhaps she could relax a little with him. She did enjoy his company.... "I guess we can be friends," she said warily. "As long as you understand I don't have the time or the inclination for dating."

His hand clasped hers warmly. For just a second she felt another tremor of emotion run through her body, but she managed to keep her fingers still in his.

"Right," he said briskly. He glanced at his wristwatch. "Perhaps we'd better go meet Tony. We have about ten minutes to plane time."

She'd forgotten all about Tony. Relieved to have something to distract her from the emotion of the last half hour, she managed a smile that felt a little stiff and gathered herself together enough to open the car door and climb out.

She wasn't completely satisfied with the answers he'd given her all the same, she realized. She definitely had the feeling that there was more behind his trip to Cape Cod than he was revealing. For one thing, he didn't seem the type of man who would vacation alone. Though of course, the resort was for "swinging singles." She would feel more satisfied if he'd explained why he'd taken her plane, which he'd avoided doing. She had a feeling he didn't intend to explain, that the reason in some way embarrassed him. What could it possibly be?

TONY EMERGED FROM THE PASSENGER RAMP peering over the top of a heavy looking cardboard carton that obliterated half of his long skinny body from view. "What on earth have you got there?" Petra demanded.

He set the box down as carefully as though it contained eggs, gave her his usual bear hug, then touched the toe of his sneaker to the box. "My computer," he said matter-of-factly. "I didn't trust the airline to get it here intact. One of the flight attendants let me put it in the coat closet." He frowned, his dark eyes narrowing in thought behind his tortoiseshell-rimmed glasses. "Alice," he recalled triumphantly. "She said to say hi to you."

Petra looked at him lovingly, enjoying the sight of him. He looked a lot like those old photographs of their father—extraordinarily tall for sixteen, and skinny as a scarecrow in his university sweat shirt and blue jeans. Like Petra he had their mother's large dark eyes, though his had the myopic look of one who was usually tuned inward to the workings of his own brain. His black hair was as curly as Petra's, though much shorter. "I'm surprised you didn't hold that great box on your lap all the way," she teased him.

"I wanted to," he said seriously, "but Alice said it was against regulations." His brow furrowed, making him look much older than his years. Petra thought sometimes that he had been born old. How was she going to get him to let down, to relax and act like an adolescent now and again, she wondered. "I'm developing a math program for grade schools," he said earnestly. "It's really innovative. My professors are all pretty excited about it. It's a book with software supplements. It starts out with—" He broke off, looking sheepish, finally realizing that she was shaking her head in exasperation. "I guess I'd better not go into it now, huh?"

He turned shyly toward Dan, and Petra introduced him, smiling as she saw the astonished expression on Dan's face. She should have warned him that Tony was a little unusual, she thought as they headed for the baggage claim area. A gifted student, he'd raced through high school and had just, at sixteen, completed his sophomore year in college. Their father had been a brilliant man, and Tony was just as bright, though his interests were vastly different. He was a prime example of a person born in just the right era. Enthralled with the whole world of data processing and computer engineering, he could speak what Petra called the technological age's Latin as though it was his mother tongue.

Naturally Tony was thrilled by Dan's car. It was a computerized marvel, after all. As soon as he saw it, he let out a long low whistle and pronounced its name in tones of awe, complete with all its numbers and letters. Immediately Dan warmed to him. She could see it happening.

Tony insisted on sitting in the front seat, which relieved Petra even if she did have to sit with her knees up to her chin. Dan seemed to have forgotten she was there anyway; he was so busy explaining the various instruments on the dashboard as they pulled away from the airport. Before long, he and Tony were eagerly discussing digital feed-ins and readouts, gas-plasma displays and drag coefficient.

Petra sat back and let them go at it by themselves, tuning them out, willing herself to stop looking at the way Dan's hair curled inward toward the nape of his neck, to stop remembering the touch of his sensual mouth on hers, to concentrate on thinking about her hotel and the plans she had for it.

It was a while before she realized Dan and Tony had finally exhausted the subject of the car and were discussing sailing. "You're welcome to come along," Dan was saying. "I've always wished I had a kid brother I could teach to sail. Maybe you'd like to learn."

"Hey, that would be great," Tony said. Then doubt clouded his voice. "I should probably tell you that I'm much better at the theory of recreational activities than I am in actual practice."

"I was a bit of a klutz myself when I first started," Dan said seriously, evidently not a bit put out by Tony's somewhat intellectual way of expressing himself. He was so self-assured. Most of the men Petra had introduced Tony to were threatened by his startling intelligence, as were his peers.

"Well, I'd certainly enjoy the challenge," Tony said slowly. "But I'm probably going to be pretty busy for a while. I expect Petra has three thousand chores waiting for me."

"You'll get some time off," Petra promised from the back seat. Then she hesitated, not sure if she wanted to encourage this friendship that seemed to have sprung up between Tony and Dan. Yes, she wanted Tony to make friends on the Cape. And she wanted him to have fun. But the idea was for him to have fun with kids his own age. In his rather isolated school world, where the students were all much older than he was, he'd become something of a loner. He didn't seem to have much interest in a social life at all. Petra was afraid he was neglecting a side of his development that he would need in later life. She wanted him to turn into a more well-rounded person.

"I'm not sure," she started hesitantly, but before she could complete the thought, Tony turned to Dan and said, "I guess as long as Petra's going sailing with you, I ought to be able to take time off too."

"I haven't said I'd go..." Petra began, but again she was interrupted, this time by Dan.

"It will be good for Petra to get away from the inn," he said as though she wasn't even there. "She's taken on a very tough job. I don't think she realizes how tough. She's going to need a safety valve."

Her mouth open to protest this taking over of her spare time and the repeated implication that she wasn't going to be able to handle the hotel, Petra subsided as Tony enthusiastically started asking intelligent questions about sailing before the wind and off the wind and on the wind, proving at once that he did understand the theory if not the practice.

Settling herself as comfortably as she could in the shallow back seat, she contented herself with fuming silently, deciding finally that she wasn't going to get into any more philosophical arguments with the superconfident Mr. Dan Halliwell. She was simply going to be too busy to see him. Let him try to talk her out of that.

CHAPTER FIVE

SARAH MERRIWEATHER TOOK ONE LOOK at Tony, struggling in through the front door of the inn with his oversized box, and registered an expression that said as clearly as though she'd spoken aloud, "Poor wee bairn."

Petra felt herself relaxing. Tony had found another mother. Sarah was bustling around his luggage, looking at him with a decided glint in her eyes. "We're going to have to get some meat on your bones," she said as she preceded him up the stairs to his room. "We'll see what a few dumplings can do and some good meat and potatoes. I thought your sister was thin enough, but you. . . ."

As her voice faded away on the next flight of stairs, Tony paused on the landing, looking down at Petra, his eyebrows jerking in his Groucho Marx imitation. Knowing exactly what he was thinking, she laughed out loud. "People are always wanting to fatten Tony up," she told Dan, who was looking at her in a questioning way. "What they don't realize is that he goes through groceries like an out-of-control Pac-Man. Yet he never gains weight."

"Lucky boy," Dan said. He was leaning casually against the newel post at the foot of the stairs, one elbow hooked over the banister, looking completely at ease as usual, gazing at her speculatively.

Nervously she turned over papers on Sarah's roll-top desk, trying to look busy. "You and Tony get along well?" he asked after a while.

"Yes, we're very close. Unusually so, considering the difference in our ages."

"Tony was very young when your parents were killed."

Her stomach tightened in a familiar way, but she managed to answer. "He was five and a half."

"Must have been tough for you. You were sixteen, weren't you? What exactly happened? I'm not sure I know."

"I prefer not to talk about it," she said levelly, averting her eyes.

"I see." She thought he'd drop the subject but he didn't.

"You must have been very shaken up. How on earth did you cope?"

How had they got into this? What business was it of his? She took a deep breath and prepared to tell him her coping mechanisms had nothing to do with him, but then thought better of it. Probably all he wanted was to get her to reveal more of herself so he could file some information under the heading "rapport," subheading "self-revelation," and count another step forward in this relationship he'd programmed for the two of them.

"I managed fine," she said evenly. "Naturally it was very traumatic for me, but I was able to keep busy and. . . ."

"And you've kept busy ever since?"

"There's something wrong with that?"

"It depends on whether you've left time for play."

"When necessary," she said coolly, hoping to discourage him from making suggestions about her leisure time again. Before he could respond, she added, "I hope you'll excuse me. I'm grateful to you for taking me to pick Tony up, but I do have an awful lot to do right now."

He studied her face for a minute, then nodded thoughtfully and came forward to shake her hand, which surprised her. "I enjoyed the drive," he said mildly, smiling down at her, holding on to her hand with both of his.

"I did too." It was the truth, she realized. "Rapport," her own mind supplied. It would really be rather nice if they could be friends, but that was obviously impossible. The sexual attraction between them was too strong. She might choose to deny it, but she couldn't ignore it. In which case, it would be better if they didn't see each other again.

"I see a 'goodbye forever,' coming on," he said lightly. "You might as well know, Petra, that I've thought our relationship over and I've reached a decision. We can start out as friends, but just to prove it's impossible, I'm going to make you fall in love with me." There was that engaging, eye-crinkling smile again.

The man was incorrigible. "I'm sorry, Dan," she said slowly. "I'm flattered by your interest, but the fact is I've sworn off men for a while."

"So your friend Janie told me." He laughed at her

audible sigh. "Janie is quite a talker, isn't she?" His eyebrows rose. "Have you any idea what a challenge it is to be told a woman isn't interested in men?"

"I have a feeling this is all a game to you," she said wearily.

"Would you rather I treated it seriously?"

"That's not what I—I didn't mean—" She broke off. "I'm sorry. I'm a hopeless case I'm afraid."

He laughed. "I hope you don't think I'm just going to fold up my tent and quietly steal away."

"You'd probably be well-advised to."

"I don't suppose you'd like to put a bet on this? Ten dollars says I have you eating out of my hand within ten days?"

"I'm not a gambler."

"Nor am I." He paused meaningfully. "Unless it's a sure thing."

He continued to look at her with the greatest of good fellowship, and she found herself becoming more and more exasperated. She forced herself to return his gaze steadily. After a minute or so, he grinned. "Why do I get the feeling whenever you look at me that all my flaws are showing?" he asked.

Petra tried to ease her hand out of his, but he held it tightly and she wasn't about to fight for possession of it. Raising one eyebrow, she said in as nonchalant a voice as she could muster, "Probably because they are."

He laughed. "Oh, Petra, you are the most straightforwardly blunt person I've ever known. It's refreshing to meet someone so outspoken. What are my flaws?"

She didn't hesitate. "You can't take no for an answer. You interfere in other people's business. And you think no woman can resist you."

"But all of those are fairly harmless faults, wouldn't you say?"

He was trying hard to make her smile and he was succeeding. "From your point of view, maybe so. From mine, they just tell me it would be wisest not to get to know you any better than I do already."

"But you promised we'd at least be friends." There was a chiding note in his voice.

"I really do have a great deal to do," she said almost pleadingly.

He nodded. With one final squeeze of her hand, he smiled gently. "I'll call you."

"You do understand that I'm going to be working very hard and. . . ."

"I understand almost everything," he said gravely, and then he released her hand and walked away from her, leaving her to wonder exactly what he had meant.

SHE SAW HIM the next morning. Having risen at six to perform the half hour of working out with dumbbells that she routinely went through every morning, she'd gone to her window to breathe in some of the good salty air. Below on the beach a movement caught her eye. In the narrow space between the line of seaweed left by the tide and the edge of the gentle waves, Dan Halliwell, dressed only in blue swimming trunks, was running. She found herself standing very still, one dumbbell held at arm's length above her head, the other supported on her left shoulder.

Although the distance was considerable, there was no mistaking his identity. There was really no need for her to set down the dumbbells and pick up the binoculars Tony had left on her windowsill the previous evening after he'd done some stargazing. She was just going to check for sure that it was Dan, she assured herself.

She put the binoculars to her eyes, catching her breath when he sprang into focus, looking so close she might have touched him. He was running at a steady, measured pace, his feet kicking up spray to sparkle in the early sunlight. There was such joyous freedom in his running that she felt an answering thrill inside her own body and wished she had time to join him out there in the lovely morning. He was breathing easily, his body functioning so efficiently it was obvious that running was a regular part of his schedule. He had a good body; lean waisted and slim hipped, spare and hard and firm, without being grossly muscular. There wasn't an ounce of fat on him. He was tanned an even golden brown and his brown chest hair, tipped with gold at the ends, arrowed down to disappear suggestively inside his shorts. Petra's fingers curled around the binoculars as she imagined what it would be like to touch that thick mat of hair, to run her fingers over it, to. . . .

She set the binoculars on the windowsill with an audible click, suddenly feeling like a voyeur, ashamed of herself for violating his privacy, ashamed too of the liquid rush of sensation that had gone through her at the sight of his near-naked body. Janie was right. The man was a hunk. Smiling at the thought of what the irrepressible Janie would have had to say at the sight of Petra McNeil spying on a man like a sex-starved spinster, she managed to tear herself away from the window.

Okay, she admitted to herself. The man was a desirable, extremely attractive male. If she wasn't so busy, and if she didn't have the problems she had with relationships, it would be very easy to let herself accept the challenge he'd offered.

But she was too busy, and she did have problems, and she did not, oh how she did not, want to be hurt again. She needed time to heal, time to recover before taking any risks at all. So.... Shaking her head, she left her bedroom and prepared to get started on her day. Thank goodness for work, she thought as she descended the stairs. There was such safety in work.

After deciding over breakfast that while they waited for Matt Mansfield to show up she and Tony could get the two guest rooms that had not been water damaged ready for occupancy, she drove into town to buy supplies, then wrapped her hair in a red bandanna, her body in a pair of Tony's old overalls with the legs rolled up and went happily to work. Tony enjoyed spackling and sanding and wallpapering as much as she did and though the work was exhausting, between the two of them they made good progress.

She was not really surprised when she didn't hear anything from Dan during the next couple of days. Her attitude had probably discouraged him from playing his macho games, she decided. That was all to the good. She didn't have any energy left over for verbal sparring. By the time each day ended, her back ached, her fingers stung and her head felt as though it would burst if she didn't lay it down and get some sleep.

But in spite of her exhaustion she felt a compelling urge to go ahead with her plans for the hotel. She had so many ideas. A lot of them were more suited to a much larger establishment, which was frustrating, but she was bursting to try out those that were suitable. By the third day after Tony's arrival, she had decided now was the time to start instituting changes. She and Sarah were in the kitchen cleaning up after lunch. About to go back to sanding the baseboard, Petra hesitated. "What do you think about offering our guests high tea in the afternoons?" she asked Sarah.

Sarah's eyebrows almost disappeared into her hairline. "High tea? This is not the Savoy."

"It doesn't have to be anything elaborate," Petra said. "I thought perhaps tea and little sandwiches, maybe some of your mouth-watering scones. Just something to tide people over until they go out to dinner. I went to high tea at the Empress on Vancouver Island once and I loved it. People stood in line for it. I want us to establish some traditions like that."

Sarah sat down, something she rarely did in the daytime. "We've never done anything like that," she protested.

Petra sighed. She was tempted to let the whole subject go for a couple of days. But her mind, active as always with ideas, wouldn't let her back out now she'd started. "Don't you think it would work?" she coaxed. "I've noticed most people come back around four in the afternoon to rest and change before going out to dinner. They might enjoy a little refreshment. We could serve it in the sitting parlor. Later on, I thought we might...." She hesitated, then decided she might as well lay her plans out for Sarah's inspection. "Later, we can serve in the carriage house, after I've got it cleaned up."

"The carriage house!" Sarah sounded scandalized.

"I've taken a good look at it. It's really solid, Sarah. And there are lots of windows. Once I get the furniture moved back into the house, we could serve our high tea there—and after a while maybe breakfast. Breakfast out there would be easier on us than taking trays to the bedrooms as we do now. Once we get some new customs established I can raise the room rates to cover the cost."

"Aye, well, maybe so. I don't know, lass. It's all a little too much for me to think about."

"Then could you just think about the high-tea idea for now? I'm sure it would be very popular with the guests." There were nine people staying at the inn: an elderly couple from upstate New York, a widow from Rhode Island and the rest from the Boston area.

Sarah's mouth was tightening ominously. Petra took a deep breath and started in again, speaking too fast as she always did when she was nervous. "We could treat it like a family thing—everyone gathering at the end of the afternoon so they could maybe talk about what they've done that day. Now, unless they meet on the beach and get talking they don't really get together at all. Later on we might offer wine and cheese and crackers. We have the license—I checked on that.''

"You've been busy, haven't you?" Sarah said dryly. "Well, I've no doubt it could be managed. And you're the boss after all."

"Oh, Sarah, I don't want you to think of it that way. We're in this together. If you really object—"

She broke off, afraid to press too hard.

Sarah stood up, tightening the ties on her starched white apron, her mouth pursed thoughtfully. "I've no real objection," she said at last, then nodded briskly. "Aye, it's not a bad idea. We'll try it out tomorrow."

Carried away with excitement, Petra hugged the older woman and surprisingly felt the pressure of an answering hug.

It was then that the telephone rang. Petra picked it up, feeling a nervous tremor go through her when she heard Dan Halliwell's voice. Determinedly she took a deep breath. "I'm sorry, Dan," she said when he invited her to have dinner with him. "I don't have time."

Sarah paused on her way through the doorway. "Go out with him, lass," she said. "You deserve a break."

Petra shook her head and Sarah lifted her hands in apparent disgust. "Why not?" she persisted.

Petra lowered the telephone and put one hand over the mouthpiece. "Sarah, I'm much too busy. You know that."

Sarah's hazel eyes glinted behind her glasses. "You like him, don't you?"

Petra laughed tiredly. "Is it that obvious?"

Sarah's mouth turned down in one of her dry smiles. "I stopped by your door the other day," she confided. "I saw you watching him through your binoculars."

"Oh, Sarah." Petra lifted the telephone to her ear again as Sarah left the room looking smug. "I'm sorry, Dan. Sarah had a message for me."

"You have to eat," he pointed out, using the same ploy that had captured her for lunch several days before.

"If I eat here I don't have to bother with makeup and dressing up."

"You could invite me to join you," he suggested.

She swallowed. She was tempted—how she was tempted! But she had her evening all planned. She and Tony had almost finished one bedroom. She'd managed to find some high baseboard that matched the original—she was determined to restore where she could rather than replace. She'd planned to nail the sanded baseboard into place after dinner, then countersink the nails and get the holes filled with wood putty before she went to bed, so she could stain it the next day. If she put all that off until tomorrow...no, she couldn't do that—she had to get ready for the inn's first high tea.

"Petra?"

"By the time I get through with all I have to do today, I'll be too tired to even make conversation," she said at last.

There was a silence. "We don't want our relationship to stagnate," he said lightly.

Petra sighed. "We don't have a relationship," she said wearily. "Maybe you should search elsewhere. I've seen a few nubile-looking wenches on your beach there. I'm sure one of them would be delighted...."

"If I wanted a wench I'd find a wench," he said sternly. "I want you."

How exactly did he mean that? Silly question. She knew how he meant that. "I'm not making excuses, Dan," she said abruptly, honestly. "I'm absolutely exhausted. Your timing is really incredibly bad."

To her surprise he laughed. "If timing's all it takes, I can handle that. I'm known for my patience." He paused a second, then said with a smile in his voice, "I'll be in touch," and hung up the phone.

He was so damn sure of himself, Petra fumed as she hauled herself up the stairs, one hand pressed to her aching back, wishing she could go soak in a hot tub for thirty or forty hours. She hadn't realized how long it had been since she'd done any really hard physical work. Even though she kept her body in good shape, she was using, or rather overusing, muscles she didn't normally use. She'd get conditioned eventually, she assured herself. And as for Dan Halliwell...he'd just have to realize all by himself that she wasn't going to go out with him. Apart from anything else, she didn't approve of his game playing. What a nerve he had, telling her he was going to make her fall in love with him! He had some crazy ideas of what constituted entertainment for his vacation.

Next year maybe, if he came back to the Cape for
another vacation—next year, when she had everything organized and going nicely and could sit back
and look around at other areas of her life—maybe
then she'd be willing to play games with Dan Halliwell. " 'Tomorrow and tomorrow and tomorrow,' "
she quoted dramatically aloud.

Tony, putting the finishing coat of varnish on a
windowsill in the bedroom she'd entered, groaned.
"Slave driver," he said.

Petra laughed. "The quote was for me, not you!"
she told him and laughed again when he straightened
from his bent-over position and gave her a puzzled
frown over his glasses.

THE HIGH TEA was not going well, even though all
nine of the guests had shown up. They tended to hud-
dle in their own twosomes, barely glancing at the
others, evidently waiting for someone to break the
ice. So far the only people they'd talked to were herself and Sarah and Bonnie, who'd been pressed into
service and was neatly dressed in a white shirt and
navy skirt, and all they'd managed to say to them was
an occasional please and thank-you and a comment
on the weather.

The entire day had been a dead loss, Petra decided.
Matt Mansfield had not arrived as half promised and
so far, all efforts to track him down had proved
unsuccessful. And she'd had an argument with Tony.
He'd been working every bit as hard as she had, from
early morning until late at night, so she'd insisted he
take a half day off to get some fresh air, and then had

discovered him in his room after lunch, hunched over his computer. She'd had to argue with him for a half hour before he would switch off the machine. "Go out. Take the car, explore, meet people," she'd ordered.

He'd pleaded that he'd much rather work on his precious program, but Petra had stood firm. "The whole idea of moving out here was to get us both out of our self-defeating ruts," she'd reminded him. "I have to find a way of life I can enjoy, and you have to discover machines aren't life partners. There are people in the world."

Grudgingly, he'd at last agreed to take himself out for a while. Now she wished he was here to help, though knowing Tony, he would probably stand around looking bewildered, as though he didn't speak the language of ordinary people.

The Captain Mac's guests were a motley bunch, Petra thought, as she circulated with a plate of Sarah's scones. Mrs. Menniger, the outrageously outspoken widow from Rhode Island, was eighty years old, she'd confided to Petra on the stairs the morning before. She certainly didn't look it. In her bright yellow pants and flowered blouse, her white hair cut in a casual style and makeup impeccably in place, she could have been taken for late fifties in any but the brightest light. She'd nursed her husband through a long illness and had decided to treat herself after his death to a season at the Captain McNeil Inn, where she and her George had spent every summer for the last ten years. "I'm sure George would want me to enjoy myself," she told Petra as she helped

herself to a scone, the diamonds on her fingers sparkling in the bright sunlight that was flooding the
room. "After all, we had sixty years of making
whoopee. How many people have that?"

She lowered her voice confidentially and glanced
across the room. "Will you look at that young man?
Can you imagine having to make whoopee with
someone like that?"

Petra didn't have to look to see whom she meant.
The young man in question, Tom Lyman, was an insurance salesman from Boston. He was so terribly
overweight that she'd wondered how he rated on his
company's actuarial tables. His wife, by contrast,
was a little bird of a woman with a permanently worried expression. "Probably thinking about how she'll
have to do it with him for the rest of her life," Mrs.
Menniger whispered irrepressibly.

Petra laughed and shook her head in mock ad-
monishment, then carried her tray to the Lymans.
Mrs. Lyman refused, so her husband helped himself
to two scones, saying with a rather fatuous grin that
she never did eat, so he just had to force himself to
manage her share as well as his own. If they kept that
up he'd weigh three hundred pounds before he was
thirty, Petra thought, and his wife would probably
fade away.

Sitting next to the Lymans, but somewhat apart,
were the honeymooners, the Bentleys. They were almost a storybook couple: he was tall, dark and handsome and she petite, red-haired, gorgeous, and a
snob. Petra saw Mrs. Bentley glance calculatingly at
the simple cream-colored silk dress she'd put on for

the occasion. She herself wore only designer clothes, she'd informed Petra. She'd also made it clear that it hadn't been her idea to come to Cape Cod. She'd wanted to go to the Bahamas, which her daddy had been more than willing to pay for, and she certainly wouldn't have chosen this little old place, but her husband had insisted on paying for the honeymoon himself, so she'd indulged him, this once. Petra had received the impression that it wouldn't happen again.

She was fascinated by the various personalities of her guests. She was beginning to feel something like the matriarch of a large family, interested in everybody's comings and goings and the revealing comments they made about themselves. Now, if she could only manage to get them talking to each other!

She headed toward one of her favorite guests, an elderly man who'd told her he and his wife came there every year because Will always let them bring their Bedlington terrier, who was all the family they had now that their children were grown and busy with their own affairs. The usually friendly dog was sitting at his master's feet at the moment, nose between front paws, not socializing either, not even looking around.

Just as she reached Mr. Carrington, she saw someone take the front steps outside two at a time and heard the front door open and close. A moment later, Dan Halliwell, looking his elegant self and twice as self-assured as usual in a khaki safari suit and black turtleneck, strode into the room as though he was quite sure of a welcome. "I seem to have improved my timing," he said with one of the dazzling smiles that lit up his lean face and turned his green eyes to phosphorescent glory. "Are those Sarah's scones I see?" Helping himself to one, he smiled winsomely at Petra, then said, "Why don't you introduce me to your guests, love?"

Feeling a mixture of emotions in which annoyance predominated over discomfort—what the hell did he mean coming in here as though he owned the place, and where did he get the nerve to call her "love"— Petra performed the necessary introductions through what felt like a very stiff smile.

"Providence, Rhode Island?" he repeated in a wondering tone to Mrs. Menniger as she gazed saucily up at him. "Do you know, I've never been there. Isn't that shameful?"

"I have a sister lives in Rhode Island," Mr. Lyman volunteered. "Phyllis Tomlinson."

"Any relation to the Tomlinsons in Kingston?" Mr. Carrington asked, which brought a few remarks from Dan about Rhode Island University, and suddenly everyone was talking, the dog was circulating, being petted and admired, and Mrs. Menniger and Mrs. Lyman were laughing together over his resemblance to a little gray lamb. At Dan's urging, little Mrs. Lyman ate a scone.

Dan stood in front of the fireplace, next to Petra, beaming goodwill like a beacon, obviously taking full credit for all this jollity, which he deserved, Petra reluctantly had to admit. But just as she was telling herself she should feel grateful to him for getting her venture off the ground instead of resenting his interference, he put an arm around her shoulders and pulled her close to his side. "What do you think you're doing?" she asked through her teeth, holding her body stiff.

"The lady beside the piano is after me," he murmured.

Petra followed his glance. Red-haired Mrs. Bentley was indeed eyeing Dan with a speculative look, which changed to one of disappointment as Dan turned his head toward Petra and deposited a kiss on her hair. "Help, save me," he whispered in her ear.

Petra was torn between a desire to laugh and annoyance at herself for the wave of feeling that swept over her whenever this man touched her. Mrs. Menniger, she could see, was taking in the whole scene with narrowed and delighted eyes. Sarah was positively beaming.

"Will you stop," she demanded under her breath.

His eyes met hers, unsmiling, stern. "No," he said.

Nervously she pulled away from him and crossed the room to speak to Mrs. Bentley. She could feel Dan's gaze following her, but she refused to look at him.

"Aren't you going to thank me?" Dan asked when her guests finally, and with obvious reluctance, dispersed to their rooms.

"For what?"

"Your little gathering was dying on its feet when I came in."

Indignant, she glared at him. "Are you implying I'm not capable of running something as simple as a high tea? Given a little more time, I'd have had the guests talking to each other. It was our first time, after all.'' She looked at him with sudden suspicion. ''What did you come over for, anyway?''

His expression was open, candid: George Washington, incapable of telling a lie. ''Just a friendly visit,'' he said innocently. ''What else?''

Before she could question him further, he lifted her chin and studied her face very earnestly. ''You look tired,'' he announced. ''More than tired, actually. Pooped.''

Petra bristled and pulled her chin away from his fingers. She'd thought she looked pretty good. This was the first time in days she'd managed to get every speck of paint washed off herself, and she'd blow-dried her black hair so it curled softly around her face, taken special pains with her makeup, worn what she felt was a becoming dress. ''I'm not at all tired,'' she lied.

Both eyebrows lifted. ''What was that discussion we had about honesty?''

Exasperated, she shook her head. ''The thing I'm really tired of is your constant implication that I'm not up to running this place,'' she said.

''I'm getting on your nerves, aren't I?'' he said with immense satisfaction. ''That's good. Anything's better than indifference. Annoyance can easily lead to love.'' Before she could respond to that, he gripped her shoulder, leaned down to kiss her very gently on the mouth and then said, ''My dear tough Petra. I really do admire you, you know.''

It was some time after he'd left before Petra recovered her composure, and then she realized his timing had been a little too coincidental. On a hunch, she went looking for Sarah and found her scrubbing out the downstairs bathroom. "You told Dan Halliwell about the high tea, didn't you?" she accused.

Sarah sat back on her heels on the floor and tilted her head to one side. "Well, now, I might have mentioned it when he took coffee with me this morning," she said slowly.

"Didn't you think I could manage it myself?"

"Well now . . . ."

"I'd rather Dan Halliwell didn't know too much about what's going on here," Petra said forcefully. "He's inclined to be bossy and interfering and I don't need his advice."

"He gave you advice?"

"Well, no, not exactly, but you see, he's trying to—" She broke off. She could hardly tell Sarah that Dan Halliwell had some crazy idea of making her fall in love with him. Given Sarah's fondness for him, she'd probably think that was the most normal thing in the world. "He's just looking for excuses to come over and—" She broke off again as Sarah looked up with an inquisitive glint in her hazel eyes. "Just don't tell him anything," Petra warned.

Sarah nodded without turning her head, and Petra had the decided feeling her warning had fallen on purposely deaf ears.

Coincidentally, according to him, Dan just happened to drop in at the same time for the next two days. He charmed her guests with tales of far places, stuffed himself with Sarah's feather-light scones, and acted at all times as though Petra was the most important person present, gazing at her fondly until she almost dropped whatever tray she was handing around, talking to her in a voice softened by affection, generally behaving as though he was her oldest and dearest friend.

And his tactics began to tell on Petra. She found herself watching for him at teatime, felt her tired spirits lift when he walked into the room, so that when he didn't show up for a couple of days, she felt grouchy and out of sorts and annoyed out of all proportion. He hadn't left the Cape yet, she knew. Every morning she watched him running on the beach, though now she closed her door first against Sarah's snooping. He had more exciting things to do than visiting Petra McNeil and her run-down inn, she supposed. As Sarah had suggested when she spoke of his many women since his divorce, he had a short interest span. She chided herself for the direction her thoughts were taking. She'd wanted him to stop bothering her, hadn't she?

Hastily she decided her annoyance was due to the fact that Matt Mansfield had apparently disappeared from the Cape along with his uncle. His teenage assistant swore he had no knowledge of his whereabouts, and Petra's drives around the area had turned up no trace of him or his elderly crew.

The only good thing was the weather. It continued fair and warm, so warm that Petra got in the habit of sitting out on the veranda whenever she had spare moments, grateful for the breeze off the sea.

Late one evening, after a hard day of wallpapering, she treated herself to a soak in a hot tub, then pulled on a comfortable floor-length beach robe made of white terry cloth and settled herself wearily on the veranda glider to watch the night creep outward over the sea. The twilight sky was cloudless, so the sunset wasn't spectacular, but she was so exhausted it felt good just to sit and not think. Faintly, on the breeze, she could hear the sound of the band playing in the resort nightclub. It seemed a long time since she had danced. She wondered if Dan was dancing. She thought that if she wasn't so tired, it would probably be exciting to dance with Dan Halliwell. She thought that she must stop thinking about Dan Halliwell. She would be glad when he left the Cape.

She dozed a little finally, waking with a start to find that night had arrived and only the porch light illuminated the veranda. In the dark of the trees at the corner of the inn, something moved.

Her first thought was that the tall shadow might be Dan, but in the next second she realized the shadow was not quite tall enough, and it was a little stooped. Gradually, as her eyes strained to probe the darkness, she made out the figure of a man with silver hair to his shoulders, a man dressed in what looked like an old-fashioned frock coat. Had the ghost of one of her ancestors arrived to give her a belated welcome? she wondered sleepily, then laughed as the figure moved and spoke in a soft but totally human-sounding voice. "I couldn't tell if you were sleeping or not," he said.

"I thought for a minute you were a ghost," she answered.

He gestured at her white gown. "I wasn't too sure about you either."

"Were you wanting to register?" she asked.

"No."

"Would you like to come up?"

"Sure." The two-syllabled "shu-wah," proclaimed her visitor to be a local man. He climbed the steps, glancing rather furtively at the front door. For a second Petra felt alarm stirring, but then she saw the gentle, weathered face and that beautiful mane of silver hair and knew she had nothing to fear from her visitor, whoever he might be.

"Name's Nathaniel Jenkins," he said in a voice that was still so low she wondered if he might be deaf and afraid of overcompensating for it. "You may call me Admiral—everyone else does."

Petra held a hand up for him to shake. "Petra McNeil," she said. "I guess you're retired from the navy now?"

"I was never in the navy, Miss Petra. But you must not think me a fraud. The title is an honorary one. Admiral means commander of a fleet. Fleet means a number—not specified—of boats. I was for many years commander of two commercial fishing boats, both engaged in shellfishing out of Wellfleet. I retired a year ago and returned to my native village for well-earned rest and recuperation."

"I see." Petra was enchanted with her visitor and his courtly way of talking. She especially enjoyed the dry humor that lay beneath everything he said. She still wasn't quite sure he was real. She smiled up at him. "Did you come to see Mrs. Merriweather?"

He shook his head. "I would not dream of disturbing that dear lady. I ventured to address you only because I saw you out here alone in the night."

Had she conjured him up out of her imagination? Petra wondered. She looked at his odd clothing curiously. As well as the frock coat, he wore a starched white shirt with a high collar and wide cravat, trousers with a thin stripe down the outside and a green plaid waistcoat with six buttons. He was handsome in an "aging poet" way: small boned and rather frail looking, not as old as she'd first thought—sixty or so maybe. "Do you live nearby, Mr. Jenkins—Admiral?" Petra asked.

"Indeed I do. This inn was built in 1812 and my own residence in 1790—which makes us practically neighbors in time." As Petra frowned, wondering if after all he was an escapee from some local nursing home, a sweet smile lit up his features. "In point of fact, now, my residence is across the street behind you."

"Oh?" Sitting up straight as light finally dawned on her, Petra smiled delightedly at him. "The historical society's house. That's why you're dressed this way."

"Unfortunately yes. I'd have preferred that you believe I had strolled through some time warp especially to chat with you, but the truth is that I'm curator of the house in question. Thought I ought to come and welcome you to Cape Cod. Will's niece, aren't you?"

"Yes. Did you know my uncle?"

"Not well. As I said, I've been away. For upwards

of twenty years. And I haven't always been welcome in the Captain McNeil Inn.''

''You and Will didn't get along?''

''Will was a good man.''

She'd lost the thread of this conversation somewhere, Petra thought, but before she could clear her mind, Mr. Jenkins, still talking so softly that she had to strain to understand him, invited her to come and see the house he took care of, which he explained had once belonged to his family.

''It's a museum now, you understand,'' he told her as they walked together across the wide road that ran between the two properties. ''We're open noon till four on weekdays, all day long on special holidays. I donated the old place to the historical society many years ago. But now, in exchange for my duties, I'm allowed to live here and will for the rest of my life if I so choose. It's a fine arrangement all around.''

Petra had noticed the historical society's sign outside the house and had promised herself a visit as soon as she had time. It was a dignified Georgian house with a widow's walk, white-painted, surrounded by well-kept lawns and rosebushes.

Inside, Mr. Jenkins showed her around on the official tour, beginning with a room in which quilts of every description were hung on walls and draped across tables and chairs and towel racks in a riotous display of color and design. After she'd admired the quilts, especially the crazy quilts with their intricate embroidery and the friendship quilts with their autographs, he led her on to see bed warmers and old irons, ancestral portraits by the dozen, dolls made of cloth and wax and a wonderful collection of elaborate shell valentines brought home from Barbados by whalers. One of the valentines, Nathaniel told her, had been brought by Josiah McNeil for his wife, Nell, who was a fine woman with yellow hair and a pleasing disposition. She had suited Josiah immensely, which was to the good for he had been a hard man to please.

"You knew him well?" Petra asked teasingly.

"In a former life," he said with a twinkle. He sighed. "It was a far more romantic age, that one."

"Josiah doesn't look romantic in any of my old portraits of him," Petra said.

"Probably thought it wasn't manly," Nathaniel said. "Men had a very masculine image of themselves in those days." His faded blue eyes twinkled again. "That was long before you modern young women started trying to change our minds about how we should act. We knew our roles then and felt secure in them."

"Are you telling me you're not a liberated male, Admiral?" Petra asked.

He shook his head, laughing gently. "I'm possibly one of the least liberated men you'll ever meet," he informed her. "I'm a total prisoner, you see."

Petra frowned at him. "Of the past you mean?"

"That and the present."

"I don't think I understand."

"I don't expect you to." His gentle smile illuminated his lined face. "I'm making a mystery for you, Miss Petra. It will come clear to you someday."

She stared at him for a minute, hesitating, then

said thoughtfully, "I noticed when we were at my place you were whispering, but here it's evidently not necessary to whisper. Is that part of the mystery?"

"It could be indeed."

"I thought perhaps you were hard-of-hearing."

"Don't confuse old-fashioned ways with senility, my dear. I'm hale and hearty, I assure you."

They had passed on into a room that held doll-houses and furniture made by whalers, and Petra was fascinated by the detailed work the men had done. The room itself held her interest too. It was the largest room, being the parlor in its original state, finely paneled with pine wainscoting. On the walls hung mourning samplers, each with an embroidered scene and a sort of tombstone plaque with the name and dates of the deceased. "Someone took a fancy to some of these," Nathaniel said, indicating some vacant spots on the wall.

"You mean someone stole them?"

"Half a dozen." His lined face mournful, he gestured at an empty oak cabinet. "Used to be a couple of Saratoga trunks there, initials in nail heads on the top. The thieves took those too. Now what do you suppose anyone would want with such things? They've no monetary value, but they mean a lot to the people who donated them to the museum. The thieves also messed up every room in the house. Took me days of work to straighten everything out. Senseless vandalism makes me purely angry, Miss Petra. Especially so when items are irreplaceable."

"When did all this happen?" Petra asked.

"Last week. Wednesday night. While I was sleeping. I put in an alarm, but it was too late of course.''

Petra made a mental note to install an alarm at the inn as soon as possible. She hadn't thought it would be necessary. Somehow the fact that the inn was so old had made her think, at the back of her mind anyway, that she could leave the doors open and not have to worry. She might have known the twentieth century would intrude. ''The man who rented me my car told me about some vandalism in town,'' she told Nathaniel. ''Could the incidents be connected?''

''I'd have no way of knowing. Not a week goes by in summer we don't have some kind of problem. Just yesterday, according to the *Falmouth Enterprise*, someone stole fishing and boating equipment from a boat in Falmouth Harbor—a Loran depth finder and a digital sounder. Whoever took the items also ransacked the boat, pulled food out of the cupboards, spilled cereal and flour and sugar and other goods on the floor. Seems we have a very malicious mischief maker in our midst.'' He sighed, then patted Petra's shoulder. ''I doubt you have need to worry as you've so many people around. Seems this person is more likely to go where he thinks there are no people—not looking for trouble, I guess.'' He paused, looking glum. ''One of the summer people, no doubt. I know all the folks hereabouts—straight as tall masts, they are—and not one of them would think of harming a neighbor or his property.''

''Do you know Dan Halliwell?'' Petra asked.

''The handsome scion of the Braden Corporation Halliwells? Something of a scoundrel with the ladies?''

"That's the one."

His forehead wrinkled above his faded blue eyes. His mouth pursed comically. "Well now, and what would be your interest in young Mr. Halliwell, Miss Petra?"

"I've no real interest," she said carefully. "His family owns the resort, you know. I'm just curious...."

"Uh-huh." He put a world of meaning into that one expression, and Petra felt herself flushing slightly.

"All right, Admiral," she admitted jokingly. "You've got me. The man turns me on, as we say in my century."

"An eloquent expression. Is the young man aware of your regard?"

"Not entirely," Petra said. "He's so determined to seduce me, it's more than my life's worth to let him see how much I'm attracted to him."

"I had thought women nowadays to be more straightforward, not so secretive about their feelings."

"In some ways, but we still have to protect ourselves, Admiral. If we wear our hearts on our sleeves, the daws will peck at them."

His eyes lit up with pleasure. "Ah, you are a reader of the great bard. I recognize the allusion—*Othello*, was it not? Iago speaking?"

"Were you acquainted with Shakespeare in your former life too?" Petra asked, smiling.

He shook his head sadly. "He was a century or two before my time."

Petra studied the man's lined, mischievous face.

"Admiral Jenkins, you didn't really answer my question. Do you know Dan Halliwell?"

"Well now, I might and then again, I might not."

"What does that mean?"

"It means I ain't talkin', sweetheart." Nathaniel's sudden switch from his courtly nineteenth-century manner to a hip imitation of Humphrey Bogart was so abrupt and so unexpected that Petra burst out laughing.

But then, as Nathaniel laughed with her, something in his expression triggered a suspicion that she'd once more been carefully distracted from her line of questioning. Determinedly she brought it up again. "How long have you known Dan?"

"I knew him when he was a boy," he answered after a short hesitation. "I renewed the acquaintance when I came back. It was Dan who arranged for me to reoccupy my old house. The Halliwell name has a lot of influence hereabouts."

"You're telling me you like him?"

"I do indeed. And he likes you, Miss Petra."

"Oh, you've discussed me?"

He sighed deeply and looked very sheepish. "I informed Dan I was useless as a secret agent, but he wouldn't believe me. Now the cat is out of the sea chest and I must confess all. Yes, Miss Petra, we've discussed you. He asked that I call on you, make your acquaintance and offer my friendship. He's worried that you are working too hard."

"He doesn't give up, does he?"

"I beg your pardon?"

She shook her head. "It's nothing, Mr. Jenkins.

It's just that Dan Halliwell won't believe I'm capable of taking care of myself and my duties without his interference.'' She hesitated, sensing her annoyed tone had hurt the old man's feelings, which she certainly hadn't intended. She managed a smile. "I'm glad you came over," she assured him, "but I'd rather it was because you wanted to visit me than any other reason."

He was suddenly serious. "I did want to visit you, Miss Petra. How can you doubt it?"

His thin face was so earnest that she had no choice but to believe him. All the same, she thought, as she was escorted back to her inn, her hand kissed and the front door opened for her, she was getting fed up with Dan Halliwell interfering in her life. And next time she saw him, she would tell him so.

WHEN SHE POKED HER HEAD INTO THE KITCHEN to ask if there was coffee left, Sarah, seated at the round pine table, greeted her with a vexed expression and a clipped "How should I know?"

Sarah was often inclined to be a bit on the sour side, but she wasn't usually rude. And the coffeepot, still plugged in, was on the table beside her. "What's wrong, Sarah?" Petra demanded.

Huffily Sarah averted her gaze, but she relented enough to pour Petra a cup of coffee and pass it and the cream across the table. "Sarah?" Petra probed.

Sarah's long face had flushed a blotchy red. She was obviously very angry. Petra couldn't think what she'd done. "What for were you *consorting* with yon fool Jenkins?" Sarah demanded at last, her Scotish accent even more obvious than usual.

"Consorting?" Petra echoed. "You make it sound as though I was doing something illegal. Mr. Jenkins—the Admiral—was very nice. He's a really sweet man and certainly no fool. What on earth do you have against him?"

"That's my business. But I'll thank you to stay away from yon troublemaker, lass."

"What kind of trouble has he made?"

"He's a disreputable old rascal. I've forbidden him the house. The nerve of him, creeping around here when he thought my back was turned. I'd have taken a broom to him if I'd seen him soon enough. He knows it too...."

Nathaniel Jenkins's whispering voice was explained. Was this the mystery then—that Sarah didn't like him?

"You must promise me you'll stay away from him," Sarah said.

"But Sarah, you haven't explained...."

"Nor am I about to. You must take my word for it. He's not a good person. You must stay clear of him. Promise me now."

"He spoke well of you," Petra said, more and more puzzled by Sarah's odd behavior. "He called you a dear lady."

"And well he might..." Sarah said. And that was all she would say. Setting her mouth tightly, she pulled her old blue chenille robe around her stocky body and took herself off to her bedroom, wishing Petra a very thin "Good-night."

Petra sipped her milky coffee slowly, unable to make any sense out of Sarah's outburst. It wasn't like the housekeeper to get so upset over anyone. She must have grounds for her anger, but what could they be? Was this also part of the Admiral's mystery? If so, it would have to wait for a solution. She was much too tired to puzzle it out tonight.

CHAPTER SIX

HORRIFIED, PETRA STARED AT MATT MANSFIELD, who had arrived unexpectedly without explanations or apologies for the delay. She couldn't possibly have heard him correctly, she decided. She'd worked so hard lately her senses must have become addled.

"Vinyl siding?" she repeated, her voice rising to a squeak. "Your uncle never once mentioned vinyl siding. He agreed with me that the inn should be restored as close to the original as possible."

"Like I said, miss—Carter isn't responsible for what he says."

They were standing on the lawn looking at the front of the inn, while Mansfield explained in detail what he thought needed to be done. Petra had already suffered one shock when she found out his uncle's estimate, though fair enough, was not high enough to cover the cost of the new roof Matt insisted she needed. Even though she was almost sure that only one section of the roof actually needed replacement, she'd finally agreed to pay the difference after Mansfield pooh-poohed the information Carter had given her about pressure cleaning and moss-retardant treatment.

She'd also agreed that the shutters should probably

be thrown out and new ones put in their place. But vinyl siding was something else again.

"You can't be serious," she told the young man. "Any value this inn has is historic. How can you possibly suggest putting vinyl siding on a building that's a hundred and seventy years old?"

"Mebbe you're right. Mebbe it's not worth the expense," he said, pulling his cap down over his eyes as he peered at the inn.

"Not worth it! I didn't say that. It would ruin the whole look...." She stopped and glared at him, suddenly aware that he'd deliberately misunderstood her. "Is this supposed to be some kind of joke?"

He raised his cap and scratched his pelt of curly blond hair—a gesture Petra was becoming familiar with. "Vinyl doesn't ever have to be painted," he said. "Keeps out drafts, keeps in heat, maintenance free...."

"Mr. Mansfield, there's no use discussing this. I'm not about to let you use any synthetic materials anywhere on my inn."

"Well now, that might make another difference to the price, if I have to replace that old shiplap. Lot of work there."

"It doesn't need replacing. It needs sanding and repainting, that's all."

"Lot of work." His voice allowed no argument.

Petra had been trying to hang on to her temper, but she was rapidly losing the battle. Looking up at the sturdy old building, she felt pretty sure the whole roof did not need to be done, and also that many of the shutters could be reclaimed, with a little work.

Matt Mansfield was trying to make an unholy profit out of her, simply because she was a woman alone, and vulnerable. It was also coming clearer by the minute that the young man didn't have his uncle's feeling for the place, nor his sense of history. "Don't you care that this building is one of the old ones on the Cape?" she asked him. "Can't you see that I don't want to change anything about it? I just want to make it as lovely as it once was. Can't you go along with me, even if you don't understand that?"

He was shaking his head stubbornly. "Too much sentiment about old buildings, if you want my opinion. Best thing you could do here, miss, is tear the place down and start over. Put in something modern, something up-to-date."

"I'll do the repairs myself," Petra blurted out.

Mansfield laughed, hands on hips, head thrown back. "That I'd like to see."

"You won't see it," Petra said tightly. "You won't be here to see it."

Eyes glimmering with amusement, he brought out a pack of cigarettes, lit one and regarded her silently through the smoke. "You firing me already?" he asked at last.

"I never did hire you," she pointed out. "I hired your uncle, for whom you disclaim all responsibility. Obviously the contract between your uncle and me isn't worth anything, so I'm nullifying it now."

Totally unmoved, the young man nodded a couple of times, then grinned again. "I guess I'll get back to Doc Mullins's place then."

Petra looked at him, narrow-eyed. He'd taken her decision very lightly. "Is that the house you were working on when I came to see you? That monstrous contemporary?"

He nodded. "Doc decided we did such a good job on the roof we should repaint the whole interior. Twenty rooms, he has there. There's a real house now—cathedral ceilings, solar heat, everything new."

"You never intended working on my inn, did you?" Petra accused him.

Rather than answer, he simply grinned again, then sauntered off toward his dilapidated old truck, which he'd parked at the side of the inn.

Petra gazed blankly for a while at what was rapidly becoming her beloved inn, realizing she'd really burned all her bridges now. Having dismissed Matt Mansfield, she was probably stuck with managing the whole job herself. "I don't care," she murmured aloud. "Vinyl siding, for heaven's sake."

Approaching the front entry, she smiled grimly up at the inn as though it were a person in need of reassurance. "Don't you worry," she said. "I may not be an expert, but I do care what happens to you. I'll get you fixed up somehow. You see if I don't."

Her mind immediately produced an image of Scarlett O'Hara shaking her fist at the sky above Tara. . . "'As God is my witness!'"

She laughed out loud. Was she never going to grow out of her tendency to overdramatize? Having laughed, she felt much more cheerful and went back into the inn determined not to let this latest setback discourage her.

Tony was in the kitchen with Sarah. Petra could hear his voice the minute she entered the inn. At first disappointed that he'd returned so soon when she'd sent him off with strict instructions not to come back until he'd talked to at least two people, Petra smiled again when she realized he sounded animated, as cheerful as though he'd just won a game of chess with his beloved computer. He looked cheerful too, she saw as she went into the kitchen. His face was flushed with what she thought at first was excitement, but realized was actually the beginnings of a suntan. "I don't believe it," she said, laughing. "You actually got out of the car."

"I not only got out of the car, I got into a boat," he said, looking up from the bowl of fish chowder he'd been wolfing down when Petra entered. "You'll never guess what happened, Pet."

Delighted, she smiled at him. He hadn't called her Pet since he was a small boy, and then only when he was extra happy. She'd decided long ago that Tony was born formal and there was no changing him. "A pirate kidnapped you and carried you off on his clipper ship," she suggested.

"Not quite, but almost as unexpected." His suntan deepened with what most certainly was a flush this time. "I met a girl."

"Uh-huh!"

"No, nothing like that," he interrupted hastily. "She's only fourteen. But what an incredible girl. She's so down to earth, so levelheaded. I've never met anyone quite like her. She's pretty too, and she doesn't wear a lot of gucky makeup.''

"Nothing wrong with makeup," Petra objected.

"Not for someone as old as you maybe," Tony agreed, "but the way some young girls plaster it on, they look like raccoons. But not Lori. That's her name: Lori.'' Behind his tortoiseshell glasses, his dark eyes shone. "She's very sweet and a really straightforward person, like you.''

"One insult and one compliment acknowledged," Petra said. She slid onto the chair opposite Tony and grinned at him, winking at Sarah as Sarah put a bowl of chowder in front of her. "Has our Tony fallen in love, do you suppose?'' she asked. "Look how pink he is. It must be love.''

"Cut it out Pet. I told you she's only fourteen. She's a friend, that's all. And she's not my only new friend. She has a brother, Seth, who is eighteen and really super. He's in Mensa, no less—the high-IQ organization. He thinks I ought to join too. He's going to be an architect. He goes to Boston U. He was telling me all about it. I told him I might end up there myself, if I don't go to M.I.T. There are four other guys in their crowd. I don't remember all their names, but they are all crazy about boats and they've promised to take me out any time I want to go. We went out to Hyannis Port this morning. Their boat is a real sporty cruiser. It belongs to Seth's Dad, who's a stockbroker. Seth gets to use it all summer. You wouldn't believe the instrumentation in the cockpit— and the power—it goes from zero to plane in seconds!''

Enjoying his eagerness, Petra was smiling at him, but her smile faded when he suddenly hit his forehead with the heel of one hand and said, "I have a message from Dan. I almost forgot."

Petra swallowed. "Dan Halliwell? You saw him too?"

"He was coming into the harbor about the same time we were." His mouth had developed the crooked twist that meant he was embarrassed about something. "We got in his way. You're not supposed to do that with a sailboat—sailboats have the right of way. But he was very nice about it. Just told Seth to hold back a bit next time."

"What did Seth say to that?"

"Just 'yes, sir.' What else? You don't have to worry Petra. My friends aren't a bunch of creeps; they've got good manners. Anyway, Dan has a fantastic sailboat—a twenty-five-foot sloop. Gosh, she's a beauty. He had a woman aboard, a real knockout. Reddest hair I ever saw, straight and thick. There must have been about ten yards of it all the way down her back." He frowned. "He said a funny thing when he introduced me to her. He said, 'Tony, this is wench—I mean Wendy.' She didn't look too pleased."

"I'm not surprised." It seemed Dan had taken her advice. She should be pleased about that, shouldn't she?

"He invited me on board to look at her," Tony went on, and then laughed. "The boat, not the woman." He sighed. "As far as the boat is concerned, I think I *am* in love."

He was in awfully good spirits, Petra marveled. She couldn't remember ever seeing him this relaxed, this elated. She was determined not to ask him anything about the woman.

"Dan wants us to go out with him on Wednesday to Nantucket," Tony added as he stood up. "That's tomorrow, I guess. I said we'd love to go. He's going to call you later."

"Tony!" Petra put down her spoon and stared in shock at her gangling brother. "I can't possibly go tomorrow. Or any other day. I've just fired Mr. Mansfield. He was trying to make too much profit from this job, and I told him we'd do it ourselves. I'm going to call around and see if I can find another contractor, but I don't have much hope. Which means we may have a lot more work to get through this summer than we bargained for."

Every once in a while Tony acted like any other sixteen-year-old. He did so now. "Gosh, Petra," he complained, "right when I've started to find friends. After all the times you've nagged me to spend time outdoors—" Evidently hearing the whine in his voice, he broke off, made a face, then reached down and awkwardly hugged Petra's shoulders, his young face earnest. "I'm sorry, Petra. That was dumb of me. I'm sure if you fired Mr. Mansfield, then he deserved it. And you don't have to worry. I'll pull my weight. When do we start on the roof?"

"First I have to find some of the right kind of shingles." She sighed. "And we still have to finish the bedroom we're working on. But you're not going to work all the time. I do want you to have friends.

And if you want to go with Dan tomorrow, that's okay. I think I'll advertise in the local paper for a handyman. I just meant that *I* don't want to go to Nantucket. You shouldn't have accepted for me.''

Tony straightened, shaking his head. "If you don't go, I don't see how I can, and I'd really like to. I've never sailed. And Nantucket, Petra. That's where all the whaling used to be. You know you've always loved historical places. There's a museum, Dan told me—a whaling museum. You'd enjoy that. And cobbled streets. Come on, Petra. I'll work extra hard all the rest of the week. We're nearly finished with that second bedroom now. Anyway, I doubt Dan will even take me if you don't go. It sounded like a package deal.''

"You wouldn't be practicing a little emotional blackmail, would you?" Petra asked.

"Of course. It's always worked for me in the past." He gave her his rare smile, with an endearing edge of pleading to it. "I'm not being completely selfish. You deserve a break too. You can't keep working all the time either." He turned to Sarah, who was working at the sink, but had her head turned to catch every word. "Tell her she needs some time off, Sarah," he pleaded.

"You do, lass," Sarah said sharply. "Those shingles have been missing off the roof for a while, so another day isn't going to hurt anything. There's no rain in the forecast. You won't be able to get an advertisement in the *Falmouth Enterprise* for a handyman before tomorrow, and I'll be here if there are any replies, so it's a good day to go. You worry about

Tony not getting any social life and you insist I keep going to my quilting bees and card parties, but what about *your* social life?''

"I'll catch up later on, Sarah," Petra protested. "I've had enough social life to last me a while. Tony hasn't.'' She looked up at her brother, steeling herself against the renewed pleading expression on his thin face. "I can't do it," she said. "But don't worry. If Dan does follow through on the invitation, I'll try to arrange for him to take you.''

"That wouldn't be the same, Petra," he said with a falsely miserable expression on his face. He sighed hugely, dramatically. "I couldn't possibly go without you, even if Dan said it was all right. I'd feel so guilty.''

Petra shook her head at his playacting, but couldn't hold out any longer just the same. "All right," she said in accents as martyred as his, "if it means that much to you, I'll try to make time to go—*if* Dan asks me.''

"He will." Tony bent down to give her a rib-crushing hug. "You'll have a good time, Petra, I know you will. It's a fabulous boat. You'll see.''

With a fabulous skipper, Petra added nervously to herself. She shouldn't be going, she knew. Now more than ever she had more to do than she had time to do it in. But Sarah was right. She had been working without a break. The thought of getting outdoors for a whole day, of sitting for a while, relaxing.... And in any case, she couldn't possibly bring herself to wipe that look of eager expectation from Tony's face. He was finally reaching out toward people. She had to encourage that.

She chose to ignore the nervous anticipation that had started her heart pounding the moment Tony mentioned Dan's name. She was not going to allow that man to get to her. He was nothing but a wealthy playboy who liked to play games with women's emotions. Evidently he really was merely taking a vacation—he certainly seemed to have plenty of time on his hands. If he called, she would be friendly but distant, she decided, thus setting the tone for any boat trip they might make.

SHE DIDN'T GO to her bedroom until three-thirty, when she went to clean up for high tea. The daily event had proved very popular with everyone, even though there had been some changeovers in the guests. The honeymooners were gone, and the Lymans. A middle-aged and very sociable couple had replaced the honeymooners, but the other room was still empty. The couple from Virginia who'd booked it had canceled out at the last minute, even though they had spent their two weeks at the Captain Mac for the last five years.

"Why?" Petra had asked bluntly when the woman called to tell her she and her husband had changed their booking to the Pine Village Resort.

"We just changed our minds," the woman had hedged. "We talked it over with our travel agent and the resort seemed more suitable."

More suitable. Why did those words sound so ominous? Petra had wondered. Why did she feel so threatened suddenly? Why did she feel that if she wasn't so tired, if she just had a minute to think, she would find this particular cancellation very worrying? She'd been counting on the bookings that were already made. In order to make ends meet, she had to keep as many rooms as possible filled during the season. After five years of coping with Uncle Will, why had these people decided they couldn't cope with Petra?

Worrying about this and about the roof, because she hadn't been able to find another contractor who could do anything but make promises to come in a couple of months or so, she was all the way inside her room before she noticed the flowers.

Lips parting involuntarily with wonder, she backed up a couple of steps and leaned against the doorjamb, staring in awe at the garden she'd walked into. Sometime during the afternoon her bedroom had been magically transformed. Yellow roses were everywhere, dozens of the long-stemmed variety thrust into tall crystal vases that circled the floor, white straw baskets of rosebuds on the round table by the window and on the nightstands at each side of her wide bed, an Oriental dish garden filled with miniature, perfectly formed blooms on the windowsill. One huge basket of tea roses had been set majestically on top of the quilt in the middle of her bed, another on the seat of her armchair. It was a sight so beautiful it was numbing to all senses except the sense of smell. And the smell was wonderful, a heady natural fragrance no perfume manufacturer could possibly duplicate.

Stunned, Petra stood motionless in the doorway of her bedroom for what seemed a very long time. She was brought to her senses by a voice at her elbow. Mrs. Menniger, trim in a lavender pantsuit and deep purple silk shirt, was peering around her with avid interest. "There must be five hundred dollars' worth of roses here," she said in a voice tinged with awe.

"At least." Petra cleared her throat. "I'm not sure I believe the evidence of my own eyes. Am I seeing things, Mrs. Menniger?"

The old woman chuckled. "If you are, then I'm sunstruck too. May I ask who they're from? I don't suppose the local welcome wagon is this generous. Did you find a card yet?"

"I haven't looked."

"Well come on, girl, aren't you curious?"

Petra smiled at the little woman. She had known the instant she saw the bower of flowers who had ordered them for her. But for Mrs. Menniger's sake she made a show of hunting for a card, having to edge sideways around the many beautiful vases of flowers.

The card turned out to be with the miniature garden. It was signed, "Dan, the discouraged farmer."

Puzzled, she must have stared at the phrase for several seconds before she understood she was being challenged as she had challenged him on the drive to Boston. He'd won this challenge. Though "the discouraged farmer" rang a bell somewhere in her memory, it was a faint bell and she couldn't come up with the source.

Mrs. Menniger cleared her throat in an exaggerated manner, and Petra remembered with a start that she was not alone. The old woman had followed her across the room. Her button-bright eyes were fixed on the card. "Young Mr. Halliwell, right?" she asked, adding when Petra nodded, "What wouldn't I give to be forty years younger!" She patted Petra's arm briskly. "Don't let him get away, dear. Any man who makes grand gestures should be treasured."

She returned to the doorway, adding over her shoulder, "I mean *treasured*, held on to, clung to, penned up in a room with the door locked and the key thrown away." Her voice faded along the hall. "Never let him go," was the last instruction Petra heard.

Standing in the middle of her bedroom, surrounded by roses, Petra sank onto her bed. The huge basket of tea roses sank with her, and she had to catch it to stop it from falling. She could barely get her arms around it. She had never in her entire life seen so many roses in one spot, unless it was on one of the floats in the Pasadena Rose parade.

She had a sudden vision of her entire room, with her in the middle of it, moving majestically along while she, dressed in Tony's overalls and her bandanna, with white paint on her nose, waved graciously to the cheering spectators. Setting the huge basket of flowers on the floor with the rest, she started to giggle and found that she couldn't stop. It was such a crazy thing to do, to send this many roses, an extravagant, impossible, wonderful thing to do....

She was still laughing when the telephone rang. She gurgled uncontrollably when she heard Dan's voice, feeling absolutely giddy and light-headed, all barriers let down. "You're out of your mind," she told him.

"I take it my floral offering arrived safely?"

"Arrived? It's taken over. Dan, you must have bought out all the yellow roses in Massachusetts. How on earth did you know that yellow roses are my favorite flowers?"

"You're feeling warm toward me, would you say?"

"Meltingly so." What ever happened to "friendly but distant"? her mind chided.

"Uh-hah. Then you'll have dinner with me tonight?"

An alarm bell clanged stridently in her mind. "Whoa. Wait a minute. Tony said you wanted to take us to Nantucket. Dinner wasn't mentioned at all."

"A last-minute idea. Dinner at the Coonamessett Inn tonight, Nantucket tomorrow."

"Is Tony included in the invitation?"

"Nantucket, yes, dinner tonight, no. I planned an early dinner—about six o'clock. How does that sound to you?"

He was being very high-handed, taking over, giving her no choices. "There's something I'd like to talk to you about—a favor I'd like you to do for me, if you will," he continued when she hesitated.

That was intriguing. She was weakening, she knew. But really, how could she refuse him? Only a particularly mean-spirited woman could resist a room full of roses. And whatever else Petra McNeil was, she was not mean-spirited. "I'd love to have dinner with you tonight,'' she said recklessly, wondering even as she hung up the phone if the perfume of the roses had affected her sanity.

Nothing had changed, she reassured herself. She was as determined as ever to concentrate only on her business, and not let any man distract her. But there could surely be no harm in having dinner, especially at such an early hour. And no harm in sailing tomorrow on a public stretch of water to a very public tourist spot.

She stood up and gazed helplessly around at the roses, wondering what on earth she was going to do with them all, starting to laugh again even as she wondered.

THE COONAMESSETT INN—built in 1790, the same year as Nathaniel's house, Dan told her—was about half a mile from Falmouth center. It was a gracious yet stately place, situated on a pond, with shrubs and trees all around. Petra, looking over the exterior with a newly professional eye, decided that even though it was much larger than her inn, it was still small enough to have a hospitable, welcoming air.

The interior was as elegant as the outside, featuring many plants, a huge brick fireplace and cream-colored planked paneling on the walls. Tall mullioned windows overlooked the shady grounds, and old-style candelabra lighting cast shadows onto the high beamed ceiling. The tables were covered with green cloths and an array of silverware and delicate crystal that indicated gourmet dining at its best.

As Dan pulled out a ladder-back chair for her at

their table by the window, Petra looked around her with pleasure, glad she'd dressed well enough for the sophisticated atmosphere of the place. After a lot of thought she'd chosen to wear a dress her Aunt Sophia had bought her and she had never worn. It was made of a hot-pink silk that made a perfect foil for her black hair and creamy skin. She hadn't worn it before because its plunging neckline made her look more well endowed than she really was and also precluded the wearing of a bra, which made her feel very sexy and reckless. Admiring herself in the mirror of her dressing table before she'd left, recognizing that the daring neckline could be interpreted as an invitation, she had felt curiously reluctant to change into one of her more demure dresses.

After all, she'd reminded herself, Dan's vacation or business trip or whatever it was must be coming to an end. Surely, just for one evening, she could let herself be vulnerable and feminine and unsuspicious of motives. Though even now, she was wondering why. . . .

"Why did you want to eat so early?" she asked, lifting one hand toward the few diners who were scattered throughout the large room. They were mostly young couples with small children.

"So we can watch the sunset," he said promptly. "I've an idea it will be pretty spectacular tonight."

She looked at the lawns and trees beyond the window. "How can we possibly see the sunset from here?"

His eyebrows arched above eyes that were as impossibly green as the inn's landscaping. "I hadn't intended that we should. I have in mind an old dock—a place where I used to fish when I was a little boy. There's a bench we can sit on. The place is usually deserted, which is why I've always liked it.''

His gaze was holding hers steadily, almost daring her to object to his plans. Her heart had started beating more loudly, pounding like the drum that accompanied aristocratic victims on their way to the guillotine during the French Revolution.

His eyes were asking a question. If she didn't look away right now, she would be giving him an answer. And she couldn't look away. He was particularly attractive tonight, she thought with dismay. He was wearing a whiter than white shirt with a dark tie and a light gray suit that fitted his elegantly lean frame as though it had been made for him—which it probably had. His light brown hair was smoothly brushed. His time spent outdoors was beginning to show. His face was now a deep tan that emphasized the clear whites and dancing green of his eyes. ''You didn't mention deserted docks before,'' she said in a suddenly breathless voice.

''You didn't ask.''

He wore such an obviously false air of innocence that she couldn't stop herself from laughing aloud. What a rogue he is, she thought, and the thought was enough to make her feel quite safe. Rogues were rarely dangerous. Rogues didn't get serious enough to be dangerous.

''This is a beautiful place,'' she said, trying to regain control of the conversation.

He nodded. ''I knew you'd like it.''

"The same way you knew I'd like yellow roses? Sarah gossiping about my likes and dislikes?"

His eyes shone with appreciation. "You're quite right," he said. "I cheated on the roses. I asked Sarah to tell me your favorite flowers. Did you understand the reference to the discouraged farmer?"

A faint smile hovered around his mouth, heralding one of those eye-crinkling grins. She shook her head, hating to admit defeat. "It sounds vaguely familiar, but I can't quite place it," she said.

The grin came through as promised, as meltingly attractive as she remembered. "James Whitcomb Riley," he prompted.

The arrival of the wine he'd ordered gave her a moment to consider and by the time he'd sniffed, tasted and approved the chardonnay to go with their oyster appetizer and roast duckling, she had figured out the connection—"The Discouraged Farmer," by James Whitcomb Riley.

"'Fer the world is full of roses,'" she chanted aloud, so delighted to have remembered the quote that she forgot she was in a public place. "'And the roses full of dew, and the dew is full of heavenly love that drips fer me and you.'"

As several heads turned across the room, she realized she'd declaimed a little too loudly. She felt heat rush to her face.

Dan applauded, drawing more stares, then raised his wineglass to her. Feeling considerably embarrassed, she accepted the toast and took a sip from her own glass. "I would never have remembered it if you hadn't told me the author," she admitted.

He grinned. "Actually, I called home and had our housekeeper look up roses in *Bartlett's Quotations* before I went to the florist's shop. I wanted to have something to impress you with." He lifted her hand and kissed the back of it gently. "I salute you. Your brain is obviously sharper than mine."

The hand-kissing gesture was casually performed, but it brought a rush of sensation to Petra's body. The room, which had previously seemed pleasantly cool, was suddenly stiflingly hot, as though all the air had been sucked out of it. A knot of anticipation established itself in her stomach, a premonition of disaster connected with the charming man sitting opposite her. She was quite suddenly not so sure it was harmless to have dinner with him.

Her feeling was confirmed a little later when he speared one of his oysters with a fork and offered it to her lips saying, "Try this."

Automatically she bit into it, chewed and swallowed, wondering why he should think his oysters tasted any different from hers. She looked at him enquiringly. His smile alerted her—there was something triumphant about it. "Didn't I tell you I'd soon have you eating out of my hands?" he asked softly.

She could have dismissed the small incident as a joke—on her—if his eyes hadn't held hers so steadily, and her body hadn't responded with a stillness like the calm before a storm. She should have stayed at the inn, she thought desperately. She should have worked on the last of her varnishing, painted the golden eagle Tony had got down for her, sanded the woodwork in the next guest bedroom on her list. Almost any occupation would have been safer than sitting here with this dangerously attractive man.

MOST OF THE BOATS in the harbor were small sailboats, riding at anchor, their sails furled, their masts starkly etched against the glorious sky.

It was a small harbor, embraced by arms of land on which the lights in small cabins and one or two larger houses winked in the gathering dusk.

Petra and Dan sat side by side on a bench in front of a large equipment locker and watched the sun slowly sinking, shedding light in a wide golden path across the calm water. Across the sun's face wispy gray horsetaillike clouds drifted lazily. There was no wind at all. Everything was still, as though waiting with bated breath for night to fall.

Since their arrival, fifteen minutes before, neither Dan nor Petra had said a word. The sky, golden when they got there, changing gradually through almost every color in an artist's palette, flared orange and crimson now, turning the calm water in the harbor to molten flame. The sight was so breathtakingly beautiful, it seemed sacrilegious to speak. Until Dan moved, the only sound was the quiet lapping of water against the dock pilings, the occasional soft twittering of birds in the trees on shore.

Dan produced a tall bottle and two delicate stemmed glasses from the small cooler he'd brought along. "Château Lafite-Rothschild," he announced as he expertly uncorked the bottle.

Another grand gesture—seventy-five dollar-a-bottle wine.

After letting the wine breathe for a few minutes, he handed a glass to her and raised his own. "To the sunset," he toasted.

"To the sunset," she echoed, her eyes still on the wonderful display of colors in the western sky.

It was a marvelous wine, with a distinctive odor of violets and almonds, a rich body and a delicate taste. The color had nuances of orange when she held the glass up to the light, as though the sunset itself had been distilled in the glass. Sipping it, she decided it even tasted like a sunset—like the liquid red gold of sun on water, clean red gold flowing down into her body, warming it, relaxing it.

She savored the wine as she had so far savored the entire evening, as something special, to be remembered pleasantly, beginning with the roses. When she and Dan had been able to converse naturally for the remainder of their time at the Coonamessett Inn, she'd decided that she'd been foolish to think of him as dangerous. He was just a man, an attractive man. It was perfectly possible to enjoy his company without worrying about dire consequences. There weren't going to be any dire consequences as long as she kept her wits about her.

There certainly hadn't been any dire consequences so far. She might have been enjoying the sunset with Tony, though she couldn't imagine Tony wanting to watch a sunset with her or sending her hundreds of dollars' worth of roses. She laughed softly, explaining to Dan when he queried her with raised eyebrows, "I was remembering the roses. I put some in every room in the inn and still had some left over. Do you always send hundreds of roses to a woman before you ask her for a date?''

He smiled and shook his head. ''Special people require special tactics.'' There was a look in his eyes that flustered her. Silence threatened to enfold them again, and again there was tension in the silence, dangerous tension.

Petra stirred. ''I do hope you won't think....'' She paused, uncertain how to phrase her warning that the situation hadn't changed.

He touched his fingers to her mouth. ''Hush and watch the sunset, woman.'' Petra felt one of his arms settle casually around her shoulders as he refilled her wineglass. No, not casually, she amended in her mind. Nothing this man did was ever casual. She sat very straight, watching the sky, willing herself not to lean back against his arm.

The sun slid slowly below the horizon, back lighting the clouds in a sudden blaze of color, like the final spectacular display at a fireworks exhibition. Ribbons of pale blue mingled with pink and orange and crimson and aqua and purple, intensified for several long moments, then darkened to charcoal gray and gold in the last of the sun's rays.

Almost immediately, a breeze sprang up. Petra shivered, not so much from the cold as from the wonderful experience of the sunset. Dan pulled off his suit jacket and placed it gently around her shoulders. ''I should have thought to bring a blanket,'' he murmured. ''I never would have made a Boy Scout, I'm afraid.''

She felt curiously unthreatened by the intimacy of

the moment, even though his arm was around her, holding the jacket in place, even though the heat of his body lingered inside the jacket, folding around her in an embrace more potent than his actual touch.

"That was so beautiful," she said on a long sighing breath, her gaze still held by the spot where the sun had disappeared. "It was like watching art happen—as though the greatest artist in the world was working on a huge canvas just for our pleasure."

Dan laughed softly. "The last woman I brought here complained the whole time that I should have reminded her to bring a camera."

"How awful." Petra exclaimed. "I can't understand people who have to use a camera constantly to record beauty like that. They're so busy fussing around with their f-stops they miss seeing the real thing and only have the copy to look at afterward."

His grip tightened around her. "I thought I was the only person in America to have heretical thoughts like that. Not that I've anything against cameras, or photographers—but as you say, if the photograph becomes a substitute for the actual experience, it's like watching two lovers kiss on a movie screen and never experiencing a kiss yourself."

His voice had dropped seductively and his mouth was very close to her ear. Sitting very still, Petra said nervously, "You have a unique way of interpreting the things I say."

"Suggestive, would you say?"

Keep it light, her defense mechanisms dictated. "My very thought," she said.

"You don't want me to be suggestive?"

"How did you guess?"

"Why not? Are you jealous because I mentioned bringing another woman here?"

"That's not such a good guess, Dan. I have no reason to be jealous. Jealousy implies caring."

"You don't care for me, Petra?" His voice was still very low, his mouth so close to her face that when he spoke his breath was warm against her cheek.

It wasn't fair of him to play word games with her when her mind was still filled with the glory of the sunset. "I didn't say I didn't care," she said. "I meant that I don't—I don't have the strong feelings of someone who.... Oh forget it," she said, laughing suddenly. "How can I possibly explain what I mean when you're breathing down my neck?"

"Such a pretty neck," he said, touching it with his lips.

"Dan," she said in what was meant to be a protest, but somehow came out as a long sigh.

"Petra?"

There was hardly any light suddenly. Only the faint glimmerings from houses, none of them very near. Again she was conscious of a waiting in the air, but knew that this time it was something in her that was waiting for him to make a move.

He would make a move, she had no doubt. She hadn't yet made up her mind how she would react when he did. As it turned out, she had no desire to stop him when he gently took the wineglass from her hand and set it somewhere. Nor did she protest when his long fingers closed around her wrist and he turned her hand over and touched the tip of his tongue to the soft vulnerable spot at the center of her wrist.

Shock waves reverberated through her body, rendering her powerless to move. When he raised his head, he murmured indignantly, "You have calluses on your hands!"

She laughed. "Sorry, I didn't have time to go for a manicure."

"You've been working too hard." He had raised both her hands now and was studying them in what light was left, a frown puckering the skin between his eyebrows.

"A little hard work never hurt anyone," she said jokingly.

"Too much can kill you," he said. He looked stern, she thought. Then there was no more thought as he closed her hands together, gave them a little tug to bring her closer to him, then put his arms around her and brought his mouth down gently on hers. Almost immediately her entire body responded as though it had been programmed to do so. Like soft curling shavings planed from a piece of wood and touched with a match, she went up in flames the moment their lips met.

There had never been a man who affected her as quickly, as completely as this one did. In his presence, she apparently had no will, no mind of her own, no control. With his searing kiss, she returned to primitive times; she was simply, single-mindedly, woman to his man.

Of course, she told herself vaguely, this couldn't possibly be happening, because Petra—logical, level-headed, practical Petra had made up her mind she would not let it happen. So it must be a fantasy, a waking dream, brought on by a combination of two different kinds of wine, aphrodisiacal food, several dozen roses and one glorious sunset. How else could one kiss cause her heart to start racing at twice its normal speed, send currents of energy through all her veins, send torturing heat to tighten the tender area between her thighs? When he lifted his head, it was as though all the breath in her body left, as though he'd sucked all breath from her in that one gentle kiss. No doubt about it; this must be a fantasy. A wonderful fantasy. A sigh escaped her, and she saw the white of his smile against the darkness.

Moving in slow motion, as though he was afraid of startling her, his fingers brushed over her nipples, which stiffened in immediate response beneath the thin fabric of her dress. Then he touched lightly at the top of the soft valley between her breasts, tracing downward with one finger until he reached the first button and unfastened it, then the next and the next. She felt the cool night breeze caress her breasts and knew they were naked to his touch, a touch that was sending signals to every part of her body—signals that were received and understood and acknowledged, without thought of refusal.

Somewhere far at the back of her mind a voice was clamoring to be heard, shouting a warning that she was forgetting her vow, forgetting past pain, forgetting, forgetting. But it was a very small voice and it couldn't quite penetrate this fantasy that seemed so natural to her right now.

His fingers trailed fire across her body, circling, stroking, teasing with their delicate touch until she could stand their torture no longer and reached to press both his hands firmly and tightly against her breasts. At the same time, a small soft moan escaped her lips and she recognized it for what it was, a moan of surrender.

As though the sound had inflamed him, Dan suddenly discontinued his patient touching. As his arms enfolded her, his hands spread behind her and he pulled her sharply against his body, so that her naked breasts pressed against the crisp cotton of his shirt, and her lower body was raised from the bench to be held captive between his hard, demanding thighs. His mouth pressed harshly against hers, demanding all she had to give and more. She gave to him gladly with her mouth, aware that she had never in her life given so much in a kiss, had never known it was possible to give so much in a kiss. It even seemed natural that while her own mouth was still filled with the wonderful lingering taste of the red Bordeaux wine, she could taste it on his tongue—surely the most sensuous feeling that had ever accompanied a kiss.

Wanting to be closer to him, she unfastened his shirt. He'd already removed his tie. When had he done that, she wondered. It didn't really matter—it was all part of the fantasy. Pressing her breasts against the soft matting of hair on his chest, she crooned his name softly against his lips and felt his mouth curve in a smile. "You are a very sensual woman, Petra McNeil," he murmured.

"Mm-hmm." She didn't want him to speak. Words created thoughts and thoughts got in the way of primitive responses. She didn't want to think. For just a little longer she wanted only to feel the teasing movement of his body against hers, the soft night air lifting her hair against his face, the quickness of his breath against her lips, the heat of his hands on her, burning through the flimsy silk of her dress.

"Petra," he said, as she eased herself more comfortably against him. "I think we'd better change locations, don't you?"

Cradled in his arms, her head resting against his shoulder, she became aware of sounds. There were cars moving along the road behind the dock. People were returning from dinner in town, or going to movies, theaters. At any moment one of the cars could turn off toward the dock. He was right. It was time to wake up from the dream. Sighing, she straightened and slid back onto the bench, her fingers going automatically to fasten her dress.

Dan's jacket had fallen from her shoulders. She found it crushed down between the bench and the wooden equipment locker and handed it to him, not needing it anymore. She was still so warm.

"We could go to my suite," he murmured.

For a moment she was sorely tempted. Her entire body was still yearning toward him, wanting to return to the fantasy, wanting him. If there had been some magic way to transport them from the bench to his room without physical effort, without having to separate and get in his car and drive on a road where there were other cars—a whole real world—she would probably have become his lover that very night. But the real world had intruded and Petra the realist was in charge again. The interlude had been nice, very nice, but she'd be foolish to let it go any further. She'd already let it go too far.

"I don't think so," she said with more than a little regret.

"Why not?"

"I'm being practical, Dan. I'd really rather be your friend. Let's not mess up our friendship just when it's begun, okay?"

"You look upon lovemaking as messing up?"

There was a caustic note in his voice that let her know he was far from amused by her change of heart. Typical male, she thought. After buying all those flowers, paying for her dinner, he probably felt she owed him. . . .

"Perhaps I didn't word that properly," she apologized. "I guess what I'm saying is I'd prefer to enjoy your company without getting too intimate about it. I'm really adamant about this, Dan. As I've already told you, I don't want to get too involved."

"And I've already told you we can't let our relationship stagnate," he protested. "I don't have a lot of time left. Another couple of weeks is all."

"Two more weeks?" Her alarm came through clearly in her voice and she thought he smiled in the dark.

"Didn't I tell you?" he asked in a surprised voice that sounded totally phony. "I'm going to be staying longer than I thought."

"Why?"

He didn't answer for a minute, as though he was trying to decide on the proper answer. When he did speak, his voice had suddenly become stern, almost bleak sounding. "I have to stay on because of Kelly."

Ah-huh, she thought. There was indeed more to his visit than just a vacation. Her first suspicions had been correct after all. "Kelly?" she asked, trying not to show how interested she suddenly was.

"Kelly O'Connor, the resort manager." His arm was around her shoulders again. "Petra, are you sure..." he began.

Easing herself away from him, Petra directed the conversation back again. "I've been meaning to go over and introduce myself to your manager. It seems the neighborly thing to do. What do you think?"

His arm dropped away. "I don't think it's a good idea."

"Why not?" Exasperated when he didn't answer, she repeated the question. "Why not?"

"He's not someone you'd like at all."

"How can you possibly know who I'd like and who I wouldn't like?" she demanded. "You're not my keeper, Dan. I wish you'd stop behaving as though you were. Apparently you don't care for the man, but that has nothing to do with me. Except that I don't understand why you want to stay on because of him if you don't care for him."

He sighed. "It isn't Kelly's idea that I stay on. Actually, Kelly's trying out a few new programs and head office wants my opinion."

"That's part of your job as a troubleshooter, to look over new programs?"

He was silent for a minute, then he laughed shortly, his face clearing. "I keep forgetting how smart you are, Petra. No, that's not part of my job."

He sighed again. "I might as well come clean, I guess. I'm just enjoying my time here so much, I requested an extension. I hope you don't think that's terribly lazy of me."

He was lying to her and not even trying to disguise the fact very cleverly. Which was damned insulting, any way she looked at it.

"You're right," she said bluntly. "It is none of my business."

He winced, probably because she'd shown she'd recognized his lie.

"What was the favor you were going to ask me?" she asked abruptly.

"Favor?"

"You said you had a favor you wanted...."

"Oh yes, that." He was sounding distinctly uncomfortable again. Why? "As a matter of fact, that had to do with Kelly," he said evenly. "I just wanted to ask you, if you do happen to run into him, well, perhaps you'd go along with whatever he says about me, about my reasons for being on the Cape."

"You mean you lied about your reasons to him too?"

He winced again, then sighed. "Not exactly. I let him believe certain things that were not exactly true, perhaps. Anyway, if you do go to see him, though I certainly wouldn't recommend that you do...."

"Let me get this straight," Petra interrupted. "For some reason which you don't want to tell me, you don't want Kelly O'Connor to know why you are staying on the Cape."

He gave a sigh of relief. "That's it, yes."

"What does he believe?"

"I'm not really sure, so I don't want to pass on any conclusions that might be false. I'd really just as soon...."

"Okay, Dan," she interrupted again. "I don't think I want to hear any more. What did you call it when I did it? Fudging? If I see Mr. O'Connor and he asks about you, I'll simply play dumb. That ought to be in character, don't you think?"

He ignored her sarcasm completely. "Thank you, Petra," he said gravely. Then he lifted her hand between both of his. "Now that that's over, what about you and me?" It went to prove, Petra thought, how little he thought of her common sense. Did he really think she could overlook the fact that he was a liar, no matter how little it might involve her personally?

"There is no you and me," she said firmly. "I'm sorry. I didn't mean to lead you to think.... I guess the sunset got to me." She looked into his eyes. "Nothing has changed, Dan. All I'm prepared to offer is friendship."

He let out his breath on a long exhalation. "Okay." There was a pause, then he said briskly, "You'll still go to Nantucket tomorrow, won't you?"

There was a coaxing note in his voice now and it affected her so strongly that she wanted to tell him she'd do anything he wanted, anything at all. But she wasn't going to give in to those urges again. Obviously he still wanted to play games with her, but she wasn't going to play any more.

"Of course, Dan," she said firmly. "I promised Tony I would."

CHAPTER SEVEN

DAN'S SLOOP was rigged for single-handed operation, because, he explained to Petra as they came on board, when he managed to get time for sailing, he usually preferred to sail alone.

As she had always insisted on time to herself, Petra could identify with his feelings, though his statement surprised her. He'd struck her so far as a very gregarious type.

Standing in the cockpit while Dan and Tony stowed a few supplies in the tiny galley, she looked around with delight at the sparkling brightwork and scrubbed teak decks of the *Odyssey*, thinking how her classics-oriented father would have approved the sloop's name. She was looking forward to the day. Her spirits seemed to lift in the clear, salty air. She was amazed as always at the incredibly clear light of early morning that seemed to be peculiar to the Cape. There was a chill to the air though, and she was glad she'd dressed warmly in her dark-blue-and-white sweat suit. Dark curls blowing in the brisk breeze, her head tipped back, she looked up at the crystal blue sky and stretched her arms toward it, breathing deeply.

"Ready for takeoff?" Dan asked behind her.

Startled, she turned to look at him and laughed nervously, immediately remembering her first sight of him, as he'd probably intended her to do. How long ago that meeting aboard the airplane seemed. Another world. Another life.

He stood smiling faintly, looking down at her as he had then, the green of his eyes accentuated by the grass-green sweat shirt he wore with his tight-fitting jeans. He held her gaze for a moment, then raised one eyebrow as his glance dropped to her mouth. Immediately she knew he was thinking about the previous evening.

Increasingly nervous, she was glad to hear Tony's voice close by, asking a question about the sail covers. She glanced up at him as he peered at Dan through his thick-lensed glasses, smiling at the lovable picture he made, so loose boned and lanky in cutoffs and his favorite old university sweat shirt. He was waiting for an answer to his question, but Dan ignored him, his eyes half-hooded, still watching her mouth, which had become extremely dry. With an effort she resisted the temptation to moisten her lips with her tongue, which she was afraid he would construe as an invitation.

When Tony repeated his question in a tone of voice that indicated he thought Dan must be hard-of-hearing, Dan laughed, lightly touched her closed lips with one unhurried finger, smiled crookedly at her and turned away to talk to the boy.

Petra sat abruptly on the raised helmsman's seat, conscious that a shot of adrenaline had gone through her in that single intense moment. *I'm not interested in Dan Halliwell,* she told herself firmly, and ignored the answering jeer that came immediately from the back of her mind.

Dan took the *Odyssey* out of the harbor under power, explaining to both of them, as he maneuvered between the dozens of large pleasure boats, exactly what he was going to do and what he wanted them to do once they were under way. His instructions were clear and concise, delivered calmly in his crisp Boston accent. To Petra's delight, he apparently accepted automatically that she was part of the crew and perfectly capable of helping out.

Once clear of the harbor, he gave her a heading and left her in charge of the tiller while he and Tony saw to the sails. He let Tony operate the winch, much to the boy's obvious pleasure. "Keep her pointed into the wind, Petra," he called over his shoulder, then stood back and watched the mainsail go up, encouraging Tony with a word or two, before moving lightly and surefootedly forward to bring up the jib sail himself.

As soon as everything was secure, he returned to Petra's side, turned off the engine and let the wind take over, smiling with obvious exhilaration at the powerful slapping sound of the wind in the sails.

The boat skimmed through the water effortlessly with barely a touch on the tiller necessary to keep her on course. Because the tiller was so sensitive, Petra mostly allowed the boat to feel her own way among the swells, which she seemed perfectly capable of doing.

"She's wonderful, Dan," Petra said, feeling a rush of exhilaration more heady than champagne.

"Awesome," Tony agreed over his shoulder. He was beaming from ear to ear, delighted with himself, as he had every right to be. Under Dan's tutelage he'd performed creditably, especially considering the fact that his lanky body wasn't always too well coordinated. He'd only flubbed once, when he got an overbite on a line, but he'd managed to sort it out himself after a calming word from Dan. He moved to the foredeck now and stood there, feet braced, squinting through his glasses out to sea, the wind blowing in his hair. He looked for all the world like an experienced sailor, which was probably the way he wanted to look.

Dan Halliwell had a certain way about him that was irresistible, Petra admitted to herself. Self-confident himself, he managed to imbue others with confidence simply by expecting them to be able to perform the tasks he assigned them. And there was no macho posturing about him. He seemed as much at home on the boat as he had at the wheel of his car and as he would chairing that board meeting she'd imagined when she saw him for the first time.

Petra liked the way he was treating her today—as an equal in intelligence and in common sense. In fact, when she thought about it, he treated her that way most of the time.

Aware that she was showing signs of softening toward him, she recited his faults to herself: he was inclined to be bossy a lot of the time...bossy and high-handed and interfering and far too sure of his own sex appeal.

She shook her head, checked the compass and let

her mind open to the crystal blue-and-silver vista before her. This was too beautiful a day to spend time trying to analyze Dan Halliwell's faults.

The Sound was fairly clear of traffic, though she could see several sailboats off Martha's Vineyard and more toward Nantucket. A large ferryboat was heading that way too, but it was well ahead of them. The *Odyssey* was sailing close to the wind now. Above her mast a couple of gulls swooped and mewled. Studying the action of the wind in the sails, Petra suddenly understood for the first time that the boat was being lifted by the action of the wind moving across the sail—in the same way an airplane is lifted by the action of air moving across the wing surface. She said as much to Dan and received an approving nod and a smile. His reaction pleased her. Given any such comment, Brad would have made some sarcastic remark and David would have looked at her as though she'd grown two heads. Dan took it for granted that she should be able to reason things out. Petra's face glowed suddenly, not only from the wind, and she felt tremendously glad to be alive on such a glorious day.

"What are you smiling at?" Dan asked.

"How wonderful this is. How lucky we are to have such a good wind. How glad I am that I let Tony talk me into coming."

"You didn't really want to come, did you?"

She gave him an apologetic smile. "So much to do," she explained.

He looked at her with narrowed eyes. "Remind me sometime to tell you why my marriage failed," he said obscurely. He spoke again before she could react. "It is great isn't it? Though I'm afraid we'll have to go back to power soon if we want to spend any time on Nantucket." He grinned at her, reached over to ruffle her hair in a brotherly way, then yelled forward to Tony. "Hey, shipmate, are you ready to learn how to come about?" Another grin for Petra. "You too," he said sternly. "No slackers allowed on my ship."

"Aye, aye, skipper," she said obediently, and for the next few minutes Dan took over the tiller and called directions while she and Tony handled the jib sheets, managing by the skin of their teeth to avoid backing the jib. During the next hour Dan put them through several more procedures, showing as always the calm attitude that made him a perfect teacher. At last, satisfied with their prowess, but anxious to get them to Nantucket, he surrendered the tiller—to Tony this time. He and Petra dropped the sails, furling the mainsail and bagging the jib, and then they proceeded under power for the rest of the trip, making it possible for them to relax and enjoy a snack and a pot of coffee.

Obviously feeling high-spirited, Tony led them into a contest naming nautical terms, such as "leeway," "half-seas over" and "three sheets in the wind," which had come to be used in everyday language. After that Dan entertained them with tales of sailing adventures and misadventures, including one hair-raising account of a time he'd been caught at sea in a howling "no'theaster."

Hours later, when they tied up at the yacht club on

Nantucket, they were close friends, totally at ease with each other, a state of affairs for which Petra was very thankful. She felt comfortable, relaxed and happy walking along the wide cobbled street toward the restaurant that Dan had promised would serve them the best crab rolls in the country. Dan walked between Petra and Tony, holding Petra's left arm lightly at the elbow to help steer her through the crowds of people who had disembarked from the earlier ferry.

In spite of the crowds of tourists strolling the tree-lined Main Street and crowding the shops in search of ivory carvings and scrimshaw, Nantucket had exactly the atmosphere she'd expected, the truly salty flavor of a Colonial seaport. The cobbled streets were there as promised, the cobbles brought almost 150 years ago from Gloucester in England, Dan told her.

Petra's ready imagination kindled a picture of a young Nantucketer standing on the cobbles, gazing out to sea. He lived in one of the huge, gracious mansions that lined the street, of course—his father had built it with his whale-oil profits. His father and uncles and brothers were whalers, and he too would soon be sailing away aboard some whaler bound for the South Pacific. So real was the image in Petra's mind that she could almost smell the sickening odor of processed whale and boiling blubber. Hardly a romantic ambience.

It seemed amazing to Petra that this small island, only fourteen miles long and three and a half miles wide, should at one time have been the whaling capital of the world. Ship captains had returned here from voyages to the Azores, the Caribbean, Brazil and the Gulf of the St. Lawrence. In these streets had walked coopers and riggers and blacksmiths and carpenters and sail makers and others whose trades linked them with ships and the sea.

And the women. How strong they must have been! Left alone to raise their families while their men risked their lives at sea. Kissing their sons goodbye when they were seventeen, and not seeing them again until they were grown men of twenty-two. Petra took a deep breath of the salty air and decided she was glad she lived now instead of then.

As they passed a beautiful old brick house that had been converted into a general-goods store, walking sideways to get through the customers who had spilled out onto the sidewalk, a female voice hailed Tony. He called out "Lori!" in a delighted tone of voice, and halted in his tracks until a young girl managed to shoulder her way to his side.

The girl was of a type Petra had always admired— cool, contained and confident. She was fairly tall and slender, with shoulder-length honey-blond hair that curved faultlessly around her oval face under a floppy brimmed denim hat. She wore no makeup, and had no need of any. Once they'd all regrouped themselves beyond the knot of people, she offered Petra a firm small hand for shaking and acknowledged Tony's introductions with a polite, "How are you?" in a cool little voice that duplicated Dan's accent.

With her was a boy a few years older who turned out to be her brother, Seth. They were dressed identically in blue Izod shirts, khaki Bermuda shorts and loafers. Seth's hair was cut short and brushed as neatly to one side as his sister's. He was eighteen years old, Petra remembered, and Lori was fourteen. They both looked older, not because of any physical characteristics, but because of the serious expressions on their young faces, coupled with their superb manners.

"Tony has told us so much about you, Miss McNeil," Seth said with a charming smile. "I feel I've known you for ages."

Petra melted. "I'm glad Tony's making friends on the Cape. He told me you took him out on your boat. Did you bring it over today?"

He nodded. "As a matter of fact we telephoned Tony, but your...housekeeper...said you'd both left with Mr. Halliwell." He looked at Dan. "I guess you didn't remember me the other day when we... met, Mr. Halliwell. My father's John Cartwright. I believe we first met at the Warburtons'."

"Cartwright, Stennis—stockbrokers?" Dan asked.

The boy inclined his head. Petra was amazed at his poise. His manner was just right—confident without being pushy, assured but with a hint of deference.

Dan, on the other hand, was palpably not impressed. Why that was, she couldn't imagine, but she'd felt his hand tighten on her elbow shortly after the Cartwright boy opened his mouth to speak, and it hadn't relaxed yet. Surely he wasn't still annoyed about the boat incident Tony had told her about?

They had obviously lost Tony. He was gazing at Lori as though he'd never seen anyone quite so per-

fect. She was smiling prettily up at him, telling him
they were on the way to visit a friend whose grandmother had a cottage in 'Sconset, on the eastern
shore of the island. "Tucker Channing, remember?"
she added. "You met him on our boat."

Tony nodded agreement, though Petra had an idea
that at this moment he had no idea who Tucker
Channing might be and didn't really care. He would
have agreed with anything young Miss Cartwright
said. So much for his "Nothing like that" denial,
when she'd teased him about being in love, Petra
thought. If those weren't the painful pangs of first
love creasing Tony's thin scholarly face, she didn't
know her own brother.

Lori had turned toward Seth, her smooth young
brow puckered in a charming frown. "Why don't
we take Tony with us?" she suggested. "Tucker
wouldn't mind." She smiled up at Tony again.
"Would you like to come? We're invited for lunch.
We're riding those." She pointed to the corner where
a couple of mopeds were propped against the brick
wall of the shop. "We can rent one for you at
Snow's, right here on Main Street."

"Hey, that would be great!" Tony exclaimed, obviously forgetting all his former enthusiasm about
the whaling museum and other historical treasures.

Petra was beginning to feel torn. She wanted Tony
to be with young people. Riding a moped to somebody's grandmother's cottage sounded like just the
sort of thing Tony should do. But on the other hand,
if he left she would be alone with Dan and she wasn't
sure that was a good idea. Dan didn't seem to think

so either. When she glanced at him she saw that his face had darkened considerably. "I don't know, Tony," she demurred. "We did come with Dan and...."

"Tony shouldn't feel obliged to me," Dan said at once, but in such a clipped manner that he left no doubt that he expected Tony to feel exactly that. "Although I would think—" He broke off and looked from Seth to Lori with a very stern expression on his lean face. Something was bothering him, that was for sure, but he seemed uncertain of what it might be.

Petra looked at him, frowning. Uncertainty was not something she associated with Dan Halliwell. "Well, if you really do object..." she began.

"Gosh, Dan," Tony interrupted. "Of course I won't go off after you've been so kind if you...."

"Good," Dan said.

Tony's face fell. Petra had suspected his heart wasn't in the statement he'd made to Dan. She was surprised Dan hadn't sensed that too. He certainly hadn't needed to make it so impossible for Tony to ease away gracefully. His whole attitude since Seth and Lori had arrived was beginning to make her angry. Why should Tony have to be denied the company of his friends just because Dan Halliwell.... "I don't really think it would matter..." she began again. "Someone's grandmother's cottage, you said?" she asked Lori.

The girl nodded, smiling. "It's a darling old cottage, Miss McNeil, with roses all over it." She smiled breathtakingly up at Tony. She had wonderfully even teeth. Petra was willing to bet she'd worn braces until quite recently—and she'd probably looked just as attractive in them as she did now.

Petra sighed. "I really can't see that there's any harm in your going," she said to Tony, ignoring Dan. "As long as you're back at whatever time Dan decides we have to leave."

"Three hours from now," Dan said tersely. He was obviously annoyed, but Petra was sure once she'd explained her reasoning about Tony needing to be with kids his own age, he would understand.

But he didn't. "That was damn rude, Petra," he exclaimed the moment the three youngsters left.

"I know, Dan," she soothed. "But you see, I've wanted so badly for Tony to make friends with people his own age. One of the reasons we moved to the Cape was that I was afraid Tony was getting too withdrawn. He's in school with people much older than him, you see. It makes difficulties for him socially. I know he should have stayed with us after you brought him here, but I thought you wouldn't mind once I explained."

"You don't know anything about those kids," he said coldly, apparently ignoring everything she'd said.

"I got the impression you knew the family...."

"I've heard of their father, that's all. You know how kids are nowadays, Petra—drugs and drinking and...."

"For heaven's sake, did they look as though they were on drugs? They certainly weren't drunk."

"That doesn't mean they never indulge."

She looked up at him, exasperated. They had continued walking after Tony left, Dan striding out so rapidly in his annoyance that she was getting out of breath trying to keep up with him. "I thought you told me you never lost your temper," she grumbled.

"I said rarely, Petra. I've never pretended to be a saint. And I have a right to be annoyed. You shouldn't have given Tony permission to leave with people you know nothing about."

"He's not a child," Petra exploded. "I was very impressed by those kids. They had super manners. You'll have to admit that."

"Did you ever see any reruns of an old television series called 'Leave It to Beaver'?" Dan asked abruptly.

She nodded, puzzled. "What's that got to do with anything?"

"There was a character named Eddie Haskell. He was always polite to the Beaver's parents remember, but in a smarmy way, and he encouraged Wally to disobey family rules as soon as his parents were out of sight."

"You think the Cartwright kids are like that?"

"The boy, anyway. The girl is more likely to take Tony to bed."

"Dan! She's only fourteen."

"So was Juliet. I'm telling you, Petra, that girl gave me a come-hither look that singed my eyelashes. When she gets hold of an innocent like Tony anything could happen."

"You're acting like a father."

"Somebody has to look out for him."

Petra stopped dead in the middle of the street, hands on her hips. "Are you saying I don't?"

"Obviously not as much as you should."

"May I remind you, Dan Halliwell, that this is none of your business anyway?"

Narrow-eyed, he glared at her. Then he laughed and took hold of her arm and shook it a little. "Listen to us. We sound like parents squabbling over how to raise the baby. I'm sorry, Petra. You're right. It's probably good for Tony to be with young people. I'm sure he'll have a terrific time." He glanced at her sideways. "And we're alone, after all. We shouldn't waste time quarreling."

Petra ignored the innuendo. Contrarily, now that she'd defended the Cartwright kids so vigorously, she was suddenly assailed by doubts about them. "You don't really think they might be into drugs, do you?" she asked worriedly.

Dan laughed shortly and put an arm round her shoulders, pulling her close to his side. "Tony will meet us in three hours," he assured her. "In the meantime I'm about to starve to death and the restaurant is only one more block's walk away. So what do you say? Shall we stop worrying about Tony and try to enjoy ourselves?"

Petra nodded. "Let's do that," she agreed.

But all the same, she decided, she would be glad when the time had passed so that she could see Tony again and be sure he was all right. Had she been irresponsible?

"Petra," Dan said warningly, tightening his grip around her shoulders.

She looked up into his face and managed a smile. "Aye, aye, skipper," she said.

He gave her one of his superpowered smiles, and as her traitorous body responded with a flush of warmth that spread all the way down to her toes, she realized with a sinking heart that she had more to worry about than Tony's absence. This man kept opening chinks into her defenses. There seemed no way to close him out.

Their lunch was superb—the crab rolls every bit as marvelous as Dan had promised. The restaurant was crowded, but Dan managed to commandeer a corner table that gave them a semblance of privacy. Once seated, he set himself to draw her out, and to her amazement, Petra found herself telling him all about her former boyfriends, offering the same reasons for the disintegration of her relationships with Ted and David as she had with Janie.

To her relief he didn't try to psychoanalyze her, as she'd half expected him to. He accepted what she had to say at face value, thoughtfully, but without commenting one way or the other. He even seemed to understand that after being let down twice, she'd naturally prefer not to get too involved with another man for a while. As they drank coffee, he told her a little about his own past.

His present job as troubleshooter, he explained, was the latest in a long line of different types of work in the hotel industry. He'd handled public relations, corporation sales and catering, and had managed a couple of the corporation's hotels himself. His father wanted him to have a thorough knowledge of the hotel business before he settled down in the home office in Boston.

Watching the enthusiasm on his lean face, listening to his crisp voice detailing his experience, Petra found herself admiring his clear-cut goals, the steady progression he had mapped out for himself after graduating from Cornell. Yet at the same time she realized that she'd been right about him all along. He was a superachiever, a go-getter, like Ted and David. And men like that, she had learned to her cost, were unable to allow the same ambitions in the women in their lives.

"How wonderful to be so sure of what you want to do," she said wistfully when he paused. "And to be so certain of how to achieve it. I've always looked up to ambitious people who aren't afraid to go all out for what they want."

He looked at her approvingly as though she'd passed some kind of test, but all he said was, "I'm not too sure about going all out. I've learned, painfully, that—"

He broke off and shook his head. "I guess I'm not ready to talk about that," he said ambiguously, which made her feel intensely curious. But he was obviously reluctant to go on and she didn't press the point.

A certain amount of resentment was mixed in with her admiration, she admitted to herself as he resumed talking. Though she had enjoyed every job she'd had, she couldn't ever seem to get a handle on what she wanted to do with her own life. And until she did, she reminded herself, she'd be stupid to get mixed up emotionally with anyone so sure of himself as Dan Halliwell. If she did, she'd never find her own way. He'd make sure of that.

Following lunch, they walked around the quaint old town some more. Petra was fascinated by the stories Dan told her of fortunes that had been wrested from the sea, of brushes with death, or death itself, and the meteoric rise of the whaling industry and its subsequent decline when the discovery of petroleum administered the economic coup de grace.

"Personally, I hope to see an end to all mammal killing very shortly," Dan said as they paused inside the whaling museum, looking at a poster that called for able-bodied seamen, coopers, carpenters and blacksmiths to join a sperm-whaling voyage that was due to set sail on July 2, 1846. He turned away to look at the skeleton of a whale that was displayed behind a roped-off area. "But whatever you might think of whaling itself," he added, "Nantucket's industry was a vital part of our history and I have to admire the strength and sheer endurance of the men who took part in it."

"And the women," Petra added.

"And the women," he agreed, with the loaded sideways glance that always caused her to miss a breath or two.

Their next stop was an art gallery on South Beach Street, which Dan had told her featured mostly local art including pottery and sculpture.

Petra enjoyed walking around the gallery. She'd always wished she had some talent in that direction.

At least she had an appreciation of other people's work, she reassured herself.

After a while she came across a foot-high sculpture that she particularly admired because of its graceful curves—an abstract figure carved from pale green stone set on a walnut base. It was a while before she realized the figure represented a woman, nude, gracefully curled around on herself, her hands clasping her ankles, her head resting on her knees. Something about it reminded her of her Aunt Sophie. She touched the stone lightly with one finger, liking the cold smooth surface of it.

"Nice," Dan said beside her.

She nodded. "Unfortunately it's also six hundred dollars."

"You wanted to buy it?"

"There's something about her—something that appeals to me."

He looked at her in a measuring way, then studied the figure very intently. "I see," he said obscurely.

Puzzled, she glanced at him. "What do you see?"

He pointed to the small card on the wall above the sculpture, his finger resting on the title of the piece. "Retreat," he said solemnly.

"So?"

He raised his eyebrows in the annoyingly superior way he had. "You don't see the resemblance to yourself?"

"I'm hardly trundling around in the fetal position," she said acidly.

"Not obviously so, perhaps, but psychologically...."

"That's nonsense," she interrupted, suddenly very angry, then realized she had spoken much too loudly. She glanced around the gallery and was relieved to see that the only other person there was the young male attendant who was busily dusting some picture frames in a far corner. "You've no right to inflict your pop psychology on me," she said in a lower tone. "You don't even know what I'm really like."

He smiled at her, completely unruffled as always. "I know you better than you think, Petra. For example, those stories you told me over lunch about the other men in your life—all those reasons you gave for the ending of the relationships. Did you really fool yourself into believing all that? Those men didn't stand a chance. Right from the start you were prepared to turn them down."

Wasn't that just like a man? She'd made herself vulnerable by answering his questions about her former men friends and now he was taking advantage of her honesty. "I did not turn them down," she said angrily. "Neither of them could cope with a strong woman. They turned me down."

He shook his head. "Petra dear, a woman lets a man know in countless ways how she feels about him. It doesn't matter if anything is said or not. A man knows if a woman loves him. And he knows just as well if she doesn't. Judging from the way you've behaved with me and what you told me about them, I'd say you probably put up a barrier between yourself and them from the minute they first showed serious interest in you. Admit it now. I'm right, aren't I? You're in full-scale retreat from love and always have been. Just like this cold lady here."

His fingers brushed sensuously across the gracefully curved body of the sculpture, and Petra flinched as though he had touched her. Her anger had dissolved abruptly, leaving in its wake the sick awareness that there was truth in his statements. But she didn't have to let him know that.

"That's crazy," she said, then turned abruptly on her heel. "It's about time we met Tony, isn't it?"

She thought he might push her to pursue the conversation but he didn't. He merely glanced at his watch and said, "I guess it is."

TONY WAS ON THE WHARF ahead of them. In response to Dan's question, he said he'd had a good time. His smile was cheery enough, but he seemed subdued during their return trip and if Petra hadn't had so much to think about herself, she might have worried more than she did about him. Perhaps he'd had a fight with Lori, she decided. If he didn't perk up by the time they got back home, she'd ask him about it. In the meantime, she wanted to think about the sculpture she'd seen and the comments Dan had made.

Had she really erected a barrier between herself and the men she had known? She could remember Ted saying, "Why are you so annoyed that I decided to marry Leona? You never cared about me, not really." And David: "You didn't write all those speeches because you loved me—you wrote them to prove you could do them better than I could." Was Dan right?

Was she like the sculpture? She certainly didn't like to picture herself all curled in like that, closing out feeling, closing out emotion. No, he'd had no business implying that she was a cold woman. Like Aunt Sophie. Sophie had brought a lot of men friends home over the years, but the relationships were all brittle, sophisticated, easily terminated when the men started making demands. Petra wasn't like that. Dan had already told her she was a sensual woman. She'd responded to him warmly enough the night before, hadn't she? Too warmly.

By the time they reached Falmouth Harbor, she was angry with him again. He knew it too. He could hardly fail to. Although she'd responded politely enough whenever he spoke to her, she'd been fairly short with him and hadn't cared if he thought her rude. All she wanted was to get home, back to her inn, where she could bury herself in work and forget all about Dan Halliwell and his damned psychology.

But then as Tony walked away toward Petra's rented car, Dan held her back with a detaining hand on her arm and eased her around to face him, his free hand tucking and stroking her windblown hair behind her ear in the most caressing, intimate way possible. She was suddenly short of breath. Annoying as he could be, he still had the power to affect her when he touched her. She wished, oh how she wished, that he wasn't such an attractive man. The sheer strength of the physical attraction between them was almost impossible to resist. "I know a charming little bar near here," he said. "How about a glass of wine? I think I need to apologize to you."

"It's not necessary," she began, but then he smiled again and touched her face with the back of his hand in another softly caressing movement, and she found herself walking over to the car to tell Tony to drive on back to the inn himself. He didn't seem to mind at all, just nodded absently. "Are you okay?" she asked him.

"I'm fine," he answered in a firm voice that brooked no argument. Petra had no choice but to accept his word.

THE BAR WAS INDEED CHARMING and very comfortable, with high-backed armchairs upholstered with bright flowered cushions. They sat at a small round table overlooking the harbor. Darkness was gathering, shrouding the dozens of tall masts, etching mystery into the still water. Lights began coming on here and there, reflecting, shimmering. It was a dramatic sight and they sipped their wine in silence for a while. Then Dan said quietly, "I offended you terribly, didn't I, there in the art gallery?"

She looked at him. His lean face was solemn, and he was frowning down at the table where his hand was idly moving his wineglass around in small circles. "I'm not used to having home truths pointed out to me quite so bluntly," she said quietly.

Letting go of his wineglass, he picked up her hands and held them between both of his. "I'm sorry, Petra." A roguish expression crossed his face, lifting one corner of his mouth into a crooked smile. "You do agree they were truths though?"

"Not all of them." The thought crossed her mind

that he'd achieved one of the things he'd set out to do. He'd brought her to the stage of making revelations about herself. That, she knew, as he knew, could lead to a much more intimate relationship. There was still time to hold back though. If she refused to reveal anything more of herself, the danger would pass.

All that was very logical, except that as long as his hands were holding hers, her heart beat rapidly and her bones began to melt again and her mind refused to work properly.

"Which of my assertions do you disagree with?" he asked formally with a mocking light in his green eyes.

She was determined not to let him joke about this. "I'm not a cold woman," she said stiffly. "You implied that I was."

"Did I really? How very stupid of me." His hands had tightened on hers and he was leaning forward. He was going to kiss her. She could see the intention in his eyes, which were as green as a moonlit sea as he bent forward to touch his lips to hers. There was no longer any mockery in them.

Aware that there were several people in the bar, and that conversation around them had paused momentarily as though those people were finding the spectacle of a man kissing a woman to be of the utmost interest, Petra couldn't seem to dredge up enough will to break away. His lips moved against hers, setting alight a slow fuse of passion that twisted throughout her body, reaching for the hidden core that was deep inside her, waiting to explode. She wanted him. Oh, how she wanted him.

"I didn't mean cold sexually," he said gently when the kiss was ended. "You're demonstrably not that." He released her hands and touched her mouth with one delicate finger. "I meant cold emotionally. You do tend to back away when I get too close to you, Petra. You must admit that."

Petra hesitated. Was it safe to be honest with him? She wasn't sure, but it would be such a relief to be honest for once. "I guess I do tend to hold a part of myself back," she said slowly. "I've always been scared to death that if I didn't I'd end up doing something stupid like falling helplessly in love—the way we discussed. It would be so dreadful to give someone that much control over my feelings, to let someone so close that. . . ." Again she hesitated and he covered her hand with one of his.

"Go on, Petra."

She shook her head, suddenly filled with a nameless panic. "I don't really know what I wanted to say." She glanced up at him, knowing full well there was a look of pleading in her dark eyes. "I don't really want to be like that sculpture, Dan," she said. "I don't want to retreat."

She heard the swift intake of his breath. His hand tightened over hers and his eyes held hers intently. For a long moment, he studied her face. His own face was totally empty of expression and she remembered the first impression she'd had of him. The words she'd associated with him then echoed again in her mind. Powerful. Predatory. Confident.

She was amazed at the sensations his touch evoked. She could feel the blood pulsing in his hand

and hers as though they shared a common system of veins and arteries. And now she could not tear her gaze away from his eyes, those green, green eyes that seemed to see all the way inside her. His hand was raising hers now, bringing it to his lips to be kissed. And she was trembling uncontrollably. He had to know she was trembling. His lips brushed across her fingers, delicately, warmly.

"I've got it all figured out, love," he said softly. "You want to hold back, and I don't want to make any commitments. All my jokes aside, I did go through a divorce fairly recently, remember? So, as long as we both know that there's no big love story or happy ever after planned, then there's no danger of us getting hurt if we do make love. All we have to do is keep it light. That way we satisfy this chemistry that's so strong between us, and we protect ourselves from disappointment at the same time."

"What happened to all that stuff you told me before?" she asked abruptly.

"Stuff?"

"The things you said about, well, about starting to fall in love...."

He looked at her levelly for a moment, making her wonder, and then he laughed shortly. "I did come on rather strong, didn't I?" He raised both eyebrows, his smile breaking through. "Don't avoid the issue. What do you say?"

"We agree it's just a game?" She paused, choosing her words carefully. "I guess as long as we both recognize that, then...."

"You do want me, Petra, don't you? Admit it,

love. Don't fight me. Tell me. You want me, don't
you?''

She pulled her hand free, reached for her wineglass
and drained its contents. Then she nodded, totally
unable to hold out any longer. He let out a long
breath and smiled wickedly. "My place or yours?"
he asked, and she recognized that he was joking
again in order to release some of the tension that had
built up between them.

She found a need to take in a deep breath herself.
All her oxygen had been used up in the past few
minutes. And she was waking up to the fact that
she'd just about offered herself to him. She wasn't
quite sure how it had happened. It had something to
do with the sculpture, perhaps more to do with the
touch of his hands and lips. Whatever the cause,
she'd made some kind of commitment to play the
game. Surely it wasn't too bad an idea. At least if
they made love she could get him out of her system.
Then when he left Cape Cod she wouldn't be left
with a load of regrets for what might have been.
You're rationalizing, Petra, a small voice whispered
in her mind.

"I wouldn't want Sarah to—" she found herself
saying and then broke off, not knowing how to ex-
press herself without embarrassment.

"My place then," he said at once. Standing, still
holding on to one of her hands, he tugged her gently
to her feet.

CHAPTER EIGHT

THE ENORMOUS LOBBY of the Pine Village Resort was as busy as though it was midday. People milled around, talking, gesticulating, sizing each other up as though they were at some informal cocktail party. Petra wasn't quite sure if it should even be called a lobby—it looked more like an outdoor courtyard, paved with tiles and attractively furnished with lots of basket-weave armchairs and a preponderance of plants and lily ponds.

Dan didn't linger. With one hand under Petra's elbow, he led her briskly around the perimeter of the area. As they passed a tulip-shaped fountain, they were hailed by a noisily laughing group of people in evening clothes. They all smiled and said hello, glancing in a friendly way at Petra. One man in particular—a tall, thin, nervous-looking man with a close-cropped beard and rather small brown eyes behind thick glasses—let his gaze linger on her, then winked at Dan. The woman next to him wore a sleek black dress that revealed everything anyone could possibly want to know about her figure. She had a warm smile for Dan and long red hair that hung straight and thick down her back. Tony had been right. "Wench" alias Wendy was a knockout.

"Who was that man?" she asked as they went on toward a back hall. Dan escorted her into a small cocktail lounge, and she thought they were going to stop for a drink, but he kept going, taking her out through another door into a hall that led to a staircase. She understood the trip through the bar had been intended as camouflage.

"That was Kelly O'Connor," he said as they started up the stairs.

Preceding him, Petra gave him an exasperated glance over her shoulder. "The manager? Dan! You might have introduced me. He probably thought— well, he might have thought...." She let her voice trail away, choosing to ignore the fact that the manager's thoughts were quite certainly correct.

Dan raised one eyebrow and smiled crookedly. "It seemed more politic to keep going. We didn't want to join him and his party, did we?"

She could hardly argue with that. But still.... "Was that his wife with him?" she asked.

"His secretary."

"Really."

Dan laughed. "That was a very disbelieving note in your voice, Petra dear. Don't tell me you are guilty of sexism. Just because a woman is gorgeous doesn't mean she can't hold down a good job, you know."

Petra felt herself flushing. She *had* been guilty of sexism. Probably because the woman had smiled in such an intimate way at Dan. Was jealousy worse than sexism? She'd thought herself free of both.

What is she to you? Petra wanted to ask, but of course didn't. In any case, the woman didn't seem very important to her right now. Neither did Kelly O'Connor. Dan had turned toward a door at the end of the upper hall. They had evidently reached his suite. Once she crossed that threshold, she knew, there could be no turning back. Dan Halliwell would not take kindly to a woman who promised and did not deliver. She didn't think much of that kind of woman herself.

Swallowing hard, she preceded him through the doorway. The corner suite was even more luxurious than she had expected. Dan had turned on a couple of genuine Tiffany lamps illuminating an eclectic mixture of antique and contemporary American furnishings that added up to a charming and costly looking decor. The color scheme was mostly of cool blues and greens that seemed to bring the sky and sea indoors. The rug was a genuine Persian, the watercolor landscapes on the walls originals. A long bay window overlooked the water. "I'm glad I don't have to pay the rent on this," she said lightly to cover her nervousness.

"This is the VIP hospitality suite, not meant for the hoi polloi," Dan murmured, pocketing his key. "I'll thank you to preserve a properly humble attitude. Actually," he added as he reached around her to pull the draperies closed, "this isn't so grand. Wait till you see the bedroom."

She swallowed. "Aren't you going to offer me a glass of wine?" she asked in a suddenly tight voice.

"No."

Frowning at the terse note in his voice, she turned to demand an explanation and found herself in his arms. "You don't really want any more wine—you're using delaying tactics," he accused. She couldn't deny the accusation. She couldn't deny anything when he was pressing her close to his lean, hard body, lifting her chin with curled fingers for his kiss.

They sank together onto a softly upholstered sofa as their lips met. The first touch of his mouth on hers told Petra that he was going to take his time. In response she felt all the tension go out of her body. In one brief flash of logical thinking before she gave in to the pressure of his lips and opened her mouth to him, she decided that she wasn't going to think again this evening. She was going to do as Janie had once advised her and "go with the flow."

For no apparent reason she suddenly remembered a short story she'd read in college—Wanda Hickey's "Night of Golden Memories." It was one of the most hilarious stories she'd ever read. It had dealt more with a young boy's rites of passage into manhood than with the heroine, but for some reason it seemed to fit her current situation. Perhaps it was because all she was likely to get out of this night was a golden memory. So be it, she thought, not altogether rationally.

A little nervous giggle escaped her, and Dan drew back and looked at her enquiringly. But she wasn't going to explain. Reaching up, she let her fingers tangle in his thick hair and pulled his head down to hers until their noses touched. He smiled. "I'm going to make a study of your mouth," he told her slowly. "It has a wistful look to it sometimes that is quite beautiful. And it's very well defined around the edges. That's unusual, you know.''

The tip of his tongue traced the edges of her lips and she drew in her breath sharply. "Dan," she said, but he wouldn't let her speak.

"This is a serious scientific research project," he interrupted, brushing one finger between his mouth and hers. "You mustn't interfere." He smiled again. "I like the way your mouth lifts at the corners even in repose. That would seem to indicate a basically good-natured personality, wouldn't you say?''

"I'm not saying anything," she breathed. "If you're going to torture me by talking to me with your lips right against mine, I guess I'm going to have to bear it, but I'm not going to contribute...."

"I wish you'd be quiet and kiss me, Petra," he said sternly, jokingly, and she obeyed at once and was immediately lost in a sensual excitement greater than any she had ever experienced.

After a long while he held himself away from her and looked into her face very solemnly. As his hand reached for the zipper of her sweat suit and drew it slowly down, she felt a rush of intense emotion that started low in her body and shot upward to her heart. His eyes were boring into her, devouring her, and once more she knew there was definitely no turning back.

"How do you get this thing off?" he asked irritably, and she realized the zipper had jammed at the bottom as it always did. Swiftly she released it and pulled the jacket off. She wished there were some magical way to make clothing disappear. It was awkward to disrobe in front of a man, to fuss with all the buttons and things and try not to look too eager or too awkward or too uncomfortable. . . .

Dan seemed to sense some of her thoughts as she fumbled with her cotton blouse. Gripping her wrists suddenly, he kissed each of her hands, then set them aside and began to undress her himself, making an erotic game out of the process, kissing each part as it was laid bare, so that her clothes did seem to disappear magically after all.

And after a very short while it seemed only natural to offer him the same service. Lifting the hem of his sweat shirt, she tugged it up and over his head. Discovering that he wore nothing beneath it, she touched her tongue to each of his nipples in turn, delighting when they hardened as hers had, going on to nuzzle gently the thick hair on his chest.

"Petra, Petra," he murmured thickly, "how forward you are."

"Not cold?" she asked teasingly as she struggled with the unfamiliar buckling of his belt.

"Not cold," he agreed. His fingers moved to help her and he pulled jeans and shorts down in one economical movement, managing to get his shoes and socks off at the same time.

"Very clever," she marveled. "You must be more used to stripping than I am."

"You talk too much, Petra McNeil," he said shortly and pulled her roughly into his arms. And then he kissed her passionately and for a very long time, holding her naked body tightly against his.

There must be a window open somewhere, Petra

decided. She could feel a small draft threading across
her flesh and she could hear, very faintly, the sound
of waves splashing lightly onto hard sand. Somewhere in the distance a foghorn called a melancholy
note of warning, and nearer at hand the band played
in the resort's nightclub. She strained to hear. "You
Light up My Life." Fitting, she decided.

Heat was flaming through her. She was responding
more ardently to Dan's mouth than she had ever responded to David's kisses, though it was true that she
had never been cold in lovemaking. She had, after
all, inherited her mother's passionate nature, even if
it was tempered with Scots' caution. Her need for
him, the need she had felt the moment she first saw
him, was rising urgently, yet she felt she would be
just as content to stay in his arms, being kissed and
lightly caressed forever, without moving on to any
other stage.

Dan, however, was not about to settle for less than
total lovemaking. After some time had passed, she
felt a rippling movement go through his body. Then
he was standing up with her in his arms, cradling her
easily and comfortably against his chest. "I've never
been carried before," she murmured. "I feel like
Scarlett O'Hara." She laughed, remembering the
melodramatic quotations she'd borrowed from that
spirited woman. "You won't drop me, will you?"
she asked when Dan looked a question at her.

"I won't drop you." He hesitated, gazing down at
her with a smile in his green eyes. "Unless you misbe-
have of course."

"I can't think what would constitute misbehavior

under these circumstances,'' Petra said, furrowing her brow.

He laughed, his arms tightening around her as he turned her to go through the bedroom doorway. ''Between you and Tony, you must have swallowed a couple of dictionaries,'' he teased, kissing her lightly.

She laughed too. This was fun, she thought, surprised. This really did seem to be a game. With Dan there was none of the awkwardness she'd suffered through before. The few men in her life had felt there was no place for laughter in the bedroom—perhaps they had been afraid the laughter might be directed at them. She hadn't known that sex could be playful.

And they owed each other nothing. They had made no promises, no vows. ''This must be how sex was in the beginning, before people started messing it up with false expectations and too much solemnity,'' she said as Dan knelt on the floor and laid her down on the surprisingly low bed.

He didn't comment but merely raised his eyebrows as he lifted her and pulled out the bedcover and blanket from beneath her, so that she was lying on a dark blue sheet. He began to kiss her slowly and hungrily all over. ''Don't move,'' he ordered when she started to reach for him. Obediently, she lay back, stretching herself languorously, and looked up at the ceiling. The room was full of shadows, though the light from the living room of the suite fell on their bodies. Even so she could see that this room was even more luxurious than the other. Brocaded draperies—blue and green—hung at each corner of the low king-size bed and were repeated at the windows. It was there that the window was open. She could smell the sea air. The sound of the waves was louder now.

After a short time, Petra began to trail her fingers lightly over his body, drawing erotic designs on his flesh. He had a beautiful body, firm and lean hipped and hard in all the right places. She was suddenly glad she'd spent time every morning as long as she could remember exercising to keep her own body toned and firm. Her idea had been to keep herself physically fit, but the bonus at this moment was that she didn't have to worry about how she looked to him.

As first her fingers and then her lips played over his warm flesh, a tremor ran through him and he raised himself up on his knees. Leaning over her, he placed each of his thumbs on each of her nipples and pressed downward very, very delicately, and she thought that she would burst with the sudden tide of longing and passion that went through her. She realized she could no longer hear the sea or the foghorn or the soft strains of music. There was only the sound of their breathing as they came together on the bed and wound around each other. He entered her slowly and tenderly and with the greatest restraint.

A soft moan of pleasure trickled out of her throat, and he smiled and bent his head to her breast and kissed it and caressed it with his tongue, first moving his tongue in slow maddening circles around the nipple, then trailing a row of kisses across to the other breast and giving it the same ardent care. At the same time he was thrusting rhythmically inside her, and her heart was thundering in her chest. She moved with him and her hands roamed over him, reveling again in his smooth male flesh, reaching up to touch the iron-hard muscles in his upper arms, now straining as he leaned his weight on his hands to spare her body.

Petra was intoxicated with him, filled with him. "Dan," she murmured softly, hardly knowing that she spoke. Then she caught her breath as he lifted his head and she saw desire clearly revealed on his face, a desire so blatant, so real, so overpowering that she was momentarily staggered. This was not a game to him, no matter what he had said. This was serious.

The thought terrified her and she felt an abrupt withdrawal inside herself. But then as she stared at him, aghast, his eyebrows twitched over those grass-green eyes of his in a comical expression of lust. She realized then that she had been mistaken, and she was able to join him in a sudden bubble of laughter.

Seconds later, heat began spiraling through her again, drawing her up against him to meet each thrust of his body. Pressure was increasing inside her, building to an unbearable pitch, drawing the feeling in her whole body together and around that one rapierlike thrusting mechanism that felt as though it were about to explode—and did, in a series of spasms that found echoes in her own body. Faster and faster, not thinking, hardly breathing, holding tightly, tightly to each other, they hurtled upward together, then spiraled down into one long joined sigh of contentment and fulfillment. "Petra," he moaned softly.

"Dan," she whispered, her body still shuddering,

like his, her face damp with perspiration, her arms clutched around him in a viselike grip that she thought might never come free.

It was a long time before either of them moved. Then Dan eased his body off hers and she felt a chill for a second until he pulled the covers over both of them, and tucked her close in to his side. "Sweet Petra," he murmured.

She looked up at his face, wishing there was more light. He was smiling crookedly, his eyelids hooding his eyes. "It occurs to me," he said, "that the human race wastes an awful lot of time with mating games. If we'd just go to bed with each other as soon as we realize we're attracted to each other, we'd save a lot of energy."

She felt a chill. And wondered why. *She* had wanted to keep their relationship light. What was she expecting from him? More of his joking references to love? He hadn't teased her like that for some time. And she didn't want him to. Did she?

"Would you like your glass of wine now?" he asked.

She nodded, feeling suddenly awkward. Should she get up and leave? Did he expect her to spend the rest of the night? She couldn't do that. Sarah would wonder. Tony might have waited up. . . .

He brought the wine bottle in an ice bucket, switched on a small lamp beside the bed, then handed her a tulip-shaped glass full of shimmering, bubbling liquid. "Champagne?" she asked.

He grinned. "I can't think of a better time for it. It's supposed to celebrate special occasions." He sat

down on the edge of the bed, supremely unselfcon-
scious about his nudity, and lifted his glass to touch
hers in a toast. Their eyes met over the rims of the
glasses, and she felt again that tremendous awareness
of him that she'd felt at their first meeting. His
thoughts must have been similar. "Are you finally
ready to admit it, Petra?" he demanded. "I turned
you on the minute you saw me, didn't I?"

The choice of words was too much of a coincidence.
"Nathaniel told you what I said," she accused.
"What a rat. I'm in the middle of a conspiracy, aren't
I? Nathaniel and Sarah are tattling about everything I
say."

"They have encouraged me when my spirits were
down," he confessed. "Sarah especially kept cheering me on. That's why I didn't give up even in the
face of overwhelming odds." He touched her nose
with a playful finger. "Come on, confess. You
wanted me the minute you saw me."

"Okay," she conceded with a laugh. "I felt something. I don't know what it was. A forewarning of
disaster, maybe."

He gestured at the rumpled blue sheets. "You
think this is a disaster?"

"Not so far, but. . . ."

"Hey." He grabbed at the sheet and pulled it
down and her naked breasts were suddenly pressed
once more against that wonderfully, sensuously
warm mat of hair. His mouth moved against hers.
"You were beginning to sound serious again," he
complained when he finally came up for air. "That's
verboten, remember?"

"Aye, aye, skipper," she agreed. "No more serious talk."

They had both set their champagne glasses down and his hands were moving over her again, stroking her at first softly, then more roughly as they both became aroused again. This time was more relaxed, the earlier sharp hunger for each other satisfied. They moved together slowly, almost languorously, looking at each other, kissing lightly, murmuring incoherently. In the diffused light of the bedside lamp, his features were softened, younger, more vulnerable than she had ever seen them. Even as she recognized the stirring inside that would lead to increased excitement, Petra felt the most incredible sense of peace lying there in his arms, moving with him slowly, rhythmically. She could imagine they were back on the *Odyssey*, rocking slowly together over the swells as the wind filled and lifted the sails above them. He was looking at her very intently, as though he was trying to memorize every feature of her face.

He held her gaze for a while, then he whispered, "You are so very beautiful, Petra," and kissed her gently on the mouth. She felt a strange sensation in the area of her heart, an expanding, flowering, yearning sensation that was unfamiliar to her. She focused her thoughts on the feeling as he lifted her and began to increase the pace of his loving. And as she responded to him with instant white-hot desire, her breath held with wonder at the tumult of sensation that was gathering and spreading throughout her entire body, even to her fingers and toes, she suddenly had the strangest conviction that the yearning sensation was love.

Following the thought, words went through her mind of their own accord, like a streamer following an airplane with an advertising message—words not consciously presented to her brain, but rather drifting across it so that all she had to do was read them off one by one. *I'm in love with Dan Halliwell.*

Immediately she knew also that Dan was not someone she'd be able to get over as easily as she had the other men in her life. And a passion like this was not destined to last. She remembered once when she'd sympathized with her mother that her operatic career was fragmented because of her love for her husband and family, her mother had laughed and said, "But Petra darling, nothing glorious lasts forever."

Frightened by the sudden memory, disoriented, she pulled back from Dan for a heartbeat and immediately started struggling to be free. But he wouldn't let her go. Within seconds her passion was rising again and she felt warmth filling her as her body arched and fitted itself to his, and her mind blanked out all thoughts, all words, all crazy ideas as it readied itself for the next passionate explosion.

"'AND ALL THAT'S BEST of dark and bright meet in her aspect and her eyes,'" Dan quoted, looking directly into her face, his own face half-buried in the pillow beside her head. "Although, actually, right now you look a little glazed," he added in an everyday voice that brought her abruptly out of her thoughts.

She tried to think of something else from Lord Byron to answer him with, but all her mind produced was: " 'In her first passion woman loves her lover, in all the others, all she loves is love.' " And that didn't seem nearly light enough to offer to him.

What did she know of love after all? He was certainly the last person in the world she should even think of loving. Not only was he the same type as the others who had let her down, but he'd loved his wife. . . helplessly. Possibly still did. Not to mention the fact that he was merely passing through on his way to his next assignment in some glamour capital of the world. How much pain did one person need in a lifetime? She could still sense that the pain of losing him was going to be far greater than any pain she had ever felt before.

"What are you thinking, pensive maid?" he demanded and she opened her eyes to see him smiling at her. His hair was quite unruly. She couldn't resist reaching to run her fingers through it. Even when they were sailing it hadn't looked this untidy. She liked it this way, tumbling over his forehead. He looked less formidable, less powerful.

She wanted to smile back at him, but she had the most awful feeling that if she attempted it she would burst into tears. There was a definite prickle behind her eyelids. God, she mustn't let him see. . . .

"Petra?" he said tentatively, and she realized he was wondering why she hadn't answered him.

She searched her mind for something to say to him, and to her horror heard herself blurt out, "Tell me about your wife."

She'd had no intention of saying any such thing and she could have bitten off her tongue, especially when he said immediately and abruptly, "No way."

Awkwardness descended between them. "I guess I'd better go," Petra said at last, turning away from him to swing her legs out of the opposite side of the bed. "Perhaps you'd bring me my clothes."

"Hey, it's okay, Petra. I'm sorry. I didn't mean to bite your head off. You surprised me. I wasn't ready to...."

"It's all right. I understand."

"No, you don't. Even I don't understand."

"It doesn't matter, Dan."

He slid off the bed, went out of the room for a minute, then returned with her clothes draped over one arm. He handed them to her, then stood looking at her as she started to put them on, a contrite expression on his face. "We're still friends, aren't we, Petra?"

Friends. She thought of the expression she'd seen on his face while they were making love. Had she been mistaken about the depth of his feelings? Whatever happened she mustn't let him know she felt more for him than.... Making an effort, she smiled up at him. "Friends," she said.

Refusing to think anymore, she finished dressing, tidied her hair in the mirror over his dressing table and prepared to leave. He put his arms around her. Their lovemaking had not diminished the electricity between them, Petra discovered. In spite of the passion they had just shared, he could still set her pulse clamoring just by touching her. The thought made her feel claustrophobic. She had to get away from him for a while. She had to sort out what was happening to her.

"We *are* going to see each other regularly, aren't we?" he murmured into her hair.

See each other. Was that a euphemism for making love? "I guess so," she said awkwardly.

"Tomorrow?"

Panic immobilized her for a second. She had to have time to think, she had to.... Somehow she found the ability to laugh. "Dan, I've told you again and again, I've got a lot of work to do. I've already taken a whole day and two evenings. I don't have time...."

"Okay, okay." He touched his fingers to her lips, then kissed her lightly. "Soon though?"

Still managing to act convincingly, she frowned at him and shook her head at his persistence. "Soon," she promised.

CHAPTER NINE

A VERY BUSY WEEK LATER, Petra straddled the peak of the inn roof, her jeans-clad knees gripping the top rows of shingles, her heart in her mouth as she watched Tony clambering precariously toward her up the steep grade. "What do you think?" she asked when he lowered himself cautiously beside her. He was breathing heavily, his face pale, his dark eyes enormous behind the thick lenses of his glasses.

"I think I've never been so terrified in my life," he said flatly. "This is a hell of a time to find out I have acrophobia."

"I don't think it's a height phobia. I think it's a family failing," Petra said, nerving herself to look down again. The ground seemed terribly far below. In her mind she saw images of herself and Tony rolling over and over down the steeply pitched roof, their bodies hesitating over the rain gutters, then hurtling down to the unyielding ground.

They looked at each other helplessly. Then Tony said, in a limp imitation of John Wayne, "Well, I guess a man's gotta do what a man's gotta do." He attempted a smile in her direction that didn't quite succeed. "And a woman too."

She nodded. "It shouldn't take too long. We only

have ten rows of eight shingles to replace. If we start in the morning after the guests are up and gone, we could probably be through by dinnertime.''

''Sure,'' Tony said bravely, making two syllables out of the word as the Cape Codders did.

''I'm glad I was able to get some shingles to match. What luck to find some that were all weathered and everything. They're a lovely smoky gray, aren't they?''

''Right.''

''I'll hold them in place and you'll hammer the nails in, right?''

''Right.''

Neither of them moved. They might have sat there forever, frozen in place, if Nathaniel Jenkins hadn't appeared on the front lawn below.

They recognized the Admiral by his long silver hair. He was wearing a blue work shirt and jeans rather than his old frock coat. It must have been after four o'clock and the museum had closed. Petra spared a thought for high tea at the inn below. She hoped it was going well without her. The custom was pretty well established now, and Sarah treated it as though it had been her own idea. Petra was sure her guests could all get along fine without her, especially considering the low mood she was in.

Nathaniel waved gaily. Petra and Tony both called weak hellos, but neither of them waved back. After staring up at them for a minute or two, Nathaniel started toward the corner of the inn.

''Don't tell me he's coming up,'' Tony said in a horrified voice. Tony had met Nathaniel several days before and had been given the museum tour. The Admiral had told Petra he'd formed a liking for the boy immediately. According to Tony, the feeling was mutual.

Before Petra could nerve herself to shout to Nathaniel, she heard him coming up the extension ladder and then neither of them dared speak, afraid the frail man would slip and fall. He wasn't a young man, after all.

A moment later, his head appeared at the top of the ladder, followed a second later by the rest of his spare body.

"Be careful, Admiral," she called. "The roof's steeper than it looks. For heaven's sake don't try to come up here."

He took no notice of her at all. Walking nimbly as a mountain goat up the roof toward them, he stood there looking down at them, his lined, weathered face as relaxed as though they'd all met in the middle of Main Street. "Young Bonnie tells me your contractor let you down," he said in his soft, flat Cape voice.

Petra nodded, still gripping with her knees. "I thought I could replace the shingles myself, but I'm afraid...." She hesitated. "I'm afraid—period."

"Me too," Tony added glumly.

"I see."

He frowned down at the single bundle of shingles Petra and Tony had managed to bring up between them, then smiled at Petra. "I heard you advertised for a handyman? I'm applying for the job. Want me to start on those shingles tonight or tomorrow?"

"Oh, Nathaniel, I do appreciate your kindness, really. But I hardly think...."

"Don't think I'm up to the job, Miss Petra? Want to check out my muscles?" Rolling up the right sleeve of his blue shirt, he flexed a very presentable biceps. "I'm not exactly ready to be beached yet," he said firmly. "And heights don't bother me. In my former incarnation I used to climb up to the crow's nest without hesitation. Reckon I'll do?"

"But you have your own work...."

"Not enough to keep me busy. Naught to do until noon and I was always an early riser. Now, do I get the job, or do I sit around listening to my arteries harden the way I've been doing lately?"

Petra grinned at him. "Well, if you put it like that, what can I say?"

"You mean I can get off this roof?" Tony breathed.

"You certainly may," Nathaniel said. "I don't want any weak heads cluttering up the decks."

"You're sure you can manage alone?" Petra asked.

He pointed in the direction of his own house. "Did *my* roof this spring."

She eased herself around and followed the direction of his hand. His roof looked eminently weatherproof. She let her breath out on a long sigh of relief. "I don't know how to thank you, Admiral."

"I'm not offering charity," he drawled. "I'm asking five dollars an hour. Not minimum wage, but not too high, I'm thinking. And I promise you I can have this roof shipshape and Bristol fashion in no time—

moss and all. And whatever else you want done be-
times. What do you say?''

''I say you're hired,'' Tony said loudly.

Petra laughed. ''It'll probably be best if you start
tomorrow morning, Admiral. I'd planned to wait on
the hammering until all the guests were out of the
inn.'' She looked up at him sheepishly. ''In the
meantime, I think your first job is figuring out a way
to get us off this roof.''

When she was finally on the ground, having literally crawled down backward as far as the ladder, she
turned to Nathaniel. ''Was it really Bonnie, or Dan,
who told you we needed help?'' she asked.

His eyes shifted uneasily. ''Bonnie confirmed it,''
he said defensively.

''Uh-huh.''

''Dan's still a problem for you?'' he asked.

Petra looked around. Tony had gone into the inn,
groaning that he needed a cup of Sarah's strong tea
to help him recover from his ordeal. ''He's a problem,'' she confirmed.

''I knew you and he were seeing each other,'' he
volunteered.

She looked at him, frowning. ''Did you? How?''

''Truth be told I've seen you leaving in his car once
or twice, and I saw you together in Woods Hole last
week, eating lobster at the Fishmongers. I almost
joined you. I purely love lobster myself. But I've no
wish to interfere with Cupid's designs, so I kept my
distance.''

''You could have joined us, Nathaniel,'' Petra
said. ''I'd have loved seeing you.''

"Thank you." His sailor's blue eyes twinkled. "I appreciate it when a pretty lady lies for the sake of my pride."

It wasn't a lie at all, but she didn't want to tell him that.

On an impulse, after they'd fixed a time for him to start work the next day and he'd gone off to prepare his own tea, Petra took the path down to the beach instead of returning to the inn. She pulled off her sneakers, rolled the legs of her overalls to her knees and ran into the shallow surf, gasping when the cold water numbed her feet. Yanking off her bandanna, she ran a hand through her dark curls and left them uncovered to the sun's warmth. It had been another glorious blue and silver day, though she'd hardly had a chance to enjoy it. The sky was clouding a little now, forming a yellowish haze in the distance, but the sun was still bright overhead and the breeze was warm.

Deliberately she avoided looking toward the resort beach where the chaises were still covered with tanned bodies and young couples frolicked in the shallows. Wading out a little way, she climbed on the huge flat rock that had been memorialized in Will's photograph album and sat leaning back with her weight resting on her hands, her face lifted to the sun, her eyes closed against the brightness. She had tried very hard not to think about the relationship between her and Dan, but she couldn't avoid thinking it through anymore. She was uncomfortable with the constraint that was between them. What she had told Nathaniel was quite true. She and Dan probably would have enjoyed having him join them. More than that, his company might have alleviated the awkwardness that had come between them ever since they'd first made love a week before.

They had indeed eaten lobster in Woods Hole—the most delicious lobster Petra had ever enjoyed—dripping with butter, tender as it was possible for lobster to be. Petra loved Woods Hole. It was such a vigorous little village with a college-town atmosphere due to the many students attending the oceanographic institute. Yet it retained a seaside, day-tripper atmosphere too. Tourists enjoyed photographing the little drawbridge that came up on Water Street, walking the narrow crooked streets, watching the gulls skimming the water.

Petra and Dan had also spent an afternoon antiquing in the charming town of Dennis where Petra had been unable to resist buying a lovely old pitcher-and-bowl set of a pristine white with delicate blue flowers. One evening they had taken the long drive "down Cape" to Provincetown. And they had talked: about the history of the Cape, the geography of the area, even the geology of the area. They had discussed the shifting shorelines, the effects of oil spills on marine life, the importance of wetlands, the impact of too much housing development. And they had also covered most of the world's problems as revealed on the eleven-o'clock news each night.

The only subject they had not discussed was themselves. And they had not made love again. They had not even kissed. The fault was hers. Knowing that she had fallen in love with Dan had frightened her. She wasn't ready for love—not yet. And she wasn't at all sure she ever would be. Because of her fear, she'd suppressed her emotions deeply and was unable to respond anymore when Dan joked about their relationship. Like the stone lady who had jolted them into making love, she had folded in on herself and was unable to uncurl. She didn't like the situation, but she seemed unable to do anything about it.

All week she'd followed her usual idiotic practice of tucking the problem away in her I'll-tackle-that-tomorrow file, but she suspected that Dan was soon going to insist on a reason for her coldness and then she would have to break off with him. It would be infinitely preferable, she had decided, for her to break off with him rather than to wait for the inevitable blow of the ax from him. At least she would have kept her pride intact. And even though pride was solitary company, it was better than nothing.

Why hadn't she stuck to her vow? she wondered, clasping her knees to her chest and looking out at a lone sailboat tacking across the bay. Why had she opened herself up when she knew she wasn't capable of handling a serious relationship with a man?

It was better to let him think the problem was sexual. Even though it certainly wasn't. She still thrilled to Dan's touch. Even imagining him kissing her would start her heart beating deliciously fast, sending thrills of excitement along her veins. But if he suggested they should go somewhere where they could be alone, something inside her threw a circuit-breaker switch and closed off all feeling, all response.

Dan had recognized there was a problem right

away, but when she told him she didn't want to discuss it, he'd respected her wishes—until the day before. A delivery boy had brought her a crated package, which had proved to be the sculpture she'd admired on Nantucket—the lady in retreat. Dan's message was clear.

Looking at the gracefully curved figure form of the smooth, cool green stone, she'd felt a deep panic rising that was so overwhelming, so potent, that she'd had to bury the sculpture frantically in its Styrofoam chips, feeling that she couldn't even bear to look at it. She'd returned the sculpture at once through the same delivery service. She couldn't accept a six-hundred-dollar gift, symbolic or not, she'd rationalized.

He would be leaving Cape Cod soon. He would forget all about her. He might even go back to loving his wife. . . helplessly. And that was another reason it was best if—

She broke off her thoughts, impatient with herself. She was making up stories for herself again, trying to fool herself as Dan had accused. And she was through fooling herself. She'd decided that during the long nights of the past week. Inside where it counted, she knew that she was afraid she'd lose herself, the essence that was herself if she allowed herself to feel too deeply. She'd always known that the only person she could really count on was herself.

"Hello Petra."

She was not surprised to hear his voice. Had she hoped, subconsciously perhaps, that he would see her sitting on the rock and would come along the beach to join her so that she could break it off now, while her resolve was firm?

She turned self-consciously, running a hand through her hair, wishing she'd thought to put on some makeup, at least brush her hair before coming down. She must look an awful sight.

He was carrying his shoes, wearing khaki shorts and a white Izod shirt that reminded her of Seth and Lori. The expression on his lean sharp-featured face told her nothing, except that his mouth was stern. For a brief moment she fantasized kissing the sternness away, imagined how his lips would soften against hers, warm to her touch, open. . . .

His eyes didn't meet hers. She would have to wait to find out if he was angry with her for returning the sculpture—if he'd heard yet that she'd returned it.

He climbed on the rock and sat down beside her, fairly close, but not touching her. She felt his presence there as though he'd pressed intimately against her, as though the air between them contained a magnetic extension of his body, pulling her toward him. "How are you, Dan?" she asked nervously when he didn't speak.

"I'm not sure."

His tone was clipped, frosty. Her breath froze in her throat. Yes, he'd heard about the sculpture. She concentrated her gaze on his long legs, stretched out in front of him, crossed gracefully at the ankles. Below his knees the silky brown hair was wet, clinging to his flesh. His feet were long and angular, his toes slender. There wasn't a part of him that wasn't attractive to her. Still, why had she let herself become so deeply involved?

Recognizing that she was acting like a coward, hoping he'd avoid talking about the sculpture, she took a deep breath and plunged into the subject herself, forcing herself to turn and look directly at his face. "I'm sorry I had to return the sculpture," she said in a rapid, nervous voice. "It was very generous of you, but I just couldn't let you. . . ."

His eyes were ice green, his mouth a straight, grim line. "Don't fudge, Petra," he said tersely. "Generosity had nothing to do with it and you know it. I wanted to wake you up to what you were doing. Did I at least succeed in that?"

"I don't know what you're talking about," she began.

He sighed. "Petra. My beloved Petra." He paused and her mind rejected the word. He didn't really mean it. "This is the first time in my life a woman ever treated me like a one-night stand," he said after a moment.

"I didn't do any such thing. I. . . ."

"What else would you call it?" he demanded. "I wish to hell you would try to be honest with yourself, even if it's impossible for you to be honest with me."

"I know I closed you out afterward," she blurted out.

"Now we're getting somewhere," he said gently. "Do you know why you closed me out?"

"Yes," she said miserably. "I just can't surrender myself to someone. I have my own life to lead."

He was shaking his head as his curled fingers reached to touch under her chin, turning her face toward him. For a moment she thought he was going to kiss her—and wanted him to, even while something over which she had no control at all made her chin stiffen and her gaze shift from his. Abruptly, he dropped his hand and sighed deeply. When he spoke again, he had changed the subject. "This rock is in the pictures in your uncle's photograph album, isn't it?"

There was a sudden stillness inside her. "Yes," she said warily.

"I remember one particular photograph that always seemed to sum up for me the whole spirit of your family." His voice had a conversational tone. There was nothing threatening about it, but Petra felt more and more wary as he went on. "It was the picture of you and your mother and father together on this rock. Your mother was pushing your father off the rock. You were all laughing."

"Yes."

His hand pressed on her shoulder and she stiffened against the tingling excitement that immediately radiated from the spot, but he was merely changing his position and had leaned on her for support. Once he was settled with his legs crossed in front of him, his hands clasping his own ankles, she felt safe again.

"Why are you forever wanting to talk about my parents?" she demanded.

He didn't answer for a moment. He seemed to be lost in thought and she fixed her gaze on a gull that was diving over and over into the swells in search of food, crying out in frustration when it came up with an empty bill. A cool wind was rising and the smell of salt was strong in the air. "I never did tell you why I caught your flight that day, did I?'' he said abruptly, in an almost defiant way.

Warily, she looked at him, wondering what he was leading up to now. ''You told me it was a coincidence,'' she said at last.

''But you didn't believe me?''

''Not for a minute.''

''That's what I thought.'' He paused, looking at her in a rather calculating way that made her feel very nervous. ''I believe Sarah told you that I used to come over to the inn when I was a kid and look at photographs of you and your parents, didn't she?''

She nodded.

''Did she tell you why?''

''I don't think she knows why.''

''Yes she does. I told her. I guess she felt I wouldn't want you to know. And I'm not sure I do. It's rather a childish reason, I'm afraid.'' He took in a deep breath. ''It's a little embarrassing,'' he admitted. ''I used to pretend your parents were part of my family and you were my little cousin.''

Startled, Petra stared at him. ''Why?''

He had averted his gaze. ''You always looked so happy, all of you,'' he said slowly. ''There was a warmth between you that spoke of deep caring, of love, even in the photographs.''

She felt a softening inside her. ''You don't have that in your own family?'' she asked gently.

''It's there; it just doesn't show. My parents are very ambitious, capable people. They're both very involved in the Braden Corporation.''

He sighed deeply. ''My parents always loved me,

Petra, but they never did quite know how to show emotion. So I made up my own fantasy family. *Your* family.'' He hesitated. ''I held on to the fantasy even after I was grown up. I felt you were all close to me and would feel affection for me if you knew me.'' He paused. ''So naturally, when Sarah told me you were coming to Cape Cod, I couldn't resist taking your plane. I'd been recalled from Chicago at about the same time anyway, so I was curious to see what my 'little cousin' was really like.'' He paused again. ''I didn't expect our meeting to affect me the way it did. It was pretty startling, wasn't it? I stopped feeling cousinly right away.''

The sudden glimpse of himself as a boy and a young man, a lonely young man, that he'd given her moved her tremendously. She had felt so desperately lonely herself for so long now.

Clasping her knees, she watched the gull swooping again, skimming the top of a wave, rising sharply. ''My parents are dead,'' she said flatly. ''I don't have a family anymore.''

His voice held sympathy. ''There are people who love you, Petra.'' When she didn't answer, he sighed. ''I can't blame you for missing them. I was very upset myself when they died, almost as upset as Will. That must have been a terrible time in your life.''

''I prefer not to talk about it,'' she said flatly.

She felt rather than saw his gaze sharpen on her averted face. ''You said that to me before, Petra. I've thought about it since. I'm sure it hurts you to remember your parents' accident, but I think you need to speak of it to someone who cares. I think that when it happened, you closed off the bad feelings to avoid pain. The trouble is that no one can select which feelings to close off. If you close off one you close off all of them, good as well as bad. I think perhaps you've deliberately stopped yourself from feeling anything, Petra. And I think that's why you returned the sculpture.''

Obviously he had no idea that she had learned how very much she could feel. For him. And as long as he didn't know how much she loved him he wouldn't be able to hurt her. She was still in charge of her own life. She could make her own decisions.

''I've asked you before not to inflict your pop psychology on me,'' she said coldly.

There was a silence broken only by the splash of waves against the rock, the voices calling to each other on the resort beach. ''So you have,'' he said finally and there was no expression in his voice at all.

She stole a glance at his face. The lines on it were more noticeable now, so that he looked every one of his thirty-five years.

''Maybe it would be best if we didn't see each other for a while, Dan,'' she suggested stiffly. ''Maybe when I've got my problems with the inn straightened out....''

''As I remember saying once before, Petra dear, life can't be put on hold.'' He stood up and she could feel his gaze on her bent head. But she couldn't look at him. ''I'm going now,'' he said curtly. ''But I want you to think about something. Another quote—not from our nineteenth-century friends this time but from a man you might allow was just as wise. 'Give

sorrow words,' Shakespeare said. 'The grief that
does not speak whispers the o'er-fraught heart, and
bids it break.' '' He paused and she had to bite her lip
hard to keep tears from starting up in her eyes.

"My feelings about my parents are no concern of
yours," she said stonily.

He sighed. "We obviously aren't going to get anywhere in our relationship until you can trust me
enough to talk about what's troubling you. I won't
bother you again until you let me know you're
ready."

She heard his feet splash through the shallow
water, sensed that when he stopped to pull his shoes
on he looked back at her, but she couldn't turn
around. She was remembering another quote from
the same source. *Macbeth*, she thought—somewhere
toward the end. "I cannot but remember such things
were, that were most precious to me."

Her throat was so tight she could hardly breathe.
But she wasn't going to let herself cry, she told herself even as moisture overflowed from her eyes and
trickled down her cheeks. Dan was right, of course.
Her parents' death had been a great shock to her. At
sixteen she'd been left suddenly alone. She'd learned
that accidents weren't always things that happened to
someone else. She'd learned that if you loved someone you were susceptible to pain. If she'd ever allowed herself to think through her problems with
love, she'd have arrived at a similar conclusion to
Dan's. Not that she couldn't feel, couldn't love, but
that she was afraid to give in to love because that
would make her vulnerable to the pain of loss.

Wasn't it natural to avoid pain? Did he have to make her sound sick or frigid, just because she was sensible enough to want to protect herself?

Sighing, she wiped her cheeks with the backs of both hands and shivered suddenly, sitting there alone on the rock in the hot sunshine. Deliberately she closed off any more thoughts of Dan. He was out of her life now. She wouldn't be calling him to say she was ready to confide in him. She wouldn't ever be ready.

She must return to the inn. She had work to do. She and Tony had finished three of the bedrooms now, but there were still two left to go. The furniture for those two rooms was still in the carriage house, though she had managed to get it straightened out and cleaned. But until she got the rooms redecorated and moved the furniture back in, she couldn't go ahead with her plan to convert the carriage house into a dining room, and she was anxious to see how that would work. And sometime soon she had to sit down and figure out how to attract more guests to the inn. Only four rooms were rented right now. Another couple, due to arrive next week, had canceled out without any explanation. She had a feeling that if she could check, she'd find they'd be turning up at the Pine Village Resort.

She couldn't really blame them. Who would want to stay in an old inn that smelled of paint and varnish—a place where the proprietor ran around in dungarees looking like a refugee from a work farm?

She sat up straight, suddenly conscious of urgency. She had to get the work finished. Now.

There was relief in the thought of work, she decided as she slid her feet gingerly back into the cold water. And she mustn't forget that Nathaniel had volunteered to help. That had taken a huge load off her shoulders. If she could just ignore the stone that had taken the place of her heart, she'd survive. Of course she would survive.

She waded slowly to shore, conscious of the happy carefree sounds coming from the resort beach, aware that the sun was still shining and the gulls were still wheeling and squabbling overhead. But all these sounds were distant and had nothing to do with her. She had sealed herself back in her bubble of protection, her cocoon of safety, and she wasn't going to venture out again.

SARAH WAS SITTING AT THE TABLE in the kitchen, her arms folded across her chest, an expression of sheer outrage on her long face. The little knot on the back of her head seemed to bristle when she looked at Petra as she entered. "Is something wrong?" Petra asked cautiously, while her heart sank even lower than it had been before, something she would not have thought possible.

The older woman sniffed self-righteously. "I understand from the laddie that you've hired that misbegotten wretch to work on the roof." Every *r* rolled to its fullest extent.

Petra stared at her blankly for a moment. She had completely forgotten the feud between Sarah and Nathaniel. Having asked the Admiral for an explanation of Sarah's hostility and been gently refused, she'd dismissed the whole thing from her consciousness. And she wasn't going to worry about it now, she decided, her chin coming up to meet Sarah's annoyance head on. "If you're talking about my friend Nathaniel," she said firmly, "I certainly have hired him. And I'm glad to get him."

"Then you'll be wanting to replace me," Sarah said just as firmly.

Aghast, Petra stared at her. "I don't want to do anything of the sort, Sarah."

"It's me or him."

Petra sat down at the table opposite her, put one hand on her folded arm. "Sarah dear...."

"Don't try to soft-soap me, young lassie," Sarah said grimly. "I'll not be changing my mind. It's him or me. Choose now."

She meant it. She really meant it. And without her the inn would fall apart. There was no possible way that Petra could run the inn without her.

Having spent part of the day in abject terror on the steeply pitched roof and the rest of it having her guts taken out for examination by Dan Halliwell, only to be greeted by this ultimatum, Petra did the only thing possible. She folded her arms on the table, put her head down on top of them and burst into tears.

It was probably the smartest move she could have made, even though she hadn't done it deliberately. In spite of Sarah's somewhat sour disposition, the woman had a heart that was as soft as butter, especially where her "lassie" and "laddie" were concerned. "Oh whisht now, whisht," she muttered, jumping up at once to come and put her arms awkwardly around Petra. "You have no business doing this. It's not fair. It's not."

"I can't manage without you, Sarah, you know that," Petra sobbed. "And I can't manage without Nathaniel. I was so relieved when he offered to help. You've no idea how scared I was up on that roof. I thought I could do anything, but I should have known I'd freeze up there. I've never been able even to ride a Ferris wheel."

Her voice trailed off on a wailing note and Sarah hugged her tighter. "Of course you must not be climbing around on the roof," she said soothingly. "I'll manage to overlook that scoundrel if it means that much to you. I canna leave you, you know that. It was just an idle threat. I was so angry at the idea of him being here."

Petra raised her face, her tears miraculously drying now that she knew Sarah hadn't really meant to leave. "Why?" she asked gently. "Why don't you want Nathaniel around? He seems such a nice man. So kind and gentle and funny."

"Aye," Sarah said heavily. "There was a time I thought so too." She'd resumed her seat opposite Petra and was pouring tea for both of them from a round brown pot. She swore by her brown pot, Petra remembered irrelevantly, insisting always that good tea could only be made in a brown teapot that had first been heated with boiling water.

Staring at the older woman while this thought went through her mind, she suddenly realized what she should have known all along. There was only one reason that a woman would profess extreme dislike for a man who seemed perfectly likable to everyone else. "You're in love with Nathaniel Jenkins," she said wonderingly, her tears forgotten.

Two bright spots of color appeared on Sarah's cheeks, like patches of rouge slapped on by a careless hand. "I am not," she said heatedly.

"Then you were."

For a second longer, Sarah stayed sitting rigidly upright, her hands clasped in front of her. Then she relaxed and let out the breath she'd been holding in a drawn-out sigh. "Aye, there was a time when I thought he was the finest man in the world—God's gift to woman, you might say. I can only excuse myself with the fact that I was reasonably young at the time, though I was thirty, which was probably old enough to know better."

"Nathaniel lived across the street when you moved in here to work for Uncle Will?" Petra prodded gently.

"He did. It wasn't a museum then of course. A fine house it was."

"He was married?"

"Aye." Sarah sighed heavily. "Not that there was any joy in the marriage. A poor excuse for a woman, his wife was. He'd married her when they were both twenty. She was pretty enough. But that was all she had going, her looks. Hours she spent in front of her dresser, always fussing with her hair and face—when she wasn't sipping her gin."

"She was an alcoholic? Oh, poor Nathaniel."

"Aye. Well, I'm not sure she was an alcoholic," Sarah said, obviously striving to be fair. "She was dainty in her ways, you understand. She didn't drink from a bottle or anything like that. But she did like her gin and tonic. And it seemed to me that she drank a fair amount in a day's time, especially toward evening, sitting out on the porch there.''

"Nathaniel wanted to divorce her and marry you?"

She nodded. For a brief moment, nostalgia softened her somewhat pinched features and Petra caught a sudden glimpse of the young woman she must have been, never beautiful, but comely—yes, that was the word, comely and slender and shy. Her hazel eyes had a light in them for a second that must have been even brighter then. "What happened to Mr. Merriweather?" Petra asked. "I take it he was out of the picture by then?"

Sarah looked startled, then she smiled sadly. "There never was a Mr. Merriweather, lass. It's traditional for a housekeeper to be called Mrs., you know. I simply tacked it on to my name. I never did marry. After Nathaniel, nobody ever quite appealed to me again." She pursed her mouth and snorted. "Silly fool. He was thirty-five and should have known better just as I should have done. He kept saying, 'Say the word, Sarah, and I'll ask Amy for a divorce.'"

Petra shook her head. "What you wanted of course was for him to divorce her because he didn't want to be married to her and then come to you. Because that way you wouldn't be responsible for another woman's losing her happiness."

Sarah's hand reached out and clasped Petra's in a

rare gesture of affection. "I suppose it takes another woman to recognize that," she said softly. "Nathaniel never did. When I refused to do as he asked, he went away. Amy died a year ago and he came back. They never did have children. She told him she couldn't, but I've an idea she didn't want to ruin her figure. She was certainly proud of her figure."

"You've never forgiven Nathaniel then?" Petra asked.

"Oh, I suppose I have. It was all a long time ago. But then when he came back he kept hanging around here as though I'd snap him up right away, and I finally had to tell him to stay off the property."

"You mean he asked you again to marry him?" Petra exclaimed. "Sarah, why didn't you...."

"He hasn't done anything of the sort," Sarah said bluntly. "All he did was hang around, looking for some home cooking and making compliments about the way I looked. Silly old fool. Let's not talk about him any more." She patted Petra's hand once more as Petra looked alarmed. "You've no need to worry, lass, I'm over my tantrum. I'll stay on even if he's working here. I can put up with him for your sake, as long as I'm not expected to socialize with him. I've no time for his foolishness."

I believe I told you I wouldn't have time for socializing, Mr. Halliwell, Petra's voice echoed in her memory. How could she question Sarah's attitude when she was just as—what was the word Dan always used—prickly...that was it. She was just as prickly herself.

"I'm sorry, Sarah," she said softly. "I'm glad you

told me though. Of course I won't expect you to
spend time with Nathaniel, though I must say...."

"Don't say it, lass." Sarah stood up, briskly rety-
ing her apron strings, tucking stray hairs into her
braided bun. "If you start having the idea that it
wouldn't hurt to do a little matchmaking, I'll not be
able to put up with it. I do have my pride, you
know."

"Okay, Sarah," Petra said at once, alert to the
possibility that she could still lose Sarah. "I'll stay
out of it altogether. How's that?" She hesitated.
"And in return you won't be encouraging Dan Halliwell to come around, okay?"

Sarah gave her a long measuring glance in which a
great deal of sympathy showed. "It's like that then,"
she said heavily.

Petra nodded. "It is."

"All right then. It's agreed." She reached out to
touch Petra's shoulder with her usual brisk pat, but
instead, she pulled her into a hug that was almost
Petra's undoing. Holding on to Sarah's solid form,
she had to take several deep breaths to hold back the
tears that were threatening to fall again. But whether
these tears were for herself or for Sarah, she had no
idea.

CHAPTER TEN

THE SOUND OF HAMMERING on the inn roof was the most reassuring sound Petra had ever heard. Pausing in the middle of applying adhesive to a strip of wallpaper that she'd spread on a plywood board supported by sawhorses, she lifted her eyes toward the sound in a brief prayer of thanksgiving. Nathaniel had managed to get the rest of the shingles unpacked and up on the roof the previous morning and had promised today he'd start fixing them in place. And there he was, bless him.

She had the strip of pastel striped paper up and smoothed into place before it dawned on her that Nathaniel was making an awful lot of noise for one man. Wiping her hands on the seat of her overalls, she ran lightly down the stairs and out to the front lawn and was amazed to see a familiar-looking stocky figure, clad in shapeless overalls, up on the roof beside Nathaniel, the two of them working companionably away in perfect rhythm. "Carter Mansfield," she called in astonishment.

He stopped hammering and lifted his painter's cap in a gesture that duplicated his nephew's, disclosing a mop of curls as thick as Matt's but as gray as a woolly sheep. "Mornin'," he called down to her.

"What on earth are you doing here?" she shouted.

He looked puzzled, glanced at Nathaniel, then back down to her. "Said I'd be here," he pointed out. "Just a little late mebbe. I got delayed in Boston." His blue eyes twinkled. "Our Mr. Halliwell appealed to my sense of chivalry, when he sought me out yesterday, Miss Petra. Damsel in distress, he said. Told me that nephew of mine wasn't disposed to help, churl that he is. So naturally I came back to the Cape as soon as I could."

Dan again. Just once she'd like to accomplish something without Dan Halliwell's interference. But she couldn't really hold a grudge. She needed Carter Mansfield too desperately. "I'm glad you're here," she called up to him. She grinned at Nathaniel, who smiled back at her. "Looks like I've got all the help I'll need," she said. "Thanks a lot, both of you."

Her heart felt lighter than it had for some time as she returned to her wallpapering. Now she could begin to make progress. Now things would start happening, falling into place. And perhaps she could take things a little easier, a little slower.

So Dan had gone back to Boston, she mused as she measured the next strip of wallpaper. She had wondered if he might have gone home. True to his word, he hadn't come near her after their talk on the beach. Nor had he run on the beach yesterday, not at a time she was looking out at any rate—and in spite of herself she'd looked out several times. Had he gone for good? It would be best if he had, wouldn't it? He'd said he wouldn't bother her again, and she had accepted that, even been glad of it. Unfortunately he

had added, "until you're ready." Surely that had indicated he would be available, if by some chance she
was ready? It just went to show that she'd been right
to break off with him. Even in this small thing he
hadn't proved reliable.

She straightened her body, which was showing a
distressing tendency to slump. Forget Dan Halliwell,
she ordered herself once again. What she needed was
a distraction of some kind. As long as she had some
help now, maybe she should take the afternoon off,
part of it anyway, and go visit Kelly O'Connor. That
way she'd take care of an obligation, and also find
out if Dan had gone for good. If he had, then she
could set herself to forgetting about him altogether.
She never had liked loose ends. That was all that was
upsetting her, the not knowing, not being sure....

She sighed as she folded the pasted strip of paper
loosely together and carried it to the wall. Was she
ever going to stop rationalizing where Dan Halliwell
was concerned, she wondered. She could at least admit to herself that she hadn't wanted him to give up
on her, that she'd wanted him to be more persistent
than the other men in her life had been—even if she
couldn't understand why it should be necessary.

KELLY O'CONNOR SEEMED DELIGHTED to see her when
she knocked on his office door at four o'clock. He
seated her with great ceremony in a squashy-soft armchair, one of two set in a cosy space in front of the
room's deep bay window overlooking the Olympic-
size swimming pool. Then he insisted on sending for
refreshments, offering first the hotel's famed screw-

drivers, then wine, which Petra agreed to. The wine came accompanied by a platter of grilled morel mushrooms on tiny squares of toast, one of Petra's weaknesses. "Mmm, delicious," she sighed as she tasted one. "You have a superb chef, Mr. O'Connor."

"Kelly," he insisted, settling himself a little too closely in the chair opposite and crossing his long legs.

There was something about him that was not objectionable exactly, but not likable either—something a little too intimate in the glances his rather small brown eyes were giving her through the thick lenses of his glasses, something too knowing in his smile. He kept flicking glances at her as though he was imagining what she would look like naked, and she had to keep reminding herself that she was perfectly respectable in her yellow cotton dress and low-heeled sandals. She had the feeling it was as well she'd come to visit Kelly O'Connor during daylight hours. She wouldn't trust him an inch at night.

Yet he was a nice-looking man, tall and slender. His beard was neatly trimmed, his hair impeccably in place. He was well dressed too, as well dressed in his charcoal-gray suit as Dan had been when she had first seen him, though without Dan's air of being born to such well-tailored elegance. Kelly O'Connor's gloss seemed more contrived, which of course was not something anyone should criticize. Few people could be born to the Halliwells' brand of silver spoon.

Perhaps what was putting her off was his nervousness. Even when he was sitting, he didn't seem quite at ease—as though given the slightest provocation he would jump to his feet again.

"I thought I should come in and say hello as we're neighbors," Petra explained as soon as the initial pleasantries were over. She didn't want him to get the wrong idea about her visit, and he seemed the type who would.

"I'm glad you stopped by," he said smoothly, smiling at her. "I don't know when I've had such a pretty neighbor."

"Neighbors should enjoy a good business relationship," Petra said hastily, putting plenty of emphasis on the word "business."

"You are so right," he said gravely. He seemed amused, which annoyed her. She'd almost made up her mind to leave, and then he started talking about the hotel business and she was able to relax.

"I'm hoping to get filled up pretty soon," she told him when he asked how business was going. "I had to do some repairs, and I still have a couple of rooms to finish, but it's coming along. My main problem at the moment is that I have room for four to eight more guests than I have."

"Perhaps I could alert our front office to refer any overflow to you," he suggested. "We're totally full at present and I understand we are still getting requests."

"That would be kind of you," Petra said, wondering if she'd misjudged him. "I'd certainly appreciate any help. Perhaps you'd like to come over and see what I'm doing with the place, so you'll know any commendations would be backed up by. . . ."

He chuckled softly in a way she didn't quite like. "Did I say something funny?" she asked stiffly.

He shook his head. "Not in itself. But I certainly wouldn't dare poach on Dan Halliwell's preserves, Miss McNeil. I'm quite sure he wouldn't take kindly to my paying you a call, much as I'd like to do so."

She stared at him. "I don't have to get permission from Dan for someone to come to see my inn."

He raised dark eyebrows above his thick-lensed glasses. "Had a spat, have you? All the more reason for me to stay out of the picture. Evidently you've no idea how territorial the Halliwells are, Miss McNeil. They shoot trespassers on sight."

"I'm not Halliwell property."

"No? That's not the story I heard."

"What did you hear?"

He leaned forward, carafe in hand. "More wine?"

Anxious to hear what he would say, she nodded impatiently and held out her glass for more of the Chablis, even though it wasn't one of her favored brands. He took his time pouring it, one hand touching hers where it held her glass, ostensibly to steady it. No, she hadn't misjudged him. She felt a tremor of distaste go through her, but tried not to show it.

"You have to realize, Miss McNeil," he said with another of those annoyingly knowing smiles, "gossip is very important to small communities, especially encapsulated communities like this resort. It was only natural that we'd hear Dan was courting you with roses and dinners at the Coonamessett Inn. After all," he added when she let her annoyance at this intrusion into her privacy show, "Dan Halliwell is our boss—not the big boss, but his right-hand man. When he shows up, we all tremble in our shoes and look for the reason behind his visit.''

"But I'm not, I've never...." She hesitated, suddenly hearing in her memory Dan's voice saying, "Go along with whatever Kelly says...." Was this what he'd meant?

"Maybe you should have asked Dan about our relationship," she said dryly.

His eyebrows rose. "But I did, of course. And he was quite open about it. I realize you probably feel you have to protect him, because of who he is, but believe me, it's okay. He was very open. He told me quite frankly that the only reason he was staying on was that he wanted time to...." He hesitated. "Shall we say, 'court' you. You weren't being too amenable, he said, and it would take time to break you down." He leaned back in his chair, leering at her—there was no other word for his expression. "I was glad to see the other night that you *had* become more amenable," he said. "A happy boss is an easy boss."

Somehow Petra managed to keep herself from slapping that leer off his thin face, even though the temptation was great. She felt soiled. Something that had been beautiful was being tarnished by this man's tongue. And Dan had told him, had used what was between them as an excuse to....

She stood up abruptly. "I've kept you long enough, Mr. O'Connor," she said crisply. "I have to get back."

"Please don't hurry away. I may not be able to come visit you, but as long as you're here and it can appear to be a business call...."

"It *is* business," she said flatly, looking him right in the eye.

He laughed, unabashed. "I thought you said you weren't Halliwell property."

About to say something very insulting and unfeminine, Petra paused. He had promised to send guests her way. Business was business. She would have to ignore his insults. It wasn't his fault that he'd been led to believe certain things about her. However, she didn't have to expose herself to any more of this man's innuendos. "I really must go," she said in as pleasant a voice as she could manage.

He nodded and rose, insisting on escorting her to the door. With his hand on the doorknob, he hesitated and looked at her. "May I offer a word to the wise?" he asked.

Wanting only to get away from him, but feeling it might be best to hear what he had to say, Petra nodded.

"I'm not sure Dan's motives are all they appear to be," he said in a rather unctuous tone of voice. "The Braden Corporation would love to get their hands on your strip of land, you know."

"I know that they offered to buy it from my uncle," Petra agreed. "But so far no one's even asked me...."

"The Halliwells are not always straightforward. Having once been refused, they are more than capable of underhanded practices. In order to sway your thinking...."

She thought of the two couples who had canceled their reservations. No. Dan had assured her that no one in the Braden Corporation would make trouble for her. And she had believed him. Completely.

"You're wrong, Mr. O'Connor..." she said, wishing her voice sounded a little firmer. Surely she didn't still have doubts....

"Kelly. I insist."

She hadn't noticed before how oily his smile was. Unable to avoid showing her distaste, she managed a nasty smile of her own. "Kelly," she amended. "I've already accused Dan of going after my hotel and he flatly denied any such action. And I believe...."

"You don't *look* naive," he said with another smile that set her teeth on edge. "The Braden Corporation didn't get its billions by worrying about the little people like you and me," he went on before she could continue. "They own resorts and hotels in Europe, Tel Aviv, Hawaii, Japan. Do you really think they'll take no for an answer when they want a few feet of beach that happen to belong to someone else? Do you really think you aren't wasting your time with all your repairs and efforts? They'll get that place away from you, one way or the other. You might as well give up now as later."

"I'm not giving up at all," she said firmly. "And I'm quite sure you are wrong about Dan."

"Love is indeed blind."

He said this with such an exasperatingly smug expression on his face that Petra came close to yelling at him that love wasn't involved in any way. But luckily she was so annoyed that she had to pause long enough to catch her breath, and that gave her time to realize it didn't matter what Kelly believed. And she didn't have to dignify his innuendos with any response at all. Managing to hold out her hand in a manner that she hoped appeared friendly, she thanked him for his time and for his promise to recommend the inn, and smiled when he expressed the hope she'd come calling again.

She was outside by the swimming pool before she let herself give vent to the anger that had been building up inside her. Even there she couldn't manage any more than a sudden explosion of breath—the area was so crowded with happy young people taking in sun and screwdrivers in almost equal proportions. Walking briskly past them all, she went down the steps to the beach, pulled off her sandals and then ran through the deep white sand to the water's edge and hunted for a handful of rocks that she could throw one by one, with more force than she'd have thought she had in her, into the water.

"Damn, damn, damn," she exploded with each splash. Even if she didn't believe Kelly O'Connor's assertion that the Braden Corporation was after her property, she was still shaken by the things he'd said. It had occurred to her almost as soon as the words were out of his mouth that Dan might not just have used their affair, if it could be called that, as a convenient excuse for staying on the Cape, but might have engineered the affair for that reason alone. That made him far less than the rogue she'd thought him—it made him lower than the lowest creep she'd ever met.

IT WAS A WHILE BEFORE SHE FELT CALM enough to return to the inn. By the time she did, high tea was over. She could hear Sarah talking to someone in the kitchen. Bonnie and Terry perhaps, or Tony. She hesitated in the lobby, trying to decide if she should go straight up to her room. She didn't really feel like being sociable right now. But as she hesitated she heard Dan Halliwell's distinctive voice saying, "Okay, Sarah, it's a deal."

Without stopping to plan any strategy or think through what she was going to say, she stalked into the kitchen and confronted Dan before he even had a chance to get to his feet at the table where he'd been chummily sharing a pot of tea with Sarah and Tony. "What are you doing here?" she demanded.

Maddeningly imperturbable as always, he peered up at her as though he wasn't quite sure who she was. "Petra, how are you?" he asked in that annoyingly calm voice of his, his Bostonian accent as noticeable as ever.

"I'm furious," she told him. "What the hell do you mean telling Kelly O'Connor, telling him—" She broke off, suddenly aware that Tony and Sarah were both staring wide-eyed, hanging on every word. She directed a glare at each of them. "I'd like to speak to Mr. Halliwell alone," she announced.

Tony grinned. "Aw, come on, Petra. You're always telling me my social life needs revamping. How can I learn how to have a rattling good row if you don't teach me?"

Dan laughed. "Tony, I don't think your sister...."

"Go to your room," Petra ordered her brother, not caring that he was no longer six years old.

And he had the sense to realize he'd better obey, though he did pull a face at her as he whisked out of the door.

Petra transferred her gaze to Sarah, who was pulling herself to her feet as slowly as though she was bothered by rheumatism, which she never had been to Petra's certain knowledge. "Now lass, there's no call for you..." she began, but as her eyes caught Petra's she let the rest of the sentence trail away. Shaking her head, she went briskly out of the room.

Dan rose to his feet and pulled out the chair Sarah had vacated. "What's the problem, Petra dear?" he asked politely.

"I am not your dear," she snapped. "And I don't want to sit down. This won't take long. I've had about enough of you interfering in my life. Kelly O'Connor was the last straw. You used me, didn't you? You wanted Kelly to believe I was the reason you were staying on the Cape. Probably you started that whole thing with me just so you'd have an excuse."

"That's not so," he interrupted. "As I told you before, I let him believe certain things—but I didn't ever discuss you with him. What kind of rat do you think I am, Petra? Did you really think I'd discuss our private lives with someone like Kelly O'Connor?"

"He says you did."

"And you think he always tells the truth?"

"How else would he know?"

"This is a small area. People gossip...."

"Kelly did say something like that himself," she admitted.

"Well then...."

She sat down abruptly, suddenly running out of steam, which she regretted. It was far better for her to stay angry with Dan Halliwell. Especially when he was looking again like the captain of industry she'd first met. He was dressed in his blue pin-striped suit again—he must just have arrived from Boston. Once again, she wished he wasn't so damned attractive.

Could she believe that he hadn't used her, hadn't talked about her to that unsavory man? "Well," she said lamely. "If you'll tell me what you are really doing on the Cape, I might be able to believe you."

His eyes met hers with a rueful expression in them. "I wish I could tell you, Petra, but I'm not quite ready to. Could you hang on for a while until I'm free to tell all?"

His green eyes were candid, direct—otherwise free of expression.

"It's just a matter of time?" she asked, reluctantly deciding she might have to give him the benefit of the doubt.

"Absolutely."

"I suppose I'll have to wait for an explanation then." She was letting him off far too lightly, she knew. After all Kelly had said, after all her anger.... Perhaps she was doing so because the main reason for her anger had been the fear that Dan had denigrated what had been between them. Why that should upset her, she had no idea, because it wasn't all that important to her, was it? It couldn't be. She wasn't going to let it be.

"From the look on your face when you came in

here, I'd say you didn't care a whole lot for our Kelly O'Connor,'' Dan said.

Petra nodded. ''You're right about that. A thoroughly nasty piece of goods. Why on earth did you employ him?''

''I didn't. I'm a troubleshooter, remember. I've got nothing to do with personnel until they. . . .''

''Until they go bad? Did Kelly do something?'' She leaned forward, suddenly curious, but Dan was in control of himself, immediately ready to cover up his slip. ''Until they require my help,'' he finished smoothly.

''He doesn't think much of the Braden Corporation,'' she told him, suddenly wanting to be nasty.

''Oh?''

''He told me your family was after my land and would stop at nothing to get it from me. They don't care about little people, he said.''

A look of utter distaste showed on Dan's face. ''What else did he have to say about us?''

''That was about it. It made me wonder though,'' she added and then stopped.

His green gaze sharpened on her face. ''Wonder what?''

Should she say anything? Why not? What at this point did she have to lose? ''It's probably coincidence, but I've had a couple of cancellations. One couple definitely went to the resort instead. The other pair I don't know about.''

His eyes had narrowed. ''You think somebody's influencing people to cancel?''

''I didn't say that, Dan. I just—well I guess I'm

worried about it. Lord help me if it turns out to be a trend...." She tried to laugh, but didn't quite succeed. There was such an odd expression on Dan's face. His mouth was grim, but there was a sudden light of understanding in his eyes. "Dan, you don't think the Braden Corporation...."

"Absolutely not," he said with utter conviction. But all the same, he wouldn't quite meet her eyes. And his brain was working very busily behind those abruptly hooded eyes. "Did you mention this to Kelly?" he demanded in the frostiest voice she'd ever heard him use.

"No. I wouldn't have mentioned it to you, except that...."

"Friend Kelly will be—" he interrupted, then broke off, but not before Petra had noted the implacable tone of his voice. She shivered suddenly. She couldn't imagine Dan ever losing his temper, his sometimes rigid control, but she wouldn't want to be his enemy. She had the feeling he'd be an unforgiving one.

"Well, he's not all bad," she said lightly. "He did offer to send overflow guests my way."

"You can forget that," Dan said flatly.

"Why?" Her temper was rising again. Maybe she had calmed down too quickly.

"He won't do any such thing. He's just trying to make points with you. He's not in any way a helpful type."

"Not like you, then?" she said spitefully.

He winced at the sarcastic note in her voice. "You refuse to believe I have your best interests at heart, don't you, Petra?"

"Don't patronize me, Dan Halliwell."

He looked at her levelly. "Did that sound patron-izing? I'm sorry."

"You don't have to be sorry. Just leave me alone to run my inn." There was a sympathetic expression on his face that was irritating her tremendously. "You still don't believe I can bring it off, do you? You think I'm going to fail."

"I've never suggested you would fail."

"You've never suggested I might succeed."

"Petra love, I know how tough it's been for you, how tough it will be in the future, and I wish I could do more to help, but. . . ."

"I don't need your help. I don't need anyone's help." That wasn't at all true of course, but it felt good to say it. And it felt good to see that smug look of sympathy leave his face.

There was a silence that she didn't attempt to break. After a while he stood up. "I have a feeling I've worn out my welcome again," he said. "And I do have several telephone calls to make, so I guess I'd better take myself off to my room."

Something in the way he'd said that caught her attention. "Your room?" she asked.

He hadn't used his dazzling smile on her for a while. And their conversation so far hadn't led her to expect any kind of smile from him, so it was all the more devastating when the smile appeared. She felt her entire body warm from the top of her head down to her toes, as though she'd suddenly been bathed in tropical sunshine. "I guess we didn't have a chance to tell you," he said slowly. "I've rented a room here, at the inn, for a few days. The one with the charming wild-flower patterned wallpaper. I understand you applied it. You did a marvelous job, Petra. The seams are almost invisible. You really are talented...."

"I'm sorry. I don't think it's a good idea for you to stay here," she said stiffly, shocked to the core. "I wasn't consulted. If I had been, I would have told you that it's absolutely impossible for you to stay here...."

"No it's not. I'm doing it. I've already signed the register. I'd hate to have to tell the chamber of commerce you discriminated against me for some unknown reason...." He let his voice trail away.

Petra glared at him. "That's blackmail."

"No it's not," he repeated. "Blackmail is to demand payment by threats." He tilted his head to one side, considering. "Perhaps it would qualify as blackmail. Payment being the use of a room." He nodded solemnly. "Yes, you are quite right. Blackmail it is."

Petra closed her eyes and let out her breath on a long sigh of exasperation. "I suppose I can't throw you out legally," she said at last. "But I certainly don't see why you'd want to stay where you're not welcome."

"It suits my purposes," he said lightly.

She looked at him very directly. "You always do what suits your purposes?"

"Always," he answered, standing up. And then he had the gall to bend down over her and lift her chin with very gentle fingers and kiss her lightly but intimately on the mouth. Before she could even catch her breath after that assault on her senses, he was gone and she was left staring after him, filled with a sudden yearning for what might have been.

Oddly enough though, she realized, she hadn't flinched away from him as she'd done previously. Why was that?

She sat for a while thinking it through and finally came up with an answer that dismayed her because it revealed that her problems were as complicated as she'd always suspected. Now that she'd found out Dan might have used her—now that it seemed clear that he didn't care deeply for her at all, she didn't feel threatened by him. As he'd so astutely pointed out, it was only when people came too close to her that she felt threatened.

Sighing, she managed to move at last and went in search of Sarah, feeling she needed to apologize for her earlier behavior.

Sarah pooh-poohed her attempts at apology when she tracked her down in the sitting parlor. Straightening from her dusting—a task she wasn't supposed to get involved in, but invariably did immediately after Bonnie or Terry had completed it—she smiled rather sheepishly. "I suppose Dan told you he's staying with us a while."

"He did," Petra said coldly. "Whose idea was that?"

"His, of course. Seems he's tired of the noise over at the resort. Needs a little peace and quiet, he says."

"And you believed him?"

Sarah looked indignant. "Dan would not lie."

"If you'll believe that, you'll believe anything," Petra said flatly. Then, before Sarah could argue the point, she looked around vaguely and asked where Tony was.

At once Sarah frowned and put her dusting cloth aside. Arms akimbo, she looked at Petra directly. "I've been meaning to speak with you about that. Tony's off again with his friends. What are their names? Seth someone, and a young girl."

"Lori," Petra supplied.

"Aye. He's seeing a lot of them, have you noticed?"

"I've not only noticed, I've encouraged him to do so. He needs young people, Sarah. We can't expect him to work all the time. He does quite a bit."

"Och, I'm not complaining about his work," Sarah protested. "He's a good lad and he does his share. It's the kids he's associating with. What do you know about them?"

"Has something happened?" Petra asked, alarmed.

"Not yet, but I've a mind it might."

Petra sat down heavily on the arm of one of the wing chairs, suddenly very weary again. "Don't tell me there's a problem," she begged. "What happened?"

"Nothing happened, lass. It's just that . . . well, that Seth boy drives a Mercedes. Did you know that?"

Petra shook her head. "I'm not surprised. He's just the type. I suppose it's his father's."

"You think it's all right for a lad his age to be driving a car like that?"

"It's not something I'd provide for a child of mine," Petra said. "But I don't really think it's any of our business, Sarah. Seth's father seems to be indulgent. He lets Seth use his boat. . . ."

"Aye, that's another thing. Those children running around on the water by themselves, no supervision. How do we know what they're up to? Mark my words, lassie, no good comes of rich children with time on their hands."

"Have you discussed this with Dan?" Petra asked on a sudden suspicion.

"I have. And why not?" Sarah had taken an immediate defensive stance, arms folded across her chest, head tilted at an aggressive angle. "He agrees with me."

"I'm sure he does," Petra said, letting her exasperation show. "He's already told me he's not impressed by Seth and Lori, but as far as I can see, there's nothing in the world wrong with them except that their parents allow them too many privileges. You can't really condemn the kids for that. And," she added, holding her palm up as Sarah began to interrupt her, "I've got a lot of faith in Tony's judgment. He's mature enough to exercise it, so I don't want to hear anything more against Seth and Lori from you or Dan, whether you approve of them or not."

Sarah sniffed. "Well, no doubt you know best, lassie." She picked up her container of polish and her dustcloth and flounced toward the doorway, where she turned and sniffed audibly. "Or you think you do," she threw over her shoulder just before she disappeared through the doorway.

Petra laughed. Trust Sarah to have the last word.

She sat where she was for a minute, trying to decide quite how she felt about Dan Halliwell staying at her inn. She was annoyed that he'd taken advantage of her short absence, of course, annoyed that Sarah and Tony had made the arrangements with him without consulting her. But if she was to be truthful with herself, underneath her annoyance, she was excited, and hopeful. And that just went to show she hadn't got over being stupid yet, not by a long shot.

CHAPTER ELEVEN

PETRA WAS DESCENDING THE STAIRS to the lobby when she saw the young woman enter through the front door. She recognized her immediately: Wendy, the woman from the resort—the "wench" Tony had seen sailing with Dan. She had exchanged her sleek black dress for a yellow terry-cloth playsuit that left her creamy shoulders and long legs bare. Her straight red hair seemed to glow with a life of its own in the sunlit lobby.

Petra was immediately conscious that she was just wearing her usual garb of glue- and paint-stained overalls, a gray "save the whales" T-shirt she'd bought in Woods Hole and a bandanna over her dark curls. For a second she was tempted to bolt back up the stairs, but then sanity prevailed and she continued down. "May I help you?" she asked frostily.

The woman smiled in what was obviously a genuinely friendly way. Transferring the canvas beach bag she was carrying to her left hand, she held out the other to Petra. "You must be Miss McNeil," she said. "I'm Wendy Barstad."

Her handshake was firm. Petra began thawing.

Wendy's smile had spread to her beautifully made-up eyes and seemed to indicate admiration as she looked around.

"I've heard you've been doing a tremendous job with this place," she said warmly. "This is a lovely little inn. I'd enjoy working on a place like this myself. I really admire you for doing it."

The thaw was complete. Gorgeous she might be, but she was obviously a very nice woman too. Petra smiled. "Thank you. Sometimes lately I've thought I was crazy to take the job on, but...."

"There you are," Dan Halliwell said, emerging from the sitting parlor.

Both women turned toward him. Petra's breath caught in her throat. The late-afternoon sunlight was pouring in through the front door and windows of the inn, gilding his hair and shining into his eyes, so that they seemed especially green against his lean tanned face. He was wearing a green Izod shirt today—the exact color of his eyes—and white chinos that hugged his lean hips suggestively. He looked devastating.

"I'm sorry I'm late, Dan," Wendy said breathlessly. "I couldn't get away." She frowned. Even her frown was attractive, Petra noted. It crinkled the freckled skin above her straight little nose in a piquant way that was most appealing. "I'm not sure I should have come at all," she added.

"Of course you should have." Dan had approached her and now he put his hands on her bare shoulders and looked down into her eyes with that compelling expression Petra knew so well. "You wanted to, didn't you? It's worth the risk. Admit it." One of his eye-crinkling grins accompanied the demand.

Wendy softened just as Petra always had. Petra

could almost feel the vibrations as the young woman responded to his touch. "You're right," she said softly.

"Good," Dan said. He put one arm around her shoulders and began walking her toward the sitting parlor, then stopped and glanced at Petra who had listened to this exchange openmouthed. "I'm sorry. I didn't introduce. . . ."

"We've already met," Petra said, with the frosty note that had returned to her voice.

Raising both eyebrows in the superior way he had sometimes, he glanced again at her and then at Wendy, then back to Petra. He laughed, and then his green gaze swept her with an all-encompassing look that she felt sure noted every detail of her messy appearance. "You don't mind if we use the parlor for a while, do you?" he asked. "High tea's all finished with."

"Be my guest," she said nastily.

But her sarcasm was lost on him. He simply smiled gratefully and then he and Wendy disappeared into the front room.

Petra glared at the closed door. She supposed she should be glad he hadn't taken the young woman up to his bedroom. Perhaps even Dan Halliwell didn't have that much nerve. But it had taken considerable nerve to bring another woman into her inn, after all that had happened between them. There wasn't anything she could do about it, though. Any guest was permitted to have visitors. This was a hotel, not a jail. All the same. . . .

Shaking her head, she forced herself to turn toward the passage to the kitchen. By her own choosing, what Dan decided to do with his spare time was none of her business.

Sarah and Nathaniel were both in the kitchen, Nathaniel in his work clothes sitting at the table drinking a cup of coffee, Sarah at the sink, rinsing tea things for the dishwasher, her head and neck at a stiff angle, her starched white apron tied tightly.

Petra had insisted that Nathaniel be given refreshments whenever he desired them and Sarah had reluctantly agreed to serve him. Petra had wished since then that she hadn't been so adamant. Whenever Nathaniel was in the house, Sarah behaved as though she'd been asked to serve food to some indigent who'd wandered in off the street. "Hello, Admiral," Petra said warily.

He smiled his gentle smile at her. "Miss Petra," he said courteously. "Will you join me in a cup of this excellent coffee?"

Sarah sniffed loudly. Petra could almost hear her saying under her breath, "Flattery will get him nowhere."

"I'd love to," she said. Hoping to lighten the palpably heavy atmosphere she added, "Is Tony around?"

"Gone to town with those friends of his," Sarah said in her most disapproving tone.

Petra sighed. That hadn't helped at all. "What are you doing here this time of the day?" she asked Nathaniel. "You're only supposed to be working mornings."

"Had a little finishing up to do," he explained.

"We got all the moss off and Carter sprayed the roof with retardant. I came back after the museum closed. Carter wanted to finish so he could start on the siding tomorrow."

Petra let her breath out on a sigh of relief. At least something was going right. "I'm so glad that roof's done," she said.

"Drop-dry," Nathaniel asserted, adding when she looked a question at him, "That's a nautical term, Miss Petra. Means it's waterproof."

Another loud sniff from Sarah. "Seems to me some people ought to give over pretending they've had naval experience when all they've done is operate a couple of fishing boats." Her words might have been formed of dry ice.

"Now, Sarah," the admiral said, winking at Petra.

"Don't you now Sarah me."

"Hey you two," Petra objected. "I came in here looking for relaxation."

"Dan and I were discussing the annual Falmouth Road Race this noon," Nathaniel said, obviously trying to smooth things over. "It's a foot race, Miss Petra. Starts in Woods Hole and ends at Falmouth Heights. Runners of all ages, from world class to weekend joggers. It will be held in a couple of weeks' time. It's something to see."

He paused, looking at her calculatingly as she sipped her coffee. "Dan thought it might be a good idea for you to contact the chamber of commerce and remind them you have rooms available. Lots of people come to town for the race. And if you were to tempt them with one of Sarah's good nutritious breakfasts...."

"We dinna serve but a continental breakfast," Sarah said firmly. Petra had noticed before that her Scottish accent became more pronounced when she was annoyed, but she'd never heard it this thick.

"I've been meaning to talk to you about that," Petra said. "You do cook so well, Sarah, and there's no need for you to be doing housework. Bonnie and Terry do a good job and I can always help. If you were to concentrate on cooking at least for breakfast . . . it's not a bad idea. We do need the rooms filled up."

She was conscious of a feeling of relief. Her trust in Dan had not been misplaced in this instance. If he was making suggestions about how to fill the inn, then he was certainly not involved in any conspiracy to spirit guests away. All the same. . . . She looked at Nathaniel and sighed. "I wish the suggestion hadn't come from Dan. I know he doesn't think I can make a success of this place and it galls me when he. . . ."

"When advice is good, it's best to accept it wherever it comes from," the admiral said gently.

"I suppose you're right, but. . . ."

"Am I not to be consulted then?" Sarah demanded. She had finally turned from the sink and Petra saw that her face was red. What a fine line she had to tread all the time, she thought with dismay. Now she'd offended Sarah again.

"Of course you're being consulted," she said. "By the time the race guests come, Tony and I could have the carriage house cleaned out. We could serve breakfast in there." Her heart sank at the thought of how much work that entailed, but she went on doggedly. "We can get it done somehow."

"I'll help," Nathaniel said.

Sarah sniffed again. "You stick to your outside work," she said. "The lassie and I can handle the carriage house."

"You'll do it then? Oh, thank you, Sarah!" Petra jumped up and impulsively hugged Sarah's unyielding figure. "I'll go call the chamber of commerce right away."

"They're closed, Miss Petra," Nathaniel reminded her.

"So they are." Petra sat down again. "In the morning then."

And in the morning, she realized, she'd have to swallow her pride and thank Dan for his suggestion. If he'd emerged from the sitting parlor by then, of course.

An image of Wendy Barstad—all friendly smiles and freckles and glorious figure—floated through her mind. What were the two of them doing behind that closed door that was "worth the risk," she wondered, and then wondered if she really wanted to know.

Once all of the current guests were out for the evening, she decided to indulge herself by playing the piano in the parlor. She was not checking to see if Dan and Wendy had left clues to their activities, she assured herself. She'd seen Dan walk Wendy out to the porch an hour earlier. No doubt Dan had taken her out to dinner—the Coonamessett Inn perhaps, followed by a viewing of the sunset. Tony hadn't returned, but she wasn't worried about him. He was perfectly capable of taking care of himself, and she was glad he was beginning to develop a social life.

Sitting at the old upright, letting her fingers ramble over the keys, she felt herself relaxing for the first time in several days. Cool air was blowing in through the open windows, bringing with it the uplifting tang of the sea. She was freshly showered and shampooed, comfortably dressed in a cool blue cotton blouse and white linen pants. She was playing one of Chopin's nocturnes. Sensitive and dreamy as whisperings at dusk, the music sounded as though twilight had entered the room and found expression through Petra's fingers.

"I've always liked Chopin," Dan Halliwell commented from behind her. "But something more cheerful might be nice. We could have a rousing sing-along. What do you think?"

Her fingers stilled on the old ivory keys. "You do have a habit of making unexpected appearances," she said without turning around, conscious that her heartbeat had increased the moment she heard his voice.

His hands touched lightly on her shoulders, pressing her gently back against him. "Disconcerting, would you say?"

"Very." To her annoyance, her voice sounded breathless. "You've deserted your friend?" she asked.

He didn't reply for a moment and her hands grew progressively stiffer on the piano keys. Then he sighed and turned her around on the stool to face him. He'd changed his clothes, she saw. He was wearing the light gray suit he'd worn when he took her out to dinner at the Coonamessett Inn. Had he realized that he looked most attractive to her when he was smartly dressed like this? She sighed inwardly.

His expression was one she couldn't read. But his eyes seemed very green in the lamplight, sea green, with darkness in their depths. When he spoke his voice was even, giving away none of his thoughts. "Did you ever read a novel that was full of conflict, but you felt all the way through that if the main characters just sat down and talked everything over they could straighten it out?"

"I don't know what you're talking about."

"I know you don't." He paused. "I'm about to explain why you don't have to make snide remarks about Wendy."

"I did not make—" She broke off. "You're right. I implied snide. I'm sorry."

Taking a step backward, he seated himself in one of the wing chairs and smiled at her. There was a sardonic edge around the smile, she noticed, and something more—anger?

"I've been investigating Kelly O'Connor," he said. "I know you guessed that, but I couldn't admit to it until I had something solid to go on. The man's as slippery as—" He broke off, disgust clouding his face. He was angry. But not with her.

He gave her an apologetic smile. "Kelly was getting altogether too suspicious of my hanging around the resort. I couldn't accuse him until I had proof, and I couldn't tell you what I was up to because I was afraid you'd let something out unwittingly if you met him—your attitude alone might have been enough to forewarn him. I didn't want him to have a chance to cover everything up.'' He looked at her directly. ''I will admit I let him believe you'd encouraged me to stay. No more than that however. I was getting ready to deck him over his innuendos about you and me,'' he added as she started to interrupt. ''It seemed a good idea to switch locations, but I wanted to be close enough if Wendy decided to cooperate.''

''Wendy was helping you?''

He nodded. ''She brought me the proof I needed. It took me some time to persuade her. She was afraid. Kelly had something on her. It was nothing so terrible but something she didn't want known—a movie she made when she was too young to know better. Kelly is the type to use that kind of thing.'' He made a grimace of distaste. ''Today Wendy brought me Kelly's personal books. They told the whole story. I'd found out some of it already, but it was all gossip and I'd already heard the gossip. That's why I was sent here. Unfortunately I couldn't find anyone willing to swear the rumors were true, until Wendy.'' He sighed. ''Kelly O'Connor has been using hotel funds to 'entertain' young women of questionable character who in turn 'entertained' certain important guests out of Boston and New York and Washington, D.C.''

Petra stared at him, aghast. ''Prostitution?''

He inclined his head. ''Prostitution.''

He paused, raising both eyebrows expressively. ''Do you wonder I didn't want you to get involved with him?''

''What happens now?'' Petra asked, not wanting to dwell on her own stupidity.

He thrust the fingers of one hand through his thick hair in a tired gesture that made her want to reach out and touch him. "I'm only the middle man. I'm taking a report in to my father tomorrow. Our main problem will be to preserve the reputation of the hotel and the corporation. Whatever happens—my sleuthing days are almost over." He paused and seemed about to say something more, so she waited. After a moment he shook his head. "One way or another I'll have the whole thing wrapped up in a few days."

And what about her, Petra wondered. Would she be all wrapped up at the same time? Or did he consider she was already "wrapped up"? That was stupid, she scolded herself. *She* was already through with *him*.

He grinned at her suddenly. "In the meantime I still don't want friend Kelly O'Connor to get any inkling of what I've been up to. So I was wondering. . . ."

He looked unsure suddenly, something that always softened her. Perhaps he knew that by now. There was a glint in his green eyes that told her he was about to make some kind of proposal, or proposition, that she might not like. Refusing to make it easier for him, she waited.

"I wouldn't ask you if I thought there was any problem there at the moment," he said hesitantly. "Kelly has naturally been extremely cautious while I've been in the vicinity. There's certainly nothing of an odious nature going on right now. So. . . ." He hesitated once more, then blurted out, "I wondered if you'd go dancing with me."

"At the resort?"

He smiled his most dazzling smile and she could feel herself weakening. If Kelly did have suspicions, they'd be alleviated if she turned up there with Dan. He was probably right about that. And as that was obviously his reason for inviting her, there was nothing for her to feel nervous about. She would really enjoy dancing for a change anyway. And an evening of dancing would end their association on a more friendly note. All the same. . . .

"I was intending to start work on the carriage house this evening," she said slowly. "I'm going to change it into a dining room, for breakfast. . . ."

He was nodding. "Sarah told me."

Was there anything Sarah hadn't told him? "Maybe I could help you with the carriage house before we go," he suggested.

Images of the beds and bedroom furnishings that filled the carriage house floated across her vision. "No, I don't think so," she said slowly. Then she looked up at him. "Thank you for suggesting the road-race people by the way," she added. "That was very thoughtful. I'm going to call—"

She couldn't continue because in one swift, unexpected movement he had stood up, leaned over her and kissed her full on the mouth, which had the effect not only of cutting off her words but her breath too. Whatever psychological quirk had closed her away from him physically had disappeared now, that was for sure. His mouth on hers felt so right, so wonderfully tender. Even if he hadn't forcibly stopped her from talking she would have forgotten what she was saying. He was arousing her rapidly, his kiss becoming more persistent, deeper, his tongue venturing into her mouth tentatively, then searchingly. Sighing, she raised her hands to clasp his neck and allowed her mouth to respond to his, following his tongue with hers as he withdrew it, teasing, playing, coaxing.

He straightened abruptly, pulling her with him, setting her away from him, his hands on her shoulders. He was smiling, his lids heavy over the glint in his green eyes. "Are we going dancing or am I going to undress you right here in Sarah's sitting parlor?" he asked thickly. "I'm not leaving until the morning. There's plenty of time...."

He was leaving. She must not forget that. The past week had given her a little distance. It would probably be better to keep it there. But she wanted to go dancing with him. And he had been very helpful to her, making suggestions for the hotel, helping with the high tea. Rationalizing again, she conceded.

She looked down at herself. "If we're going dancing, I'll have to change. From what I saw that night...." Better not to mention that night. "From what I've seen, the resort gets pretty dressy."

He nodded. "How about the pink dress you wore before?"

He *would* think of that. Even apart from its extreme décolletage, the dress had too many sexual associations now.

His face was a study when she returned in a full-skirted, white, handkerchief cotton dress that buttoned all the way to its deeply pointed collar. But to her surprise he didn't comment apart from a grave,

"Very pretty." She had been quite sure he would say something caustic about virginal trappings. But then he never had been predictable.

The lobby of the resort was as crowded as ever. She wished briefly she could grab about three of the couples milling around and take them forcibly over to rent the empty rooms at the inn, but in the next breath she realized that such "beautiful people" wouldn't be happy at the Captain Mac, and she wanted only happy guests around her. The inn deserved satisfied people.

There was a six-piece band playing in the nightclub and the dance floor was full. As Dan commandeered a table and ordered cocktails, she looked around for Kelly O'Connor, but didn't see him. His absence was explained a few minutes later when the band went off for a break and the nightclub show began. Dressed in impeccable evening clothes, Kelly appeared on stage and proceeded to host the show in a highly competent way, with a steady stream of witty remarks that soon had the sophisticated audience howling with laughter. It was obvious that the tall bearded man was popular, deservedly so.

"He's good," Petra whispered as they applauded a monologue about Provincetown that made gentle fun of the Puritans who had once lived there. They had objected to bearbaiting, Kelly said in his closing remarks, not because of cruelty to the bear, but because of the pleasure of the onlookers.

Dan nodded. "That's one of the reasons he's lasted this long. We had our suspicions about some of his activities, but he *is* good at what he does and we didn't want to believe the worst."

The show was excellent. There was a husband-and-wife singing team that Petra had seen on television several times, a comedian who was almost as famous and an Irish tenor who persuaded the audience to sing along with him. "I told you a sing-along would be more fun," Dan said softly, touching her arm with one hand.

He didn't raise his hand at once and she looked at it lying on her bare arm, elegant and long, brown against her creamy skin. She remembered the way his hands had felt on her body, touching, stroking, caressing. She raised her eyes to his under eyelids that felt suddenly heavy and heard the quick intake of his breath.

And then there was a final burst of applause and the band returned to play as Kelly announced, "for your dancing and listening pleasure...." Kelly passed their table with a smile and conspiratorial wink at Dan, and then Dan stood up and gave her his hand and they walked together to the dance floor.

If Petra had thought the sudden resumption of music would ease the sexual tension that had returned between them, she soon found that she was mistaken. The tune was slow and dreamy and Dan, as she might have expected, proved to be an excellent dancer, smooth and confident, his hand on her spine giving her unmistakable signals of his intentions whenever he turned or sidestepped. She followed him faultlessly as though she had been dancing with him all of her life.

He held her fairly close, but not too close. There was a sensuousness in the distance. She was far enough away from his body to feel the soft material of his suit pants brush against her leg when they turned, far enough away to be able to look up at his face and see the stern expression on it and wonder exactly what he was thinking. His eyes held hers. She couldn't look away. His right hand was warm at her waist, his other hand now pulling her right hand in close to his chest, raising it so that he could lightly kiss her bunched fingers while his gaze held her spellbound.

"It's a good thing someone invented dancing," he said softly. "If they hadn't I'd have had to invent it myself."

At the intimate note in his voice, her pulse, already beating erratically, began throbbing through her and every nerve end ignited. His tone drowned out the inner voice of caution that was supposed to protect her.

And then Kelly O'Connor returned to the microphone and announced a twist contest. His announcement was greeted by groans from all sides. Petra could understand why—most of the audience had been born after the twist's heyday. The only reason Petra was familiar with it was that one of her sorority sisters had inherited a library of records from a rock-and-roll-mad relative and had insisted on playing them frequently and making all her friends dance madly around the sorority lounge, convinced that this would help them to maintain good figures.

"The prize is a bottle of Veuve Clicquot," Kelly said into the mike. A round of applause greeted that statement, and a few people started drifting reluctantly toward the dance floor. Seeing Dan and Petra still on their feet, Kelly called out, "It seems we have a leader, people. Our own Dan Halliwell and his lovely lady will show us the way."

"Oh no," Petra protested, but she was too late. Dan, evidently not at all averse to public attention, had raised their joined hands in acknowledgment and was already positioning himself in front of her.

The band swung into a spirited rendition of Chubby Checker's best, and Petra and Dan swung just as easily into the ridiculous dance. Evidently impressed by the fun they were having, others joined in, but there was never any real contest. Fifteen minutes later, Dan and Petra walked off with the bottle of champagne and a severe case of exhaustion. By unspoken consent, they headed for the outside door. "Ah, that's better," she exclaimed, breathing deeply, noticing that fog had crept in while they were inside the resort. The lamps around the swimming pool wore halos and nothing beyond was visible. The sound of their footsteps seemed muffled as they walked across the concrete toward the edge of the bluff.

"Where are we going?" Petra asked.

"I thought we'd walk back along the beach, if that's okay with you."

"Sure." She glanced at his face, puzzled by the terse note in his voice. Was he annoyed about something? she wondered as they started down the path to the beach. She'd thought they were just coming out for a breath of air and would return to dance some more. Now it seemed he was through with her for the evening. He didn't speak at all on the way down.

Surely he couldn't still be out of breath from their exertions. No, he was breathing easily, but his profile looked almost grim.

"Is anything wrong?" she asked as they reached the bottom and he fell into step beside her.

"Yes. I've tried to be patient and understanding, but it's no use. I want you."

She stumbled in the deep sand. They were moving beyond the resort's lights now, and there was only a faint silver glimmer from the sand to guide them. His hand shot out to support her elbow and she gave a nervous laugh. "There are times when you are pretty straightforward yourself, Dan Halliwell."

"I don't have time for games now. I'm leaving tomorrow. I don't know when I'll be back. I planned to leave without bothering you again. In fact, I was determined to do so, but I can't. Holding you, watching you dance...." His hand increased its pressure on her elbow and her breath caught in her throat. "There's passion in you when you dance, Petra. I want some of that passion for myself tonight."

"Dan, I don't...."

She was never sure afterward what she'd been about to say. *I don't think it's a good idea? I don't have passion in me? I don't want you to go?*

The retaining wall in front of the resort's share of the bluff was concrete. It felt cold through the thin cotton of her dress when Dan pressed her against it. She shuddered when his hand touched lightly against her breast, but the shuddering was deep and had nothing to do with the cold wall. Dan held her arms to her sides so that she couldn't move away. Not that she seemed to have any intention of moving away.

His mouth met hers in a demanding, intrusive kiss that called up an immediate passionate response. She couldn't get enough of his mouth. Such a beautiful mouth. Her own mouth moving under his, she heard herself making little incoherent sounds that seemed to inflame him even more. His arms came around her, holding her against his body, his hands moving down her spine, across her hips, pulling her to him, moving her against him as he gave her insistent, impossible-to-ignore proof of his desire for her.

"Where?" he murmured against her lips when the kiss ended for lack of breath.

She didn't remember answering him, but she must have done so. She must have told him where the keys to the carriage house were in the kitchen because she remembered his going there while she scooped up two champagne glasses from the cabinet in the sitting parlor. But she didn't ever remember coming up the steps from the beach to the inn, except she did have a thought somewhere about needing to put in stronger lighting. And she did remember stopping to kiss him every few steps, stopping to move her hands over his body while he did the same to hers. And she also remembered with a feeling of embarrassment that by the time they reached the carriage house, his jacket was off, and his tie, and his shirt was pulled halfway out of his pants. Her demure dress was unbuttoned to the waist, and she'd taken off her panty hose somewhere along the way.

Shameless, she thought afterward, but not with

much conviction. Anything that felt so wonderful, so free, had to be all right. When they did get into the carriage house, they struggled hilariously to open the bottle of champagne in the dark, not wanting to put on lights and reveal their whereabouts. A great deal of the champagne spilled before they could catch any in the glasses. In any case they were able to toast each other with it for no more than ten seconds before they literally fell on each other, somehow managing to land huddled together on one of the stored beds as though they'd been picked up by a particularly high wave and deposited on an island that was barely big enough to contain them.

"Do you realize we've started a tradition?" Dan murmured in her ear. "We always drink champagne before making love."

And then there was no more talking for a long time. And there was no gentleness or tenderness in either of them. This was sheer raw need, consuming in its demands. Dan's hands were rough against her breasts, stroking in exquisitely punishing circles, rougher still as they moved lower and his mouth followed them. There was nothing passive about her response either. She was every bit as unrestrained as he. Repeating his name over and over, she moved with him, against him, in opposition to him, arching and stretching like a cat, wanting to touch every part of him, to kiss and taste every part.

It was a mindless time. And yet it was one of great communication. Instinctively each seemed to know when the other was ready for a change of position, a change of technique. Without thinking about it, each knew the source of the other's pleasure at each particular moment and concentrated on it until the time seemed ripe for change.

At last Dan lay still on the sheet-draped mattress, waiting. She understood as clearly as though he'd spoken that this time he was leaving it up to her to initiate the final intimacy. If she wanted to she could stop now. But she didn't want to stop. She hadn't allowed herself to think about what she was doing and she wasn't going to start now. She would think about it tomorrow after Dan left for Boston. Tomorrow.

She couldn't see him in the darkness. She could hear him though. She could hear his ragged breathing, hear the rasp of whiskers as he evidently ran a hand across his face. In the distance she could hear the sound of a gentle surf echoing the beat of her heart and Dan's. And she could smell the foggy air, damp and gray, safely locked out beyond the closed double doors.

"Petra?" Dan asked.

She nodded, then realized he couldn't see her any more than she could see him. "Yes," she whispered, then positioned herself above him. He lifted his hands and held her gently at each side of the waist while slowly, carefully, she welcomed him into her own moist darkness.

For a while the urgent brutal heat of their passion seemed to have lessened. They were gentle with each other, palms barely brushing against heated flesh, mouths meeting in sweet-tasting delicacy, bodies moving in a gentle undulating rhythm. He smelled wonderful to her, a heady mixture of fog-dampened hair and honest sweat. She could even smell herself. The faint odor of the Raffinée she'd applied to her pulse spots had been released by their exertions and wafted around them in the still dark air. All of her senses seemed sharper in the darkness. The comforting humming of the springs in the mattress, the soft sliding sound of body against body, the erratic ragged murmur of their breathing mingled to form an erotic music that was background for the glory of touching him, of sliding her fingers over a firm shoulder, a smooth hip, a muscled thigh. Her mouth tasted the tang of salt on his body, the sweet cleanliness of his breath, and she felt his own similar sensuous enjoyment in the touch of his fingers and mouth on her own warm naked flesh.

And then at last another giant wave caught up with them and lifted them and carried them so high Petra thought her body would break in two at the exact moment that Dan called out her name, and there was a long rushing that came from somewhere in the darkness and entered into her and became part of her and tossed her high into the air again and left her stranded there only as long as it took for Dan to move in her one more time.

Slowly, infinitely slowly, they slid back down the side of the wave together.

CHAPTER TWELVE

IT WAS TWO IN THE MORNING when Dan left her, buoyant with happiness, at the door to her bedroom. Kissing her very gently on the lips, he whispered, "I'll be back as soon as I can, Petra. I don't know exactly when that will be, but I'll be back."

She watched him walk away from her along the hall to his room, his back erect as always though his shirt was far from its pristine self and his slacks had lost their perfect crease. He was carrying his suit jacket over one shoulder, one finger hooked under the collar, his shoes in his other hand. At his door he waggled his free fingers at her, smiled once and was gone.

She took his promise to bed with her without questioning it and slept without dreaming, waking with a smile on her face. But in the clear light of seven in the morning, when she descended to the kitchen dressed in her blue blouse and white pants, hoping to have breakfast with Dan before he left, Sarah told her he had already gone to Boston. "He drove off at five-thirty," she said flatly. "I was barely up. He wouldn't stop for a meal; seemed in a powerful hurry to be gone." She looked a question at Petra.

Somehow Petra managed to smile and said she

knew he'd intended leaving. "Did he take a suitcase?" she asked in a voice that didn't sound as
casual as she'd tried to make it.

Sarah frowned. "He did. Said he wasn't sure when
he'd be back, so not to hold his room if anyone
wanted it."

With an effort Petra managed to shrug. "Probably
no one will, but maybe we'd better have Bonnie clean
it and change the sheets, just in case."

Sarah nodded and bustled out to make the arrangements, though not without darting another
questioning glance at Petra's face.

Standing at the sink, looking out of the casement
window at the cloudless sky, Petra felt all of her confidence and happiness drain away. In their place
came doubts to plague her. Had he left so early to
avoid seeing her? Had the wild lovemaking of the
night before been intended as a farewell perfor-
mance? Would he really return as he'd promised?

She was still standing there when Sarah returned,
her gaze fixed unseeingly on Nathaniel's house across
the street. Catching Sarah, who had busied herself
with coffee making, looking at her oddly, Petra managed to rouse herself enough to say with false brightness, "I was just thinking I'd go to the chamber of
commerce this morning. I think it would be better to
make a personal call rather than to telephone, don't
you agree?"

Sarah nodded. "Are you feeling up to some breakfast first?"

"Well of course I want breakfast," Petra said with
a laugh that sounded false even to her own ears.

Turning away from Sarah's sharp scrutiny, she began
pulling cups and plates out of a cabinet, talking
rapidly about the relative merits of cereal or bacon
and eggs, aware even as she babbled on that she
wasn't fooling Sarah one bit.

A couple of hours later she was discussing the road
race with the pleasant middle-aged lady who had
been so helpful to her before, marveling that she
could sound so enthusiastic when all life and color
had gone out of the day. She had already secured an
agreement from the woman to mention the vitamin-
rich breakfasts Sarah would fix for race visitors.

"Sarah's a kind woman, isn't she?" the woman
said, which at once reminded Petra of Dan saying
much the same thing. She could see him smiling at
her, see the teasing glint in his green eyes.

Feeling her throat close at the reminder, she turned
hastily away to check that there were still enough of
the inn's brochures in the racks that covered one wall
of the room.

There were none of her brochures there.

At first she felt a lift of her spirits, thinking she
might expect a rash of calls, while at the same time
congratulating herself for her foresight in bringing
more pamphlets in. But then it struck her that she'd
had Tony check the number of a few days earlier and
he'd reported only one gone.

"Did my inn suddenly become popular?" she
asked the woman behind the desk, pointing out the
bare space in the rack.

Frowning, the plump pink-and-white woman came
out from behind her desk, put on her glasses and ex-

amined the rack closely. "That's odd," she said slowly. "I tidied these up when we closed yesterday and there were a dozen or more for your inn. I noticed particularly because I really love that photograph on the cover—it reminds me of my grandfather's place in...." Her voice trailed away. "I guess someone must have...." She paused. "That *is* odd, because we haven't had but two people in this morning and they would hardly...."

"Did you notice who those people were?"

"Not particularly. They didn't really talk to me. Said they didn't need any help. A young man and a pretty girl. Yes. He was very tall. My goodness, it does seem that young people are taller than they were when I was a girl. It must be all the vitamins mothers...." She shook her head. "There were a couple of teenage boys in, last night, just before I left. Very brown, good-looking boys. They wanted a map, I remember, and they browsed for a while, but I wouldn't think—though of course nowadays kids do seem to do things just for the mischief of it."

Her mild pretty face brightened. "It's a good thing you brought some more brochures in. Just set them in there, dear, and before you know it, someone will be just as attracted as I am by that photograph. Your visitors are going to love Sarah's breakfasts. I remember her apple-sauce bread—she brought some to a quilting bee once." She sighed gently as she fanned herself with one of Petra's brochures. "My, it's getting to be a hot day, isn't it?"

Somehow Petra stopped herself from making a fuss about the missing brochures. The woman was hardly responsible for watching to see that someone didn't take more than necessary. Their disappearance might just have been someone's idea of mischief, she supposed, though it seemed strange that no other hotel had been affected.

On a hunch, feeling rather foolish, but determined to follow her instincts, Petra drove next to the car-rental agency and discussed a small problem she'd been having with one of the Dodge's door catches. "I'll have to buy a car as soon as I have time," she told the young man who had driven her to Falmouth when she arrived.

After he fixed the door, he recommended a dealer and she thanked him, then blurted out her suspicions about her brochures. "Do you suppose anyone could have taken them deliberately?" she asked. "Would someone do that?"

He looked immediately embarrassed and she put another sudden suspicion into words. "You know something, don't you?"

He nodded slowly, reluctantly. "I've been thinking I should maybe telephone you, Miss McNeil. Someone called me. I don't know who. He said he was representing the Braden Corporation. They're the people who own the Pine Village...."

"I know," Petra said grimly.

"He offered me...well, it amounted to a bribe, I suppose, if I'd talk people out of staying at the Captain Mac." He pulled awkwardly on the brim of his Pennzoil cap and smiled rather sheepishly. "I know you chided me that first day about speaking up about the Pine Village Resort, but I didn't know then, I mean I was just speaking as one young person to another. Because you're so pretty and.... I wouldn't really try to talk anyone into staying away from the Captain Mac.''

''When did this person make the offer?'' she asked sharply.

He thought a minute, then shrugged. ''Three, no— maybe two days ago.''

''Did he give a name?''

''Just the Braden Corporation.''

''Do you know if he called anyone else? Taxi services perhaps?''

''I wouldn't know, Miss McNeil. But believe me, I gave him short shrift. We don't like that kind of goings-on on the Cape. Everyone here is trying to earn an honest living and....''

Mulling over what he'd told her, Petra answered him absentmindedly. It seemed clear to her that all the incidents were connected—the cancellations, the missing brochures. Someone was trying to stop people from staying at her inn. Kelly O'Connor's thin bearded face appeared in her mind. He could have called the car agency right after she'd visited him. Of all the double-dealing, two-faced....

Somehow she managed to reassure the young man that she didn't hold him responsible in any way for her problems, and then she drove slowly back to the inn, trying to decide how she was going to combat this insidious warfare.

Warfare wasn't too strong a word, she decided. Though she couldn't think why O'Connor would want to close her down, especially without the knowledge or blessing of the Braden....

No, she would not believe anyone else was behind

it. Kelly was acting alone; she was certain of that.
And she would have to forget her first impulse,
which was to go to the resort and confront the man
with her knowledge. Dan was already working on
ousting Kelly O'Connor, she reminded herself. She
would report this to Dan and let him handle it. He
would be as outraged as she was, she felt sure. Or almost sure.

It was frustrating to wait. She thought of telephon-
ing Dan in Boston, but decided it would be better to
wait until he returned. He had said he'd be back
soon. She had to believe he had meant it. But how
long was soon? she wondered.

To fill in time, she started emptying out the carriage house, with Tony's help. It was very hot work.
For once there was no breeze and the temperature
had soared. Halfway through the afternoon Petra
called for a lemonade break and changed into a
halter and shorts. Tony was already stripped to
swimming trunks. By five o'clock they'd managed to
get the furniture returned to the bedrooms in spite of
the heat. They hadn't yet finished repairing the last
two rooms, but she threw old sheets over the beds
and dressing tables and other items to protect them,
and went back to vacuum out the carriage house.

How long was "soon"? she wondered again after
dinner when there was still no word from Dan. Tony
had gone out. He was seeing a lot of Seth and Lori,
she realized, and he'd stopped telling her everything
they did together, merely mentioning that they'd
gone out on "the boat" or in "the car." Remembering Sarah's worries and Dan's concern, she thought

perhaps she should talk to him, find out exactly what they were all up to, though she was sure Tony had the sense to stay away from drugs or drinking—they'd discussed the subject many times and he was adamant....

"Why doesn't Dan telephone at least?" she demanded of the empty air in the carriage house. Now that she'd obliterated the scene of their wild lovemaking it seemed impossible to imagine it had really occurred. She didn't even know how she was going to react to Dan when he did return, if he returned. She wasn't at all sure she had any sense left where Dan Halliwell was concerned. Look at her now, waiting for a call, waiting to see him, as though nothing else mattered.

Nothing else did, she admitted to herself at last.

PETRA HAD ALWAYS LOVED PLAYING THE PIANO. In her childhood she had dreamed of becoming a concert pianist, of perhaps accompanying her gloriously talented mother when she grew up. Technically she was good, but she had learned gradually that she didn't have the necessary dedication to practice, and that something was missing from her playing—a certain emotion, a willingness to let herself "lean" on the music and let it take over. By the time she was twenty she had recognized without any great sorrow that her dream had been just that—a dream.

All the same, whenever she felt particularly troubled she retreated to the nearest piano and found comfort in the purity of music, the lack of complication in simply putting her fingers to piano keys and letting some of her feelings loose in sound.

At eight in the evening, she found herself back at the piano in the sitting parlor, where Dan had interrupted her the night before. This time she played Sousa rather than Chopin, trying to hammer out some of the day's confusion on the dignified old spinet.

The previous night had set the seal on her emotions, she realized as she thrashed her way through the "Washington Post March." She loved Dan Halliwell deeply and completely, and when she tried to imagine what the rest of her life would be like if he didn't come back, she could almost feel a cold wind blowing around her in spite of the evening's heat—a wind as cold as though it had crossed Arctic wastes to get to her.

When the telephone rang she flew to answer it, her feet given wings.

"How y'all doing?" a familiar voice asked her.

"Janie? My goodness. What a surprise."

"You don't sound altogether tickled to death."

Petra laughed. "I'm sorry. Of course I'm tickled—delighted. It was just that I was half expecting—" She broke off. "How are you? *Where* are you?"

"Boston. The Logan Hilton, where else?"

"Are you coming out? Janie, I'd love to see you. Can you take a bus out, or shall I come and get you? I could take you back early in the morning. Gosh, it's been such a long time...."

"Whoa there," Janie said, laughing. "I'd love to see you too, but I'm afraid this time I...." There was a silence that lasted a little too long.

"You're not alone," Petra guessed.

"No. Um, Brad and I just wanted to check up on you. Do y'all realize you haven't sent me so much as a postcard?"

"I've been awfully busy. And you haven't written me either." Petra hesitated. "Brad and you?"

"Yes. Well, Brad's not such a bad old boy, Petra. I know you didn't think a whole lot of him when you went out with him, but he's really a nice man under all that playboy exterior. We've both been flying out of Chicago lately, which is why I haven't called before. And well, we got to know each other better, I guess."

"Is he there now?"

"Not right now. He went to get some cigarettes, but he'll be back and.... Hey, listen," she said abruptly, "what have you been doin'? Did you ever get to see the hunk? Halliwell?"

"Yes. I see him."

There was another silence, filled with expectancy at Janie's end. Then she laughed. "I declare, Petra McNeil, you are the most maddening person I've ever known. Come on now, tell me everything."

Petra took a deep breath, and let it out. "I've fallen in love with him, Janie."

"You make it sound like a tragedy."

"I'm not sure it isn't."

"Is he in love with you?"

"I don't know. He hasn't said so. Well, he has, but that was a while ago and he was joking, I think."

"You think?"

"He left for Boston early this morning. I'm not sure when he'll be back."

"But you love him."

"Yes."

"So what are you goin' to do about it?"

"Wait and see what happens, I guess."

Janie's exasperation came clearly across the wire. "Petra McNeil, don't you know yet that you have to get out there and *make* things happen? If I'd just waited around, Brad never would have noticed me right there under his nose. I had to *tell* him it was time we got together."

"Well, we have gotten together."

"I'm not talking about dating," Janie said in the tone of an adult speaking to a child.

"Nor am I."

"Oh? Well then." Janie's sudden gurgling laugh made her so vivid to Petra that she realized abruptly how much she'd missed having her to talk to.

"Are you sure you can't come out here?" she asked. "You could both come and spend the night. It's not all that far and I have plenty of room." That was certainly true, she thought glumly.

"Uh-uh," Janie said. "I'm not exposing Brad to any other woman until I have him firmly under control." She paused. "But I will try to visit y'all real soon. It sounds to me as though you need me to push you in the right direction. Have you told him you love him?"

"Of course not. You know how men are. He'd run all the way back to Boston if I told him that."

"Well, maybe. Sometimes I think men have just gotten a bad press. They can be real old softies, given the chance."

"Brad?" Petra asked disbelievingly.

"Even Brad." Janie sounded defensive. And then she laughed. "Speaking of Brad—he's coming back in now, so I have to go. Listen now," she added in a low voice. "You don't let Dan Halliwell get away from you. I liked him right from the start, remember? You hang on to him, you hear?"

"I'll try," Petra promised.

After she hung up the phone she felt more restless than ever. It was all very well for Janie to talk, but sometimes all anybody could do was to wait and see what happened next.

But she didn't have to sit around moping, she scolded herself. Back she went to the sitting parlor and the piano and the mind-emptying intricacies of the "Washington Post March." *I'm not going to worry about the future,* she told herself with figuratively clenched teeth as she pounded away. Dan had said, "We've started a tradition." Didn't that imply a future? She concluded the march with a loud clash of discordant chords.

This time it wasn't the telephone that summoned her, but the bell in the lobby. Her heart jumped into her throat, but she forced herself not to run again. She walked slowly, hoping that it might be Dan, but steeling herself against disappointment.

The man who stood waiting for her was slender and fresh faced, with blond hair that shone under the lobby's single lamp. He was dressed in the uniform of a Falmouth policeman. His face was very solemn and he didn't respond to her tentative smile. "Miss McNeil?" he asked crisply and she felt her stomach drop not only with disappointment but with anticipation of disaster.

"Is anything wrong, officer?"

"It's about your brother, ma'am. Tony McNeil."

She walked carefully around him and sat down hard on the chair behind Sarah's rolltop desk, her legs suddenly turned to jelly. "There's been an accident? Oh, God, what happened? Is he all right?"

The young man bent over her, his face concerned. "He's fine as far as I know, ma'am. Look, I'm sorry, I didn't mean to frighten you. I didn't even know your brother wasn't here. Can I get you something, call someone...."

She must have lost all her color, she thought. She felt as though she had. "I'm sorry," she said, feeling very foolish. "It's just that my parents—" She broke off whatever she'd been about to blurt out.

"You wanted to see my brother?" she managed to ask. "He's out, I'm afraid, but I'm expecting him home soon. He was pretty tired—he said he wouldn't be late. What...."

She had to stop babbling and let the man talk. He was looking quite flustered.

He gave her a relieved smile when she took a deep breath and nodded to him to speak, and she realized he was a very handsome man, a little reminiscent of David, also blond and blue-eyed. Young though, a year or two younger than herself. "Just a few questions," he said carefully.

She nodded and stood up. "Perhaps we'd better go into the sitting parlor." He followed her and she gestured him to a wing chair, then sat opposite him. "Tony isn't in trouble, is he?" she asked.

He shook his head. "Not that I know of. It's just

that we understand he's been hanging around...associating with some young people that we suspect of...."

"Dan was right then. Good grief. Does that man have to be right every time? I should have thought...." She pulled herself firmly together. "Seth and Lori Cartwright?"

"Yes, ma'am. There are some others. Tucker Channing. Bart Stratford. Cory Winslow."

She shook her head. "I don't know them. I only know Seth and Lori. And I've only met them once. What have they done, Officer...."

"Clement, ma'am. Mitchell Clement." He hesitated. "Seems they might be involved in some vandalism and theft that's been going on in town. For kicks, probably. We've no real proof yet, just a couple of eyewitnesses who are a little confused about their duties under the law."

"They don't want to testify?"

"People rarely do unless they're personally involved, ma'am."

She wished he'd stop calling her ma'am. It made her feel ancient. "You surely don't think Tony's involved?"

"I just want to talk to him, ask him if he knows...."

"I'm sure he'll tell you whatever he does know. He's never been involved in anything criminal, not even remotely. And he's very careful of other people's property. Besides," she added, suddenly sitting forward, "your problems started before Tony and I even came here. I heard about them my first day on the Cape. Some automobiles, and then the historical house across the street, Mr. Jenkins's house...are they part of this?''

"It's possible, miss." He must have read her mind. He'd stopped calling her ma'am.

He was looking uncomfortable again. No wonder. She'd sounded like every boy's doting mother, convinced her child could do no harm. But Tony....

"Tony's a very unusual boy," she told him. "He's something of a brain. He's going to be a junior in college in September and he's only sixteen. He's mad about computers." What was she doing, giving character references?

She took a deep breath. "I'm sorry, Officer... Clement. I'm a bit distracted today. And it was such a shock...would you like to wait until Tony comes home and...."

"If I could check a couple of dates with you? You understand you are not required to answer any questions. But if you would cooperate?"

"Of course I will. And Tony will too. We have nothing to hide." Lord, she sounded like a TV drama. "What dates?"

"Well, last night for one. And a week or so ago." He pulled a notebook out of a pocket and consulted it. "Wednesday the tenth."

"Tony was here then. No, wait a minute, he was out for a while but he came home early. By eight o'clock at the latest. Last night he was out with Seth and Lori. I don't...." She paused and hoped she wasn't blushing. "I wasn't here when he came home.

I went out for a while myself, dancing, at the resort next door...." Why was she telling him that?

He smiled. "They get some good bands I hear. I haven't been to any of the dances myself, but I've heard the entertainment is pretty good."

He was making an effort to put her at ease. She must have blushed. Did he think she looked guilty? Impossible not to feel guilty when a policeman came to your home. The most upright citizen felt a flash of worry over what he might have done when....

"I could ask Sarah—my housekeeper. She'd probably know what time he came in."

The notebook had been replaced in his pocket and he was standing up. "That won't be necessary, miss." He gazed at her very earnestly, looking absurdly young to be wearing his uniform. "This is just a friendly visit, miss. I don't like to see kids get into trouble, and if your brother is...associating with these kids, it might be well to—well, I'd like to talk to him anyway. Perhaps I can wait on the porch outside. I don't want to keep you from anything."

"That's okay. You aren't stopping me from...." There was a glimmer of amusement in his eyes now, and she suddenly realized he must have heard her pounding away on the piano when he came in. "Please sit down," she said peremptorily, and he obeyed at once. "I'm sure Tony will be home soon and this can all be cleared up. Can I get you anything? Some coffee, perhaps?"

"Thank you, no."

There was an awkward silence. Petra had no idea how to fill it. The young policeman was looking at her now with an expression she recognized. Interest. He was interested in her as a person, a woman, not just the sister of a possible delinquent. She glanced down at herself, remembering with dismay that she was still wearing her very brief shorts and halter top. Not a whole lot of her was covered. Dammit, no. She wasn't going to blush again. "Have you lived here long?" she found herself asking idiotically, and then was relieved to hear the front door open and close and the sound of Tony's sneaker-clad feet on the planked wooden floor of the hall. "Tony," she called. "Come in here, would you?"

He leaned around the doorjamb. "I need sustenance, Petra," he announced. "I'm about to starve to death. Do you realize I haven't eaten in two—" He broke off as he caught sight of the policeman, who had just risen to his feet.

To Petra's dismay, he looked suddenly and unmistakably guilty. A dark flush mounted to his cheeks and as he unwound himself from the doorway, he pulled off his glasses and started polishing them on the tail of his open khaki cotton shirt after pulling it out of his cutoffs—a sure sign that he wanted time to recover composure. She'd watched him do the same thing countless times when he wanted to delay answering some question she'd asked him. Her heart sank.

"Officer Clement wants to ask you some questions about Seth and Lori and their friends," she managed to say. "I've assured him that you'll tell him anything he wants to know."

Slowly Tony put his glasses on and advanced into

the room, squaring his shoulders. Petra's heart began
to thud in her ears. She knew her brother better than
anyone in the world. She knew when he felt uncomfortable or uneasy or wary. And he was all three as he
faced the policeman. "I don't know anything," he
said carefully. "Seth and Lori are my friends. They
haven't done anything wrong."

"I didn't say they had," Clement answered.

Petra's stomach churned. The young policeman's
face was still friendly, but he was watching Tony's
face carefully and there had been marked suspicion
in his voice.

He stayed for an hour, talking to Tony, asking
questions about the activities he'd shared with his
friends. Tony's answers came promptly, unequivo-
cally. They had driven to Sandwich a couple of times
to a teenage dance club. They'd gone swimming at
Hyannis Port, taken in a couple of movies, gone out
on Seth's father's boat. That was all.

He was holding something back, Petra felt sure. A
couple of times he pulled at his tangled mass of dark
curls, something he did when he was not quite telling
the truth. He cleaned his glasses twice. And he didn't
want to sit down even after Mitchell Clement invited
him to. He kept roaming around the room, apparently unable to stay still.

Clement seemed satisfied with his answers. Pa-
tiently he explained to Tony that they'd had a report
that four boys and a girl had been seen in the vicinity
of at least four of the incidents just before there was
any criminal activity. The five had matched the descriptions of Seth and his friends. Five, Petra noted

thankfully. If the police had descriptions, no one would have been able to miss tall, gangling Tony with his curly mop of hair and thick glasses. If the kids were involved, then obviously Tony had not been with them. Which she had known all along, of course.

All the same, Tony wasn't telling the whole truth, she was certain. And as soon as Clement left, after telling Tony to be sure to call him if he thought of anything to add to his statements, she pounced on her brother. "So help me, Tony, if you lied to that man, I'll swat you, big as you are. You didn't tell him everything, did you?"

Tony sighed dramatically. "Isn't one inquisition enough, Petra? I told him everything I know."

"Then why won't you look at me? You haven't once looked at me since you came in. I want you to sit down here and tell me the truth about those kids."

"They aren't 'those kids.' They're my friends."

His mouth had set in an unfamiliar straight line, and Petra realized with a shock that he wasn't going to tell her anything either. And short of hooking him up to a lie detector, she had no idea how to go about getting the truth out of him. It had always been a relatively easy task. He'd never dissembled seriously—only in small ways, the kind of white lies all kids tell to stay out of trouble with adults. "Tony," she started again.

He shook his head. "I really am tired, Pet. Let's talk about it tomorrow, okay? All that furniture moving...."

The "Pet" softened her. He had worked very hard

today. He always worked hard. And he did look tired. Or was that worry rather than fatigue on his face?

She felt suddenly unutterably weary herself. It had been an eventful day, after a night of little sleep. Heat rose to her face as she remembered again where she had been during the night and with whom. No, she didn't want to think about that. If she had been home when Tony came back, she'd have known if....

"Maybe you're right," she said, capitulating so suddenly that Tony was taken off guard and looked immensely relieved, which of course ignited all her suspicions again. "Don't leave the inn before we've had a chance to talk, okay?"

"Okay." He hugged her before going out the door and she told herself he couldn't possibly have done anything wrong. Not Tony. Not possibly.

BUT IN THE MORNING, HE WAS GONE. "He made a phone call and someone came and picked him up— that Cartwright boy and his friends," Sarah informed her. "He didn't say where he was going. Is anything wrong, lass?"

Petra started to speak, then changed her mind and shook her head. "I wanted him to do something for me," was all she said.

She was furious. With Tony most of all, but also with herself for letting him off so easily the night before. She should have insisted on thrashing the matter out there and then. And the way she felt now, "thrashing" was the operative word.

The telephone rang in the lobby. Sarah answered it and Petra started into the kitchen, intending to get some coffee inside her before deciding what to do next. A moment later, Sarah followed her into the kitchen, her face as pale as the apron she wore tied tightly around her sturdy waist. ''Tony's been arrested,'' she said in a voice that had lost all life.

There followed one of the most confusing hours of Petra's life. She talked on the telephone with the police station, found out to her relief that Tony hadn't been charged with any crime. He'd been picked up driving out of town with the other kids, but the police had no evidence to hold him. So far all he was guilty of was refusing to talk. ''You can come and get him,'' the police sergeant told her. ''But he'll be called as a witness and if he refuses to testify. . . .''

The implied threat lent wings to Petra's feet. As soon as she hung up the telephone, she ran upstairs to change out of her overalls into something more suitable. Though what could qualify as suitable wear for getting your brother released from jail she had no idea. For a while, still stunned, she stared in confusion at the rack of clothing in her bedroom armoire. Finally she decided on a plain wheat-colored shift, put on makeup with shaking hands, brushed her dark curls into some semblance of order and started down the stairs.

Dan Halliwell stood in the lobby with his arms around Sarah. He was still wearing his gray suit, though it had obviously been pressed.

Petra didn't think she'd ever been so glad to see anyone in her life. So much for being an independent woman, she thought with some small part of her mind as she hesitated on the stairs and waited for Dan to see her. It suddenly seemed important that she wait for him to see her, rather than run down to him as she was tempted to. He was comforting Sarah very efficiently, listening to her pour out the story of Tony's troubles, not saying anything until she was done. He didn't offer any platitudes at all, but simply said "I'll see what I can do." Then he looked up and saw Petra.

He must have spent a rough day in Boston yesterday, she thought. He didn't look as though he'd had much sleep. But there was such warmth in his face as he looked at her. And she felt an answering warmth flood her entire body, reassuring her that everything, at least between the two of them, was going to be all right.

But then on the way into Falmouth, when he'd insisted on driving her, he told her bluntly, without any preparation, that he'd seen his ex-wife. "I've got to talk to you about her," he said in a tired voice. "But now's not the time." He smiled wearily. "Actually, I've a hell of a lot to tell you. For one thing, Kelly's been sabotaging your business and...."

"I knew it had to be him," she exclaimed. "The brochures were missing and the man at the car-rental agency told me...how did you know?"

"I did some checking. When you mentioned the canceled reservations, I wondered. I called a travel agent I know and put him on the job of calling around. He came up with at least five agencies that had been asked to talk people out of staying at the

Captain McNeil Inn.'' He paused, hunching forward over the steering wheel. ''You don't have to worry about Kelly, Petra. As of today, he's out. As soon as we get this thing with Tony cleared up, I'm going to personally escort him off the premises of the Pine Village Resort.''

''You look tired, Dan,'' she said sympathetically. ''We shouldn't have unloaded all this on you when you....''

''Nonsense,'' he interrupted. ''I'm as concerned as you about Tony.'' He gave her a sidelong glance that almost made her bristle—it was so like the loaded glances he'd given her from time to time ever since she'd met him. ''I did tell you I didn't trust those kids,'' he said mildly. ''You wouldn't listen.''

''I suppose I'm supposed to be all chastened and contrite now,'' she said with a flare of temper, forgetting temporarily how glad she'd been to see him.

His grin banished the tiredness from his face. ''One thing I cannot imagine,'' he drawled, his Bostonian accent never so apparent, ''is a contrite and chastened Petra McNeil.'' One hand reached to clasp hers, which were clenched together in her lap. ''And it's not something I want to see,'' he added. ''I like you just the way you are, full of spirit and bad temper and ready to defend your independence to the death.''

She could feel her hands relaxing under his grip, even while her mind dolefully pondered the word ''like.'' Nothing was changed really, she supposed. Dan would be leaving for sure now, once Kelly O'Connor was evicted from the resort. And all she'd have left were her ''golden memories.''

She'd worry about that tomorrow, she decided. She had more than enough on her mind today. "You do look awfully tired, Dan," she said again. "Did your wife. . . ."

"I had a big 'discussion' with my father," he said, his face grim. "We went at it half the night. He wants to send me off to Spain right away. He even wanted to send someone else to deal with O'Connor. It seems our hotel in Madrid—" He broke off and she saw that they'd arrived at the police station.

"We'll talk later," he said as he stopped the car. He let go of her hands and lifted her chin so that he could kiss her lightly. It was a pleasant kiss, a friendly kiss, nothing more.

What did she expect? she scolded herself as she preceded him into the police station. He'd seen his ex-wife, the woman he'd admitted to loving "helplessly," had a fight with his father, come back to fire Kelly O'Connor, only to be greeted by the problem of young Tony McNeil. Was he supposed to smother her with kisses then, tell her he'd missed her, he'd never leave her again, assure her that he didn't want to leave her. . .he loved her, of course he loved her.

Yes, she thought miserably, that was exactly what she wanted him to do.

CHAPTER THIRTEEN

THE OTHER BOYS and Lori had all been released into their parents' custody before Petra and Dan arrived. Tony was alone, upset, frightened and closemouthed. No matter how Petra harangued him he insisted on saying, "We were just going for a drive to Hyannis. We weren't doing anything but driving along."

"You must have warned them," Petra said furiously. "How could you, Tony, after I'd specifically told you to stay home until we had a chance to talk? How do you think I felt when...."

His mouth was setting in a way it hadn't done since he was four years old. They were standing outside the police station, Tony looking like a soldier who expected to be shot for desertion of his post, Dan watching both of them with sympathy in his eyes. Sympathy for which one of them, Petra wondered.

"You did warn them, didn't you?" she insisted.

Tony shrugged. "I told them the policeman came to see me, yes," he admitted. "Seth said not to worry, we'd go see his father in Hyannis and he'd set everything straight."

Petra pounced. "Then they *are* guilty."

Tony's mouth closed tight again and she suddenly wanted to shake him, tall as he was. "Someone of your intelligence,'' she began, but Dan interrupted.

"Maybe we should get off the street," he suggested mildly.

Petra felt herself flushing. People were passing, looking at the three of them curiously. She felt foolish, but all the same.... "Did you go with them on any of their...escapades?" she demanded as soon as they were in the car.

"There weren't any escapades," Tony said. "I told you and I told that policeman, we went to a couple of movies, and to a...."

"Tony!"

He wouldn't budge. No matter how Petra questioned him and scolded him, he refused to admit to any knowledge of anything. But she was determined not to let up on him until he told her the truth.

"I have an idea," Dan interposed after some time. "Why don't I take Tony with me to the resort? He can amuse himself in the video-game room while I deal with our friend O'Connor. Then perhaps he'd like to go with me to Hyannis." He turned to Tony, smiling. "I'm going to look at a Windsurfer, Tony. Have you ever tried wind surfing? It's terrific."

Tony's face had lit up the moment Dan mentioned video games, for which he had a passion. Now he was positively glowing. "I've seen Windsurfers out at Nobska Point," he exclaimed. "I'd love to...."

"Have you lost your mind, Dan?" Petra demanded from the back seat. "Don't you realize how serious this is? How can you justify offering to entertain him after the way he's behaved? Can't you see that...."

"Petra, dear, simmer down."

"Don't patronize me, Dan Halliwell."

They had arrived at the inn. Dan got out of the car, assisted Petra out, told Tony to stay put, then led her a few steps away. "Listen to me, love," he said softly, putting a hand on each of her shoulders. "You aren't going to get anywhere like this. The boy's scared to death. Can't you see that?"

"Of course I can see it. And he should be scared to death. He's going to be charged as an accessory if he doesn't...."

"He knows that."

He had no right telling her how to treat Tony. "I've almost raised that boy since he was five years old," she said angrily.

"And he sees you as an authority figure, even though he loves you. Where's your perspective, Petra? He needs some space. He needs to be left alone for a while to think things through. I think he might open up to me. He's afraid of you."

"He is not."

"Of your opinion of him, I mean." He gave her a little shake. "Listen to me. It's surely worth a try, isn't it?"

She stared up at him. He was still infuriatingly calm, but she could read concern on his face. He cared about Tony, that was obvious, and maybe Tony would talk to him. He had a lot of respect for Dan.

She shook her head wearily. "I don't know, Dan," she said. "I can't bear the thought of Tony getting into trouble, and you have other things to do anyway. Kelly...."

His face set in grim lines. "I can handle Kelly in very short order." He raised his eyebrows. "What do you say?"

She sighed. "Well, maybe, as long as you don't let him out of your sight. Maybe I should tell him...." Half turned away, ready to go back to the car, she was stopped by Dan's hand on her arm.

"Let me try first, okay?" he said.

She chewed her lower lip, trying to decide, and he smiled. "Don't worry, love. Once we have everything straightened out we can order up a bottle of champagne and celebrate." His eyes were suddenly very green in the sunlight.

Petra looked up at him helplessly. "Oh, Dan. I can't even think of champagne right now."

His hand squeezed her arm gently and in spite of her declaration of a moment before, she found herself thinking of what might follow the champagne he'd promised her. What would they be celebrating this time? she wondered despairingly. Dan's departure? "Okay," she said, giving in, and at once he released her and returned to the car.

Had she done the right thing? she wondered as she walked listlessly back into the inn. Should she have insisted? No, Dan had been right as usual. She hadn't been getting anywhere with Tony.

THE TWO OF THEM WERE GONE a long time. Petra went through the motions of cleaning out the carriage house and getting it ready for a coat of paint, but her heart wasn't in her work. It suddenly didn't seem to matter if the inn was full or not. Was she losing interest in the inn, she wondered, the way she'd lost interest in every other job she'd had?

To distract herself from worrying about Tony she joined her guests for high tea and was depressed anew by the small number of people. She'd even welcome young Mrs. Bentley back, she thought afterward—and Mr. Lyman, even if he did eat more than his fair share of scones.

The inn still did matter, she conceded as she wandered disconsolately around the lobby, picking up small ornaments, setting them down. Nathaniel was in the kitchen with Sarah. He'd been working all day with Carter on the siding, and she'd insisted he have dinner before going home. She was supposed to join them, but she didn't feel up to eating. And anyway, she could hear from the tones of their voices that they were quarreling again. She'd told Nathaniel what had happened and he'd said gruffly that the boy ought to be keelhauled, then kept on bread and water for a couple of days. He'd been teasing her, she knew, trying to cheer her, but Sarah had taken him seriously and jumped vigorously to Tony's defense.

Petra was sitting on the veranda glider, listlessly watching the lowering sky and trying to decide if it was going to rain when Dan's car drove up. She recognized the sound of its engine; she'd been listening for it all day. Tony came up the steps eagerly, looking as carefree as though he'd spent the day sailing. "Gosh Petra, you should see the Windsurfer Dan bought," he exclaimed. "It's really a beauty. He's going to teach me how...."

Petra was on her feet, hands on the hips of the

wheat-colored dress she'd changed back into for high tea. "Is that all you have to tell me?" she interrupted. "I thought you were supposed to...."

He gave her an awkward hug, totally disregarding her anger. "It's okay, Pet," he said. "I've been to the police station and told them everything."

Relief flooded her, followed by worry. "What exactly was everything?"

"He didn't do anything wrong, Petra," Dan said, coming up the steps behind Tony.

She glared at him. "Let me be the judge of that." She turned back to Tony. "Well?"

He at least had the grace to blush. "Dan's right. I didn't do anything. But I did...." He took a deep breath and squared his shoulders manfully. "I knew they were all up to something. They dropped some hints about how dull it was except when they could shake people up a bit. They joked about stuff they'd 'acquired,' said it wasn't really stealing if you didn't do anything with it. It was just for fun, they said."

"You knew about this on Nantucket, didn't you? You were very subdued coming home. I knew something was going on."

He nodded, his eyes downcast behind the thick glasses. He looked so woebegone, so contrite, that Petra wanted to reach out and hug him, but she steeled herself to continue. "You might as well tell me all of it," she ordered.

For once Dan didn't interfere. He walked around her, sat down on the glider and let her interrogate her brother in her own way. And gradually, with much hesitation and shamefaced glances of apology, the story came out.

Tony had known the group was up to no good on Nantucket. The cottage had not belonged to Tucker Channing's grandmother, "though it was covered with roses," he said as though that made any difference.

Petra heard a strange sound coming from Dan and could have sworn he was laughing, but when she darted a glance at him, his face had already assumed a stern expression. Only a faint smile hovering around the corners of his mouth gave him away.

The cottage was abandoned, it seemed, and the group had appropriated it as their "headquarters," where they planned their "adventures." They had indeed vandalized and stolen in several locations, including Nathaniel's house. Tony had started to lecture them on the difference between right and wrong, but they'd immediately become cool to him and he'd backed off. "Because," he said, "it was the first time kids my own age seemed to like me, and I *did* like Lori a whole lot, though of course I couldn't go along with what she was doing."

He'd refused to get involved and they'd accepted that, but his conscience had troubled him terribly, and he'd started leaving them as soon as they talked about anything that sounded questionable. "I know I was wrong to ignore what they were doing," he said earnestly to Petra. "But I thought if I didn't know for sure what they were up to, then I could at least still see Lori."

A look of intense pain crossed his thin face and

Petra's heart went out to him. He'd really suffered over this, obviously.

"I told the truth about what happened this morning," he said. "I did tell those guys about the policeman, and Seth came to get me and we were going to Hyannis."

He looked down and scuffed the boards on the porch with one sneaker. "They were laughing," he said furiously. "Lori as much as any of the others. They thought it was funny the police had finally caught on. They figured nothing would happen to them because their parents are all important people. I was mad, but they just laughed at me too, and then they threatened me with all kinds of stuff if I told, and I, well, I wasn't scared, but I didn't want you to know what a fool I'd been, so I promised I wouldn't tell."

"And kept your promise," Petra said with exasperation clear in her voice.

"I'm sorry, Petra. It seemed the proper thing to do. But then Dan made me see that if I didn't tell on them they'd keep committing crimes, maybe looking for bigger and better kicks until they got into really big trouble. I could see the truth of that. So I went to the police station.

"Dan was great," he added, with a shy smile in Dan's direction. "He helped me explain why I hadn't told the truth."

He sighed. "I'm dreading having to go to court," he said miserably.

She pulled him close so that she could hug him. "You did the right thing, Tony," she said. "I'm proud of you. But if you ever...."

"I won't," he said, straightening, then grinned, looking like his old self for the first time since he'd come home to find Officer Clement in the sitting parlor. "Now, could I go get something to eat? I'm starved."

Petra nodded. "And for goodness' sake, try to establish peace between Nathaniel and Sarah," she called after him as he headed for the front door. "I'm worn out with their squabbling."

"More trouble?" Dan asked sympathetically as the door slammed behind Tony.

She sank down on the cushioned glider next to him and leaned back. "Nothing too important." She turned her head to the side and smiled ruefully at him. "I'm grateful, Dan. I'm sorry I was—" she grinned "—prickly."

He touched one finger lightly to her mouth, starting up some interesting sensations she'd have thought she was too weary to feel. But almost immediately his own smile faded and his hand dropped away. "Kelly's gone," he told her. "It wasn't pleasant." His mouth curved in a grimace of distaste. "He really couldn't understand that he'd done anything so wrong," he said in an amazed voice. " 'You have to give people what they want,' he kept insisting. How on earth can we expect our kids to know right from wrong when we raise them in such a moral climate?"

He shook his head and ran one hand through his hair. "I persuaded Kelly to admit to interfering in your affairs," he said. "Seems he sent a couple of his beach boys to pick up your brochures. Then he called various agencies himself, in the name of the Braden Corporation...." His voice was indignant now.

After a moment he sighed. "I knew he was guilty of trying to sabotage your efforts, but I wanted to know why. I finally got out of him that he suspected I was here to look into his activities, so he got the bright idea that if he could somehow put you out of business and acquire the extra land for the corporation, my father would forgive him what he called his 'indiscretions.'"

A look of extreme satisfaction crossed his face. "I told him I'd try to influence my father if he handed over the film he had of Wendy. He fell for it. It didn't occur to him that I hadn't said which way I'd use my influence. I wouldn't have thought he'd be so stupid." He paused, then laughed in a way that sent a small shiver along Petra's spine. Again she'd been proven right in her first estimation of him. He could be ruthless when necessary.

He reached over and picked up her hand and held it in his own. "I'm sorry you got embroiled in this mess with Kelly, Petra. I'm just glad I was able to put a stop to it."

"What happens now?" she asked tentatively, afraid to return the pressure of his hand until she knew exactly where she stood.

He sighed again. "I don't really know. I'm supposed to call my father—" he glanced at his wristwatch "—in about ten minutes—to report how it went. I expect we'll go on from there to continue our argument about Spain." He looked at her directly. "I may have to go, Petra," he said.

She swallowed. What was she supposed to say to that? "You were going to tell me about your wife," she said carefully.

Another sigh. "It's a long story. Let's leave that for another time, shall we?" To her dismay, he released her hand and stood up. "I really do have to go make that telephone call. My father's a stickler for punctuality." He looked down at her. She hadn't moved. "I should be through in an hour or so, I hope," he said. "How would it be if I brought our champagne here and. . . ."

"I don't think that would be such a good idea, Dan," she said, then paused to wonder why her mind had immediately rejected the suggestion. She knew what would follow the champagne, of course. The warmth in his green eyes was evident even through his weariness. And then what? He'd probably leave tomorrow. He'd made no declarations. She hadn't expected him to. She didn't expect him to. No commitments, he'd said. And that had been fine with her. It wasn't his fault that she'd foolishly fallen in love with him. The trouble was, she didn't think she could allow him to make love to her again without letting him know how she felt. She knew herself well. She was quite likely to blurt out, "I love you," in the heat of the moment, and she didn't want to see him look trapped, or evasive.

She remembered suddenly what she'd told Janie that night in the Hilton: "However it ends you get involved in scenes and arguments and recriminations." She couldn't bear to go through all that again, especially not with Dan. If they could at least part as friends, maybe some time he'd come back. He'd bought a Windsurfer and promised to teach Tony. He must plan on coming back. When he did return, maybe she'd be better equipped emotionally to handle their relationship. *I'll think about it tomorrow,* she told herself as she had told herself so many times before, only this time she didn't feel like laughing.

"I'm really very tired, Dan," she said. "I worried so all day about Tony and...."

"I'm sorry about that," he said. "It took me a while to get him to start talking. And then I didn't want to call you or bring him here first before going to the police station. I was afraid he might change his mind."

"I understand. I wasn't blaming you. I'm grateful to you. But I'm not in the mood for champagne. Some other time, perhaps."

Eyes narrowed, he stared at her for a long moment. Then he nodded shortly. "Perhaps you're right. I'll see you later."

Another second and he was gone.

She sat perfectly still for a long time, watching the sun's inevitable path downward toward the water, watching the gathering rain clouds flare with orange light, fading to gray. She was there when Nathaniel came out to say good-night to her. He didn't seem inclined to linger, and she didn't feel like facing the questions she could see in his eyes. Probably Tony had told him and Sarah she was out there with Dan— no doubt that was why neither of them had come out to insist she eat dinner with them.

But now that she thought about it, she was hungry. Relieved to have something simple to do, she went inside to see if Sarah had kept anything hot for her.

AN HOUR LATER she was in the sitting parlor, listlessly thumbing through a copy of *Cape Cod Life*, wondering if she had the energy for some piano playing. Tony had gone up to his computer. Machines he could understand, he'd told Petra with a shadowed grin. He'd added, surprisingly, that Dan had promised him a part-time job at the resort. The beach boys, Dan had told him, earned fabulous tips just for setting up cushions and umbrellas. He could work outdoors a couple of hours a day, still help Petra—maybe even find new friends, whom he would "choose more discriminatingly," he'd added as he left the room.

The bell rang in the lobby. Petra waited for Sarah to answer it and then remembered she'd gone out to a card party, to "take her mind off that stupid old man," she'd offered as a parting shot.

Wearily, Petra rose to her feet, then forced a smile to her face. Maybe now that Kelly was out of the picture she'd managed to get a new guest.

To her surprise and alarm, Officer Mitchell Clement stood in the lobby, shrugging out of a drenched raincoat. She hadn't even realized the threatened rain had arrived. For a moment she almost stopped breathing, wondering if he'd come to tell her more evidence had surfaced and he had to take Tony in again, but then she saw he wasn't wearing a uniform under his raincoat. He was dressed in an open-necked sport shirt and well-pressed gray slacks. His smile was warm. "I was hoping you'd be home," he said. "Don't worry," he added as she opened her mouth to question him, "I'm not on duty."

He looked suddenly shy and very appealing. "There's a new show at the Hyannis Melody Tent," he went on. "Phyllis Diller and Anthony Newley. I was going to ask if you'd like to come and see it with me. It's supposed to be very good. But with this weather, I guess it's not a great idea."

Petra smiled, but shook her head. "Can I take a rain check?" she asked, then grimaced. "Sorry. I can't stand people who make puns. That one was unintentional. But I am rather tired anyway. Could I offer you some coffee perhaps, or something stronger as you're not on duty?"

"I'd love a beer," he said with alacrity. "Rain always makes me thirsty."

She took his raincoat and hung it on the coatrack behind the desk. "Go on into the sitting parlor," she suggested. "I'll see what I can find. A beer sounds good to me too."

When she returned with two foaming glasses, he sprang to his feet. "Thank you, Miss McNeil," he said gratefully.

"Petra, when you're not on duty," she said with a laugh.

"Petra." He hesitated, then smiled ingenuously. "My friends call me Mitch."

"Mitch it is then." She sat down opposite him, not minding at all the frank admiration in his eyes. He was such a nice young man. And uncomplicated, a refreshing change from Dan Halliwell. She didn't have to wonder what he was thinking all the time. It was obvious what he was thinking. His pleased smile reminded her of Tony's when he'd worked out a new program for his computer. He obviously felt he'd accomplished what he'd set out to do. He was safely ensconced in her sitting room, alone with her. "Tony's definitely not in any trouble now, is he?" she asked as a distraction.

He grinned easily. "Not at all. I was pleased to hear he came in and volunteered the information. I had an idea he knew what his friends had been up to, but I know how the code goes. You just don't nark on a friend." He grinned. "I have three brothers, all younger than me. We fight all the time, but when anything goes wrong we stick together."

He looked around him. "I was in here when Will McNeil was alive," he told her. "About a year ago, I guess. He'd gotten upset about people driving too fast on the road back of the inn. He sure was a crusty old guy. He'd been out shaking his fist at drivers, yelling at them that he was going to have the law on them. It seemed a good idea to drop in and see him."

Petra smiled. It felt good to smile, she thought. And it was good to sit there on a rainy evening talking to this nice young man about her uncle and the reputation he'd enjoyed in town. "Everyone liked him," Mitch assured her, "but it wasn't easy to let him know it. He wasn't a man you could get close to."

He went on to make a comment about Sarah, who it seemed was this very night playing cards with one of his aunts.

"Does everybody know everybody around here?" Petra asked, laughing.

"This is really a small community," he said earnestly. "You wait until winter—you'll find out. It's a whole different place in the winter when the tourists go."

When the tourists go. When Dan goes. Petra shook her head. "Tell me about it," she said. And he did, entertaining her with tales of hikes on windswept beaches and dances for the residents rather than visitors. "Maybe we can go dancing sometime?" he suggested and Petra answered, "Maybe we can," and saw him smile.

And it struck her then that she was a resident, not a visitor, and she would be here after all the tourists left and she would become part of Cape Cod life. If Dan Halliwell hadn't come into her life, she could have looked forward to that without reservation, but now. . . . No, it didn't make any difference. She was going to finish the work she had started, and next year the inn would hum with new life and vigor. She wasn't at all disenchanted with hotel work, she realized. She enjoyed making people comfortable, thinking up ways to make their vacations enjoyable. She liked becoming part of their lives, even for a short time, wondering about them, relating to them. Perhaps she'd finally found her true vocation.

"By next year I'll be an old hand at the hotel business," she told Mitch, who nodded agreement.

"I spent a vacation here when I was ten," she told him. "I thought it was the most fabulous place on earth. It seemed as though the sun shone all the time, and all I did was play in the water and build sand castles and ride a bicycle. Did you grow up here?"

He nodded, then launched into a series of hilarious

stories about himself and his three brothers and the great times they'd always had in an old wooden boat on Vineyard Sound. Then Petra talked about Tony and his fascination with computers and her own various careers before this one.

He and Petra each had another beer and then he asked her to play the piano. His mother had played, he told her, but she'd died seven years ago from the complications of an unplanned pregnancy. She felt an identify with him then, and sympathy, but her feelings were similar to those she felt toward Tony. She could never, she realized with a small measure of regret, take a nice young man like this seriously. He would always seem like a kid brother to her. I stopped feeling cousinly, Dan had said. *Dan.*

"What would you like me to play?" she asked, determinedly banishing thoughts of Dan.

"Well—not 'Washington Post March,'" he said with a laugh, and she made a face at him and sat down to play a selection of old familiar ballads. After a while, he joined her at the piano, standing alongside her and singing softly in a pleasant but slightly off-key voice.

And then he asked if she knew "Heart and Soul," and she grinned and nodded and he hunched down next to her and banged out the chords with his left hand while she played the melody with her right. They both made a lot of mistakes and they got noisier and noisier until she was sure that if Sarah had been home, she'd have come in demanding to know what all the "ructions" were about. The few guests were out for the evening so she didn't have to worry about them, and Tony would be lost in contemplation of his computer screen.

"How about this one?" she asked Mitch and launched into "Chopsticks."

Laughing, he joined her. "This is the extent of my repertoire," he announced.

She heard the front door open and close as they banged out the last few notes and sat laughing like a pair of children. She glanced around guiltily, expecting Sarah, but it was Dan who had walked in and he didn't look at all amused to see her sitting there with a grin on her face and Mitch Clement hunkered down beside her. Mitch turned around too and almost lost his balance. "Hi," he said with an embarrassed smile as he straightened up.

Dan nodded curtly, then glanced at Petra, eyebrows raised. It must still be raining, she thought irrelevantly. Dan's hair was damp, his suit jacket spattered with raindrops.

She became aware that both men were waiting for her to speak. "This—this is Officer Clement," she stammered. "Mitchell Clement. He came to tell me about Tony last night and...."

"I see." Dan shook hands with the young man, giving his own name, which brought an immediate look of respect to the fresh young face. Petra could almost see him standing at attention.

There was an awkward silence. Then Mitch looked from Dan to Petra and back again and said, "I guess I'd better be going. Thanks for the beer," he added to Petra. "I guess I'll be, well...." He glanced again at Dan, then back to Petra. "May I call you?"

"Of course," Petra said warmly. "I want you to get to know Tony better. I know he gave you some trouble, but I'm sure you'll like him when you get to know him."

"I could maybe take him over to meet my brothers. I've got one about his age who's a nut about computers too."

"That would be great."

She walked him to the door, then returned to find Dan still looking annoyed. His mouth was curled into the supercilious smile she hated. "I see you weren't too tired after all," he said frostily.

"He just came by to—we were talking about Cape Cod and my Uncle Will and...." Why was she stumbling through an explanation? He looked terribly tired now, even more so than before. "Can I get you something?" she asked.

He shook his head. "I brought my own bottle." He held up a napkin-wrapped bottle of champagne she hadn't even realized he was holding. "I thought perhaps I could persuade you to change your mind."

Before she could respond, he set the bottle down on a table and looked at her. "I'm sorry I drove your young friend away. I feel like the uninvited guest who put a pall on the party."

"He's just—he's a nice boy, Dan. I was depressed and he cheered me up, that was all."

He nodded. "Maybe we should have kept him around. I could use some cheering myself." He sat down on one of the long sofas and she saw that the awkwardness was over—on his part anyway. But she still felt like a child who'd been caught at some activity that was considered not quite nice by the grown-ups. It was not a feeling she relished.

She sat down beside him. "Was it rough, with your father?"

He nodded. "My father is as much a stoic as I am, Petra. He never really loses his temper, he never shouts, but he has a way of making me feel about ten years old." He grinned and she felt a thrill of response go through her at the way his whole face changed. "But I held my own, I'm proud to say. Someone else will go to Spain." He looked around for and found the champagne bottle, opened it up and poured some into the two glasses she'd promptly brought from the cabinet. "You are now looking at the temporary manager of the Pine Village Resort," he announced, raising his glass to touch hers.

Astonished, she stared at him as he sipped the champagne. "You're staying on?"

"I'm staying on." He put down his glass, took hers from her suddenly nerveless fingers and pulled her into his arms.

"I stood out on the porch for a while," he told her. "I could hear you playing and someone else singing and I didn't want to interrupt. But then I got rather cold and I was afraid Sarah would come out and find me standing on the porch clutching a bottle and be sure the devil had got me at last."

"Sarah's out," she said softly.

A wicked look of merriment came into his eyes. "Is she now? In that case...." He bent his head to hers and his mouth met hers in a long kiss that left her hungry for more. "I heard you playing some pretty old songs,'' he said as though he hadn't interrupted himself at all, ''one of which was 'Have I Told You Lately That I Love You?' Made me wonder if I had, lately.''

She sat very still.

''Is it safe to tell you now?'' he asked. ''Will you retreat from me again if I tell you that I love you? I never was joking about that—it started right away the moment I met you, maybe even before. All those photographs. I knew what you looked like at ten and fourteen and eighteen. When I saw you it was as though I'd always known I would love you. But when I told you how I felt I got the impression I'd scared you to death. So I backed off—verbally at least.'' He leaned his head back and looked at her. ''Am I still coming too close too fast?''

She stood up, suddenly feeling panicked. ''I don't know, Dan. I'm not sure I'm ready for....'' She wanted to run out of the room, she realized. She wanted to run out to the beach and keep running and....

Dan stood up and reached for her shoulders as she half turned away, her glance going to the open door. Why did the room feel suddenly smaller? Why did she feel as though the walls were closing in on her? She'd *wanted* him to love her, wanted him to tell her so.

Dan's fingers lifted her chin, forcing her to look at him. ''What is it, Petra?''

She averted her eyes. Her hands were clasped together in front of her, gripping tightly. Her whole body was trembling.

"Why are you so afraid of being loved?" he asked softly.

She shook her head so violently her hair whipped across her face. "Of course I'm not afraid. That would be ridiculous."

"Would it? Not if you'd had a bad experience with love. How many people have loved you, Petra? Tony loves you, and Sarah. Who else? Has any other man loved you?"

"Ted said he loved me," she admitted reluctantly, "and David, but they didn't mean it. Obviously they didn't—they each found someone else as soon as I . . ."

"As soon as you turned them down?"

"I didn't turn them down. I told you that." She could feel her mouth setting mutinously. She must look like Tony when he was being bullheaded. *Stubborn. Don't be so stubborn, Petra.*

Dan's steady gaze was holding hers. She felt trapped. She couldn't look away. "And your parents?" Dan persisted. "Did they love you?"

"Of course they did."

"But they died."

She tried to pull away, but his grip on her shoulders held firm. "Is that it, Petra? They died and you decided you couldn't afford to love and be loved, because it was too dangerous?"

"Yes," she blurted out. "You were right about me, Dan. I *have* retreated from love. I guess I've always been afraid if I loved someone I'd lose them the way I did mom and dad."

"You're ready to talk about the accident?"

She stared at him, taken aback, then nodded. "Yes. I think it will help if I can get my feelings out in the open and examine them. But I don't want to talk about the accident tonight, okay?"

Her voice sounded very reasonable. She was in control again even though she was still trembling. "It's been an emotional twenty-four hours," she went on just as calmly. "I'm not sure about anything right now. Maybe we can talk again tomorrow and...."

"No." His voice was still soft, but there was a determined note in it that made Petra flinch. "You're going to talk about it now, tonight."

"I can't, Dan. I'm too upset already about Tony and...."

"Now. Don't think about it, just tell it. You were sixteen, you lived with your parents in San Francisco, you were happy. What happened?"

"Nothing happened," she said. "They went out to a concert...." Her voice faltered and again she tried to pull away. "I need to get some air," she explained carefully. "This room is really too hot. I think Sarah must have put the heat on because of the rain. I should adjust the...."

"Now, Petra," he insisted. He had taken hold of her hands as she gestured toward the thermostat on the wall and was holding them tightly clasped in his own. "They went out to a concert," he repeated.

She was getting angry. She could feel her always-ready temper rising and she didn't want to lose it. She wanted to stay calm, to explain.... "Dammit, Dan," she exploded as he continued to grip her hands. "It's no business of yours."

"Tell me," he said implacably.

"They went out to a concert," she said firmly. "Their car brakes failed on one of the hills. My father couldn't stop, I guess. They crashed into a building and were killed instantly."

"You're not telling all of it."

She was shaking even more now. Tears were rolling down her face, uncontrollably. She tried to release her hands so she could wipe the tears away, but Dan still wouldn't let her go.

"I've told you everything," she said. "Please don't make me do this, Dan. It's hard for me to talk about it, but I've told you now. Don't make me go through it again."

"Did you want to go to the concert with them?" he asked unexpectedly.

She was again very still. Her mother's voice was clear in her mind. *Don't be so stubborn, Petra.*

"I didn't want to go," she whispered. "Mom was so furious. God, she scared me when she lost her temper. I was supposed to go. She wanted me to go, she'd bought a ticket for me, and the conductor was one of my favorites. It was supposed to be my birthday treat and I'd wanted to go, but John Lester asked me to go to a party with him and I'd been waiting and waiting for him to ask me out and I'd explained all that to mom and she should have understood. Dad understood, but she wouldn't. She always wanted her own way and she said I had to go but I wouldn't. And she shouted at me and dad got upset as he always did when we quarreled, and he kept putting his hand on her arm and telling her not to go on so, that

I had a life of my own to live. And finally she shook him off and stomped away and got in the car and they drove away, and I could hear them arguing still as they drove off—''

She stopped speaking suddenly and looked at Dan blankly, realizing abruptly that she hadn't even been conscious of his presence in the past few minutes. Her mind had traveled back into the past and all the painful memories had erupted into words without any conscious volition on her part—memories she had never spoken of to anyone, memories she hadn't even admitted to herself.

His eyes were filled with a sympathy that had nothing to do with pity, and they were her undoing. Laying her head on his shoulder, she started to sob agonizingly. ''They were still arguing,'' she whispered against the smooth fabric of his jacket. ''They were arguing about *me* and they probably didn't notice anything was wrong with the brakes until it was too late, because they were so busy arguing—'' Her voice broke and her whole body shook with the force of her sobs.

Dan didn't speak. He held her close to him while she cried, letting her cry, moving only once to bring the napkin that had been wrapped around the champagne bottle, murmuring somewhat about never being prepared as he pressed the soft cloth into her hand.

He continued to hold her as she cried. There was so much pain in her she thought she might die of it, yet relief was there too, because she'd told all of it and he hadn't turned away from her. He was still holding her close.

She finally realized that they were sitting on the sofa again. She had no memory of moving, of Dan moving. His arms were still around her and at some time her arms had moved around him. She was holding on to him as though if she let go she might fall into some deep hole and never surface again.

Gradually her sobs quieted until she was weeping more naturally. And then the tears stopped altogether and she hiccuped once. Dan laughed gently, removed the sodden napkin from her grip and very tenderly wiped her face.

Suddenly embarrassed, she moved away from him and sat upright on the edge of the sofa, not looking at him. "I must look awful," she groaned.

"If you're starting to worry about your appearance, you're on the mend," he said dryly. "How do you feel?"

"Empty."

"I'm not surprised. You had a lot inside you." His hand touched lightly on her head, stroking her hair. "It didn't occur to me that you felt guilty," he said slowly. "I thought you'd locked up your memories because your parents' death hurt you. There might be some resentment there, I thought, or a feeling of desertion. I remember your eyes in your graduation photograph. So much sadness for such a young woman." He was silent a moment, then he quoted softly, " 'Lost angel of a ruined paradise.' You loved them very much, didn't you?"

"Yes."

"And they loved you."

"Yes."

"Would they really have argued so long, once they left the house, do you suppose?"

She sighed. "I don't know, Dan. I didn't even know I blamed myself so totally. I knew I felt guilty of course. I was guilty, but...."

"Tony's sixteen, isn't he? The same age you were when you lost your parents?"

Puzzled, she glanced at him. He was sitting very close to her, his hand still gently stroking her hair. There was a musing expression on his face, but he was looking at her with love in his eyes. There was no mistaking the love in his eyes.

She swallowed convulsively. "What are you driving at?"

He smiled. "Simply this. Tony did something wrong, something that made you angry. Would you want him to remember that in ten years? Would you want him to feel he couldn't love another woman because he made a mistake about Lori?"

Suddenly exasperated, she let out her breath explosively. "There's no comparison, Dan. Of course I wouldn't want Tony to feel guilty the rest of his life, but there's no similarity between our experiences."

To her surprise, he nodded and grinned. "I was reaching, wasn't I? I never would have made a good psychologist, in spite of all my bold talk about relationships. I'm more of a mathematician. Two plus two equals four, so it follows that three plus three equals six. I was quite sure that if I got you to spill everything out, you'd feel free to love me the way I deserve to be loved."

"But I do love you, Dan," she said abruptly.

It was his turn to sit very still.

"I love you," she repeated wonderingly. "God, I thought I'd never be able to say that to anyone." She glanced up at him, feeling suddenly nervous.

"I'm still not sure I won't suddenly retreat again. I guess it became a habit. Logically, you know, I can see that I've been blaming myself for mom and dad's accident, and logically, I can see that I shouldn't, because I certainly didn't make the brakes fail. I mean, there was a mechanical failure. It wasn't that they weren't paying attention and collided with another vehicle, which would have been worse.... Logically, I know that if brakes fail in San Francisco, there's not a whole lot anyone can do about it, but all the same...."

"All the same, you did set yourself subconsciously to resist love, maybe feeling you didn't deserve to be loved?"

"Nonsense," she said firmly. "I deserve to be loved as much as you do."

He laughed uproariously and after a startled moment she was able to join in, realizing how prim she had sounded in her declaration, how, yes—prickly she'd been in her reaction.

There was even more relief in the laughter than the tears had brought and she began to think that maybe, now she'd revealed herself so completely to him, maybe she wouldn't panic next time he told her he loved her.

Anxious to experiment, she stopped laughing and said very clearly, "I love you, Dan."

He looked at her directly as though he knew what

she was trying to do. Then his hands reached to cup her face, and he stroked a few errant wisps of hair behind her ears. "I love you, Petra," he said, and his lips touched very delicately against hers.

She felt an almost unbearable sweetness permeate her whole body, followed by a rising excitement as his mouth hardened against hers. Her arms went around him again and she clutched him close to her, her mouth moving softly under his as his hands stroked the length of her spine and then pulled her up hard against his body.

"I would suggest," he said against her mouth after a while, "that you wash your face, which will make you feel a lot better, and then we can continue this discussion and psychological evaluation in my suite at the resort."

"I should wait for Sarah," she said hesitantly. "I don't really like to leave the inn without anyone in charge."

He lifted his head and looked at her, and she knew he was checking to see if she was still using delaying tactics. But whatever he saw in her eyes seemed to satisfy him and he nodded. "We can drink the champagne while we wait," he said solemnly. "That way we won't have anything else to do once we get to my rooms but to. . . ."

"You're a rogue, Dan Halliwell," she accused and he nodded agreement.

"An impatient rogue," he amended. Then he turned away and picked up both glasses of champagne, handing her one, raising his own in a toast. "To love," he said softly.

"To love," she echoed.

An hour later, when Sarah came home, Petra had showered and changed into her yellow cotton dress and put on fresh makeup, and she and Dan were sitting sedately in the parlor, sipping the last of the now-flat champagne.

"We're going out for a while," Petra told Sarah in her most casual voice.

Sarah looked at her, then at Dan and gave them both the broadest smile Petra had ever seen on her long face. "Are you indeed," she said dryly. "I suppose I can't stop you, but I do hope you'll not hurry back on my account."

They both laughed and Dan hugged Sarah. Then they went out to the parking lot and crossed over to the resort property, hand in hand, not speaking at all, walking quite briskly as though they were merely out for exercise in the rain, not allowing their pace to increase until they entered the resort and started up the stairs.

CHAPTER FOURTEEN

"BUT I DIDN'T WANT TO FALL IN LOVE with you," Petra protested.

Dan grinned and again she was aware of that predatory expression she'd seen on his lean face from time to time. But this time it was softened by love. Love. She still couldn't quite accept that he loved her and that she loved him. It seemed too simple. Life, she had found, in her twenty-six years, was rarely simple. In fact, it had seemed unbearably complicated to her as recently as a few hours earlier.

"It's too late now," Dan said. "It's an established fact. I heard you say it myself."

"I did, didn't I?" Petra curled herself happily against his long body in the soft brocade-draped bed. Through the open window she could hear the sound of rain really pelting down now. She spared a thought for her roof. No, she didn't have to worry about it. The admiral had assured her it was waterproof. "Drop-dry," she murmured.

Dan looked questioningly at her, but she didn't bother to explain. She was feeling—not satiated, for she had an idea she would never be satiated with Dan—but content, she decided. Her skin felt as though it had been magically coated with silk, and her body was totally relaxed, curved into his as though they had been made to fit together. Only one shadow darkened her mind. He still hadn't told her what had happened with his wife, what was to happen with his wife. And he hadn't mentioned any future. Just because he'd told her he loved her didn't mean he was even considering a future.

But he wasn't leaving. He would be here for several weeks until a new manager could be found. There was time to plan and talk and listen.

His hand stroked the length of her spine, making her shudder with renewed desire. No, she would never be satiated with this man.

Lazily, teasingly, she pulled away from him and turned over on her back. "Love me," she commanded.

"Are we establishing a pecking order?" he asked without moving.

She laughed and turned back to trace his features with her fingers, delighting in the feel of his firm masculine skin, the slight roughness of whiskers. "Are you telling me you won't take orders from me?" she asked.

"Not all the time. I believe in total equality, my love." The tip of his tongue touched lightly on her lips. Then he flopped lazily onto his back and gave her a wicked sidelong glance. "Love *me*," he ordered.

She leaned over him, lightly tracing the line of his smiling mouth with her thumb, then bent her head to kiss him. His mouth moved against hers in the most gentle way imaginable, and she felt a rush of tenderness that was new to her. She wanted to prolong this time, she thought. She wanted to touch him lovingly in places she had never touched a man. She wanted to know him completely—the feel of him, the smell of him, the sound of his breathing, his heartbeat.

Love me. She had never received such an invitation before. The men in her life had wanted always to be in control. Somehow she had accepted that. In spite of her desire for independence, she had always allowed herself to be made love to. She had never really made love to a man. It was the most erotic suggestion she had ever been given and she wanted to explore it, explore him to the fullest degree.

She seemed to know exactly what to do, as though she'd been given a map of his body. She knew where she should touch and kiss first, and where next, to bring him to a pitch of excitement that would equal hers. She began with his eyelids, touching each one tenderly with her fingers and then her lips, moved across his forehead, down again to his strong nose and then outward to each ear in turn. She had never really explored an ear before, and she marveled at the ridges and crannies that she could explore with her tongue. She noted that his breathing was quickening, but he made no move to help her or to return her caresses. When she moved her hands to his shoulders she could feel the exquisite tension of his body and knew with an inner smile that he was keeping himself determinedly immobile so that she could please herself in her journey over his body and not be guided by any particular response from him.

The skin of his shoulders was as tight and smooth

as the rest of him. It tasted clean and faintly tart to
her tongue, and she wondered at the muscular
strength below the surface. She nuzzled the hair beneath his arms and tasted cleanliness again and the
faintest trace of soap. She tasted his fingers, the
tender spot inside each elbow. She rubbed her mouth
over the mat of hair on his chest and followed it
down and down, glancing up once to see that he'd
closed his eyes. His face was relaxed, almost as
though he'd gone to sleep under her gentle ministra-
tions, but his mouth was curved in a faint smile and
his hands were clenched tightly. She could feel a
tremor go through his body occasionally as she continued to touch and kiss each part of him, even down
to his toes. Then she moved up again, after she'd
urged him to roll over so that she could explore the
soft flesh behind his knees, the hard resilient thighs,
the length of his spine. Each time she felt a tremor go
through him, she felt a heady sense of power that
finally gave her the confidence to lie down beside him
and urge him toward her and into her.

His eyes were open suddenly and all restraint was
gone from him. His mouth seized hers and ravaged
it, and she gave to him from her mouth every moment of loneliness, every ounce of pain and every
memory of unhappiness. And she let him take them
and heal her and make her whole. She tried to lie
quietly while he touched her gently with his beautifully shaped hands, stroking her as she had stroked him,
learning her body through his fingertips as she had
learned his, his fingers urgent on the tight buds of her
nipples, and again on her thighs. But she couldn't lie

still as he had done for her. The sensations of her body were becoming too piercingly urgent for that and pressure was building inside her, lifting her again and again. She couldn't get close enough to him. She wanted her body to merge with his, to become one with his, and she strove desperately to press him against her and into her.

And finally it seemed to her that she had achieved this impossible feat, and she ceased to be and he ceased to be and they were one and all her senses were exploding into a vast tumult of sight and touch and scent. The sounds of their hearts beating merged together and became one with the rain drumming on the roof and the wind-tossed sea pounding on the beach far below.

Stamina, she thought after what seemed a long time of lying clasped tightly in his arms. She needed more stamina so that she could go on loving Dan Halliwell over and over again. She resented having to stop, resented the return of thought that told her she should be going home to the inn, checking to make sure that everything was all right, checking that. . . .

His arms loosened around her and he tilted his head back and smiled at her in the dim light. "I can hear your head ticking," he teased. "What's the problem?"

She smiled at him. "No problem. I was just thinking that I should go home and make sure everything was all right."

He pulled her close again. "Petra love, you worry too much. You remind me of the way I used to be."

"You don't worry now?"

"Of course I do, but I used to be as impossible as you. I used to think nothing I worked on could go right unless I saw to every tiny detail myself, unless I was on the job morning, noon and night, giving it my undivided attention."

He rolled with her so he could lean over her, and then stroked her damp hair away from her forehead and kissed her lightly. "There are other things in life besides work," he said firmly. "I learned that late, but I learned it well. You need to learn it too."

"I've made a pretty good start," Petra protested with a laugh.

He kissed her again and she marveled at her body's instant response. Tired as she was, her body could still summon a series of explosions along her nervous system when he touched her.

But there was a shadow again in her mind. Now that they were lying quietly together, the shadow had returned to plague her with doubts and questions. Could she ask him now? Could she possibly ask him about his wife?

While she debated with herself, he moved away from her and disappeared into the bathroom. She heard the sound of water running for a moment, but then it was turned off. He wasn't taking a shower then. What was he doing?

He returned with two steaming mugs of coffee. She could smell it the instant he left the bathroom. It smelled wonderful. All her senses were heightened, she realized.

"There's a beverage maker in there," he explained as he plumped pillows behind her head and covered her tenderly with the bedcovers so that she wouldn't feel chilled. He handed her a cup and climbed in beside her. "Okay, Petra," he said with amusement in his voice. "Tell me what's going on in there behind those velvet eyes." He laughed shortly before she could answer him. "Better yet, let me guess. You want to know about my wife. My ex-wife," he corrected in a slightly grimmer voice.

"I'm sorry, Dan. I just—you said you'd seen her and I wondered."

"I'm not going to pretend I didn't care when our marriage broke up," he said abruptly. "I want to be honest with you always, Petra."

She thrilled at the "always" but didn't want to interrupt.

"I loved my wife," he said, and her moment of joy subsided. "At least I thought I did," he amended. "I wanted to share everything with her, to live a beautiful life. She was an actress—a very good actress, just getting known in England. I've always loved strong women, probably because my mother is one, and I made the mistake of thinking that because Elizabeth had a career we could form this strong partnership together. We would be independent yet interdependent."

He took a deep breath and sighed. "The day after we were married Elizabeth informed me she had given up her career and intended devoting her life to me. She had always hated acting, she announced. She wanted only to be taken care of. She would be content to live for me and because of me."

He shook his head. "I've never forgotten that moment. I felt trapped, as deceived as though she'd told me there was another man in her life. I'm not very proud of myself for my reaction, nor proud of the fact that I didn't let her see it. That's why I didn't want to talk about my marriage. I was afraid you'd think less of me.''

Petra had never imagined Dan Halliwell as afraid of anything, or concerned about anyone's opinion of him. His declaration made him ו more vulnerable, even more lovable.

He shifted against the pillows. ''I deceived Elizabeth into thinking her news made me happy. I tried to convince myself I was happy. But I made up my mind I wasn't going to change my life to accommodate her plans.''

He leaned back against the pillows and quoted softly, '''Curly-locks, Curly-locks, wilt Thou be mine? Thou shalt not wash dishes nor yet feed the swine. But sit on a cushion and sew a fine seam and feed upon strawberries, sugar and cream.'''

His smile was self-deprecating and had an edge of sadness. ''That's what she wanted. That's what she got.''

Petra sipped her coffee, not wanting to look at his face while he spoke of Elizabeth, remembering again that he had loved her ''helplessly.''

''What I didn't take into consideration,'' he went on after a moment's silence, ''was that she had expected I would give up my ambitions in order to devote myself to her. At that time my work was even more important to me. I worked—God how I worked! I'd always been ambitious. My father had made sure of that. I was the only son, the last of the Halliwells. Of course I was expected to fill his shoes. And I wanted to please him, always had. So there I was working eighteen hours a day, jetting all over the world, getting richer and richer, making Elizabeth more and more miserable."

He was silent for so long she thought he wasn't going to say any more, but then he sighed again and said, "Elizabeth was a very loving woman. She loved everybody. Everybody loved her. She tried very hard to go on loving me. I didn't realize all this at the time of course. I was too wrapped up in getting ahead. But she would give parties for me that I wasn't there for, make arrangements for theaters or concerts—and I'd come home late and tell her I had to work in my study. She didn't ever protest. She was always gentle and loving and uncomplaining. And then one day I came home from a trip to Tel Aviv and she'd gone. She left a note accusing me of making her sacrifice her career and then deserting her. She needed love, she told me. She couldn't exist without love and I hadn't given it to her. While I was away, she'd become involved with another man, a man who worked from nine to five and kept the rest of his time free for her. She explained that she loved him now. She hadn't seen enough of me in the last few years to even know me, so it wasn't possible for her to go on loving me."

He reached for Petra's hand and brought it to his lips, but she had the feeling he wasn't really thinking of her. He was still back there in his memories of Elizabeth. "Naturally I was very angry," he said with self-disgust evident in his voice. "I found out where she'd gone and followed her and tried to talk what I called 'sense' into her. But she looked at me in the serene way she had and said I was married to my career and didn't have room for a wife. It took a while, but eventually I saw that she was right. I started trying to change my life."

He glanced at Petra and smiled. "I'm still as ambitious as ever. I still want to please my father up to a point. That's the important thing—that point. I won't let him schedule my time the way his has always been scheduled. I have to have room for living—for sailing and sightseeing and getting to know people." He laughed shortly again. "It took some time to convince him, but he's finally realized I won't be pushed into devoting myself to business all the time. Winning the argument about Spain was an important step forward. He's finally giving in to the fact that I'm my own man."

He put down his coffee cup on the bedside table and put his arm around her shoulders, really looking at her this time. "That's why I was so adamant you should take some time off," he said softly. "I didn't want to see you get into the same habit—working all the time. Work can be very satisfying, but it can't fill a life. It leaves empty spaces that have to be filled."

"But I didn't ever intend to go on and on working," Petra protested. "It was necessary—is necessary for a while to devote myself to the inn, but it was just temporary. I meant to. . . ."

He finished the sentence for her. "Take time off tomorrow?" He touched her lips with his finger.

"That's what I used to say to Elizabeth. 'I'll make time tomorrow.' But as the old cliché so wisely states, tomorrow never comes."

Petra nodded slowly, not sure she agreed with him completely, not where her own life was concerned. She hadn't ever intended to devote herself exclusively to work. She would have taken time off even if he hadn't insisted—wouldn't she? She was suddenly not quite so sure. "You said you saw your wife when you were in Boston," she said slowly. "Was that very painful?"

He smiled. "There was some pain. I had loved her after all. But I could see that she is very happy now. Her husband—yes, she married him—is just the type she needs. He's not really interested in his occupation. It's just a job to him. He devotes himself exclusively to Elizabeth and she's blooming under his care. Seeing her, I realized that even if I hadn't sunk myself in work, our marriage still wouldn't have worked out. She is a lovely woman, but she needs someone who is on call twenty-four hours a day. I could never have been that person for her." He paused. "It was a relief in a way. I'd felt so responsible for the failure of our marriage, and so unfit to be any woman's husband again. But when I saw that we were the wrong people for each other, I was able to get things in better perspective and stop blaming myself so utterly. She just wouldn't complain, you see. Until she left me I had no idea I'd caused her a moment's unhappiness."

"And what about you, Dan? What about your needs?" Petra asked.

"I've thought about that, especially lately. What I need, I guess, is the new kind of woman, the kind who doesn't have to depend on someone else for complete happiness. The kind of woman who can take very good care of herself, but if she loves someone enough, could be convinced to share her life with him. Someone like you."

She was suddenly very nervous, not sure she was ready for the commitment she could hear implied in his voice. Disengaging herself from him, she set down her coffee cup and walked over to the bay window, parting the draperies a little so that she could look out. There was only the light from the bathroom in the room, but it was enough to prevent her from seeing out clearly. She could see the lights of the swimming pool, but her own face was superimposed on the view.

"Petra?" Dan queried from the bed.

She couldn't understand her own reluctance to turn and face him. She had wanted him to start thinking in terms of the future. And it was obvious to her that he had begun to do so. Why then did she feel so suddenly afraid again?

"Petra?" Dan said again behind her. He had followed her to the window. She could see the reflection of his face in the glass above hers, but she could not make out his expression, except to see that he wasn't smiling.

He put his hands on her shoulders and pulled her back against him, then put his arms around her, holding her against his warmth. She felt herself begin to relax again. As long as he held her, she had no doubts.

"Dan," she began, turning to face him, but then she felt his body stiffen and saw that he was looking not at her but beyond her.

"What the hell is that light?" he asked urgently. "Look there, the reflection—where is it coming from?" He let go of her abruptly and walked hurriedly to the side of the room and eased the drapery there to one side.

Then she could see it too. An orange light where no light should be. A light that flickered beyond the trees in the direction of the back of the Captain McNeill Inn. No, not in the direction—it *was* the back of the inn, and it was on fire. Even as they watched, stunned into immobility, the light flared up and illuminated the lower corner of the kitchen window.

"My God," Petra exclaimed, and then her immobility was gone and she was scrambling into her clothing, never being sure afterward how much she put on in the bedroom, how much she grabbed and pulled on as she was running down the stairs, with Dan close behind her.

The rain had stopped—when, she had no idea. But the wind was blowing, and as they scrambled between the trees that separated her property from the resort, stumbling and almost falling in the dark, they could see that the wind was whipping at the flames, feeding them, so that it seemed at first glance as though the entire kitchen was engulfed. "Tony," Petra was screaming as she ran, not even realizing that she was doing so. "Sarah, oh my God, what happened? How could this...."

As they came up to the side of the inn, she saw

Tony running, hauling a garden hose toward the back of the house, and she felt a moment's relief, followed by acute fear. "Don't let him go inside," she yelled to Dan. Dan was already sprinting toward Tony and Petra ran to the front of the inn, intending to go in and make sure everyone was safe.

The guests were all huddled together close to the edge of the bluff. "Sarah?" she yelled at Mrs. Menniger, and the old lady ran toward her, her light-colored dressing gown flapping around her small body, and shouted back that Sarah had gone inside to try to rescue something and Nathaniel had gone in after her.

"He was the one who saw the smoke," she said breathlessly. "He came over and got us all out and called the fire department. They're on the way," she added even as Petra heard the blessed sound of sirens approaching rapidly along the highway.

She didn't wait for the firemen. She didn't even think about danger. She headed through the front door without thinking at all, calling Sarah and Nathaniel as she went. And saw them almost immediately through a thick pall of smoke, struggling with each other, down on all fours. Surely they couldn't be fighting at a time like this! Nathaniel was holding on to Sarah's robe, almost pulling it off her as she attempted to crawl away from him. They were both coughing and choking. At the same moment Petra felt smoke sear her own lungs and she dropped to a crouch, coughing herself as she crawled rapidly toward them.

Sarah was clutching her old brown teapot, of all

things. "The table's on fire," she choked out as soon as she saw Petra. "The old oak table—it's a real antique and the curtains at the window and—" She broke off as a fit of coughing overtook her.

Nathaniel, grim faced, was still pulling on Sarah's robe, trying to get hold of her arm, which she kept yanking away from him. "Please help me get her out, Miss Petra," he wheezed, still so courtly even under such stress that she felt a hysterical burst of laughter forming in her throat and had to swallow hard to force it down.

"Of course," she answered, taking hold of Sarah's arm and helping Nathaniel to turn her around. Sarah immediately started struggling again, looking over her shoulder. "I've got to go in the sitting parlor," she insisted. "You love that piano. I know you love it. It won't take a moment to bring it. It's on castors. We canna just leave it."

"The firemen will get it," Petra assured her. Between the two of them they managed to get Sarah through the doorway, still struggling and talking about the piano.

Surely fresh air had never smelled so sweet and reviving, Petra thought. Two paramedics were immediately beside them with a canister of oxygen, leading them away.

"Dan and Tony?" Petra asked between coughs.

One of the men nodded. "They're okay, miss. Mr. Halliwell has the boy. See, they're coming now."

"The fire's out," Dan said as soon as he reached Petra. His face was smeared with soot. He must have gone far too close to the flames. He was holding on to Tony's arm as though he wanted to restrain him. "Our hero here wanted to climb in the window and take care of the fire all by himself," he said grimly.

Tony laughed. He was almost hopping up and down with excitement. "What on earth do you suppose started it?" he asked as soon as Dan stopped talking. "I'm going back to talk to the men and see what they think."

"You'll stay right here, Tony McNeil," Petra said firmly. "Let the men do the job they're trained to do. They don't need you underfoot, and I'm not letting you out of my sight. What on earth did you think you were doing with that hose? It doesn't even have a nozzle on it."

"I thought I could stick my thumb over the end and get some pressure," he said. "I had to do something. I couldn't let the old place burn." He turned to look directly at Petra. "Where were you anyway? Sarah said you'd gone to the resort with Dan, but that was hours ago. When Nathaniel started hammering on the door I went to your room first, of course, and you weren't. . . ."

"We'll talk about that later," Petra said hastily.

"The damage isn't as bad as you might think," Dan said to Sarah, who was sitting on the grass now, taking deep breaths of the night air. "Are you okay?" he asked.

She nodded. "Is my kitchen gone?"

He crouched down and took both her hands in his. "It can be rebuilt, Sarah," he said softly. "Don't you worry about it."

"And the piano?"

Puzzled, he glanced up at Petra. "She wanted to get the piano out," she explained. She crouched down to Sarah's level herself. "I'm sure it's okay, Sarah. The firemen acted so promptly—the fire couldn't have had a chance to spread."

"You're a stubborn woman, Sarah Merriweather," Nathaniel said, suddenly emerging from the oxygen mask one of the paramedics was holding to his nose and mouth. "If Miss Petra hadn't come in, you could have got us both killed from smoke inhalation with your silly worries about a piano."

"There's nothing silly about it," Sarah said promptly. And they were off again exchanging insults about the stupidity of each of them, Nathaniel defending the fact that he'd hammered on the door and shouted fire, and Sarah accusing him of "panicking everyone."

"What was I supposed to do?" he demanded. "The place was locked up for the night. Everyone in bed. Should I have let you burn so you wouldn't panic?"

Dan and Petra exchanged a glance and stood up. She wished he would put his arms around her, but he didn't and she supposed he was conscious of the guests, now crowding around them. But when she looked at him, his face was grim. "You went inside?" he said in a disbelieving voice.

"Of course I did. Sarah and Nathaniel were in there."

"You thought smoke inhalation wouldn't have any effect on you? What made you think you would be immune?" His crisp Boston accent had never been so obvious.

"Well, I wasn't hurt. I had to go in, Dan."

He looked at her for a long moment. Then the grim expression softened and he nodded. "Yes, of course you did. I'm sorry." He took a deep breath. "It was just—when Nathaniel said.... All I could think of was how thick the smoke was in there and how you might have...."

"Dan," she said softly.

And then one of the firemen interrupted them, introducing himself as Captain Aldridge, explaining that his duties included arson investigation. He held out a paper bag that contained several pieces of glass. Petra peered at it. "It looks like a whiskey bottle," she said, looking at him questioningly.

"It's what's known as a Molotov cocktail," he said grimly. "I haven't seen one of these in years. There was a rock too. Looks like someone broke the kitchen window, and then threw in the bottle. Gasoline spattered all over the place, of course. The rug went up, then that long tablecloth probably and then the curtains."

Petra stared at him, stunned.

"You have any idea who might...."

Petra began to shake her head, too shocked to speak, but then she glanced at Dan and saw the thought occur to him at the same time it popped into her mind. Dan shook his head. "Kelly's in Boston. He went to see my father, to try to change his mind."

Evidently noting the captain's alert expression, he explained about Kelly O'Connor. Then the arson officer took them both to inspect the damage. It was Petra who thought to mention Seth Cartwright, suddenly remembering Tony had mentioned threats. After a while the captain took a statement from Tony, and then they returned to the front of the inn to decide what to do about the guests. While Tony answered their excited questions, without mentioning arson, Dan slipped an arm around Petra's shoulders and drew her close to his side. She felt herself resist, which was ridiculous, considering she'd hoped he'd put his arms around her earlier. He looked at her questioningly, then smiled ruefully. "I'm sorry, Petra," he said softly. "I guess your troubles aren't over yet."

She sighed. "It looks that way, doesn't it? I certainly hadn't expected to contend with arson."

Dan laughed shortly. "The hotel business brings its share of surprises. But I suppose you do have adequate insurance."

Something in his voice aroused Petra's irritation. "Of course I have insurance. I'm not altogether stupid."

"I didn't suggest that you were."

She pulled away from his protecting arm, annoyed anew by what sounded to her like a patronizing note in his voice. "But you did expect me to fail, didn't you? You never did think I could make a paying proposition of this inn."

"I felt it would be difficult, yes, trying to manage alone. Unless you're backed up by sufficient funds, you can't just bounce back when things go wrong. You need...."

"Don't tell me what I need, Dan Halliwell," Petra said through clenched teeth, suddenly furious with

him and the patient expression that had come into his
lean soot-stained face. "I suppose you're glad to
have the chance to say I told you so. Okay, say it.
And see if it makes any difference to me."

She knew she was being unfair. She knew she was
acting stupidly, hysterically. But the shock was just
now beginning to make itself felt. If Nathaniel
hadn't seen the smoke, if he hadn't been able to
wake Sarah and Tony and the others, if the fire had
gone out of control, spread to other parts of the
inn—that old wood could have gone up in such a
short time.

She could feel herself starting to shake. "I should
have been here," she said. "If I'd been here it
wouldn't have happened. I would have—"

"Stop it, Petra," Dan said, taking hold of her
shoulders. "You couldn't have done any more than
the others did. You would surely not have stayed
awake all night watching for disaster. Don't start
blaming yourself."

She shook him off. "I'll blame myself if I want
to," she said, knowing she was being childish but unable to stop. She looked around. "I have to do something about these people. They're all catching
pneumonia. Oh God, what am I going to do? They'll
all want to leave right away and who can blame
them? I won't have any guests at all and I—" She
stopped herself abruptly. "I'll manage somehow,"
she said. "You needn't think I'm beaten, Dan. I'll
get through this. You'll see."

"All by yourself, I suppose?" he asked in a dangerously even voice.

"By myself, yes," she said vaguely, not really thinking of what she was saying.

"You didn't listen, did you? You didn't hear a word I said. You can't handle everything alone, Petra. You have to accept help when it's necessary."

He was shouting at her. So he could lose his temper then. Almost as soon as she had this thought, he took a deep breath, obviously reaching for control. But his voice when he spoke again was still tight with anger, even though he'd lowered it so that only she could hear. "I'm tired of fighting your hostility," he said bitterly. "I've tried to help you all I can and you meet me each time with anger. You're so damn set on independence, you've forgotten how to trust."

And then he turned away and talked to the others, telling them to come with him to the resort and he'd find beds for all of them and not to worry about their clothes and belongings. He'd see everything was cleaned if necessary and have it all brought to them.

Taking over, Petra thought in annoyance, though she had no idea what she'd have done with the guests without his offer. She was really very grateful, but her pride wouldn't let her tell him so.

"Petra, what about you?" he asked evenly. "I think you and Sarah had better come and spend what's left of the night, and Tony too. Nathaniel, I don't think you should be alone either. You got a lot of that smoke in you and. . . ."

"Well now, I've always wanted to stay at your fancy resort, Dan," the admiral said slowly. "But I think I'll just stay and keep an eye on things here."

"No," Petra said at once. "Dan's right. You need

to rest, Nathaniel. I'll stay if the firemen tell me it's okay. I won't sleep if I go anywhere else, so. . . ."

"I'll stay with you," Sarah said promptly, lifting her chin when Petra started to protest. "It's no use arguing with me. I'm not leaving you alone in yon place no matter what. But I agree with you about. . . about Mr. Jenkins. He'd be better off resting. I wouldn't want him to be getting sick."

"Sarah?" Nathaniel said with a softer sound in his voice than Petra had heard before.

Sarah glared at him. "Don't be taking advantage," she said firmly. "I'm merely concerned for your health as I would be for any fellow human being."

His smile was weary but dazzling. "I don't know that you've even considered me a human being for a while," he said gently.

Even in the shadows cast by the inn lights, Petra could see that Sarah's usually stern expression had softened considerably. "Och, away with you," she said, her Scotish accent thick. "I'm grateful to you for saving us all. . . ." She looked at him a moment. His eyes held hers. "We'll talk about it," she said ambiguously and again his smile lit up his lined face.

"YOU'RE REALLY VERY FOND OF THE ADMIRAL, aren't you, Sarah?" Petra said several hours later.

Sarah had managed to find an old hot plate in one of the hall cupboards and had fixed them each a cup of strong sweet tea. They sat in the parlor, drinking it gratefully, so weary, both of them, that they didn't have the strength to go upstairs even though their bedrooms didn't smell as strongly of smoke as the downstairs rooms. Petra suspected they'd have to live with that smell for some time, though the Cape's salty breezes would help.

She sighed. At least the actual damage wasn't as bad as she had expected. Only the kitchen was involved. The windows were shattered and the round oak table, a charred ruin, had been carried out along with one of the chairs. The floor was badly damaged and the braided rugs burned beyond hope. But the rest of the inn was intact. They had been very lucky, she realized.

"I've never stopped caring about that old scoundrel," Sarah said after a long silence. "But it's too late now to do anything about it."

"Too late?" Petra sat up straight, her tiredness forgotten. "Of course it's not too late. He loves you, Sarah. Any fool could see that. You just have to tell him you care about him. He'll take care of the rest."

"And then what?" Sarah demanded. "You think I want to get married at my age?"

"People do."

"I don't know that I would want to live with a man under my feet all the time." Her voice was faintly questioning, Petra noticed. She was admitting the possibility to herself. If Nathaniel would only realize that the fire had made her come to her senses and take advantage of the fact, she might just give in. A word to the wise might be justified, Petra thought smugly, echoing something Kelly O'Connor had said to her, but in a far pleasanter context. She'd talk to Nathaniel herself, suggest. . . .

"What about yourself, lassie?" Sarah asked.

Petra looked at her. "You're just as bad as me," Sarah went on. "I heard you lashing out at Dan. And just when I thought everything was going so well for you both at last. When you left here tonight, last night, I could see on your faces you'd reached some agreement. I may not be too smart about love for myself, but I can still recognize it on other people's faces. So why were you getting so riled up at him, may I ask? And don't tell me it's none of my business. I love you both."

Petra managed a smile. "I love you too, Sarah," she said. "And I love Dan. I'm just afraid...."

"Afraid? What have you been telling me just now then, if it wasn't that I shouldn't be afraid to change my life for the sake of some man. What do you want then, to be like me, to be like your Uncle Will?"

She leaned forward suddenly and fixed Petra with her sharp glance. "Do you know that foolish man was in love with your mother?"

Petra nodded.

"And so what did he do when he lost her? Did he try to find someone else? Did he and I ever once in all the years we were together here ever reach out to each other for some comfort? No, we did not," she answered herself without giving Petra a chance to speak. "We went on about our lives here, each in our own shell. We'd tried love and it didn't work, so we gave up on it. And the years went by and he got more and more bad-tempered, and I got more and more dried up."

"It's not the same, Sarah," Petra said mildly.

"It's not that I'm afraid to love Dan. It's that I'm afraid of losing him. What if I let myself love him and he gets tired of me? I'm not the easiest person to live with."

"No one is, lass. But don't you hear what you're saying? Just because there's a chance you might lose love you're willing to give it up entirely. Now does that make sense? Isn't that exactly what I did? I turned away from love all those years ago, and I've kept my face turned away from it. Do you know what happens when you do that?"

Petra shook her head mutely.

"You get dried up inside. At first it doesn't show, but after a while, it does and then it's the hardest thing in the world to let yourself relax and take a kindness from someone, or a compliment or even a cheery word. It gets harder and harder until it seems there's no way out of it, and you'll be dried up when you go to your grave."

She jumped up suddenly and hurried out of the room, returning a minute later with a gilded hand mirror that usually sat on the credenza in the lobby. She shoved it in front of Petra, forcing her to look at herself. "Look at your mouth now. While I've been talking, it's been setting in that stubborn way. Look at it now and tell me if it doesn't seem familiar."

And Petra looked...and saw. The line of her mouth that Dan had said curved upward even in repose was set straight and somehow pinched looking right now. She recognized it all right, not just from its similarity to Sarah's mouth, but to her aunt Sophie, who was as different from Sarah as anyone could be, but who had also forbidden love between herself and her men friends. She was reminded again of the sculpture Dan had sent her that she'd immediately returned. Retreat.

"I don't want to be like that," she said softly. Then she looked up at Sarah. "I'm sorry, I didn't mean...."

"I know what you meant, Petra," Sarah said.

Petra stared at her. "Do you realize that's the first time you've called me by my name?" she asked.

Sarah nodded. "I do. If I'm going to change my set ways, I have to start somewhere, don't I?"

Petra started laughing and then found she couldn't stop. What a pair they were, sitting there exhausted as they were, in a building that had caught on fire, discussing the whole philosophy of love in the small hours of the morning.

Sarah joined her in her laughter and it felt good to laugh, to look in the mirror and see that when she laughed, the line of her mouth changed to the way it should be.

At last their laughter died. Sarah's face returned to its usual dour lines. "I do want you to take warning, Petra. You don't have to be like me. Even if I am willing to change, it may be too late for me to tell that foolish old rascal that I love him, but you have time on your side—years and years of it."

"And what am I supposed to do with my time?" Nathaniel's voice suddenly queried from the doorway.

Sarah stood up as though she'd been catapulted to her feet. She looked wildly around as though searching for an escape route, her hands clasping together over her old blue robe as if she was praying for deliverance. At the first sound of Nathaniel's voice, she had blushed a deep rosy red.

While Petra stared at this phenomenon, Nathaniel came into the room and stood in front of Sarah, looking at her in a challenging way that gave his face back its youth in spite of his silvery hair and the lines on his face. He hadn't acknowledged Petra's presence. As far as he was concerned, she realized, she wasn't even there. Unfortunately he and Sarah were between her and the door, so she couldn't slip out. Not that she really wanted to. She was too fascinated by the drama that was being enacted in front of her.

Sarah's whole body had stilled. Her hazel eyes were fixed on Nathaniel's face, and there was a softness in them that brought a lump to Petra's throat. But when she spoke, the Scotswoman's voice was as terse as ever. "You're supposed to be resting, not eavesdropping," she said curtly.

"A body needs less sleep as it gets older," he said. "I couldn't sleep. I kept thinking of how you came so close to death because of your stubborn behavior."

"You took a risk or two yourself," she pointed out.

"I knew how empty my life would be if you weren't in it. No matter that you've no time for me. I want to know you are there, or where's the purpose in anything?"

"You managed fine without me for years."

His hand reached to touch gently on her cheek. "I managed, Sarah. There was nothing fine about it."

Sarah's hazel eyes were a radiant glory, transforming her. How could she ever have thought there was no beauty in Sarah's face, Petra wondered.

"Och, you're an old fool, Nathaniel Jenkins," Sarah said in a caressing voice Petra would not have believed she possessed.

"An old fool who loves you," Nathaniel said.

IT WAS POSSIBLE AFTER ALL, Petra discovered, for her to slip out of the room without disturbing them. They didn't even notice when she headed for the front porch and leaned against the front railing, her head tipped back to watch the sky begin to lighten in the east. She could not remember when she had felt so moved. If Sarah and the Admiral didn't work things out between them this time, she decided, she would crack their heads together, take a shotgun to them and get them together no matter what. But she had an idea that her interference would not be necessary. Never had two faces more clearly reflected love.

Watching the first fingers of sunlight pierce the night shadows, dimming the stars, she remembered the grim expression on Dan's face as he left her to shepherd her few guests to warmth and comfort. Was he still angry with her? she wondered. Did he realize she hadn't meant to lash out at him, that she'd been shocked and upset and afraid?

What if she'd gone too far when she shouted at him, she thought suddenly. What if he decided he didn't want to be around prickly Petra anymore?

CHAPTER FIFTEEN

CARTER MANSFIELD'S FIRST COMMENT when he arrived was that it was lucky they hadn't started work on the siding yet. "We'll have it looking good as new in no time," he assured Petra when she told him she didn't feel too lucky about anything this morning.

She nodded listlessly, wandered into the kitchen and looked at the smoke-blackened walls, the shattered windows and the charred floor coated with the remains of the rugs, which were soggy with water. She felt that she wanted to hide in a corner somewhere for a month or two and not have to worry about anything. Captain Aldridge had asked her not to try to clean up the kitchen until he'd had a chance to sift through everything, so there wasn't much she could do there anyway. And there was no point standing around feeling sorry for herself, she decided, consciously squaring her shoulders and tightening the shoulder straps of her overalls.

Everything was turning out better than she'd expected in the long hours of the night anyway. The guests had all returned—all six of them, she added disconsolately in her mind. Their belongings were undamaged, as were their rooms. Tony had had the foresight to run along the halls closing doors before leaving the premises. She would have to arrange for their clothing to be cleaned, of course. Oh yes. Dan had said he would take care of that. But there was all the furniture. . . .

She sighed. According to Tony, Dan had told her guests that the fire had been caused by arson. This had made her furious at first, but then she'd realized as she talked with sparkling-eyed Mrs. Menniger, who was very excited about the night's events, that it was better for the guests to know this was an isolated incident, than to have them worrying about faulty wiring, or careless cooking.

And it *was* an isolated incident. A call from Mitch Clement early that morning had told her that Seth Cartwright and his friends had admitted their guilt. They'd guessed Tony had informed on them and this was their way of getting even. Their parents, shocked by something that was obviously beyond youthful "high spirits"—the excuse they'd offered for their children earlier—had grounded every one of them until their joint trial could take place. Lori had not taken part, or known anything about this particular plan, Tony had been relieved to hear. "It doesn't make any difference as far as seeing her again," he'd told Petra when he returned from the resort and she gave him the news. "But at least I feel better knowing she wasn't involved."

Tony was inclined to blame himself for the night's events, but Petra had managed to convince him that he had done the right thing in coming forward and he couldn't be held responsible for Seth's revenge.

He was working now with Carter. Nathaniel had

finally gone to his own house to rest, taking Sarah with him. Tony had declared his intention of working day and night if necessary to repair the damage. Petra had sighed, ready to lecture him again on the subject of acting his age and taking time out to play, but looking at the set expression on his thin face, she'd realized that for now it was good therapy for him to be busy. Later, when the memory of the night before had lost its sharp edges, she'd make sure he took Dan up on his offer of work at the resort. At least then he'd be around young people again.

She was polishing the floor of the carriage house when Sarah appeared. After all the furniture had been moved out, Petra had discovered a beautiful though woefully dirty, planked oak floor. Evidently at some past date someone had planned to use this area as part of the inn. The sheer physical effort of rubbing paste wax into the wood she'd cleaned earlier, then buffing it to a gleaming shine, made Petra feel better, although she knew her troubles were far from over. With a damaged kitchen she wouldn't be able to fulfill her goal of offering breakfast to road-race visitors. There was no way the kitchen could be repaired in time.

"You look awful glum, lass," Sarah said when she bustled in about midmorning. Petra switched off the electric polisher and managed a smile. Sarah looked as she always did, neat and orderly in her starched apron, her hair firmly returned to its usual braided bun. But there was a difference in her expression, a softening of her features that made her look much more appealing, almost pretty.

She blushed when Petra cocked an eyebrow at her. Evidently blushing was to be a part of the new Sarah—that was twice now to Petra's knowledge. "Did you get any sleep?" Petra asked slyly.

Sarah bristled. "I did. I'm not one of you young people. The way you carry on is a disgrace." She looked suddenly wistful. "More's the pity there wasn't a sexual revolution when I was your age—my life might have taken a different route." She fixed Petra with a stern eye. "But to answer your implied question, I'm not so far gone I can forget my up-bringing to that extent. Besides—" her smile was suddenly smug "—I'm a patient woman. I can wait for my wedding."

The handle of the polisher dropped to the floor with a thud when Petra let go of it. She threw her arms around Sarah in an exuberant hug. "You *are* going to marry the Admiral. Oh Sarah, I'm so glad. We'll have the wedding right here in the inn. It will be the event of the year. We'll have it catered so we won't have to worry about the kitchen. It will be soon, won't it? You and Nathaniel aren't going to make me wait?" She stepped back as a sudden thought struck her. "Oh dear. I suppose you'll be leaving me. Whatever will I do without you?"

Sarah's arms were crossed on her chest, her chin up. "I may not be altogether up with the times," she stated firmly, "but that doesn't mean I'm going to let yon man support me. I'll be staying on as long as you have need of me, lass." She smiled her tight smile. Some things about her weren't going to change, Petra saw. "Petra," she amended.

Then her face sobered. "Now answer my question. What was the glum expression all about? Has Dan not come over or called you then?"

Petra shook her head. "I'm afraid I've really offended him this time, Sarah." She sighed. "But that wasn't what I was thinking of. I was feeling sorry for myself, I'm afraid, worrying that now we have nothing to attract the race visitors with, we won't be able to. . . ."

"My cooking is suddenly not good enough?" Sarah demanded.

Petra stared at her. "But the kitchen. . . ."

"And are you forgetting I now have use of Nathaniel's kitchen?"

She suffered another hug from Petra, then looked at her sternly. "We've a lot to do still. You keep on with your polishing now, while I see what Bonnie and Terry are up to." She started to turn away, then turned back, looking suddenly shy. "To answer your other question, the wedding will take place in the fall, after the tourists are gone. We don't want to be working so hard at the start, you understand. We thought maybe a small honeymoon—if you don't think that's too foolish?"

"I don't think it's foolish at all," Petra said warmly.

She was still smiling a few minutes later when she remembered her duties and went to pick up the floor polisher. But her smile faded as she worked. Sarah's obvious happiness had made her forget her own depression for a while, but now it came back to settle on her shoulders like a mantle of gloom. Dan hadn't

called or come over. He was probably extremely busy
of course, taking over the reins of the resort, but he
did have an excellent assistant manager. He'd told
her at some time yesterday that he'd promoted Wendy to the job and she'd already taken hold very efficiently. He could certainly have managed a phone
call—at least to check if she was okay.

"Sure he called," Tony told her when she finally
thought to ask him. They were enjoying an alfresco
lunch on the inn's porch along with Sarah and Carter
and Nathaniel and Mrs. Menniger.

"Why didn't you come and get me?" she demanded in a low voice.

"He said not to bother you. He just wanted to
make sure you didn't need him for anything. I told
him we had everything under control."

"Did he mention coming over later?" Petra asked,
sacrificing her pride.

Tony shook his head and took a large bite out of
the submarine sandwich Sarah had made him. Then
he turned away to listen to Carter, who was expound-
ing on the problems of replacing burned wood.

Petra picked at her sandwich with poor appetite.
She *had* offended Dan. Beyond repair? She could
hear his voice in her mind. "I'm tired of your hostility." Yes, perhaps beyond repair.

She wandered disconsolately back to the carriage
house, wishing she had Janie to talk to. "Tell me if
he's gone forever," she would ask her.

And Janie would say...what would Janie say?
What she'd said before, of course. *What are you
goin' to do about it?* Janie would think she was act-

ing like an idiot, waiting for Dan to call, waiting for him to make the first move. "What kind of independent woman sits around waiting for the man she loves to get over his anger and approach her again?" Janie would want to know.

As she looked around the deserted carriage house, now gleaming with polish, Petra found herself formulating a plan. The more she thought about it, the more sense it made to her. She had been the one to object to all his offers of help. She would be the one to reach out.

With Tony's help, she managed to move in, during the course of the afternoon, a sofa from the sitting parlor. "That room's too crowded with furniture," she told Tony when he questioned her. They also brought in a small walnut table and two chairs— "Just to get an idea of how it's going to look as a dining room"—and a small serving cart.

Then she went into conference with Sarah, who gave her enthusiastic blessing to the scheme and offered to prepare a dinner. "I have to cook for the family anyway," she said, her fond gaze on Nathaniel's spare frame as he labored away at a table saw Carter had set up at the side of the inn.

The next task, the hardest of all, was to telephone Dan. Swallowing her nervousness, Petra dialed the resort's number. She was connected at once. As soon as she heard his unmistakable voice she spoke rapidly before her courage could fail her. "I've got a bit of a problem, Dan," she explained. "I know you're busy, but if you could spare me some time this evening, I'd appreciate it if you could give me some advice."

"Of course. I'd be happy to help," he said.

He didn't sound happy. He sounded guarded. But nevertheless she plunged on. "It's to do with the carriage house. I—could you meet me there about eight o'clock? I won't keep you long. I know you'll be wanting to have dinner and...." She was babbling on too long, she realized. "Would eight o'clock be all right?" she asked evenly.

"I'll be there," he said. And before he could change his mind or she could blurt out anything else, she hung up the phone.

At six she took a reviving shower. By seven she'd applied makeup more carefully than she'd ever done in her life. Her freshly shampooed hair was dry and curling softly around her face. She was wearing her hot-pink silk dress and a liberal sprinkling of Raffinée.

At ten minutes to eight she took a final look around the carriage house. The blinds were closed on all windows. The only light came from a yellow rosebud centerpiece set with yellow tapers. She'd used the best silver and crystal, yellow linen place mats and napkins. A bottle of Mumm's champagne stood cooling in a silver bucket on the serving cart, next to the covered chafing dishes that contained Sarah's offerings, kept warm over Sterno. As a final touch, she'd brought in Tony's record player, hooked it up with two speakers and put on a pile of romantic records she'd put together from her own collection and the inn's. In a few minutes she'd start her first choice, "You Light Up My Life," for nostalgia's sake.

Promptly at eight, she heard Dan's footsteps in the covered breezeway, and she started to shake. But she stood her ground next to the oval table, one hand resting on its fluted edge.

He was wearing the blue pin-striped suit he'd worn when she first saw him, together with his customary white dress shirt and dark tie. He was carrying a bulky package, something that looked like a grocery bag. He stopped dead in the doorway when he saw her. Bending, he put his package down, then straightened and looked across the room at her.

He didn't smile. She had *expected* him to smile. Her pose was so obvious, so dramatic as she stood there in the small pool of light. She had been sure he would guess what she had in mind immediately. She had rehearsed in her mind how he would smile slowly. Then he would walk toward her and take her in his arms and all their past differences would melt away.

But he didn't seem to recognize his cue or even know his lines. "You wanted to see me?" he asked evenly.

She was suddenly convinced the evening was going to be an abysmal failure. Uncertainly, not at all as confidently as she had meant to say it, desperately afraid of rejection, she said, "I thought it was about time I invited you to dinner."

"I see."

He hadn't advanced a step and there was no softening in his voice. She'd made a mess of it, Petra thought dismally. What on earth had made her think she could carry it off lightly? She'd never had the kind of instinctive skills other women seemed to have when it came to dealing with men, the ability to say something provocative to disarm them, the sophistication to glide through a few opening remarks to set them at ease, to make them feel intrigued.

And this was so important to her. She loved him. She would always love him. "I wanted, I thought perhaps we could. . . ." Her voice trailed away and to her horror and shame she felt tears gathering behind her eyelids. "I just wanted to see you, to apologize, to tell you. . . ." Her throat closed and before she could even turn away to hide her face the threatened tears burst forth. Utterly unnerved, she clumsily pulled out a chair, sank into it and covered her face with her hands.

"Petra. Petra darling, I'm so sorry." His hands were pulling at her fingers, coaxing them away from her face. Presenting her with a yellow napkin he'd picked up from the table, he murmured something about needing to carry a handkerchief as a truly romantic lover would.

"I wanted it to be so perfect," she wailed into the napkin. "I wanted us to laugh and make up so that everything would be all right again."

He tugged at her shoulders, bringing her to her feet and into his arms. His face was stern still. Why wouldn't he smile? "It's not a time for laughing," he said softly. "Not yet. Later we'll laugh. But for now, I can think of many things I'd rather do."

His arms were around her, his lips kissing the tears away.

"Then it's all right? You're not still angry with me?"

"Of course not." He kissed her eyelids, her cheeks, her mouth. For a while there was no talking at all between them while he held her and touched her with fingers made gentle with tenderness. "I'm sorry, love," he said again. "I was determined not to help you. I wanted you to come to me. I was going to tell you I was sorry when you called, but you hung up so fast and I decided I'd better wait so you wouldn't think I was taking over again."

He cupped her face in his hands and looked directly into her eyes, his own very green in the candlelight. "I was smarting, I guess," he admitted. "I was determined you would have to make the first move toward me this time. I'm sorry. I promise not to play those games anymore."

"But *this* was supposed to be a game," Petra said. Her tears were under control now and she could feel the glow that must be showing on her face. "I had my plans all laid. First the dinner, then champagne and then I was going to seduce you."

His smile dazzled her. "I don't see anything wrong with that plan," he said softly as he pulled her close to him again. "Except perhaps that I suddenly don't have much of an appetite." He glanced at the table, then gave her the wicked sidelong glance she had come to watch for and to love. "Not for food at least," he added.

Setting her away from him, he looked at her lovingly. "Tell me now, Miss McNeil. If we forget about dinner for now, and we decide not to waste another full bottle of champagne, what exactly would be next on the agenda for this meeting?"

She glanced automatically at the sofa that stood in the shadows beyond the circle of candlelight and he laughed delightedly. Then he stopped laughing and bent his head and touched his lips lightly, fleetingly, to hers. "I love you, Petra McNeil," he murmured.

"I love you," she answered at once.

And then he picked her up in his arms and carried her to the sofa and laid her gently down. "I was supposed to seduce you," she protested.

He stood looking down at her, his head tilted to one side. With the light behind him she couldn't read his expression but she had the distinct impression he was smiling. "You think you could have carried me?" he asked.

"Of course," she said airily. "Haven't I been trying to tell you all along that I can do anything you can do?"

He knelt beside the sofa and started pulling off his jacket. "I'm very tempted to see what would happen if I agreed to that," he said. "I know you've thought me guilty of putting you down every time I made a helpful suggestion, which offends my sense of fair play. And I do assure you, in case there's any lingering doubt in your mind, that I accept women as the equals of men. However, now that I've got you where I want you, I find myself far too impatient to start over just so you can prove you're as physically strong as I am."

While he was talking, he had removed his tie and opened his shirt collar. Now he touched the first button on Petra's dress with one finger. "As I recall," he said slowly, "this particular dress requires that you wear nothing under it."

She nodded, her gaze on his face, now illuminated by the flickering candles. "So if I was to unfasten this dress it would be possible for me to touch your beautiful breasts?"

Again she nodded, feeling excitement rising in her, tightening her nipples under the thin fabric of her dress. Dan moved his hand long enough to touch each one delicately. "So far, so good," he murmured. "But I'm forgetting, you were supposed to seduce me."

Still kneeling, he sat back on his heels, folded his hands in his lap and waited.

"The door," she whispered. "Someone might come in."

"The door is locked."

She stared up at him. His eyebrows were raised in the supercilious expression that had so often enraged her. But now it seemed the dearest expression of all. "You rat," she said, laughing. "You knew all along." Her eyes narrowed. "Sarah told you exactly what I had planned, didn't she? Did she also tell you she is going to marry Nathaniel?"

She saw the white flash of his teeth as he bent to kiss her lightly on the forehead. "She did," he said. "And left out no detail of your scheme. She was afraid, she said, that it was too subtle for both of us. We needed to be hit on the head with a two by four, she added. But in lieu of that she thought I should at least know what you had in mind."

His face sobered abruptly and he looked at her with hooded eyes. "You were about to commence a seduction?" he reminded her.

She felt suddenly shy. Reaching up, she began to unbutton his shirt, but her fingers were clumsy and she began to feel very awkward. She reached his belt buckle and couldn't quite figure it out. "I don't think I can do it," she answered.

"That's all I was waiting to hear," he answered. "Let's try doing it together, shall we?"

"You *are* a rat," she muttered, but she was laughing as she said it, laughing as together they removed his shirt and her dress, laughing as he complained about the narrowness of the sofa. "You could at least have brought a bed in here," he grumbled.

And then there was no more laughter, only the sound of the music playing softly from the corner of the shadowed carriage house, the faint sputtering of the candles, the echo of their heartbeats as they twined around each other so closely it was impossible to tell where her body ended and his began.

With her fingers, Petra traced the outline of his face over and over, then touched his eyelids, his nose, his mouth. "I used to think you had a predatory face," she said softly.

She felt his mouth curve under her fingertips. "I'm not sure that's a compliment."

"It is in a way, because I thought you were very sure of yourself and sure of your goals and I admired that even while I was convincing myself you were a sexist." She silenced his protest with her fingers. "I know. It was all in my mind. I'm sorry I was so unjust. I guess I had to believe you were putting me down, so that I wouldn't hurl myself at you every time I saw you...."

She tilted her head, examining his self-satisfied smile. "I still think you can be ruthless," she added.

"No more than twice a year. And only when it's necessary," he assured her. Then he lifted his head and looked at her and sighed. "Don't you know there's a time when you're supposed to stop talking?"

"But we have to talk. I don't even know if you, whether you want me to...."

"I want you to do everything you want to do," he said flatly. "And if that includes becoming my wife, then I guess I'll have to let you do that too."

"Is that supposed to be a proposal?"

"No. I'm just setting your mind at rest. The proposal will come later, after I've had my way with you."

"Sarah's *waiting* for *her* wedding," she teased him.

"I'm not making love to Sarah." He laughed. "Dammit Petra, just stop talking, will you?"

And she did.

"YOU LOOK BEDAZZLED, disheveled and altogether delightful," Dan announced an hour later.

They had dressed again. Petra had made what repairs she could to her face and hair with the aid of her compact mirror and fresh candles, but she was pretty sure her attempts hadn't done much good. His words confirmed her suspicion, but she couldn't bring herself to care. "You look a little tousled yourself," she informed him. "It's good for you. Makes you look less formidable."

"Formidable?" His eyebrows rose. "You have no idea yet how formidable I can be."

She lifted her champagne glass and toasted him mockingly. "I have a feeling I'm going to find out."

"You are indeed. As soon as we're married, I intend to...."

"Just one minute," she exclaimed. "You haven't made that proposal yet."

"So I haven't." He sighed, looking down at the table. "I was hoping to have a chance to eat some of the delicious dinner Sarah prepared for us. Sole Almondine, she told me, and asparagus with hollandaise."

"She didn't leave a detail out, did she?" Petra said. "All the same, no proposal, no dinner."

"Then, in that case...." He stood up, came around the table to her side and knelt on the floor. Taking her hand he kissed it gently, then looked up at her.

She caught her breath. Her suggestion had been made lightly and he had accepted it lightly, but there was only solemnity in his face now. Solemnity and love. "Will you marry me, Petra McNeil?" he asked.

She hesitated, suddenly nervous in the face of his serious expression. "I did make a vow, you know," she said with a smile to cover her nervousness. "I wasn't going to get involved with a man until I had the inn's problems settled. Perhaps we ought to wait after all." She looked at him gravely, teasingly. "Couldn't you possibly wait and love me tomorrow when I have more time?"

To her dismay, he didn't smile. He stood up and

walked away from her toward the doorway. Too stunned to call after him, to tell him she'd been teasing, *surely* he knew she was teasing, she watched as he bent down and picked up the package he'd deposited there earlier. She'd forgotten all about it.

She heard the rustle of paper, and then to her relief, saw him turn and come back to her, carrying in his arms the sculpture he'd sent her once before. Solemnly, he set it down on the table in front of her. In the candlelight, the pale green stone seemed to glow with a frosty light. She touched it gently. . . and found to her surprise that the stone was warm after all.

She looked up at him, then stood and reached up to put a hand on each side of his face. He was still regarding her steadily, but she could see the beginnings of one of his eye-crinkling smiles in the curving corners of his mouth. "Message received," she said softly. "No more retreats. Of course I'll marry you, Dan."

He continued to look at her solemnly, though his mouth was still giving him away. "The board of directors wants me to take over the Braden Corporation in two years," he said. "My father's retiring then. He wants me to live in Boston and gradually take over the reins. How would you feel about living in Boston?"

"I think I could bear it," she said. "As long as we can come back to Cape Cod frequently." She frowned suddenly. "But what about my inn? I can't give up my inn. I've found I really love hotel work, being with people, working with them, solving problems as they come up. I really enjoy it, Dan. I can't be just a wife and I know you wouldn't want me to be, but how can I run the inn and be with you too?''

''I was wondering when that would come up,'' he said. He put his arms around her, kissed the tip of her nose. ''I've got it all thought out, love. We'll stay on the Cape for the rest of the summer. I'll be in charge of the resort for a while, and then I'll need to help the new manager get settled in. But I'll have time to help with the arrangements for repairs to the inn and the rest of the remodeling. I thought after that we could keep it in conjunction with the resort but separate, for those guests who want a quieter vacation. Nathaniel and Sarah could manage it between them for us, but you'd still be able to oversee it as your special project.''

''Special project?'' she murmured. She had wound her hands around Dan's neck and discovered once again how crisp and clean his hair felt under her fingertips. She liked him comfortably rumpled like this, she decided. She was going to make sure he spent at least some time every day looking as though he'd just got out of bed.

''Don't gleam at me when I'm talking,'' Dan said sternly and she forced an expression of exaggerated attention to her face.

''Tony will be going to school in Boston anyway,'' he went on. ''We don't have to worry about him, I'm sure. As for you—well, you *have* shown a remarkable aptitude for hotel work, especially in relating to people. Your guests were singing your praises to me last night, telling me how warm and hospitable you are at all times. That's why they were willing to come back in spite of the fire and the resulting smell of smoke.''

He pulled her a little closer against him, but still he hadn't let the smile break through. ''I've decided you'd probably do very well working for the Braden Corporation,'' he continued. ''We can negotiate a salary later. Whatever job we offer you will involve some traveling, I expect, with me, if possible. And before you object let me assure you you won't be a glorified secretary. I have several suggestions for areas you might want to explore, mostly dealing with the hospitality side of hotel work, which is where you seem to shine—as well as in painting walls, of course,'' he added with a glance for their surroundings.

''You have got it all thought out, haven't you?'' Petra said with mock indignation. ''Don't I get to say anything to all this?''

Finally he let his face relax into the smile that had been waiting. ''You can say yes if you like.''

She gave him what felt like a pretty dazzling smile of her own. ''Yes,'' she said.

His kiss awoke all of her senses again. She had the feeling his kiss always would. His mouth felt wonderful on hers, pliant yet firm, warm and loving and exciting, especially exciting. She could feel herself starting to disintegrate in the area of her knees, but before she lost complete hold on reality again, there was something she needed to make clear.

''This job you're going to offer me,'' she said against his mouth, ''it will have possibilities of promotion, won't it?''

"*Strong* possibilities," he agreed.

Laughing, he pulled her tightly against him and kissed her deeply until she was far too breathless to say another word.

ABOUT THE AUTHOR

Research for *Love Me Tomorrow* took Rosalind Carson and her husband to a favorite locale—an ocean's shore. At a Cape Cod resort very like the Pine Village in this Superromance, they managed to win a twist contest and a bottle of champagne just as Dan and Petra did. The circumstances were a little unusual, though: our intrepid author was suffering a severely sprained ankle at the time. But she insists her efforts were well worthwhile—the bottle was a very good year!

Rosalind's year has been exciting as well. On a recent trip to Japan, she wowed Harlequin readers there by addressing them in their native tongue. She has continued to pursue her studies of the Japanese language at home in Tacoma, Washington, so it is not surprising to learn that she plans to set her fifth Superromance in Japan.